Cold Feet
A Steamy Hockey Romance

Lisa Daily

Siesta Key Press

Contents

Chapter 1

I pride myself on being first in the office every morning. It's the quiet I crave – that perfect slice of time when the St. Petersburg Slashers training facility belongs just to me. No sweaty players in the hallways (yet), no coaches barking orders, no social media fires to extinguish before I've even fired up my laptop..

Just me, my caffeine addiction, and the gentle hum of the climate control system fighting back Florida's oppressive heat like a champ.

This morning was no different. I juggled my laptop bag, purse, and what was definitely too many iced coffees (one for me, one for my assistant Katie, and one with an extra shot for Coach Michaels, who would literally rather die than admit he likes anything fancier than gas station swill) as I swiped my key card at the staff entrance.

The halls echoed with that early morning emptiness I loved. Fresh floor cleaner mixed with the lingering scent of hockey – testosterone, ice, and pure ambition.

Smells like home.

In my office, I set down the coffees and allowed myself thirty seconds to appreciate the view. Floor-to-ceiling windows overlooked our practice rink, still pristine from overnight resurfacing. Championship banners hung from the rafters like silent bragging rights, including last season's Stanley Cup. Not bad for a sunbelt expansion team that every hockey purist had written off as "Disney on Ice."

I settled into my chair and powered up my computer, mentally organizing my day while I mainlined caffeine. Media availability after the morning skate. Final approval on season ticket packages. Draft talking points for Logan's ESPN hit tonight.

My phone buzzed. Coach Michaels.

"Decker," I answered, channeling my most professional voice despite having known Sully Michaels since I was in pigtails.

"Conference room. Now." His voice had that gruff edge that made my stomach drop. In hockey speak, that tone meant someone was either traded, injured, or caught doing something spectacularly stupid on TikTok.

"Good morning to you too, Coach."

"The rest of us are already here." Click.

I stared at my phone. Whatever this was, it wasn't on my calendar. And in hockey, like in PR, unscheduled meetings usually meant someone's world was about to implode.

I grabbed Sully's coffee, mine, and my tablet, mentally cataloging possible disasters as I walked. Player injury? Instascandal? *Please, hockey gods*, don't let it be another secret baby situation.

When I pushed open the conference room door, I immediately knew this was DefCon 1 serious. Coach Sully sat at the head of the table like someone had stolen his favorite whistle. Coach Rocco flanked him, both wearing worried expressions. Marcus Thompson, our GM, tapped away at his phone with his usual intensity while chatting with Ryan Keller – one of the most ruthless sports agents in the business.

And there was Cam "The Hitman" Murphy.

Hockey's golden boy. The Slashers' star left-winger. My brother's best friend since they were teenagers terrorizing college hockey together. The man whose face I'd plastered across every billboard from Tampa to Orlando as "the NHL's most eligible bachelor."

The man I'd spent the better part of a decade pretending I didn't remember naked.

Cam sprawled in his chair like he owned the place, one long leg extended under the table, arms crossed over a faded Ramones t-shirt that hugged his shoulders in a way that was entirely unprofessional for me to notice. His golden-brown hair was still damp from a post-workout shower, and when our eyes met across the table, his jaw tightened just enough for me to notice.

Those eyes. Still the same impossible shade of blue that had made me forget my own name once upon a time.

"Lana," Coach Sully nodded. "Close the door."

I set his coffee in front of him – a peace offering for whatever shit storm was brewing – and took the only remaining seat. Directly across from Cam, because apparently the universe has a sick sense of humor.

"What's going on?" I asked, directing my question to Sully while mentally cataloging everyone's stress levels. Years of crisis management had taught me that reading the room was often more useful than whatever corporate speak came out of people's mouths.

Ryan Keller cleared his throat, all business in his two thousand-dollar suit. "We have a situation with Cam's image."

My gaze snapped to Cam. Public image was my domain. If there was a problem with how the world perceived Cameron Murphy, it was ultimately my problem to fix.

"What kind of situation?" I asked, tablet at the ready.

"Redline Athletics wants to make Cam their first NHL endorsement athlete," Ryan continued. "We're talking major mainstream crossover. Game-changing money."

I nodded. Redline was massive – Nike and Adidas level. Getting them interested in hockey, let alone one of our players, was like landing a unicorn.

"That's incredible news," I said carefully, waiting for the other skate to drop.

"It would be," Ryan continued, "except they're concerned about Cam's... *personal* image."

And there it was.

"Specifically," Marcus jumped in, "there's a morality clause in the contract. They want someone stable. Family-friendly. Someone who screams *trustworthy spokesman* instead of...uh... *collect them all*."

I looked at Cam, whose eyes were now locked on mine with laser focus, intensely blue and unmistakably accusatory.

Ryan slid a contract across the table. "One-point-five million annually for three years. This isn't just sneaker money...this is positioning Cam as the face of hockey for mainstream America."

I flipped through the pages, scanning the morality language. Four-and-a-half million dollars. *Holy shit.*

"So what exactly about Cam's image is the problem?" I asked, though I had a sinking feeling I already knew.

Cam gave a short, humorless laugh. "Gee, wonder what it could be? Maybe the fact that you've spent three years marketing me as the NHL's resident fuckboy?"

"I wouldn't use that terminology in my media materials," I shot back, stung.

"No, you prefer 'hockey heartthrob' and 'the league's most eligible bachelor,'" he said, air quotes and all. "My personal favorite was 'Win a Dream Date with the Slashers' Sexiest Forward.'"

"That Valentine's promotion sold out the arena in sixteen minutes," I reminded him. "Your jersey sales are second only to Logan's, and you've got the highest likability scores in the NHL"

"And now it's costing me the biggest deal of my career." His voice stayed level, but I could see the tension radiating from his shoulders. "You know that's not who I am, Lana. I played along with this... hockey Casanova bullshit for the good of the team, and now it's biting me in the ass."

"As I recall, you weren't exactly opposed to one-night stands back in college, *Hitman.*"

Shit. The words hung in the air like a puck about to drop, heavy with the weight of everything we'd never talked about.

Cam's eyes flashed with something I couldn't name, and suddenly I was twenty years old again, waking up alone in my dorm room with nothing but the lingering scent of his cologne and a hollow ache in my chest.

"Cam and Zayne were teammates at BU," I explained quickly to the room, as if that somehow justified my highly specific knowledge of his college dating habits. "Sorry. That was unprofessional."

The truth was, Cam wasn't wrong. For all his swagger and magazine cover boy looks, he was notoriously private off the ice. I'd crafted a public image for him that worked brilliantly for the team, amplified it into something that sold tickets and jerseys – but apparently not family-friendly sneakers.

"Okay," I said, switching back to problem-solving mode. "We can work with this. Charity appearances, kids program of some sort, maybe a feature on his off-ice interests. Social media reset. Give me three months and I can shift the narrative."

Ryan and Marcus exchanged one of those looks that made my stomach drop.

"We don't have three months," Ryan said. "The NHL Awards are in two weeks. Redline will be there, watching. They need to see concrete evidence of change by then, or they walk."

"Two weeks?" I looked around the table like someone was about to tell me this was an elaborate prank. "Shoot, I forgot my magic wand at home. I can't completely rebrand someone in two weeks. I'm good, but I'm not a miracle worker."

"Actually," Ryan leaned forward with the smile of a shark who'd just spotted blood in the water, "I have a more *immediate* solution." His gaze landed squarely on me and I half-expected his undoubtedly forked tongue to flicker out like a snake's. "Cam needs a girlfriend. *A serious one.*"

I laughed, then quickly realized I was the only one.

"You want me to find Cam a girlfriend in two weeks?" I asked. "What am I supposed to do, hold auditions? Post on LinkedIn?"

"Not exactly," Marcus said carefully.

And that's when it hit me. The way they were all looking at me. The careful setup of this meeting. The strategic positioning of the only empty chair directly opposite Cam.

"Oh, hell no," I said when I finally found my voice. "Absolutely not."

"Think about it," Ryan pressed on like a man who sensed weakness. "You've known each other for years. You're at the same events constantly. Cam's close with your brother. Your family is hockey royalty... I mean, Frank Decker's daughter dating a Slashers player? The optics are exactly what we need. Plus, your position with the team explains why you'd keep it private."

I could feel Cam's eyes on me, but I refused to look at him.

"This is insane," I said, my mind already racing through the implications, pitfalls, the type of media strategy we'd need. It was sickeningly logical from a PR perspective. "You can't seriously expect me to pretend to be Cameron Murphy's girlfriend."

"Not girlfriend," Ryan corrected. "Fiancée."

The room fell silent.

"I'm sorry," I said slowly, fighting to keep my voice level. "Did you just suggest I fake an engagement to one of my own players? The media would crucify us when they found out it was fake."

"*If* they found out," Ryan amended.

"*When*," I corrected firmly. "This is the NHL. Everything leaks eventually. You *know* that Ryan."

"Six weeks, " Marcus spoke up, his voice gravelly but firm. " A few months, tops. Play nice for the cameras at the awards, let the deal get signed, then quietly break up in the off-season. Clean and simple."

"What about my brother?" I looked directly at Cam for the first time since this nightmare began. "Zayne would literally murder you. With his bare hands. On television."

"I'll handle Zayne," Marcus said confidently.

"Good luck with that," I muttered under my breath. Zayne had made it abundantly clear to every player he'd ever played with since Pee Wee that his sister was off-limits. Period. Full stop. Do not pass go, do not collect two hundred dollars, do not even think about Lana Decker unless you wanted to become intimately acquainted with the business end of his stick. The fact that he and Cam were not only teammates but best friends would make this even more complicated.

"Look," Sully finally joined the conversation, sliding my coffee closer like he sensed I needed the reinforcement. "Nobody's forcing anything here, Lana. Your job's not on the line, and we'll respect whatever you decide. But this deal..." He shook his head. "This could change everything. For Cam, for the organization, for hockey."

I looked at Cam, who'd been suspiciously quiet during this part of the conversation. "And you're on board with this plan?"

Those pale cobalt eyes held mine steady, and for just a moment, I saw past the careful control to something that looked almost... vulnerable. "I don't see another way," he said simply.

I closed my eyes, trying to think clearly. This was professionally questionable at best, ethically murky at worst. And personally? A disaster waiting to happen.

"I'll have an answer for you tomorrow," I said finally. "But I'm not committing to anything until I've thought through every possible angle."

Sully nodded, recognizing that was the best he'd get. As everyone filed out, Cam lingered by the door.

"You're really considering this?" he asked, his voice uncharacteristically soft.

"I'm considering every option," I corrected. "That's my job."

"You created this problem, you know." No heat behind it, just tired resignation.

"And you were perfectly happy to play along when it was selling out arenas and getting you the cover of *Sports Illustrated.*" I stood, gathering my things with sharp efficiency. "Maybe next time mention your secret ambition to be a sneaker mogul before I turn you into hockey's answer to Harry Styles."

A genuine laugh escaped him. "Deal."

I brushed past him toward the door, but he caught my elbow before I made my escape. His hand on my skin sent an unwelcome shock right through me.

"Lana." The way he said my name made me stop. "I wouldn't ask if it wasn't important."

We were standing too close now. Close enough that I could see the small scar above his left eyebrow from a high stick two seasons ago. Close enough to remember things I'd spent a decade trying to forget.

"I'll let you know tomorrow," I managed, pulling my arm free.

As I reached for the door, his voice stopped me one last time.

"Lana? If we do this... be my fiancée, not girlfriend."

I turned back, confused. "Why?"

The smile that spread across his face was pure Cam Murphy – devastating, confident, and entirely too knowing.

"Because if you're going to lie, Lana Banana, you might as well make it a good one."

The ridiculous nickname he'd whispered against my neck one night ten years ago hit me like a slap shot to the chest.

I walked out without answering, my heart pounding a rhythm that felt dangerously like the echoes of a mistake I'd made once before.

A mistake named Cameron Murphy.

Chapter 2

I spent the next hour staring at my computer screen, pretending to work while my mind replayed Cam's words on an excruciating loop.

Be my fiancée.

The sheer audacity. The absolute nerve. And the way those dreamy fucking blue eyes had held mine when he'd said it – like he was offering me something precious instead of a one-way ticket to career suicide. First class tickets on the *Titanic*.

I pulled up the Redline contract for the sixth time, scanning the morality clause like it might have magically rewritten itself since the last time I looked. Nope. Still crystal clear.

My phone buzzed. Katie's voice filtered through the intercom: "The social team needs approval on tonight's game graphics."

"Sending now," I replied, grateful for the distraction.

But as I clicked through the graphics, my thoughts wandered back to Boston University, to a snowy night ten years ago.

Boston University, February 2015

The party was limping toward its death – empty beer cans forming small cities on every surface, someone's forgotten playlist cycling through the same twenty songs for the third time. I'd only come because my roommate Jess had physically dragged me, insisting "Junior year, Lana! You need to live a little before we graduate into crushing student debt!"

Of course, Jess had disappeared with some pre-law student an hour ago, leaving me to navigate the social wreckage alone.

I was excavating my coat from the bedroom coat pile when the door opened.

"Sorry," said a voice that was warm honey over gravel. "Just hunting for my jacket."

I turned and nearly swallowed my tongue. Golden hair, blue eyes that belonged in a magazine, and a smile that could probably melt a whole rink. I recognized him instantly – hard not to, when the guy was basically a god on campus.

"Escaping the chaos too?" he asked, leaning against the doorframe with the casual confidence of someone who'd never been told no in his life.

"Mission accomplished, actually." I held up my rescued coat. "Time to make my exit before things get really ugly."

"That's a tragedy," he said, and I could hear the smile in his voice. "I just got here."

"Then you're about three hours late for the good times."

"Or maybe right on time for the better ones." He tilted his head, studying me like I was a puzzle he wanted to solve. "I'm Cam."

"Lana."

"Lana." The way he repeated my name, like he was testing how it felt on his tongue, sent an unexpected flutter through my chest. "Tell me something, Lana. You strike me as someone with opinions. What's the verdict on this party?"

I considered him for a moment. "Mediocre music, watered-down drinks, and at least three guys who think 'wanna see my hockey stick' is a clever pickup line. The usual."

His laugh was genuine, surprised. "Harsh but fair. What would make it better?"

"Different company," I said before I could stop myself.

The smile that spread across his face should have come with a warning label. "Well, lucky for both of us, I know where we can find some."

We ended up at a 24-hour diner off Commonwealth, sharing a plate of inexplicably delicious pancakes while snow fell outside the steamed-up windows.

"You know, earth is the only planet we know with hip hop and pancakes," he'd said as he slid into the booth right next to me. He told me about learning to skate on frozen Minnesota ponds before he could tie his shoes. I told him about growing up in hockey rinks, about my communications major, about wanting to work in sports media someday – carefully leaving out the part where my family was a legit hockey dynasty.

The conversation flowed like we'd known each other for years instead of hours. He was funny, thoughtful, surprisingly well-read for a hockey player. When he mentioned loving Kurt Vonnegut, I nearly choked on my coffee.

"Shocked?" he asked, amused.

"Impressed," I corrected. "Most guys I know think literature peaked with ESPN The Magazine."

"Most guys are missing out."

"Quick, what's your favorite Vonnegut quote," I asked, "so I know you're not completely full of shit."

"We are what we pretend to be, so we must be careful about what we pretend to be."

"I love that. Is that Mother Night?" He nodded in response, his blue eyes dancing.

We talked until the sun came up, the night dissolving around us until it was just him and me and words that felt more important than they should have. When he walked me back to my dorm, I didn't want it to end.

"This was..." I started, then trailed off, not sure how to finish.

"Yeah," he agreed softly, "it was."

When he kissed me outside my building, it felt inevitable. When I invited him upstairs, it felt right. And when we made love until dawn, it felt like the beginning of everything.

But then came the moment that changed everything.

We were lying tangled in my sheets, his fingers drawing lazy patterns on my shoulder, when his gaze landed on the framed photo on my nightstand – Dad holding his first Stanley Cup, grinning like he'd conquered the world.

"Hockey fan?" Cam asked casually.

The question shot panic through me. I'd just met him. Lie or own up to it?

"That's my dad."

I felt him freeze, though he tried to play it off. "Frank Decker is your father?"

Every defense mechanism I'd ever built snapped into place. How many guys had shown interest just to get closer to my family? How many had seen dollar signs and their NHL shot instead of me?

"You know him?" I asked carefully.

"And Zayne Decker?"

"My brother." I sat up slightly, tension creeping into my shoulders. "You know him?" I already knew the answer.

Something complicated flickered across his face – recognition, then something darker. "Yeah. We're teammates. So you're his sister? He's, uh,... protective of you."

I laughed, some of my worry easing. "That's the understatement of the century."

"How come we've never met?"

"My whole life has been hockey. I don't come to games unless my parents are here. I've been trying to steer clear since I got here. You know, find my own way outside of my family's shadow."

Cam smiled then, pulling me closer and kissing me until I forgot to worry about anything else. But looking back, I realized that smile didn't look like all the other ones I'd seen that night.

When I woke up, he was gone. No note. No explanation. Just the fading scent of his cologne and a hollow ache in my chest.

"Uh oh, Sorry, Did I catch you in the middle of a coma?"

I jerked back to the present to find Logan Rivers standing in my doorway, amusement dancing in his dark eyes. Our team captain had a way of moving through the world that commanded attention without demanding it – all steady confidence and natural authority.

"Hilarious. Sorry," I said, minimizing the Redline contract on my screen. "What's up?"

He stepped inside, closing the door behind him with the deliberate care of someone who had things to say that weren't meant for public consumption.

"You'd think after last season you'd be nicer to me," I teased.

"You'd think," he grinned. "Coco says hi."

"What's up?"

"Heard you had an interesting morning meeting," he said, settling into the chair across from my desk like he had all the time in the world.

"News travels fast around here." I kept my tone carefully neutral, though my pulse had kicked up a notch. Exactly why there's no way in hell we'd ever pull this off.

Logan leaned back, studying me with those perceptive captain's eyes that missed nothing. "Cam said you're considering the Redline situation."

"The completely insane Redline situation," I corrected. "The potentially career-ending Redline situation."

"Is it, though?" Logan tilted his head. "Seems pretty logical to me. Cam needs to fix his image. You're the best in the business at managing images. Perfect partnership."

"There's nothing perfect about pretending to be engaged to a player I work with."

"Because of what happened in Boston?"

My heart stuttered. "What do you know about Boston?"

Logan's expression softened, shifting from captain to friend. "Lana, I've been Cam's teammate for almost four years. He's one of my closest friends. You think he never mentioned the girl who got away? The one night that ruined him for everyone else?"

Heat flooded my cheeks. "It was one night a decade ago. Hardly worth ruining anyone over."

"That's not how he tells it." My heart skipped uncomfortably. "What does that mean?"

Logan leaned forward, resting his elbows on his knees. "Look, I'm not here to play telephone between you two. That's between you and him. But I am here to say that Cam Murphy is not the guy you've been selling to the public."

"I know that," I said defensively. "It's PR. I take what's there and amplify it."

"No," Logan shook his head. "You've created a complete fiction. Cam's not a player. He hasn't seriously dated anyone in years. He spends most nights at home watching cooking shows and calling his mom."

I blinked. "Calling his mom?"

"Every Sunday. Without fail. She's got MS – has for years. He checks in, manages her care, makes sure she's got everything she needs."

This didn't align with the image I had of Cam – or rather, the image I'd cultivated. Sure, I knew the public persona was exaggerated, but I'd assumed there was some truth to it. The frequent appearances with models and actresses, the flirtatious interviews, the way women flocked to him...

"Why didn't he ever object?" I asked. "To the image we created?"

Logan shrugged, but the motion seemed too casual to be genuine. "You'd have to ask him that. But my guess? He figured it was easier to play the role you assigned him than fight it. Especially since..."

"Since what?"

Logan looked momentarily uncomfortable, like he'd said more than he intended. "Since it was you doing the asking."

Something twisted in my chest; a complicated knot of guilt, confusion, and a feeling I refused to name.

"This fake engagement idea is crazy," I said, steering us back to safer ground. "It could backfire spectacularly. It could ruin my professional credibility. And there's a massive ethical issue with the team publicist dating a player."

"Which is why Coach Sully, Rocco, and Marcus were in that meeting this morning," Logan countered. "The brass knows. The agent knows. It's contained."

"For now. But if it gets out – "

"It won't." Logan's certainty was almost reassuring. "Look, I get it. Your reputation matters. Your career matters. But this isn't just about Cam being able to hawk sneakers. This is about security."

"I get it."

"Hockey's not forever, Lana. You know that better than most." He tapped his knee meaningfully – a reminder of his own surgery a few years ago that had nearly ended his career. "One bad hit, one torn ACL, and it's over. A deal like this? It's insurance. It's what comes after."

He had a point. Hockey players had short career spans at best. My brother Drake's playing career had ended after just three years. Like my Dad, he'd made the move to coaching. A major marketing deal like this could cushion Cam financially for decades.

"There's still Zayne to consider," I said, grasping at my last excuse. "You know how protective he is."

Logan actually smiled at that. "Yeah, your brother's...intense. But he's also one of the most loyal guys I know. When he understands what's at stake for his teammate, his best friend, he'll come around."

"You clearly don't know Zayne as well as you think," I muttered. My brother once broke a guy's nose at a team function for asking for my number. His protectiveness bordered on prehistoric.

"Maybe not. But I do know Cam." Logan rose to his feet. "And I know this matters to him. A lot."

"The deal, you mean."

Logan paused at the door, his expression softening. "Sure, the deal. But also... just think about it, okay? You're the only one he's ever actually cared about."

By five o'clock, I'd written and rewritten what I was now mentally calling "The Contract of Mutual Professional Destruction" at least fifteen times. The legal pad beside my laptop was filled with crossed-out clauses, revised terms, and doodled hockey sticks.

The final version stared back at me from my screen:

CONFIDENTIALITY AGREEMENT AND TERMS

The undersigned parties, Cameron Murphy and Lana Decker, along with St. Petersburg Slashers management representatives, agree to the following terms regarding the temporary public relationship between Mr. Murphy and Ms. Decker:

1. Duration: This arrangement will begin immediately upon signing and continue until 30 days following the execution of the Redline endorsement contract, the conclusion of the NHL Awards ceremony, or by mutual agreement, whichever comes last.

2. Public Conduct: Murphy and Decker agree to present themselves as a committed couple in public settings, including but not limited to team functions, social media, and the NHL Awards.

3. Physical Boundaries: Physical contact will be limited to appropriate public displays of affection (hand-holding, brief kisses, etc.). No overnight stays are expected or required.

4. Media Strategy: Neither party will explicitly state they are "engaged" to any media outlet. If directly questioned, responses will be limited to "We're very happy together" and "We prefer to keep the details private."

5. Social Media: Any relationship-related posts must be approved by both parties before publishing. A minimum of two joint appearances on social media per week is required to establish credibility.

6. Ring: A ring will be procured for Ms. Decker to wear at public appearances. The ring remains the property of Mr. Murphy after the conclusion of this agreement.

7. Confidentiality: All details of this arrangement will remain strictly confidential. All parties acknowledge this agreement constitutes a binding NDA.

8. Termination: Following the completion of this agreement, a mutual, amicable, no-fault "breakup" will be announced through approved, mutually agreed upon media channels.

9. Zayne Decker: Mr. Murphy accepts full responsibility for any negative reaction from Zayne Decker should he discover this arrangement.

The last clause gave me pause, but I knew it was necessary. Zayne would never understand – and more importantly, he'd never approve. Better to ask forgiveness than permission in this case.

I printed copies for everyone, my hands surprisingly steady considering I was about to formalize the most professionally questionable decision of my career.

My phone lit up with a text from a number I saw exactly twice a year – Christmas and my birthday.

CAM: Update?

I stared at the message, thumb hovering over the keyboard. The smart move would be scheduling a proper meeting in my office tomorrow. The safe move would be texting back a simple yes or no.

Instead, my traitorous fingers typed:

ME: Breakaway Bar, 30 minutes. Come alone.

CAM: Are you having me kidnapped?

ME: Only one way to find out.

Breakaway was a small hockey bar a few blocks from the arena, popular with staff but rarely frequented by players who preferred more upscale establishments. I chose it deliberately – neutral territory, away from both team oversight and public scrutiny.

The bar smelled of beer and decades of sports celebrations – a comforting, familiar scent that reminded me of my childhood, when my dad would take us to similar places after Zayne's juniors games. Old jerseys and memorabilia decorated the walls, including a faded Slashers pennant from their inaugural season.

I arrived first, selecting a booth in the back corner where the lighting was dim enough for privacy. I ordered a glass of pinot grigio to settle my nerves, and was halfway through the glass when Cam slid into the seat across from me.

"You came," he said, as if he'd half-expected me to stand him up.

"I said I would." I pushed the agreement across the table. "These are my terms."

He skimmed the document, expression unreadable in the dim bar lighting. The sound of a hockey game played low on the TV overhead, punctuated by occasional cheers from patrons at the bar. When he reached the end of the agreement, his eyes flicked up to mine.

"Wait. You're saying yes?"

"I'm saying I'll help you," I clarified. "Under these very specific conditions."

Cam signaled the waitress, ordering a beer before returning his attention to me. "Why? I thought for sure after this morning..."

"I thought about what you said," I admitted. "About how I helped create this image problem for you. I feel... responsible."

"Logan talked to you, didn't he?" Surprise flickered across his face.

"Apparently he considers himself your personal publicist now."

Cam's mouth quirked in a half-smile. "What did he say?"

"That you're not actually the player I've made you out to be. That you watch cooking shows and call your mother every Sunday." I paused, studying him. "That she has MS."

His smile faded. "He had no right to – "

"Is it true?" I interrupted.

Cam held my gaze for a long moment. And then..."Yes."

"Then why did you let me build this whole playboy persona around you if it wasn't accurate?" I asked, genuinely confused. "We've worked together for three years, Cam. You've never once objected to the strategy."

He shrugged, but the casualness felt forced. "It seemed to make everyone happy. The fans, the sponsors, the team. *You.*"

"Me?" I echoed.

"You seemed so...excited about it. The whole strategy. Turning me into hockey's most eligible bachelor. It was clearly working for the team, and you were..." He paused, searching for words. "You were good at it. Really good. I didn't want to mess that up for you."

The waitress delivered his beer, and Cam took a long sip, using the moment to collect himself.

"Besides," he continued, setting the glass down, "it was easier than the alternative."

"Which was?"

"Having to actually date. Having expectations. Having people ask why I was single." His voice dropped slightly. "Having to explain why I wasn't interested in..."

"In?"

"I really don't want to talk about this."

I was stunned into silence. Had I completely misread him all these years? Constructed an entire persona that he'd just... accepted? For what? To avoid awkward conversations?

"I don't understand," I finally said.

"You don't need to." Cam tapped the agreement. "So we're doing this? For real?"

I took a deep breath, feeling the weight of the decision. "Yes. All parties will sign the NDA tomorrow, and we stick to the terms. Period."

"Agreed." He looked almost relieved. "What about Zayne?"

"No," I said firmly. "Not unless we absolutely have to. You know how he is. He'd never understand. I know Marcus thinks he'll just tell him to go along and he will, but we both know he won't"

Cam nodded slowly. "Okay. When do we start?"

"Immediately. The NHL Awards are only two weeks away. That doesn't give us much time to establish a believable relationship." I pulled out my tablet, shifting into PR mode. "We'll need to be seen together gradually. Small appearances, casual settings. Build a natural progression."

"That rescheduling really worked in our favor, huh?" Cam commented. "If they'd held the awards in June like usual, we wouldn't even have had this opportunity."

I nodded. The California wildfires had been devastating, sending smoke drifting all the way to Las Vegas, creating serious health concerns and forcing the NHL to postpone the annual awards ceremony from its traditional June date to October.

"It's certainly convenient timing," I agreed. "We'll need to craft a backstory. How long we've been together, how it started – "

"How about, we reconnected after I was drafted to the Slashers. Started as friends catching up, slowly became more. Been keeping it quiet because of your position with the team and your brother?"

I raised an eyebrow, impressed despite myself. "That's... actually believable. We'll need to agree on specific details though – favorite restaurants, movies we've seen together, little things couples would know about each other."

"I can be creative when motivated," he said with a hint of the charm that made him such a fan favorite. Then, more seriously: "But we'll need more than just a story, right? We need proof. Photos. Social media. Evidence that we've been together for a while, just keeping it private."

"Yeah, I'm working on that."

He pulled out his phone. "Check your texts."

My phone buzzed, and I opened his message to find a photo I'd never seen before – Cam and me at a team charity event last year, standing close together, both laughing at something off-camera. We looked... comfortable. Happy. Like a couple.

"Where did you get this?" I asked, genuinely surprised.

"Team photographer. I asked for the outtakes months ago." He shrugged at my questioning look. "You looked nice. Happy."

"There are more?"

"A few." He swiped through his phone and showed me another – this one from the Stanley Cup celebration, one from Logan and Coco's party when she won Nationals, Cam with his arm casually draped over my shoulder as we posed with the team. Another from the holiday party, where I was explaining something animatedly and he was watching me with an expression I hadn't noticed at the time – soft, almost fond.

"These are good," I admitted. "But we'll need more recent ones. And more, you know... couple-like."

Cam nodded, suddenly businesslike. "So what's next?"

I drained the last of my wine and stood up. "Tomorrow, we get these agreements signed. Then we start being seen together – casually at first, more intimate as we get closer to the awards." I hesitated, then added, "And Cam? Outside of the people in that room today, and Logan, obviously, no one else can know. The fewer people who know the truth, the better."

"Understood." He also rose, towering over me even in my heels. For a moment, we just looked at each other, the weight of what we were agreeing to hanging between us.

"This is crazy," I said softly.

"Completely insane," he agreed, a small smile playing on his lips. "But we're doing it anyway."

I nodded, gathering my purse and the agreement. "I'll have my assistant schedule a meeting tomorrow. Nine AM, probably."

As I turned to leave, Cam caught my arm gently. "Lana?"

"Yes?" The way he said my name made me forget what I was going to say next. This was the exact reason I made it my personal mission to avoid him whenever possible.

"Thank you. I know what this could cost you, and I know you don't owe me anything. But I won't forget this."

Something warm and dangerous unfurled in my chest, and I immediately tried to stamp it out. This was business. Professional courtesy. Nothing more.

"Don't thank me yet," I said, sliding out of the booth. "We still have to convince the entire hockey world that you're madly in love with me."

His smile – slow, devastating, and, *fuck*, entirely too knowing – made my knees forget how to function properly.

"That," he said, "might be the easiest part."

As I walked out of Breakaway Bar, leaving Cam Murphy sitting in our corner booth with that enigmatic grin, I told myself the shiver that ran down my spine was from the October chill in the air. Not from the way he'd looked at me like I was something he'd been searching for his whole life.

I mean, it *was* only 84 degrees.

This was just business.

So why did it already feel like it was going to be everything but?

Chapter 3

I arrived at the arena a full hour earlier than usual the next morning, needing time alone in my office to prepare. This wasn't just another media strategy meeting or damage control session. This was professionally reckless, personally dangerous, and absolutely, completely unprecedented.

Five copies of the NDA and agreement sat neatly in folders on my desk, each with a Post-it flag marking the signature lines. My laptop displayed a PowerPoint I'd spent half the night creating – " Image Rehabilitation: Murphy Protocol." I'd gone through twelve different titles before settling on one that sounded appropriately corporate and didn't include words like "fake fiancée," "how to lie to America," or "completely insane career move."

The clock on my wall ticked like the countdown timer on a bomb. Each second brought me closer to officially agreeing to deceive the public, the media, and my own family. The PR director in me knew this was a calculated risk with a big upside for Cam and the team, and also, the potential to, you know, destroy my career. The woman in me – the one who still remembered how it felt to wake up alone after that night in Boston – knew this was emotional quicksand.

I smoothed my pencil skirt, checked my reflection in my compact mirror one last time, and headed to the small conference room I'd booked for this meeting – not the main one where anyone could see us gathered, but a smaller space tucked away in the administrative wing, where curious eyes wouldn't find us.

Coach Sully arrived first, as expected. In the fifteen years he'd coached the Slashers, he'd never been late to a meeting. His perpetual scowl softened slightly when he saw me arranging presentation materials.

"Morning, Lana. How we feeling about this circus?" he asked, dropping his worn playbook on the table.

"Optimistic but cautious," I replied with more confidence than I felt.

He grunted noncommittally and took a seat. "Your brother finds out, I'm claiming complete ignorance."

"Understood," I said dryly.

Coach Rocco arrived next, smelling faintly of coffee and the wintergreen liniment he always carried for players' muscle strains. At sixty-eight, Rocco had been with the organization longer than anyone, transitioning from player to assistant coach to hockey Yoda with the kind of grace I could only hope to emulate in my own career.

"Morning, kiddo," he greeted me with his usual gruff affection.

Rocco settled into his chair with a slight grimace, "Been around this game forty-five years, but I've never seen anything like what you kids are cooking up. Your pops know about this scheme?"

I froze slightly. "Let's keep Frank Decker out of this conversation for everyone's continued good health."

"Smart girl," Rocco chuckled. "Man finds out someone's fake-marrying the Decker princess, there'll be bodies."

Marcus Thompson and Ryan Keller arrived together, deep in conversation about salary caps, and took seats on opposite sides of the table – GM and agent, natural adversaries in most situations, now unusual allies in this scheme. Marcus nodded at me professionally while Ryan flashed his practiced agent smile.

Cam walked in, nodding casually to the rest of us. Gone was yesterday's rumpled post-practice casualness. Today he wore a midnight blue suit and a crisp white button-down that emphasized his broad shoulders and made his eyes look like the water at some exclusive tropical resort that charged $25,000 a night. His hair was styled instead of shower-damp, and he'd actually shaved. Even his socks seemed to have gotten the memo – navy blue with tiny hockey sticks, subdued by his usual standards.

He looked like a man taking this seriously. He also looked like a man who was born to be on the cover of GQ, preferably in his underwear, which made it slightly harder to stay focused around him.

Our eyes met briefly as he took the seat directly across from me. I nodded professionally, ignoring the weird flutter in my stomach. Just nerves.

"Thank you all for being here," I began once everyone was settled, pressing the power button on my presentation clicker perhaps a bit harder than necessary. "I know this is an unusual situation, but I believe with proper management, we can achieve our objectives while minimizing risks."

I distributed the folders like I was handing out death sentences, keeping my voice steady and businesslike despite the absurdity of what we were about to formalize.

"What you have before you is a non-disclosure agreement covering the arrangement between Cam and myself, as well as detailed terms of how this... partnership will function. I'd like everyone to review and sign before we proceed further."

The rustling of papers filled the small room as everyone flipped through the document. Coach Sully's eyebrows rose slightly at the clause about physical boundaries, but he didn't comment. Ryan nodded approvingly at the media strategy sections. Marcus flipped straight to the liability paragraphs – typical GM move.

Cam, however, read each page carefully, his brow furrowed slightly in concentration. I found myself watching the way his fingers turned each page, remembering how those same hands had once traced every inch of my skin.

I cleared my throat and looked away.

"Thorough and professional as always, Lana," Marcus said, reaching for a pen.

"That's what you pay me for," I replied with a small smile. "Managing public perception is my specialty, even when the situation is... unconventional."

"Unconventional," Rocco repeated with a snort. "That's one word for it."

One by one, they signed the agreements. When Cam's turn came, he read through the entire document a second time, his expression unreadable. Finally, he signed with a flourish and slid the folder back to me.

"So we're all official now," he said, clearly suppressing a grin. "Fiancée."

"Don't push it, Murphy," I replied, unable to completely suppress an answering smile despite myself. "And technically, only in public settings, as per section 2 of the agreement."

"Always by the book," he murmured, sitting back in his chair.

With the paperwork complete, I moved to my presentation, clicking through to the first slide: "Strategic Approach to Relationship Revelation."

"Our primary challenge is believability," I explained, slipping fully into PR Director mode. "The public needs to accept that Cam and I have been in a serious, committed relationship that has simply been kept private until now. To achieve this, we need to be extremely careful about what we say versus what we show."

I clicked to the next slide, which featured two columns: "Say" and "Show."

"The most important rule: we never explicitly claim to be engaged. Not to the press, not on social media, not to anyone outside this room." I looked pointedly at each person. "What we do is carefully cultivate the perception through visual cues, body language, and strategic non-denials."

Ryan shifted forward in his seat, his gold cufflinks catching the fluorescent light. "But for the Redline deal – "

"Will be completely convinced without us needing to lie," I finished firmly. "Trust me, Mr. Keller. The public reads between the lines. We don't need to say it, just show it."

"And how exactly do we do that?" Coach Sully asked, skepticism evident in his voice.

I clicked to the next slide: "Escalation Timeline."

"We'll let the public and Redline draw their own conclusions through visual story-telling, strategic non-denials, and carefully orchestrated public moments. By the end of the week, we'll have established a foundation for the revelation that we've been together for some time."

"How do we handle the team?" Marcus asked. "The guys will notice if you two suddenly start acting differently around each other."

"Cam tells Logan that we've been harboring feelings for each other but only recently decided to explore them publicly, and it will filter down through the team." I glanced at Cam, who nodded, even though we both knew Logan already knew. "That we're being careful because of workplace dynamics and Zayne's... protective tendencies. For now, we'll keep him on a need-to-know basis."

"Protective," Cam repeated with a snort. "That's diplomatic."

"Your brother's going to murder him when he finds out," Rocco said cheerfully. "Should be entertaining."

"That's a distinct possibility," Cam nodded.

I took a deep breath. "Zayne receives the same story as everyone else for now. We'll bring Zayne into the loop only if necessary."

"Better you than me," Coach Rocco laughed. "I've seen Zayne commit murders on the ice that would make the Godfather say 'whoa buddy, take it down a notch.'"

"Thank you for that helpful reminder," I said dryly, clicking to the next slide.

I continued through the presentation, detailing each phase of our plan – from initial social media seeding to strategic public appearances, from press response scripts to contingency plans.

"Sounds like you've thought of everything," Marcus observed.

"That's her job," Cam said unexpectedly, a note of what almost sounded like pride in his voice. "Best in the business."

I blinked at him, momentarily thrown by the sincere compliment, before recovering.

"And the most important visual cue," I said, reaching the final slide, "will be the ring."

"The ring?" Coach Rocco echoed.

"An engagement requires a ring," I explained, clicking to a slide showing examples of tasteful but camera-worthy rings. "Something elegant but noticeable. Something that photographs well but doesn't scream 'publicity stunt.' We'll need it by the NHL awards at the latest."

"I'll take care of it," Cam said quietly, drawing everyone's attention.

"We should discuss specifications," I began, but he shook his head.

"I said I'll handle it," he repeated, a strange intensity in his gaze. "Trust me."

Something about his tone made me hesitate. This wasn't the carefree, go-with-the-flow Cam I was used to managing in PR situations. This was... different. Deliberate.

"Alright," I conceded. "But nothing outlandish, please. It needs to be believable... "

"It will be," he assured me. Something in his slight smile made me terrified of what he was planning.

As the meeting wrapped up, I provided everyone with a printed timeline of key events leading up to the NHL Awards, including our first planned public appearance – a team charity event at the children's hospital next week.

Cam was watching me with that same unreadable expression, one finger tapping lightly on the table. The soft rhythm seemed to match my suddenly accelerated heartbeat.

"Any questions?" I asked, addressing the room but somehow looking only at him.

"Just one," Cam said, leaning forward slightly. "When do we start?"

The way he said it – low, with just a hint of eagerness – sent an unexpected shiver through my body.

"Immediately," I replied, proud of how steady my voice remained. "We have exactly two weeks until the NHL Awards. Every day counts."

As the meeting disbanded, Cam lingered near the door. Coach Sully gave me a brief nod that somehow managed to convey both approval and concern, while Rocco patted my shoulder as he passed.

"You're playing with fire, kiddo," he murmured, too low for anyone else to hear. "Just remember, in hockey and in life, sometimes the best plays are the ones you don't draw up on the whiteboard."

Before I could ask what he meant, he was gone, followed by Marcus and Ryan deep in conversation about negotiation tactics.

When everyone else had filed out, Cam approached, his movements casual but purposeful.

"So," he said, voice pitched low enough that only I could hear. "What does 'immediately' look like, exactly?"

I glanced up from my tablet, finding him closer than I'd expected. Close enough that I caught the faint scent of his cologne – cedarwood and something citrusy – and could see the faint stubble already emerging along his jaw despite his morning shave.

"It means by the time you leave practice today, people should have a reason to wonder," I said, proud of how steady my voice remained. "A social media breadcrumb. A seen-together moment. Something subtle but noticeable."

He nodded thoughtfully, his gaze dropping briefly to my lips before returning to my eyes.

"I have media availability after practice. Why don't you handle that one personally instead of sending an assistant?"

It was a reasonable suggestion. As PR Director, I often delegated routine media sessions to my staff, but occasionally supervised them myself, especially for high-profile players or sensitive topics.

"Good idea," I agreed, trying to ignore how my pulse quickened at the thought of standing close to him, playing this dangerous game in public. "That's subtle enough to not raise immediate questions but will get people looking. I'll be there."

"And after?" he asked, that slight smile returning, transforming his face from merely handsome to unfairly devastating.

"After what?"

"After media. Maybe we could grab coffee? Somewhere visible but not obvious. Start laying that groundwork."

My instinct was to refuse – to keep this strictly in the building, to minimize actual time spent together outside of necessary appearances. But he was right. We needed to start building a foundation. It was right there on my slide deck.

"Fine," I said with a small sigh. "But remember – subtle. We're easing people into this, not dropping a social media bomb."

"Always the strategist," he said, and now I could definitely hear both amusement and admiration in his voice. "See you at practice, then."

He turned to leave, but paused at the threshold. "Oh, and Lana?"

"Yes?"

"Don't worry about the ring. I have excellent taste," he grinned."

Oh gawd." My mind instantly shot back to the massive celebration after we won the Cup, and the light-up Slashers bow tie Cam had worn with his tuxedo.

Before I could respond, he was gone, leaving me with the distinct impression that Cameron Murphy had already managed to veer off-script on our carefully constructed plan.

This was not good.

I gathered my presentation materials, my mind racing ahead to our next steps. As PR Director, I'd orchestrated countless strategic narratives for the team – manufactured rivalries for media hype, carefully curated comeback stories, even the occasional misdirection to protect player privacy (*Ahem, Logan*.) But this was different. This was personal.

This was pretending to be in love with the only man in the world who'd ever made me wonder *what if?*

As I walked back to my office, my heels clicking rhythmically on the polished floor, I couldn't shake the feeling that despite all my meticulous planning, this situation was already slipping beyond my control – just like my heart had that night in Boston ten years ago.

Professional suicide or not, there was no backing out now. The NDAs were signed. The plan was in motion.

Chapter 4

T he next day was Saturday, but in PR, weekends are just another workday with better lighting.

I pulled into the parking lot of Coconut Charlie's – a beachside bar that somehow managed to be both a tourist trap and a local favorite. With its weathered wooden deck, thatched roof, and unobstructed view of the Gulf's impossibly blue water, it was just secluded enough for our purposes without seeming suspicious.

I'd chosen this spot deliberately: public enough to be seen if we wanted to be, but casual enough that our meeting wouldn't seem staged. Plus, if anyone recognized Cam, it could look like we were just grabbing lunch, not plotting an elaborate deception that could potentially derail both our careers. *Okay, fine.* Even though I'd written this stupid plan myself I was super hesitant to pull the trigger.

I spotted Cam already seated at a corner table on the deck, sunglasses perched on his nose, baseball cap pulled low – his version of incognito. Even with the disguise, he was unmistakable: broad shoulders, straight posture, that distinctive *I just want to bite you* Jensen Ackles-esque jawline that had graced so many of my marketing campaigns.

As I approached, he looked up and smiled, rising slightly from his seat in that old-school gentlemanly way he had. How he always stood when a woman entered the room, how he pulled out chairs, opened doors. Small, courteous habits that contradicted the bad-boy public image I'd helped create.

"You're early," I noted, slipping into the seat across from him and placing my oversized tote on the extra chair.

"Figured we should look eager for this date," he replied with a half-smile that did annoyingly pleasant things to his already unfair face. "Plus, I secured us an awesome table. Visible but not center ice."

I glanced around, noting his strategic choice – sheltered enough for a private conversation but with a clear line of sight from both the beach and the main bar area. The aroma of coconut rum and grilled mahi-mahi drifted from the kitchen, mingling with the salt air.

"Nicely done," I admitted. "Anyone recognize you yet?"

"Couple of autographs. The usual." He pushed a menu toward me. "I ordered us some drinks. Hope that's okay."

On cue, a server appeared with two glasses – what looked like a beer for Cam and a fruit-filled concoction for me that made me pause mid-reach.

"Mango margarita," Cam explained as I examined the drink. "That's the one you get at the after-game parties, right? Double sugar on the rim, no dorky umbrella?" He shrugged at my surprised expression. "What? I pay attention."

The realization that he remembered such a specific detail from some random night sent an unexpected warmth through me that had nothing to do with the Florida heat. I pushed the feeling aside and took a sip. It was perfect.

"We should get started," I said, pulling up my meticulously organized notes. "We need to establish our backstory. Something believable but not too complicated."

Cam nodded, leaning forward with surprising focus. "So how long have we been secretly madly in love?"

I rolled my eyes at his phrasing. "Eight months seems reasonable. Long enough to be serious, recent enough that keeping it quiet makes sense."

"Eight months," he repeated, nodding. "So we reconnected around February, maybe after the All-Star game? I remember you wore that blue dress at the reception."

I stared at him. I *had* worn a blue dress to that event – teal silk the color of the ocean with an asymmetrical neckline. The fact that he remembered made my heart take an extra beat that I immediately blamed on the frozen margarita. *Chilly.*

"That works," I said, refocusing on my tablet. "It gives us a catalyst – a special moment where our professional relationship shifted."

"We can say we started talking more personally during the playoff run, and after the win..." Cam's voice trailed off, his expression suddenly thoughtful.

"What?" I prompted.

"I finally worked up the courage to kiss you," he finished, his voice dropping lower. "At the team celebration. When everyone was distracted by Logan's Cup speech."

I looked up, caught off-guard by the specificity in his tone, like he was describing a real memory rather than fabricating one. "Seems like you've thought about this a bit."

He took a sip of his beer, eyes never leaving mine over the rim of his glass. "Just filling in details. Making it real."

Something about his intensity made me shift in my seat. "Okay. So we started dating in February, kept it quiet because of my position with the team and Zayne's..."

"Overprotectiveness?" Cam suggested delicately.

"Homicidal tendencies where my dating life is concerned," I corrected dryly.

Cam laughed, the sound bright and genuine, drawing glances from a nearby table. "Fair enough. So we've been sneaking around for eight months, and now...?"

"Now we feel secure enough in our relationship to go public."

"So, who made the first move? For real?" he asked, running a finger along the condensation on his glass.

"You already said you kissed me after the Cup win."

"I meant in our story. But in general, too." He leaned back, studying me with unexpected intensity. "I'm curious about how you see this playing out. In your mind, am I the pursuer or the pursued?"

I considered this, trying to separate my professional assessment from the strange flutter in my stomach. "With your public image, people would expect you to make the move. But for it to be believable as something serious rather than one of your... usual encounters, there should be hesitation. Respect."

"So I pursued you, but carefully. Respectfully." He nodded slowly. "That tracks. Though for the record, I don't think I'd have had the patience to wait through eight months of secret dating before telling the world."

"It's a story, Cam. Not a reality show."

He shrugged, a casual motion that somehow emphasized the breadth of his shoulders under his t-shirt. "Even fictional characters need consistent motivations." I'd forgotten he was a reader.

"Fine. You pursued. I was reluctant because of professional boundaries. You wore me down with your charm and... whatever it is your fans see in you."

"My devastating good looks and scoring record?" he suggested with a grin.

"Right. That and your humility, clearly."

We both laughed, and for a moment, it felt almost normal – just two people having lunch, not constructing an elaborate deception.

"What about the proposal story?" Cam asked after our laughter had subsided. "We need something memorable but not too public."

"We're not actually claiming we're engaged, remember?" I reminded him, tapping my pen against my tablet for emphasis. "Just... heavily implying it."

"Still need a story for the ring. People will ask." His expression turned serious. "Trust me, they always ask."

I sighed, knowing he was right. "Something simple. Spontaneous. A private moment that feels authentic."

"The beach," Cam said immediately, leaning forward. "Last month, sunset walk. No witnesses except maybe a few distant beachgoers. I didn't plan it, didn't have a ring yet, but the moment was right."

I blinked at him. "That's... actually perfect."

"Told you I could be creative when motivated." His eyes met mine, and for a brief moment, I wondered what exactly his motivation was. Oh yeah, four and a half million dollars. "What else do we need? Favorite couple activities?"

I consulted my list, grateful for the return to concrete details. "Things we supposedly do together. Movies, shows, hobbies. The little details that make a relationship feel real."

"Well, what do you actually like?" Cam asked, leaning forward again. "Might be easier to stick close to the truth."

It was a sensible approach. "I like independent films, true crime documentaries. Hanging out at Siesta Key beach with my family when I actually have time off, which is basically never during hockey season. Reading actual physical books. Boating when I can convince my dad to let me take his prized fishing boat out." I shrugged. "Pretty basic stuff."

"Not basic. Real." Cam seemed to consider. "I watch a lot of baking shows to relax. Play guitar, badly. Love anything on the water – boating, surfing here, ice fishing back home in Minnesota, skiing, snowboarding." His eyes crinkled with a genuine smile. "Have an embarrassing collection of weird socks."

"I'm familiar," I laughed. His fans sent him crazy socks by the truckload.

He grinned and briefly lifted his pant leg to reveal today's choice: little tacos with cheerful cartoon faces. The ridiculousness of it – this professional athlete, this supposed bad boy, wearing whimsical socks – made me laugh despite myself.

"We need overlap," I said, steering us back on track. "Things we both genuinely enjoy that could be couple activities."

Cam thought for a moment. "BU hockey?"

"Go Terriers!" I yelled with unexpected enthusiasm and a *bark* for emphasis that made him chuckle.

"Cupcakes," he said suddenly. "You're always bringing those fancy ones to office meetings."

"Sweet Caroline's," I confirmed, genuinely surprised he'd noticed. "They do the lavender vanilla ones I like."

"So that's something we share. You love cupcakes. I love when you bring cupcakes."

"That would imply we're actually together outside of work events," I pointed out.

"That's the whole premise, isn't it?" he countered, that half-smile returning. "That we've been seeing each other privately for months?"

"Right. Of course." I made another note. "Cupcakes, BU hockey, hanging at the beach... what else?"

"TV shows? Movies?"

I thought about my recent binges. "Schitt's Creek? It has the right balance of humor and heart. Believable couple viewing."

"Love it. David and Patrick are couple goals." At my surprised look, he added, "What? It's a good show. I'm not just muscles and slapshots, Decker."

I added it to my list, along with a few other details: favorite restaurants (we settled on a quiet Italian place near the arena and a sushi spot by the bay), weekend activities (beach walks, farmers markets), and how we communicate during away games when I'm not traveling with the team (nightly FaceTime calls, another detail Cam contributed with suspicious readiness).

"What about pet names?" I asked, working through my checklist.

Cam's eyes lit up with unholy glee. "Definitely."

"No." I held up a hand, fixing him with my best PR Director glare. "I mean, our position on them. Which is that we are absolutely not using pet names. If you call me 'babe' in public, I'm calling you 'Puck Daddy' for the rest of this arrangement."

Cam's grin widened. "I'm kinda into that, actually."

"You would be," I muttered, fighting a smile. "Let's move on. I've prepared a list of potential questions reporters might ask, so we should align our answers – "

"Lana," Cam interrupted gently. "I think we've got enough backstory for now. We're overthinking this."

"Overthinking is literally my job description," I reminded him, gesturing to my tablet full of notes.

"And you're excellent at it." His tone was teasing but kind. "But at some point, we need to stop planning and start selling this. People aren't going to believe spreadsheets and synchronized answers. They'll believe chemistry."

He was right, though I was reluctant to admit it. PR was about controlling the narrative, but romance – even a fake one – needed authenticity. Spontaneity. Which is a bit challenging to contain in neat bullet points

"Fine," I conceded. "What do you suggest?"

"Time for the world's most strategic selfie tour."

"Selfie tour?" I echoed. "Already? Don't we need time to rehearse or – Wait — is this why you asked me to bring three outfits for the beach?"

"Yes. Trust me," he interrupted, dropping a hundred dollar bill on the table for the check. Two drinks. Nice tip. "This is my area of expertise. Hockey players practically invented the strategic social media presence."

"That's not even close to..." I muttered, but I gathered my things and followed him anyway, wondering how I'd gone from meticulous planning to impromptu photo shoots in the span of a single margarita.

Outside Coconut Charlie's, the midday sun was warm but not yet oppressive, the breeze off the Gulf carrying that distinctive salt-and-sunscreen scent that defined St. Petersburg. Cam led the way along Beach Drive, his stride casual but purposeful.

"First stop, the murals at the Shore Club," he explained, navigating us toward the upscale hotel known for its vibrant wall art. "Casual, colorful backdrop. Public space but not screaming 'look at us.'"

We arrived at a wall covered in a funky beach scene – vibrant blues and greens depicting the Gulf's marine life. It was beautiful and distinctly local, the kind of spot that said "Florida" without resorting to plastic flamingoes and neon kitsch.

"Perfect," Cam murmured, positioning us in front of a section featuring rays and tropical fish. "Now, stand next to me, but not too posed. Like we just stopped to admire the art."

I adjusted my position, feeling strangely self-conscious. In my professional life, I was constantly arranging players for photo ops, coaching them on posture and expression. Being on the other side of the camera felt foreign, especially with Cam standing so close that I could feel the warmth radiating from his body.

"Relax," he said softly, picking up on my tension. "Just pretend this is real."

He slipped an arm around my shoulders – casual, easy, like he'd done it a hundred times before. The weight of it was warm, solid, and strangely comforting. The scent of his cologne – something woodsy and expensive – enveloped me.

"Look up at me," he directed, his voice low. "Like I just said something that caught you off guard."

I tilted my face toward his, all ready to manufacture a surprised expression, when he whispered, "Did you know otters hold hands while they sleep so they don't drift apart?"

The random fact was so unexpected, so charmingly odd, that I laughed – a genuine, unplanned burst of amusement that crinkled my eyes and softened my features. In that exact moment, Cam clicked the selfie.

When he showed me the result, I was startled by how... natural we looked. His arm draped comfortably around me, his face turned down toward mine with a warm smile, me laughing up at him with unguarded delight. We looked like a couple – not just any couple, but one comfortable in each other's space, happy in each other's company.

"That's..." I searched for a professional assessment and came up empty.

"Perfect," Cam finished for me, swiping through filter options. "Natural. Exactly what we need."

He was right. It was the kind of photo that didn't need a caption, that told its own story. I watched as he made minimal adjustments and saved it, not posting yet.

"One down," he said, leading me away from the mural. "Next stop: Sweet Caroline's."

I raised an eyebrow. "My cupcake place?"

"Isn't it *our* cupcake place? We established it's part of our couple lore," he reminded me. "Plus, I'm actually hungry."

The walk to the bakery took us past outdoor cafés and boutiques filled with beachy merchandise. Occasionally someone would do a double-take at Cam – a hint of recognition that he acknowledged with a friendly nod but no stopping. Just a local athlete out with his...girlfriend. The thought sent a strange flutter through my stomach.

It was a weird situation. Of course I was feeling weird. I mean, it would be weird *not to*, right?

Sweet Caroline's was tucked into a converted bungalow, with mismatched vintage furniture and the heavenly scent of butter and vanilla permeating the air. Bree was behind the counter, and her face brightened when she recognized me.

"Lana! Your usual?"

"Please," I confirmed, then hesitated. "Actually, make it one to share. And an iced coffee."

Cam's eyebrows rose slightly in surprise, but he didn't comment. Bree nodded, already reaching for the lavender vanilla cupcake with its signature mountain of pale purple frosting.

"And a coffee for me too, please," Cam added. "Black."

We settled at a small table by the window, the cupcake between us. Cam studied it with exaggerated suspicion.

He smelled it first and eyed the lavender frosting. "Does it taste like soap?"

"It tastes like heaven," I corrected, breaking off a piece. "Try it before you judge."

He accepted the bite, his expression skeptical until the flavor registered. His eyes widened slightly.

"Okay, that's actually amazing," he admitted.

"Told you." I took my own bite, savoring the delicate floral notes against the buttery cake.

Cam pulled out his phone again. "Another photo op. But this one needs to look more... intimate."

Before I could question what he meant, he leaned across the small table, closing the distance between us until our faces were just inches apart. Close enough that I could see all the different shades of blue in his eyes, the creases in his full lips. He held the phone at an angle that would capture us both with the cupcake in the foreground.

"Smile," he instructed softly. "Like I just said something sweet."

My heart thumped unevenly as I managed a smile, trying to ignore how his breath brushed my cheek. The camera clicked.

When he showed me this photo, I almost didn't recognize myself. There was a softness to my expression, a vulnerability I rarely allowed in public. Cam looked at ease, happy, his blue eyes bright with something that looked remarkably like affection.

"These are good," I admitted, suddenly needing air. "Very convincing."

He ate another bite of cupcake, and I noticed a tiny dot of purple frosting at the corner of his mouth. Without thinking, I reached across and brushed it away with my thumb.

The gesture was instinctive, intimate – the kind of thoughtless touch that happens between people who are comfortable with each other. Cam went still, his eyes finding mine. For a moment, neither of us moved.

"Sorry," I murmured, withdrawing my hand quickly. "I don't know why I..."

"Don't be sorry," he said, his voice slightly rougher than before. "That's exactly the kind of thing real couples do."

The moment hung between us, charged with something I wasn't ready to name. I cleared my throat.

"Where to next? Also, it's probably time for a wardrobe change so it doesn't look like we took all these photos in one day."

I reached into my oversized tote and pulled out a blush pink sundress – pushing down the three alternate outfits stuffed in there for today's adventure. With a nod toward the restroom, I left to change, grateful for a moment to collect myself.

I wore a simple white bikini underneath my clothes, a strategic decision in case I needed to do a wardrobe change in public. Swimsuits at the beach were hardly a traffic stopper.

When I returned, Cam had transformed as well. The baseball cap was gone, his golden hair tousled and sexy. He was now wearing shorts, and he'd removed his button down, leaving only a fitted dark gray *Letters to Cleo* t-shirt that clung to his broad shoulders and chest in such a way that was probably illegal in public spaces.

For once, I let my eyes roam leisurely over him – his high cheekbones, the curve of his biceps, the easy confidence in his posture. When my gaze finally returned to his face, I found him watching me with a knowing smile.

"See something you like?" he teased quietly.

Heat crept up my neck. "Just making sure you look presentable. Uh. For the photos."

"Of course." His smile widened. "Just the photos."

Our selfie tour continued through downtown, each stop carefully chosen for maximum believability: a bookstore where we posed with our heads bent over the same novel, a street musician's performance where Cam dropped a twenty in the guitar case and wrapped an arm around my waist as we listened. A few times we asked strangers to snap the shots, especially in places where Cam was approached for autographs, on the off chance a fan might get the rumor going on social media. Each photo captured a different facet of a relationship – casual affection, shared interests, ordinary moments made special by companionship.

With each stop, each casual touch, I found myself relaxing into the role. Cam's hand protectively on my shoulder as we crossed a street. My fingers brushing his arm as I pointed out a passing sand hill crane family that had just leisurely wandered into the street, assuming cars would stop for them as they nearly always did. The way he instinctively put himself between me and a group of rowdy college boys. Small moments, barely noticeable individually, but collectively creating a tapestry of intimacy that felt startlingly real.

Our final stop was a kitschy souvenir shop filled with shell-encrusted picture frames and t-shirts sporting jokes about Florida retirement. Cam insisted we go in, claiming we needed "something quintessentially tourist-y" to round out our collection.

Inside, he made a beeline for a display of t-shirts, rifling through until he found what he was apparently looking for.

"This," he declared, holding up a women's v-neck in soft pink. Across the chest, in glittering silver letters, it read "Hockey Wife Material" with a small puck graphic dotting the i.

"Absolutely not," I said flatly.

"It's perfect," he argued. "Cheesy enough to be believable as a joke gift, but also sending exactly the message we want."

"It's hideous."

"It's strategic." He held it up against me. "Plus, this color brings out the pink in your cheeks when you're annoyed with me."

"First, I'm *always* annoyed with you. Second, I'm not wearing that for a photo," I insisted, already knowing I was fighting a losing battle.

Twenty minutes and one unexpected purchase later, I found myself standing outside the shop wearing the ridiculous t-shirt over my sundress, Cam's arm around my shoulders as he took our final selfie.

"I can't believe I let you talk me into this," I muttered through my staged smile.

"You look adorable," he assured me, capturing the moment. "And completely besotted with your hockey star boyfriend."

"I look like I lost a bet," I countered, but there was no real heat in my words. Despite myself, I was enjoying this bizarre afternoon. The strategic planning, yes, but also the easy camaraderie, the shared purpose. The way Cam could make me laugh even when I was trying to maintain my professional composure.

"And that's a wrap," Cam announced, reviewing our collection of photos. "Now for the strategic deployment."

We found a bench along the waterfront where we could sit and select the best images. The late afternoon sun cast a golden glow over the water, painting everything in warm, flattering light that seemed determined to make our fake photoshoot feel... romantic.

"Wait, this is too perfect," Cam said, his fingers finding the hem of his shirt. My mouth suddenly went dry as he pulled it over his head in one fluid motion, revealing the sculpted torso I'd been studiously avoiding thinking about for years. Hockey had been kind to Cameron Murphy – absurdly, unfairly, viciously kind. My mouth watered.

"What are you doing?" I managed, trying to sound annoyed instead of breathless.

His eyes met mine with a naughty glint. "Selling it, right? Nobody's going to believe I'm with the love of my life and not getting in the water with her." He reached for my hand, his palm warm against mine. "Come on, Lana. Florida sunset, gorgeous beach backdrop... we'd be idiots not to use this."

I hesitated only a second before letting him pull me toward the shoreline. The feeling of his hand wrapped around mine sent a current of electricity up my arm that had nothing to do with our agreement.

When we reached the water's edge, he dropped his shirt carelessly in the sand, his eyes never leaving mine. I set my oversized tote down next to it, suddenly hyperaware of his presence, of the inches between us, of what might come next. *Business, Lana.*

"Your turn," he said softly, the challenge unmistakable in his voice.

I gathered my courage, reached for the hem of my final wardrobe change of the day, a black halter dress. Cam's eyes were on me as I untied it behind my neck and let the dress drop to my feet. The white bikini underneath suddenly felt much more revealing than it had this morning in my bedroom mirror. I flicked the dress on top of my tote bag with my foot.

Cam's eyes darkened as they swept over me, lingering in places that made heat bloom across my skin that had nothing to do with the sun.

"See something you like?" I cocked my head mischievously.

"Just making sure you look presentable," he said, his voice rougher, lower, than I was used to.

"For the photos..." I offered playfully.

"Yeah..." His smile was slow, dangerous. "For the photos."

The water lapped at our ankles as we posed with the Gulf stretching behind us, bathed in the pink and orange glow of sunset. When Cam's arm slid around my waist, his fingertips brushed the bare skin just above my bikini bottom. I inhaled sharply, my body instinctively leaning into his touch.

"That got the goosebumps I was hoping for," he murmured, his breath warm against my ear. "Very convincing."

I turned my face to his, our lips now inches apart. "Always the professional."

"Not *always*," he replied, and for a moment, I thought he might close that last sliver of distance between us.

Instead, he pulled back slightly, eyes intense. "One more for luck?"

Before I could answer, he scooped me up in his arms with athletic ease, carrying me deeper into the gentle waves as I squealed in surprise. Water splashed around us as I clung to his shoulders – shoulders I now knew felt *exactly* as solid as they looked. Damn. That memory wasn't going anywhere soon.

He snapped a few more. "Perfect," he said with a grin that turned my insides molten, setting me back on my feet but keeping his arms loosely around my waist. "These are...c onvincing."

As I gathered up my things, Cam dropped to his knees, a playful glint in his icy blue eyes. "Marry me," he said dramatically, clutching his chest. His golden brown hair ruffled in the beach breeze, and it took all I had to suppress a smile.

"Are you serious right now?" I said, trying my hardest to maintain a stern expression. "You're killing my patience today, Murphy."

His grin widened, revealing a dimple that always made my heart flutter. "I've never been more serious about anything in my life," he teased. "You know, just in case we need to go the extra mile to land that Redline deal."

As we made our way back up the beach, Cam insisted on carrying my tote. I couldn't help but stare at the way his muscles flexed under the weight, or how he didn't immediately put his shirt back on, letting the sun dry his lightly-tanned skin. His eyes kept finding mine as we walked, each glance lingering a little longer than the last. The casual brush of his arm against mine sent a spark of electricity through me. I found myself leaning into his touch, and despite my best efforts, craving more.

"You know, if we're going to pull off this fake fiancée thing," he said, his voice low and intimate, "we should probably practice making it look real."

I raised an eyebrow, trying to ignore the way my pulse quickened. "And how do you propose we do that?"

He leaned in, his voice a husky whisper in my ear. "I have a few ideas."

"Let's stick to selfies for now," I said, stepping back into my dress.

We sat down on the bench in sync and narrowed down our options to five key photos: the mural laugh, the shared cupcake, a candid of me browsing books while Cam watched with an expression of unmistakable fondness, the two of us playing in the water with the Gulf behind us, and – against my better judgment – the one with the ridiculous t-shirt.

"We don't post them all at once," I instructed, slipping back into PR Director mode. "That would seem too calculated. One today, perhaps another tomorrow. Casual. Organic."

"Which one first?" Cam asked, our shoulders touching as he leaned in to see my screen.

I studied the options, trying to ignore the warmth of him beside me. "The mural. It's the most natural, the least staged-looking."

He nodded, pulling up Instagram. "Caption?"

"None," I decided. "More intriguing that way. Let people draw their own conclusions."

"Bold strategy," he murmured, his breath warm against my ear.

I posted the photo without comment on my Instagram, where my modest following of industry contacts and friends would see it. Within seconds, notifications began appearing – likes, comments, questions.

"My turn," Cam said with a mischievous glint in his eye. He immediately reposted the same image to his much larger following, but this time with a simple caption: "Lucky guy. #OffTheMarket #CupcakeQueen"

"Cam!" I grabbed for his phone, but it was too late. The post was live, the hashtags unmistakably sending exactly the message we'd agreed to imply rather than declare.

"Oops," he said, not looking remotely apologetic. "My thumb slipped."

"This wasn't the plan," I began, but my own phone was already buzzing incessantly with notifications. "We were supposed to ease into this, not drop a bomb."

"Sometimes you need to make a splash," he argued, looking far too pleased with himself. "Besides, now everyone's talking. Mission accomplished."

I pulled up his post on my phone, watching in real-time as comments flooded in:

@FosseFan77: "IS THIS REAL?"

@hockeybaby4eva: "OMG I SHIP IT."

@rllhockeymama: "Has Cam finally been domesticated??"

@goalgettr: "Who is she???"

My own post was similarly blowing up, with teammates, colleagues, and friends all expressing variations of shock and delight. I scrolled through, a mix of professional satisfaction and personal mortification washing over me. This was happening. Really happening.

And then a very different notification appeared on Cam's phone – a text from my brother.

ZAYNE: This better be a joke.

Cam showed me the screen, his expression turning serious. "Well, that didn't take long."

"What are you going to say?" I asked, a knot forming in my stomach.

He thought for a moment, then typed:

CAM: Just messing with you, brother.

As he set his phone down, I noticed the sun was beginning its descent toward the horizon. We'd spent the entire afternoon on our "selfie tour," longer than I'd intended. Longer than I'd realized, lost in the weird little bubble we'd created.

"I should get home," I said, gathering my things. "I need to prepare for the inevitable barrage of questions."

Cam nodded, rising with me. "I'll walk you to your car."

We made our way back to Coconut Charlie's parking lot in companionable silence, the weight of what we'd just set in motion hanging between us. When we reached my car, I turned to face him.

"Well, there's no going back now," I said, attempting a light tone.

"Would you want to?" he asked, his expression suddenly serious, eyes searching mine.

The question caught me off guard. "It will look like a fling if we don't see this through now." I unlocked my car, suddenly eager to escape the intensity of his gaze. "I'll see you Monday."

He nodded, stepping back to allow me to open my door. "Goodnight, Lana."

As I drove away, I could see him in my rearview mirror, still standing in the parking lot, watching me leave. Just before I turned onto the main road, I thought I saw him shake his head and mutter something to himself.

Later, lying in bed with my phone still buzzing with notifications, I couldn't stop thinking about the look in his eyes when he'd asked if I'd want to go back – as if my answer really mattered to him. As if this wasn't just about a sneaker deal or an image rehab.

I closed my eyes, trying to ignore the memory of his arm around my shoulders, the way his laugh had vibrated through me when we stood close, the brief moment when my thumb had brushed the corner of his mouth.

This was a professional arrangement. A strategic partnership with clearly defined boundaries and an expiration date.

I wasn't making *that* mistake twice.

Chapter 5

The Las Vegas skyline glittered beyond my hotel window, a constellation of man-made stars stretching across the desert night. Twenty floors below, the famous Bellagio fountains performed their choreographed dance, but from this height, they looked like miniature splashes in a very expensive bathtub.

I pressed my forehead against the cool glass, trying to calm the nervous energy that had been building since our plane landed three hours ago. The team charter flight had been agonizingly awkward, with Cam sitting next to Logan and the rest of his teammates in the back of the plane, and me up front with our GM and Coach Sully's wife Trixie. There was no clear answer on where we should sit given our newfound status, so I decided we should keep it professional and Cam decided to "visit" me approximately six times during the flight. It felt a lot like performance art in a flying fishbowl. And every single eye was on us.

Two weeks. It had been exactly two weeks since our "selfie tour" had exploded across social media. Fourteen days of fielding calls from curious reporters, deflecting questions from well-meaning colleagues, and maintaining the carefully curated façade of new romance whenever Cam and I were in the same room.

And what a couple of weeks it had been.

The photo of us laughing by the mural had been picked up by three major sports blogs. The one of us sharing a cupcake had spawned a fan-made video compilation set to Taylor Swift's "Lover" that somehow got over two million views. Even ESPN had run a segment titled "Bad Boy Settling Down?" featuring a panel of experts seriously discussing whether Cam Murphy's apparent new relationship would affect his performance on the ice.

I unzipped my garment bag, removing the midnight blue gown I'd selected for tomorrow's NHL Awards ceremony. The silky fabric slipped through my fingers as I hung it in the closet, trying not to think about how its color reminded me of Cam's eyes in certain light, or how he'd texted "Blue is my favorite color on you" when I'd sent him a photo of options last week.

My phone buzzed with a text from my assistant:

> KATIE: Are you EVER going to give me details about you and Cam? I'm dying here. Also, the Tampa Trib wants an exclusive.

I sighed, typing back:

> ME: Nothing to tell that isn't already on Instagram. And no exclusives until after awards.

The lie came easier each time, which should have concerned me more than it did. Another notification popped up – this one from Ryan Keller, Cam's agent:

> RYAN: Redline executives confirmed attendance tomorrow. Looking good so far. Remember, happy couple vibes only.

I set my phone down, anxiety bubbling in my chest. Tomorrow night would be the real test – not just a casual selfie on the beach or a choreographed coffee run, but a formal, high-profile event with cameras tracking our every move, analyzing our body language, searching for the truth behind the carefully constructed fiction.

The past few weeks had been a masterclass in strategic public appearances. A team charity event where Cam kept a respectful but affectionate hand at my back. A practice session where I personally delivered notes to him on the ice, our conversation captured from a distance but just intimate enough to fuel speculation.

Cam had even shown up at a women's shelter fundraiser I'd organized, bringing a signed stick for the auction that fetched triple its expected auction price – and leaving with his arm casually draped around my shoulders, just in time for the local news cameras to catch us.

Each moment calculated. Each touch choreographed. Each smile measured to reveal just enough, but not too much. And yet, beneath the performance, something unexpected was happening. Something I wasn't prepared for.

Cam was... different. Not the arrogant playboy of his public persona, nor even the focused professional I'd worked with for years. This Cam laughed more easily. Listened more intently. Asked questions about my day and actually waited for the answer.

Yesterday, he'd appeared at my office door with a lavender vanilla cupcake "just because." The day before, he'd texted me a photo of socks covered in tiny monkeys wearing bow ties with the caption: *Too much for the awards dinner?*

Small moments. Inconsequential acts. Except they weren't part of our agreement, weren't performed for any audience. They were just... us.

He was pushing me way past my comfort zone.

I unpacked my toiletries, arranging them meticulously on the marble counter of the expansive bathroom. Organization had always been my defense against chaos, and right now, my life felt decidedly chaotic.

The NHL awards added an extra layer of pressure to an already stressful situation. Half the hockey world was already in town, including my brother, who was nominated for the Norris Trophy.

Zayne had been uncharacteristically quiet about the whole situation, though the stony silences whenever Cam entered the room told me he wasn't exactly thrilled.

My phone rang – a FaceTime call from Monica, the stylist I used for televised events. I propped it against the mirror as her face appeared on screen.

"Show me the dress again," she demanded without preamble, her New York accent more pronounced when she was in professional mode.

I held up the midnight blue gown with its subtle beading and elegant silhouette.

"Perfect," she nodded approvingly. "Hair up, minimal jewelry. Let the dress do the talking."

"Agreed," I said, returning the gown to its hanger. "I was thinking just diamond studs and – "

"And whatever ring your hockey boy gives you," she finished with a knowing smile. "Which I'm still waiting to hear about, by the way."

"There's no ring, Monica," forcing a casual laugh.

She raised a perfectly shaped eyebrow. "Really? Because the entire internet seems to think otherwise. Hashtag hockey-wife-material is trending, and your hot-as-sin forward has been spotted at Tiffany's."

My heart skipped. "He what?"

"TMZ caught him there this morning. It's all over socials today." She peered at me through the screen. "Wait, you didn't know? I thought you two were..." She made a vague gesture with her hands.

"I was on the plane, so my assistant is monitoring socials today," I managed, the practiced line rolling off my tongue. "It's complicated with my position on the team."

"Oh shit, sorry. She probably didn't want to ruin the surprise for you. And honey, *nothing* about the way that man looks at you is complicated," Monica replied with a knowing smirk. "That's the look of a man who knows *exactly* what he wants."

We hung up a few minutes later and I sank onto the edge of the king-sized bed, suddenly exhausted. The lie was growing, taking on a life of its own, evolving into something more complex, more entangled with my actual life than I'd anticipated.

My phone buzzed again.

CAM: Dinner in your room or mine? Unless you'd prefer the restaurant downstairs with a hundred phones pointed at us.

I smiled despite myself:

ME: Room service. My suite at 8?

His response came immediately:

CAM: See you then, CupcakeQueen.

I'd barely had time to shower and change into loungewear – sleek gray shorts with a drawstring and a matching top – when a knock sounded at my door. Glancing at the clock, I frowned. 7:43. Early, even for Cam, who was always the first guy to show up for practice. Even before Logan.

Through the peephole, I saw him shifting his weight from foot to foot, one hand thrust deep in his pocket. His usual confident posture was replaced by something more hesitant, almost nervous.

I opened the door, prepared with a quip about his punctuality, but the words died in my throat when I saw his expression. There was an intensity in his eyes I'd rarely seen off the ice, a tightness around his mouth that spoke of carefully contained emotion.

"Can I come in?" he asked, his voice lower than usual.

I stepped back wordlessly, letting him enter. He wore dark jeans and a sleek black cashmere v-neck that stretched across his broad shoulders, elegant and casual but deliberately chosen. He smelled faintly of testosterone and something woodsy – a scent that instantly transported me back to that night in my dorm room ten years ago, when those same broad shoulders had hovered above me in the darkness.

"I haven't ordered dinner yet," I said, filling the strange silence that had settled between us. "I thought maybe – "

"I have something for you," he interrupted, pulling his left hand from his pocket.

And there it was. A small box wrapped in that unmistakable Tiffany blue, tied with a perfect white satin ribbon.

My breath caught. Even though I knew this was coming – the sight of that iconic little box in Cam Murphy's hand made my heart stutter in my chest.

"The ring," I said unnecessarily, my voice sounding distant to my own ears. "Right. Nice work. I just heard about the TMZ story. "

Cam didn't immediately offer it to me. Instead, he turned the box over in his hands, studying it with an expression I couldn't quite interpret. His fingers – strong from years of stick handling – traced the edges of the box with surprising gentleness.

"I thought about having it delivered," he said quietly. "Would've been easier. But then I realized – " He paused, seeming to carefully choose his next words. "If this were real, I wouldn't do it that way."

Our eyes met, and something unspoken passed between us – acknowledgment that we were now operating in a strange liminal space between fiction and reality.

"May I?" he asked, holding the box out at last.

I nodded, not trusting myself to speak. With careful movements, he untied the ribbon and lifted the lid, revealing a nest of white velvet cradling the most breathtaking ring I'd ever seen.

A mermaid sapphire – not the expected diamond – gleamed in the center, deep blue-green and mesmerizing, surrounded by a halo of smaller diamonds set in platinum. The setting was both vintage and modern, intricate yet not ostentatious. It was just perfect.

"Cam... this is..." Words failed me as I stared at it.

He shrugged, affecting a casualness that didn't quite reach his eyes. "You said we needed to look convincing. A ring like this practically screams 'fiancée.'"

My mind raced, trying to process the logistics. It must be a loaner, arranged by his agent... something to be returned along with the tuxedo after the awards ceremony. An elaborate prop for our elaborate charade. But, holy shit, what a prop.

"It's beautiful," I managed, still transfixed by the deep blue-green stone, the color of the ocean, that seemed to capture and reflect light from depths within.

"Try it on," Cam suggested softly. "Just to see how it looks."

With slightly trembling fingers, I reached for the ring. The platinum band felt cool against my skin as I slipped it onto my left hand.

It fit perfectly. Of course it did.

I held my hand up, watching as the sapphire caught the hotel room's light, sending fractured blue reflections dancing across my face. It was substantial without being gaudy, distinctive without being flashy – exactly what I would have chosen myself if this had been...

But it wasn't real. This was business. Strategy. A means to an end.

So why did my chest feel suddenly tight? Why was it suddenly hard to breathe normally with Cam watching me so intently, his blue eyes dark and unreadable in the dim light of my hotel suite?

"The color reminded me of that dress you wore to the Stanley Cup event," he said, his voice low. "The one you had on the night we supposedly started our relationship"

The fact that he remembered that detail – had used it to select this specific stone – sent an unexpected warmth spreading through me. It was thoughtful in a way I hadn't anticipated, personal in a way our arrangement wasn't supposed to be.

I swallowed hard, fighting the sudden pressure behind my eyes. "How did you know my size?"

His mouth quirked in a half-smile. "I pay attention."

Four-carat mermaid sapphire rings from Tiffany aren't exactly standard. They're custom-fitted, and carefully measured. Which meant Cam had deliberately sought out this information – maybe Monica, my stylist? Holy hockey sticks I hope he didn't call my mother, who had my measurements from a family ring she'd gifted me last Christmas. Maybe my assistant Katie.

The thought of him going to that effort, of planning this moment so carefully, made something flutter dangerously in my chest.

"It's perfect," I admitted, still staring at my hand, at the way the ring looked sitting there as if it belonged. As if it had always belonged.

"It looks good on you," Cam said, and something in his tone made me look up.

He was closer now, close enough that I could see my own reflection dancing in his eyes, the faint stubble along his jaw. For one breathless moment, I thought he might reach for my hand, might bring it to his lips in a gesture straight out of the romance novels I pretended not to read.

Instead, he stepped back, creating distance between us again. His hand moved as if to reach for me again, then dropped to his side.

"I should go," he said, glancing at his watch. "Early press breakfast tomorrow before the ceremony. Need my beauty sleep."

"You don't want room service?" I asked, confused.

"Actually..." he said, "I'm beat."

"Of course," I nodded, relief and disappointment mingling confusingly in my chest. "I'll see you tomorrow."

He nodded, already moving toward the door. "Goodnight, Lana."

"Cam," I called as he reached for the handle. "Thank you. For the ring. It's..." I trailed off, unsure how to express what I was feeling without making it weird.

He smiled, a flash of the carefree Cam I was more familiar with. "Just doing my part for the cause. Besides," he added with a wink, "now everyone will know you're off the market."

Before I could respond, he was gone, the door clicking shut behind him.

I stood frozen for several long moments, the weight of the ring on my finger suddenly the only thing I could focus on. It wasn't excessively heavy – the design was too elegant for that – but its presence was undeniable. Impossible to ignore or forget.

Much like the man who had given it to me.

I moved to the bathroom, standing before the full-length mirror. The woman who stared back at me looked strangely transformed – still me in comfy loungewear with slightly damp hair, but my eyes were brighter, my cheeks flushed. And on my left hand, catching and reflecting the light with every small movement, was a ring that signified me as belonging to someone else.

As belonging to Cam.

My heart thudded heavily in my chest as I turned my hand this way and that, watching blue fire flash from the sapphire's depths. For one fleeting, dangerous moment, I allowed myself to imagine what it would feel like if this were real – if tomorrow night wasn't a performance for sponsors and cameras, but a genuine celebration of love found and claimed.

I imagined Cam's arms around me, his voice low in my ear as we danced. Imagined the weight of the ring as I rested my hand against his chest, feeling his heartbeat beneath my palm. Imagined what it would be like to return to this room afterward not as colleagues maintaining a professional deception, but as lovers with nothing between us but truth.

The fantasy was so vivid, so alluring that I physically shook my head to dispel it.

"Get it together, Lana," I muttered to myself. "It's not real."

I prepared for bed, setting the ring carefully on the nightstand for safekeeping, but I couldn't ignore the sudden emptiness I felt when it was no longer on my finger. Nor could I explain away the last thought that drifted through my mind before sleep claimed me:

The ring might not be real, but the way it made me feel – the way he made me feel – was becoming harder and harder to pretend away. Tomorrow, we would stand before the hockey world as a madly in love, newly engaged couple. I was no longer absolutely certain where the performance ended and the truth began.

Because the truth was, there was a teensy, tiny but very real part of me that didn't want it to end at all.

Chapter 6

"Stop fidgeting with your ring. It looks like you've never worn one before."

Monica batted my hand away as she made final adjustments to my hair, pinning the last strand into the elegant updo she'd spent forty-five minutes creating. I'd been unconsciously twisting the stunning mermaid sapphire ring on my finger – a nervous habit I'd developed in less than twenty-four hours since Cam had placed it there.

"Sorry," I murmured, forcing my hands to remain still in my lap. "Just...I don't know...freaking out about tonight a little."

Monica stepped back, giving me a critical once-over before nodding with satisfaction. "You don't need to be. You look perfect."

"Thank you," I smiled, taking deep breaths through my nose to calm my nerves.

"I could lower the neckline a bit for your big night if you want – what do you think? Professional boob? Or WAG boob?"

A short laugh bubbled up, despite the fact that I was trying to hold my breath in my belly. "Professional boob. I'd like to keep my job once all this is over."

"Over? What do you mean? The announcement?"

Shit. I realized my slip immediately. "You know, like, once we're *married*."

"Mmmhmm." *Shit, shit, shit.* That could not happen again.

I stood, smoothing the midnight blue fabric of my gown. The silhouette was classic – fitted through the bodice with a subtle flare at the hips that created movement when I walked. The neckline dipped just low enough to be elegant without crossing into inappropriate territory (aka *professional boob*), and the back featured delicate beading that caught the light with every slight movement. It was exactly my style – understated but unmistakably expensive, projecting the polished confidence expected of a woman in my position.

A woman who also happened to be the fake fiancée of one of hockey's biggest stars.

"Remember," Monica said, packing up her styling tools, "shoulders back, stick out the rack, and for God's sake, make America swoon. Look deeply into Cam's eyes on that red carpet like he spent all afternoon spoon-feeding you cheesecake."

I rolled my eyes. "I know how to work a red carpet, Monica."

Monica just smirked. "Sure you do, honey." Before I could formulate a response, my phone buzzed with a text from Cam:

> CAM: Waiting in the lobby. You ready for this?

I took a deep breath, gathering my courage along with my small clutch.

> ME: On my way down. Try not to look too terrified.

His response came instantly:

> CAM: The only terrifying thing about tonight is how much I'm going to enjoy watching you tell people we're madly in love.

My stomach did that strange flip it had been doing with increasing frequency whenever Cam said things like that – playful words that somehow felt weightier than they should, as if laden with meaning I wasn't supposed to decipher.

Cam was a total charmer and an incorrigible flirt. That's all it was. It was stupid that I kept reading something more into it.

The elevator ride to the lobby gave me one last moment of privacy to collect myself. I'd attended countless NHL events over the years – first as Frank Decker's daughter, or Drake and Zayne Decker's little sister, then as a PR professional, and now as... whatever this was. I knew the drill. Knew how to field questions, how to position myself for optimal photography, how to deflect and redirect when conversations ventured into uncomfortable territory.

But tonight was different. Tonight, I wasn't just representing the Slashers or managing someone else's public image. Tonight, I was going to be the story.

The thought made my palms sweat despite my professional training. I forced myself to take slow, deep breaths as the numbers on the elevator panel counted down. Ten. Nine. Eight...

When the doors finally opened to the opulent lobby of the Bellagio, my eyes found him immediately.

Cam stood under the Chihuly glass sculpture, his back to me, hands in the pockets of a perfectly tailored tuxedo that accentuated shoulders so broad they could block out the sun and a backside that deserved its own Instagram fan account. *Keep it professional Lana.* His golden-brown hair was styled in that deliberately tousled way that definitely took three products and twenty minutes to achieve, but looked like he'd just rolled out of bed after doing deliciously unspeakable things. I lingered on that thought a second too long, and when he turned at the sound of my heels clicking against marble, the world seemed to slow around us.

His eyes widened as he took me in, his gaze traveling from my face down the elegant drape of my gown and back again with such deliberate appreciation that I could practically feel it – like a physical caress. Something flickered across his expression: surprise, hunger, and something darker, more intense... that made my breath catch and heat pool low in my belly. Well, *south* of my belly.

"Holy... wow," he said softly. "I was going to say something smooth, but my brain just short-circuited."

"You clean up pretty well yourself," I replied, aiming for cool detachment but hearing the breathless quality in my own voice. "Though I have to say, I'm curious about tonight's sock choice. Did you go with the monkeys in formalwear?"

"Better," he winked, and charm radiated off him. He lifted his pant leg slightly to reveal vibrant teal socks covered in little purple and white cupcakes. "You like? I got these just for you."

They looked almost exactly like the one we shared from Sweet Caroline's.

"Sweet," I say, as a blush crept up my cheeks. *Cupcakes. He wore them for me. Don't fall for it.*

He stepped closer, close enough that I could smell his cologne – that same masculine, woodsy citrus that had lingered in my hotel room last night, that same intoxicating scent that had clung to my sheets for days after our one night together all those years ago. I swallowed hard.

"Ready to be the envy of every woman in Vegas?" he murmured, his voice dropping to that low register that made my toes curl in my stilettos.

"Please. You should be asking if *you're* ready to be the envy of every man in the room," I shot back, finding my footing. "This dress wasn't exactly off the rack."

He laughed, eyes crinkling at the corners in that way that made him look boyish and devastating all at once. "Nice block. Always keeping me humble, Decker."

Without further discussion, he offered his arm. The gesture was old-fashioned, courtly – classic Cam with his door-opening, chair-pulling, standing-up-when-you-leave-for-the-ladies-room, unexpectedly chivalrous ways.

As my hand settled into the crook of his elbow, the sapphire on my finger caught the light, sending blue reflections dancing across the polished marble floor. Cam's eyes followed the movement, his expression softening into a smile that made my heart triple axel in my chest.

"Let's give them something to talk about," he said, leaning down until his lips nearly brushed my ear, sending tingles racing down my spine. "I promise to behave... mostly."

The ten-minute drive passed in a blur of last-minute preparations – Cam confirming which reporters we should prioritize, me reviewing potential questions and optimal responses. It was familiar territory, the kind of strategic planning we'd done together dozens of times over the years. Only this time, we were the subject, not some player needing guidance.

"Remember," I said as our car approached the venue, "we're not explicitly claiming to be engaged. We're just..."

"Not correcting anyone who assumes we are," Cam finished, his knee brushing mine as he shifted in his seat. "I know the plan, Lana. Trust me, okay?"

Trust. Such a simple concept, yet so complicated between us. I'd trusted him once, with my body and my heart, and had woken to an empty bed and ten years of wondering what I'd done wrong. Now I was trusting him again. But this time with my career, my reputation, and if I was being honest, something dangerously close to my heart *again*.

"I do," I said softly, surprised to find I meant it. "But *please* don't fuck this up."

The car slowed to a stop. Through the tinted windows, I could see the flashbulbs already popping, the crowd of reporters and photographers lining the red carpet. My pulse quickened, adrenaline flooding my system – that familiar mix of anxiety and excitement that came with any high-stakes public appearance. It was fine. I had a lifetime of training to look relaxed and happy on the outside. The usual, *just happy to be here for the team.*

Cam reached across the seat, his fingers finding mine and squeezing gently. "Ready?"

I took a deep breath, centering myself. "Ready."

The driver opened the door, and we stepped into the chaos.

The red carpet was a gauntlet of lights, cameras, and shouted questions, but with Cam's hand holding mine, I navigated it with practiced ease. We paused for photos, him tall and devastating in his tuxedo, me smiling my carefully calibrated PR smile, the sapphire ring prominently displayed on my left hand.

"Cam! Over here!" A photographer called, motioning for us to turn slightly. "Lana, hand on his chest!"

I complied, placing my palm against the solid warmth of Cam's chest, feeling his heartbeat quicken through the layers of his tuxedo. His arm tightened around my waist, drawing me closer until we were pressed together from shoulder to hip, a study in coordinated elegance.

"Perfect!" another voice called. "Now look at each other!"

Cam turned toward me, and I tilted my face up to his, prepared to offer the camera-ready smile I'd perfected over years of public events. But the expression in his eyes – intense, focused entirely on me as if the cameras and chaos had disappeared – caught me off guard. My smile faltered, replaced by something more genuine, more vulnerable.

"You're doing great," he murmured, his breath warm against my ear.

More flashes exploded around us, but in that moment, I barely noticed them. All I could focus on was Cam – the blue of his eyes, the delectable curve of his mouth, the way his hand at my waist felt both protective and possessive.

We moved down the carpet, stopping for brief interviews along the way. The questions were exactly what we'd prepared for:

"How long have you two been together?"

"When did you know it was serious?"

"Can we see the ring?"

We delivered our rehearsed responses with practiced ease, letting Cam take the lead when appropriate, stepping in when needed. We were a well-oiled machine, finishing each other's sentences, exchanging fond glances, playing the perfect couple with an ease that should have concerned me more than it did.

As we neared the end of the carpet, a reporter from *Hockey Night* called out to Cam.

"Murphy! Your contract renewal is coming up soon, and there are rumors about that big sneaker deal with Redline. Any comment on how your new relationship status might affect those negotiations?"

Cam's expression remained perfectly neutral, but I felt his body tense slightly beside me. This was it – the moment this whole charade had been designed for.

"I'd say my personal life has made me more focused than ever," Cam replied with just the right balance of confidence and humility. "When you find someone who believes in you, who challenges you to be better both on and off the ice..." He looked at me, his expression softening. "It changes your perspective. I'm playing the best hockey of my career right now, and I think any brand would want to be associated with that kind of positive momentum."

It was a perfect answer: authentic without being schmaltzy, confident without being arrogant, and it neatly sidestepped the direct question about our relationship status while still conveying exactly the message we wanted to send.

Pride swelled in my chest, followed immediately by a pang of something that felt uncomfortably like guilt. Cam was good at this – too good. So good that for a moment, even I found myself believing the fiction we'd created.

As we finally entered the venue, leaving the red carpet chaos behind, Cam leaned down to whisper in my ear. "How'd I do, Coach?"

"Not bad for a hockey player," I replied, my voice steadier than I felt. "You might have a future in PR if that whole Cup-winning, scoring-goals thing doesn't work out."

He laughed, the sound warm and genuine, and I found myself smiling in response. Despite the pressure, despite the stakes, there was something undeniably enjoyable about working with Cam like this – our minds in sync, anticipating each other's moves.

Inside, the ballroom was transformed into a glittering wonderland of crystal and candlelight. Tables surrounded a central stage where the awards would be presented, while a dance floor and bar area occupied one side of the vast space. Teammates, coaches, executives, and their plus-ones mingled throughout, creating a buzz of conversation punctuated by occasional bursts of laughter.

Cam guided me toward the Slashers' designated tables, his hand never leaving the small of my back. The gesture was possessive, intimate – stating clearly to everyone watching that we were together. That I was his.

We were almost to our table when Cam's thumb accidentally (or accidentally on purpose) brushed the bare skin on my back. And even though I'd been holding on to his arm all night, the unexpected touch sent warm tingles through me.

"Lana!"

I turned to see Logan approaching, resplendent in a charcoal gray tuxedo, his dark hair swept back from his forehead. As team captain, he wore the mantle of leadership as naturally as he wore the formal attire – with easy confidence and understated authority.

"You look gorgeous," Logan said, kissing my cheek before turning to Cam with a knowing smile. "And you look like a fucking movie star like you always do you glorious bastard."

"Careful, Cap," Cam replied good-naturedly. "I might just beat you for best-dressed tonight."

"Not a chance," a new voice interjected as Coco appeared at Logan's side in a stunning emerald gown that complemented her auburn hair and brought out the green in her eyes. "But nice try."

She hugged me tightly, stealthily whispering in my ear, "That ring is ridiculous. We are talking about this later."

I squeezed her back in silent acknowledgment, grateful for her friendship and discretion. Despite being engaged to the team captain, Coco hadn't pressed me for details about my sudden relationship with Cam, and I wondered how much exactly Logan had told her.

As we made our way to our table, I caught sight of my brother standing near the bar, deep in conversation with Coach Rocco. Zayne looked up as we approached, his expression darkening slightly when his eyes landed on Cam's hand at my waist. By the time the 4-carat sapphire caught his eye, he looked positively homicidal.

"Brace yourself," I murmured to Cam as we neared them. "He's been giving me the silent treatment since those photos went up. And he just spotted the ring."

"The guy's one of my best friends, but seriously, when has your brother ever *not* looked at me like he wants to check me into the boards?" Cam replied with forced lightness, though I felt him tense beside me.

Before I could respond, we reached Zayne and Coach Rocco. My brother's handshake with Cam was just a fraction too firm, his eyes fixed somewhere over Cam's shoulder.

"Looking sharp, Z," Cam said, unfazed by Zayne's chilly reception.

"Yeah? Looking like we need to have a discussion in private after the event," Zayne responded coldly.

Zayne's nomination for the Norris Trophy, aka Defensive Player of the Year, was well-deserved – he'd had a career season, leading the league in blocked shots and contributing significantly to our Stanley Cup win. But my brother had never been comfortable with public speaking, preferring to let his play on the ice do the talking.

Cam nodded. "Ready to give your acceptance speech?"

"As ready as I'll ever be," Zayne replied tersely before turning to me. "Mom and Dad are here. Somewhere."

The news hit me like a bucket of ice water. "What? They weren't supposed to arrive until tomorrow's press day."

Zayne shrugged. "The story is Dad got a call from ESPN about some last-minute commentary gig. They flew in early. We both know Mom wanted to see the awards."

Panic fluttered in my chest. My parents, my very perceptive, very involved parents, were here. Tonight. When they were supposed to be in *Florida*. When Cam and I were pretending to be engaged.

They didn't know about our arrangement. My mother, with her uncanny ability to detect even the slightest hint of dishonesty. My father, with his very protective instincts where his family and legacy were concerned.

And they were here, somewhere in this ballroom, about to discover that their daughter was apparently engaged to Cam Murphy, the teammate my father had once described as "talented but undisciplined" when he and Zayne played together back at college, and whom my mother had clucked over as "such a shame, all that potential and no real family to ground him."

"Breathe," Cam whispered, his hand finding the small of my back again. "It's okay. We can handle this."

I turned to him, anxiety evident in my expression. "Cam, they will think this is real. They're going to have questions... "

"So we'll answer them," he said calmly. "Just like we've been doing all night. Trust me, Lana. We've got this."

Before I could respond, the lights dimmed slightly, signaling that the ceremony was about to begin. An announcer's voice boomed through the speakers, welcoming everyone to the annual NHL Awards and asking all attendees to take their seats. Saved for now.

Cam guided me to our table, where Logan, Coco, Zayne, our goalie Nick Fosse, and a couple of other teammates were already seated. I waved to our newest trade, Axel "Reaper" Blackwood, sitting slightly apart from the others, his brooding presence unmistakable. The intricate tattoos crawling up his neck stood in stark contrast to his immaculately tailored black suit – like a gothic haunted house nestled inside a gated community.

"Blackwood," Cam nodded as we passed, his tone friendly but cautious. The defenseman responded with a nearly imperceptible tilt of his head, dark eyes assessing us briefly before returning to his whiskey.

"Hey, congratulations you two," Nick said, offering a toast. The rest of the group joined in and we all clinked glasses.

"Thanks," we said in unison.

As I sat down, straightening my gown carefully around me, I felt Cam's fingers brush against mine under the table – a small gesture of reassurance that somehow steadied my racing heart.

The ceremony proceeded with its usual mix of heartfelt speeches, highlight reels, and carefully scripted banter from the hosts. I found myself watching Cam more than the stage – the way his eyes crinkled when he laughed, the respectful attention he gave to each winner's speech, the occasional glances he sent my way, as if checking to see if I was enjoying myself.

When Logan won the Lady Byng award, Cam was the first on his feet, applauding with genuine enthusiasm. Logan's acceptance speech was gracious and brief, thanking his teammates, coaches, and especially Coco and Poppy for "teaching me what real leadership looks like – putting others first, even when it's hard."

As he returned to our table, trophy in hand, Cam stood up and clapped him on the shoulder with obvious pride. Their friendship – built over years of shared ice time, victories, and defeats – was evident in the wordless exchange of nods and smiles. It was one of the things I'd always admired about Cam: for all his playful bravado, he was genuinely happy for others' success.

"And the winner of this year's Ted Lindsay Award for an outstanding player selected by the NHL Players Association is... Cam Murphy of the St. Petersburg Slashers!"

The announcement sent a wave of applause through the ballroom. Cam looked genuinely surprised, his eyes widening slightly before a grin spread across his face. I felt a surge of pride that had nothing to do with our pretend relationship and everything to do with knowing how hard he'd worked for this recognition.

He turned to me, eyes bright with excitement. Without thinking, I leaned forward and pressed a quick kiss to his cheek.

"Congratulations," I whispered, the words meant only for him. "You deserve this."

Something flickered in his eyes – surprise, gratitude, and something deeper I couldn't name. Then he was standing, making his way to the stage amid continued applause, every inch the confident star athlete in his perfect tuxedo and easy smile.

At the podium, he accepted the trophy with characteristic charm, thanking his coaches, teammates, and the Slashers organization. Then his expression became more serious.

"I also want to thank the people who believe in me – even when I don't always believe in myself," he said, his eyes finding mine in the audience. "Who see more in me than just what I can do on the ice. Who challenge me to be a better player, a better teammate... a better man."

My breath caught in my throat. This wasn't part of our script. This wasn't planned. Yet there was a raw sincerity in his words that couldn't be faked for cameras or sponsors.

"Success isn't just about talent," he continued. "It's about who's in your corner. Who you're fighting for. And I'm lucky enough to have found that..."

The ballroom erupted in applause as he finished, but I barely heard it over the blood rushing in my ears. When Cam returned to the table, trophy in hand, his eyes sought mine immediately, as if gauging my reaction.

"Was that okay?" he asked quietly as he sat beside me. "Not too much?"

I swallowed hard, fighting the unexpected emotion in my throat. "It was perfect," I managed, peeking over his shoulder stealthily as I hugged him. "Looks like the Redline executives are definitely impressed too. They're smiling."

"Good," he said, but something in his tone suggested that hadn't been his only concern.

The ceremony continued, and when Zayne's category was announced, I squeezed Cam's hand in nervous anticipation. My brother's face remained impassive as the nominees were listed, but I could see the tension in his shoulders, the way his knee shook restlessly under the table.

"And the winner of the Norris Trophy is... Zayne Decker of the St. Pete Slashers!"

Pride surged through me as my brother made his way to the stage, accepting the trophy with his characteristic understated intensity. His speech was brief, thanking the coaches, his teammates, and our father – "who taught me that defense isn't just about stopping goals; it's about protecting what matters."

As Zayne's eyes scanned the audience, they paused briefly on Cam and me, narrowing slightly before moving on. The subtle challenge in that look was unmistakable – a warning that said clearer than words: *Touch my sister, and there will be consequences.*

When the ceremony concluded, we moved to the afterparty where a live band was already playing.

Cam leaned close, his breath warm against my ear. "Dance with me?"

Before I could respond, a familiar voice called my name, sending a jolt of panic through me.

"Lana! Darling!"

I turned to find my mother approaching, elegant as always in a pale gold gown, my father trailing in her wake. Her eyes were already fixed on my left hand, widening at the sight of the sapphire ring.

"Mom! Dad!" I managed, forcing brightness into my voice as I hugged my mother. "I thought you weren't coming until tomorrow."

"Change of plans," my father said, hugging me. His eyes moved from me to Cam with thoughtful assessment. "ESPN called, and we didn't want to miss Zayne's big night, so here we are. Cam, nice to see you. Congratulations. Great night for the Slashers."

"Thank you, sir." Cam replied. "It's good to see you both again."

My mother barely seemed to hear, her attention entirely captured by the ring on my finger. "Lana Elizabeth Decker," she breathed, taking my hand in hers to examine the sapphire more closely. "Is this what I think it is?"

I opened my mouth, prepared to launch into our carefully crafted non-explanation that would imply without confirming, but Cam stepped forward before I could speak.

"Mrs. Decker," he said, kissing her cheek in an old-world gesture that made my mother actually blush. "It's so lovely to see you again. You look radiant tonight."

My mother, typically composed and articulate, actually giggled. "Please, call me Diana, Cam. You and Zayne aren't in college anymore. And this – " she gestured to the ring, " – is breathtaking. Almost as breathtaking as the fact that my daughter hasn't mentioned a single word about your relationship until those photos appeared last week." She glared at me teasingly.

Cam's smile was apologetic but not overly so. "That's my fault, I'm afraid. Given my position on the team and Lana's role as the team's publicity director, we thought it best to keep things private until we were... *certain.*"

The way he said "certain" – with just the right gentle emphasis – left no doubt as to what he meant. My mother's eyes softened, and even my father's stern expression relaxed slightly.

"And now you're certain?" my father asked, the question directed at me rather than Cam.

I felt three pairs of eyes on me, awaiting my response. Cam's hand found the small of my back, a warm, steadying presence.

"Yes," I said, surprised by the conviction in my voice. "We're certain."

My mother beamed, pulling me into a tight hug that smelled of her signature perfume and years of unconditional love. "Oh, darling. I'm so happy for you."

Over her shoulder, I caught Cam's eye. He was watching us with an expression I couldn't quite decode – something warm but wistful and complicated.

"Thank you," I murmured, guilt twisting in my stomach at the genuine joy in my mother's voice.

When she released me, my father stepped forward, offering his hand to Cam. "Congratulations on your award tonight, Cam. And on..." he gestured vaguely between us, "...this development."

"Thank you, sir," Cam replied, his handshake firm and respectful. "I know how important your family is to Lana. I hope you know I'm the guy lucky enough to be in her life right now, and I don't take that lightly."

My father studied him for a long moment, his expression unreadable. Then he nodded once, a gesture that conveyed both acknowledgment and warning. "See that you don't."

An awkward silence threatened to descend, but my mother, ever the social butterfly, clapped her hands together. "Well! This calls for a proper celebration. You must come with Lana to Siesta Key this weekend. The whole family will be there for our annual end-of-summer gathering. Zayne will be there of course. And Drake."

Panic flared in my chest. A weekend with my entire family? Pretending to be engaged to Cam? It was one thing to maintain the façade for a night, quite another to sustain it for an entire weekend under the watchful eyes of the people who knew me best.

"Mom, I don't think – " I began.

"We'd love to," Cam interjected smoothly, his smile dazzling. "Wouldn't we, Lana?"

I could only stare at him, words failing me as I processed the enormity of what he'd just committed us to.

"Wonderful!" my mother exclaimed, clearly delighted. "We'll expect you Friday afternoon. The good bedroom is already made up. She leaned in close to Cam for a stage whisper, "We've been hoping Lana would finally bring someone special home."

"Mom!"

With promises to call with details and congratulations on the "engagement," my parents moved on to greet other acquaintances, leaving me standing in stunned silence beside Cam.

"The good bedroom?" he murmured, amusement dancing in his eyes. "Should I be honored?"

I found my voice at last, turning to face him fully, whispering, "Are you out of your mind? A weekend with my family playing happy couple? This was *not* part of the deal, Cam. We're having a serious discussion about this later. Stick to the plan. It's showtime."

His expression sobered, but there was still a warmth in his eyes that made my heart beat faster. "Would it really be so terrible? Think about it – if we can convince your family, we can convince anyone. Including those Redline executives over there who have been watching us all night."

I followed his subtle nod to where two sharp-suited men stood near the bar, their attention indeed fixed in our direction. Well, at least the scene with my parents was probably convincing from afar.

"Besides," Cam continued, his voice dropping to a more intimate register, "wouldn't it be nice to have a weekend away from the rink? Just us, the beach, maybe a sunset or two..."

The band began playing a slow ballad, and without waiting for my response, Cam took my hand in his. "Dance with me?"

"Yes, I just..." I trailed off, my heart pounding traitorously in my chest as Cam's gaze held mine. I did not want to argue in front of my parents, my bosses, or the Redline executives, so I let him lead me to the dance floor, where other couples were already swaying to the music. His arm slid around my waist, drawing me close until we were heart to heart. His hand held mine against his heartbeat.

The solid warmth of him surrounded me, the scent of his cologne making my knees weak. Had he always smelled this good, or was this some new torture specifically designed to make me lose my mind?

"You're staring at my neck," Cam whispered, a smile in his voice.

"Just making sure your tie is straight," I lied, quickly looking up to meet his eyes. Big mistake. The amusement dancing in those ocean blues was worse than the cologne.

"My tie has been straight for four hours," he murmured, his thumb now making small, devastating circles against my lower back. "But please, feel free to keep checking."

I rolled my eyes, trying to ignore how perfectly we fit together, how his body seemed to remember mine from that one night so long ago.

"Where'd you get your dance moves?" I asked. "From all those models from your calendar shoots?"

His eyebrow shot up. "You've seen my calendar?"

"It was research," I said primly.

"Thorough research, I hope," he replied, pulling me a fraction closer. "Did you spend extra time on August? That's the one where I'm shirtless on the beach with just a hockey stick."

I nearly tripped over my own feet. "There is no August beach photo."

"Gotcha." His grin was downright wicked. "But now I know for sure you looked through the whole thing."

Heat flooded my cheeks. "That's just good PR."

"Sure it is, Cupcake Queen."

When he spun me, the movement was so smooth and controlled it felt like flying, I couldn't help the small gasp that escaped my lips.

"See? Not so bad," he murmured against my ear, his breath sending a tingle that worked its way down my neck and was now pooling low between my thighs.

"Not bad at all, Murphy," I admitted, my voice embarrassingly breathy. I could feel the rumble of his chuckle against my chest, the vibration doing absolutely nothing to help my composure. *Keep it together.*

"You look exquisite tonight, Lana," Cam said, his voice low and intimate. His eyes traced over my face like he was memorizing it. "But then, you always do."

"Flattery will get you nowhere, Hitman," I said, trying to sound unaffected while my body was actively staging a full rebellion.

He leaned in closer, his lips brushing the shell of my ear. "Is that a challenge, Ms. Decker?"

My breath hitched, and I swore my heart was pounding so hard he must feel it. "Maybe it is."

His eyes darkened, and for a moment, I thought he might kiss me right there on the dance floor. I found myself tilting my chin up, just slightly, an involuntary invitation I wasn't ready to acknowledge. I snapped it back down to my clavicle in self-defense.

"Game on, then," he murmured, his voice filled with promise. But instead of kissing me, his hand slid just a fraction lower on my back, still perfectly appropriate but somehow infinitely more intimate.

"You realize what you've done, right?" I asked quietly, desperate to break the tension. "A whole weekend with my family. They'll expect us to be..."

"Happy? In love?" His mouth curved in a smile that sent my stomach into a triple axel. "I think I can manage that. The question is, can you handle me for a whole weekend, Decker?"

"I manage you every single day of my professional life," I countered.

"But this is different," he said. "This weekend, you have to pretend you actually like me."

"Who says I'm pretending?" The words slipped out before I could stop them.

His step faltered – barely noticeable, but there. I'd surprised him. Good. Let him be the off-balance one for once.

"Still think we're faking this?" he asked, his voice a low rumble that vibrated through me like a bass line.

I swallowed hard, fighting the urge to look away from the intensity in his gaze. "Convincing doesn't mean real," I whispered, but even to my own ears, my voice wavered with uncertainty.

"Keep telling yourself that," he said softly. His thumb brushed across my knuckles, sending another jolt through me. "But that dress has been saying something else all night."

The dance ended, and he stepped back, breaking the spell that had momentarily surrounded us. I felt oddly bereft without his arms around me, like I'd lost something essential that I hadn't known I needed.

"I need a drink," I muttered.

"That makes two of us," Cam agreed, his eyes never leaving mine. "Do you need something cold?" he winked.

The rest of the evening passed in a blur of congratulations, small talk, and carefully maintained appearances. Cam played his role perfectly – attentive but not overbearing, affectionate but appropriately restrained, charming everyone from veteran coaches to rookie players' nervous dates.

By the time we finally made our excuses and headed toward the exit, my feet ached from hours in heels and my cheeks hurt from smiling. The weight of the ring on my finger felt both foreign and strangely right, a paradox I didn't have the energy to examine too closely.

In the relative privacy of the hotel car, I finally turned to Cam, unable to contain myself any longer.

"*We'd love to come to the beach*?" I hissed, mindful of the driver just feet away on the other side of the privacy shield. "Really, Cam?"

He had the grace to look slightly abashed, but there was a stubbornness in his jaw that told me he didn't regret his decision. At all.

"What was I supposed to say? 'No thanks, Mrs. Decker, we're only pretending to be engaged for a sneaker deal'?"

"You could have let me handle it," I countered. "Instead, you've committed us to an entire weekend of... this." I gestured between us. "With my family. Who know me better than anyone."

Cam's expression softened, his hand finding mine in the darkness of the car. "Lana, it's going to be fine. We've got this. And honestly? It's better this way. The more people who believe we're actually together, the more convincing it is for everyone else – including Redline."

I knew he was right, logically speaking. The weekend at Siesta Key would solidify our cover story, provide more social media opportunities, and further the narrative we were trying to create. But the thought of maintaining this charade with my family – of basically lying to the people I loved most – felt like a step too far.

"Hey," Cam said softly, noticing my distress. "If you really don't want to go, I'll call your mom tomorrow. I'll make up an excuse. We can find another way."

His willingness to back down should have made me feel better. Instead, it made the knot in my stomach twist tighter. Because the truth was, despite all my reservations, despite all the reasons it was a terrible idea...

Part of me wanted to go.

Wanted to pretend, just for a weekend, that this was real. That Cam and I were actually engaged, actually planning a future together, actually in love in the way he'd described so convincingly to my parents.

"No," I said finally. "You're right. It makes sense... strategically. We'll go."

Cam studied me for a moment, as if trying to determine whether I meant it. Finally, he nodded, a slow smile spreading across his face.

"Too late now anyway," he said, leaning back against the leather seat. "Better pack that bikini, CupcakeQueen."

I rolled my eyes at him dramatically, "Whatever you say, Puck Daddy."

He roared with laughter, his features lighting up like he was up on the big screen, "That's my girl."

And despite everything – the stress, the confusion, the growing fear that I was in way over my head – I couldn't quite suppress the smile that tugged at my lips.

Because as much as I wanted to deny it, there was something terrifyingly real hiding beneath the surface of our carefully crafted lie. And the longer we played this game, the harder it became to remember where the act ended and the truth began.

Chapter 7

The night air felt electric as we arrived at the team's hotel. Exhaustion hit me like a Mack truck, but somehow, with Cam's hand resting lightly against the small of my back – each brush of his fingers sending shockwaves through my spine – I wasn't quite ready for the night to end.

"I really can't believe we pulled that off," I murmured as we stepped into the hotel elevator, acutely aware of how close we were standing in the confined space. "I mean, I can, but I can't."

Cam's reflection grinned back at me from the mirrored wall, his eyes lingering on mine with unmistakable heat. "Told you we'd be convincing."

"A little too convincing, maybe." I twisted the ring absent-mindedly, the weight of it already feeling dangerously familiar. "My mother is already mentally planning our wedding. Pretty sure she's picking out centerpieces as we speak."

"Is that so terrible?" he asked, his voice dropping to a husky whisper as he leaned closer, his broad shoulder brushing against mine. "The thought of being stuck with me?"

My pulse quickened traitorously. "I've been stuck with you since college, Murphy. What's a lifetime more?"

His eyes darkened at the reference to our shared past, and for a breathless moment, I thought he might close the distance between us right there in the elevator.

The elevator dinged before I could find out, saving me from having to unpack the molten heat suddenly between my legs. We stepped out into the plush corridor, the silence between us crackling with electricity neither of us seemed willing to acknowledge.

"Thanks for walking me back," I said as we reached my door, fumbling with the key card, my fingers suddenly clumsy and uncooperative. "It's been quite a night."

"Yeah," Cam agreed, leaning one shoulder against the wall beside my door, making no move to leave. His tie was loosened just enough to expose the strong column of his throat, and I had to forcibly drag my eyes away. "Quite a night."

The hallway felt impossibly narrow, the air between us charged with ten years of unspoken want. I glanced up, finding his eyes already on me, darkened to midnight blue in the dim corridor lighting. He was standing close enough that the now faint scent of his cologne wrapped around me like an embrace – familiar and intoxicating.

"Zayne seemed pretty unhappy," I said, panicky for a safe topic. "Did you see his face when my mom mentioned the ring?"

Cam winced. "Hard to miss. I think he was mentally reviewing which penalty box would be the best place to hide my dismembered body parts."

"He's just protective."

"I've noticed," Cam murmured, his eyes never leaving mine, tracing over my features with such intensity I felt physically touched. "It must be nice, having someone care that much."

There was something nakedly vulnerable in his voice that made my heart twist painfully.

"It can be suffocating sometimes," I admitted, swallowing hard. "But yes, it's nice."

His gaze dropped to my lips, lingering there long enough for heat to bloom from my cheeks all the way down to my chest. "Lana..."

"Yes, Cam," I breathed, not pulling away as he leaned closer, the wall cool against my bare back as my body instinctively arched toward his.

His fingertips brushed mine, a whisper of contact that sent liquid fire racing through my veins. The space between us seemed to evaporate, the world narrowing until all I could see was the flicker of raw hunger in his eyes.

"This doesn't really feel like pretending," he whispered, so close now that I could feel his breath feathering against my parted lips.

My heart hammered against my ribs like it was trying to stage a prison escape. We were crossing a line, obliterating the carefully drawn boundaries of our arrangement, and I couldn't find it in myself to care. Not with the memory of his strong arms around me on the dance floor still branded into my skin, not with the weight of his ring on my finger, not with the way he was looking at me now – like I was everything he'd ever wanted but couldn't have.

He leaned in slowly, agonizingly, a millimeter at a time, my breath suspended in my lungs and desire coiling tight and hot between my legs. Just as his lips were about to claim mine, a voice like a thunderclap shattered the moment.

"What the HELL is going on?"

We sprang apart like teenagers caught making out in the basement to find Zayne storming down the corridor toward us, still in his suit pants and dress shirt, tie gone, top buttons undone, face like a gathering storm.

Lightning fast, he closed the distance between us and shoved Cam hard against the wall, forearm pressed against his chest.

"I knew it," he growled, eyes blazing. "What the hell, Murphy? I thought I could trust you.."

"Zayne!" I hissed, glancing frantically at the neighboring doors. "Not here!"

Cam raised his hands in surrender, making no move to fight back despite being perfectly capable of it. "Easy, man. Let's talk about this."

My key card forgotten, I grabbed my brother's shoulder. "Zayne, stop it. You're making a scene."

"I'm making a scene?" He laughed bitterly, but eased the pressure on Cam's chest slightly. "That's rich coming from you two and your little performance tonight."

I managed to get my door open, practically shoving both men inside before any curious hotel guests or – worse – reporters could investigate the commotion. The door clicked shut behind us, and I leaned against it, heart racing.

"Have you lost your mind?" I demanded, kicking off my heels to better stand my ground. "Attacking him in a hotel hallway? Really? One more move like that and you're getting a week of mandatory media training."

Zayne paced the length of my suite, rubbing his hand through his dark beard. The suite was spacious but suddenly felt claustrophobic -- a dangerously combustible mix of testosterone and tension filling the air. The midnight skyline of Las Vegas glittered beyond the windows, oblivious to the drama unfolding inside.

"When were you going to tell me?" my brother demanded, turning to face us. "Or was I supposed to find out from SportsCenter that my sister and my best friend since college are apparently engaged?"

Cam straightened his jacket where Zayne's grip had wrinkled it. "It's not what you think."

"No?" Zayne's voice was dangerously controlled. "Because what I think is that my *former* best friend is taking advantage of my sister. That sound about right?"

"I was actually coming to talk to you about that," Cam said firmly.

Surprise flickered across Zayne's face – and mine. This wasn't exactly part of our plan.

"You were?" I asked.

Cam nodded, his expression serious. "Yeah. I figured I owed Zayne an explanation face to face. Man to man."

The show of respect seemed to mollify my brother slightly. "Talk, then."

Cam glanced at me, a silent question in his eyes. I nodded almost imperceptibly. The truth, then.

"The engagement isn't real," Cam said simply, no preamble, no excuses.

I held my breath, watching my brother's reaction.

Zayne's expression remained neutral, but his shoulders tensed. "Go on."

Cam explained everything – the Redline deal, their concerns about his image, the publicity strategy. He didn't sugarcoat his role or try to shift blame; he owned it completely.

"It was my idea to ask Lana," he finished. "She said no at first. I pushed."

"And you agreed to this batshit plan?" Zayne turned to me, his voice carefully controlled. "Knowing how it would look? What people would think?"

I straightened in my chair, professional pride kicking in. "It was a calculated risk. One I evaluated thoroughly before agreeing to."

"Bullshit," Zayne said again, but with less heat this time. "You're letting him use you to fix his reputation."

"She's helping me," Cam corrected, a slight edge to his voice. "Because that's what teammates do. What friends do."

"Also, it's my job, Zayne. It was my media strategy that got him into this mess in the first place."

"Friends," Zayne repeated, the word dripping with skepticism. "Is that what you two are?"

The question hung in the air between us, loaded with implications. What were we, exactly? Colleagues? Co-conspirators? Something else entirely?

"Yes," I said firmly, ignoring the strange twist in my chest. "Friends."

Cam's eyes flickered to mine briefly before returning to Zayne. "Look, man, I know this isn't ideal. But the alternative was watching a deal fall through that's good for the team, good for my career, good for the league, and frankly, good for Lana too. This benefits everyone."

"Everyone except my sister when it blows up in her face," Zayne countered. "When the press finds out it was fake. When her professional reputation and our family's reputation gets dragged through the mud."

"That won't happen," Cam insisted. "We've taken precautions – "

"Nothing stays secret in this league," Zayne interrupted. "You know that."

"We signed NDAs," I interjected. "Sully and Marcus approved the plan. The timeline is limited. There's minimal risk."

Zayne looked at me incredulously. "There's nothing *minimal* about this risk."

"It's just until the deal is signed," Cam said. "A few more weeks, maybe a month. No drama, no harm done."

I moved to the minibar, suddenly desperate for something stronger than water. Finding a small bottle of whiskey, I poured it into a glass and took a fortifying sip before turning back to face my brother. I'd usually offer Cam and my brother some, but I was pretty sure I was going to need it all for myself.

"It's for work," I explained, in my most non-nonsense PR Director voice. "It's a mutually beneficial arrangement with a set timeline and clear parameters."

"Parameters," Zayne repeated, gaze moving between us. "Like what I just walked in on in the hallway?"

Heat crept up my neck. "That was... just..."

"Obviously," Cam interjected, somehow managing a hint of his usual charm despite the circumstances. "Your timing has always been impeccable, Z."

My brother ignored him, focusing on me. "So this whole thing – the ring, the dance, that speech he gave – it's all fake?"

I twisted the sapphire absently. "It's an arrangement. A temporary solution to a specific problem."

"The Redline deal," Zayne said, understanding finally dawning. "It's that significant?"

Cam nodded. Zayne sank into the armchair by the window, the fight seeming to drain out of him. "So you two geniuses decided to pretend to be engaged. To each other." He ran a hand over his face. "Christ."

"It's just until the deal is signed," I explained, perching on the edge of the bed.

"And Mom and Dad? They think this is real."

The genuine hurt in his voice made guilt twist in my stomach. "That... wasn't part of the original plan."

"They were so happy for you," Zayne said quietly. "Dad called me after you left. Said he hadn't seen Mom that excited in years."

I swallowed hard, the weight of the deception suddenly feeling much heavier. "I know."

"And now you're going to Siesta Key to continue the lie."

It wasn't a question, but I nodded anyway. "We have to. It would look suspicious if we didn't."

Zayne turned to Cam, his expression hardening. "Let me be clear: if this hurts my sister – her career, her reputation, anything – I will end you. Friend or not. Teammate or not."

"I understand," Cam said, meeting Zayne's gaze steadily. "If it makes you feel any better, I'd do the same in your position."

"You don't have siblings, idiot."

"No," Cam acknowledged. "But I know what it means to protect the people you care about."

Something passed between the men then – a moment of understanding, or at least détente. Cam never had the family stability the Deckers took for granted, but he understood loyalty. It was what made him such a valuable teammate, why players like Zayne and Logan trusted him on the ice.

My phone buzzed in my lap, breaking the moment. I glanced down to see a message from Ryan Keller, Cam's agent.

> RYAN: Redline execs over the moon. Meeting fast-tracked for next week.

"It's working," I said, showing the message to Cam and Zayne. "Ryan says the Redline meeting is happening next week."

Some of the tension left Cam's shoulders. "That's good. Faster than expected."

"Great," Zayne said dryly. "So you just need to keep this up a little longer. Should be easy, right? *Since it's all for show.*"

Something in his tone made me look up sharply. "What's that supposed to mean?"

Zayne shook his head, a knowing look in his eyes. "Nothing. Just that you two seem pretty convincing for people who are just pretending."

Heat crept up my neck. "That's the whole point."

"Right." My brother looked between us, his expression unreadable. "Well, as long as we're all on the same page."

Cam cleared his throat. "About Siesta Key..."

"I'm not covering for you," Zayne said immediately. "I won't lie to Mom and Dad."

"We're not asking you to lie," I assured him. "Just... don't volunteer the truth."

Zayne considered this, then sighed heavily. "Fine. But PG only, understand? And separate rooms."

I winced. "Mom already said we're in the good bedroom."

My brother's face darkened. "I don't want to hear it. Just... " he made a vague, grossed out gesture, " ...keep things appropriate. And if anyone asks me directly, I'm not lying."

"Fair enough," Cam agreed, looking relieved that the immediate crisis had passed.

"And when this is over, you both come clean. To the whole family. No collateral damage."

I nodded, some of the tension easing from my shoulders. Having Zayne's tacit approval, well, perhaps "approval" was too strong a word, but at least his lack of active opposition, made the whole charade seem more manageable somehow.

"Thank you," I said softly.

Zayne grunted in acknowledgment, then checked his watch. "It's late. I'm heading to bed. Try not to get engaged to anyone else before morning."

He moved to the door, pausing to give Cam one last warning look. "Remember what I said, Murphy."

"Crystal clear," Cam replied.

As the door closed behind him, I exhaled slowly, sinking back onto the bed. "Well, that was..." I trailed off, searching for the right word.

"Terrifying?" Cam offered, loosening his tie. "Your brother is intimidating on the ice, but off it? Whole other level."

Despite everything, I laughed. "He's protective. Always has been."

"Oh, I'm familiar." Cam hesitated, then sat beside me on the edge of the bed, careful to maintain a respectful distance. "For what it's worth, I meant what I said. I won't let this hurt you."

The sincerity in his voice made me look up, finding his eyes already on me, warm and earnest in a way that made my chest tighten.

"I know," I said softly, and was surprised to realize I meant it.

We sat in silence for a moment, the events of the day settling between us. The awards ceremony, the dancing, the almost-kiss in the hallway. It was a lot to process.

"So," Cam finally said, his tone deliberately lighter. "Siesta Key. Your family home. Should I be worried?"

I welcomed the change in subject, pushing away the lingering warmth of his nearness. "Terrified, actually. My entire extended family will be there. Aunts, uncles, cousins, my very unusual grandmother."

"Sounds intense."

"It is. We Deckers don't do anything halfway." I smiled ruefully. "Hope you're good at remembering names."

"I think I can handle the Decker family roster," he replied with a confidence that seemed genuine. "What else should I know?"

I considered this, absently twisting the ring on my finger. "My dad will pretend to read the newspaper while actually analyzing your every move. My mom will try to feed you until you burst. And my Aunt Margaret will absolutely try to get you drunk on her 'special punch' to extract embarrassing stories."

Cam laughed, the sound warm and genuine. "So, a typical family gathering."

"For the Deckers? Pretty much." I stifled a yawn, the emotional and physical toll of the day finally catching up with me.

Cam noticed and stood, adjusting his cuffs. "I should let you get some sleep. Big day tomorrow with the press breakfast."

I nodded, suddenly reluctant to see him go but knowing it was the sensible thing. "Goodnight, Cam."

He moved to the door but paused with his hand on the knob. "About what happened in the hallway..." he began, his voice low.

My heart skipped. "We don't have to talk about it. Heat of the moment. Part of the performance."

He studied me for a long moment, something unreadable flickering across his features. "Right. The performance."

Before I could respond, he opened the door. "Sweet dreams, Lana."

As the door clicked shut behind him, I sank back onto the bed, fingers unconsciously touching my lips where his almost had, the phantom sensation of a kiss that never happened lingering like a promise – or a warning.

I took my shoes off, hung up the spectacular dress, and slipped into a nightie. I carefully washed my face and pulled the pins from my updo -- my hair cascading down, one soft ringlet at a time.

The sapphire caught the light in the mirror, sending blue fire dancing across the ceiling. It was beautiful, substantial, perfect – and utterly meaningless. A prop in our elaborate charade.

So why did it feel so right on my finger? And why did the thought of eventually giving it back make my chest ache with a hollow, nameless loss?

I closed my eyes, trying to sort through the tangle of emotions Cam always seemed to evoke in me. Attraction, frustration, camaraderie, suspicion... and something deeper, something dangerous that had been there since college, something that had never fully disappeared despite my best efforts to forget.

Friday, we would head to Siesta Key as a couple, continuing our performance for my entire family. And then, when it was over, when the deal was signed, we would return to our carefully constructed professional relationship as if none of it had happened.

As if we hadn't almost crossed a line tonight.

With a sigh, I reached over and switched off the bedside lamp, letting darkness envelop the room. In the distance, the Las Vegas Strip continued to pulse with neon lights and endless possibility, much like the sapphire still glinting softly on my finger: beautiful, brilliant, and ultimately an illusion.

Chapter 8

"I think we need a nice, romantic, social media-friendly beach walk today."

"If I didn't know better, Murphy, I'd think you were trying to get me alone."

I glanced over at Cam as he navigated the gentle curve of the Siesta Key bridge, his capable hands relaxed on the steering wheel. The water below us sparkled in the afternoon sun, stretching out in a panorama of blues that matched his eyes perfectly. We were almost to my parents' beach house, and the closer we got, the more my intestines twisted into knots.

"And if I were?" He shot me a quick look, voice dropping to that low rumble that did dangerous things to my pulse. "What would you do about it?"

The car's air conditioning couldn't quite compete with the heat creeping up my neck. Through the open sunroof, the breeze carried the scent of salt and Cam – a combination that made my head swim more effectively than any mango margarita ever could. For a moment, I forgot this was all pretend, that we were headed to my parents' beach house to engage in a charade for the benefit of my family and a sneaker deal.

I forced myself to look away, out at the shoreline coming into view. "I'd remind you of our very professional, very detailed agreement."

He laughed, warm and rich and far too knowing. His hand left the wheel to adjust the car's navigation system on the console, and for a fraction of a second, his fingers brushed against my bare knee. It was barely a touch, probably accidental, but it sent electricity racing up my thigh.

"My mom has already texted me three times about dinner seating arrangements," I said, desperate to change the subject. I held up my phone as evidence. "The last message says 'Frank insists you sit next to him so he can get to know C better.' She's abbreviated your name to save time. That's how you know she's in full event-planning mode."

Cam chuckled, the sound low and warm in the confines of the car. "It's cute that you're nervous."

"I'm not nervous."

He flicked a skeptical glance my way, one eyebrow raised in perfect challenge.

"Fine. I'm mildly concerned about the structural integrity of this ruse," I admitted. "My family is... a lot."

"I've met your family, Lana. Your dad's been giving me the eye from the owners' box for three years. And for four years before that, when Zayne and I played at BU."

"That's Work Dad. This is Beach House Dad. Completely different species."

The teasing glint in Cam's eyes softened into something more genuine. "Hey." He reached across the console to squeeze my hand, his palm warm and unexpectedly reassuring against mine. "We've got this. I'll charm your dad, compliment your mom's cooking, and remember all your cousins' names. What else?"

I swallowed, distracted by the casual intimacy of his touch. His thumb brushed a rhythm against my skin, and I wondered if he was even aware he was doing it.

"Um... don't mention the 1994 Rangers. Dad's still bitter about that Cup run. And definitely don't bring up Drake's knee injury. Mom still tears up."

"Got it. No '94 Rangers, no knee talk." His thumb continued its absent pattern across my knuckles. "What else?"

Something about his earnestness, the way he was actually trying to memorize my family's peculiarities, made my chest ache a little. This was meant to be performance, a business arrangement. So why did his hand feel so right on mine?

"My grandmother is obsessed with astrology," I continued, forcing my voice to remain steady. "If she asks for your birth time, just make something up. Otherwise she'll spend the entire weekend trying to determine our cosmic compatibility."

"August 12th, 2:17 AM," he replied without hesitation.

I blinked. "That was...specific."

He shrugged, looking slightly embarrassed. "My mom was big on birth stories. It's one of the few things she remembers consistently."

Right. Cam said his mom's MS had progressed significantly over the past few years.

"Well, prepare for Nana Decker to tell you exactly why an August Leo and a January Capricorn are either soul mates or mortal enemies. There's no in-between with her."

A grin spread across his face. "So which is it? Soul mates or enemies?"

The loaded question hung in the air between us. I was saved from answering by the GPS announcing our upcoming arrival, and seconds later, Cam was turning into the shell-paved driveway of my family's beach house.

The sprawling, weathered-blue structure sat nestled among palm trees and sea oats, its wraparound porch and multiple balconies offering views of the Gulf's turquoise waters just beyond the dunes. It wasn't the largest or fanciest house on Siesta Key, but it had been the Decker family's sanctuary for three generations.

"Wow," Cam murmured, killing the engine. "This is... not what I expected."

"What were you expecting? A hockey rink in the backyard?"

"Kind of, yeah." His eyes roamed over the cheerful exterior with its white trim and blue shutters. "It's charming. Homey."

"It's seen better days," I admitted. "But we've never been able to bring ourselves to update beyond what's necessary. Too many memories."

"Does it have a name?" Cam asked, his eyes bright with curiosity. "Like 'Casa del Sol' or 'Paradise Point' or something? I love that beach houses always have names."

"Yeah," I grinned. "Her name is Stanley."

Before I could say more, the front door burst open, and my mother emerged, waving enthusiastically. She was followed closely by my father, who maintained his characteristic reserve but couldn't hide the genuine smile beneath his silver-flecked beard. Zayne lurked behind them, arms crossed, watching us with narrowed eyes.

"Brace yourself," I whispered to Cam as we exited the car. "Hurricane Diana incoming."

My mother descended upon us in a flurry of floral perfume and excited chatter, enveloping me in a hug before turning her attention to Cam. To his credit, he handled her effusive welcome with easy charm, accepting her embrace and presenting her with the bouquet of sunflowers we'd picked up at a roadside stand along the way.

"My favorites!" My mother pressed a hand to her heart, genuinely touched. She shot me an approving glance. "He's a keeper, sweetheart."

Next came my father, whose handshake with Cam was firm but less intimidating than I'd feared. "Good to have you here, Murphy," he said, his expression inscrutable but not unwelcoming. "Hope you're ready for some familial bonding and competitive volleyball that's been known to end friendships."

"Wouldn't miss it, sir," Cam replied with exactly the right balance of respect and confidence. "Though I should warn you, I'm terrible at volleyball. Like, embarrassingly bad."

My father barked a laugh. "Perfect. You can be on Drake's team. Even the playing field a bit."

And just like that, the ice was broken.

As Zayne helped unload our luggage from the trunk, making a point of carrying mine while letting Cam handle his own, and I felt some of the tension ease from my shoulders. Maybe this weekend wouldn't be the flaming ball of disaster I'd feared.

Then my mother linked her arm through mine and lowered her voice. "I've set you up in your old room, honey. I've been redecorating, and I think you'll find it much more... accommodating for two."

The significant look she gave me sent alarm bells ringing.

"Mom, you didn't have to... "

"Nonsense! It's not every day my only daughter brings home her fiancé. Now come along, I want to show you what I've done with the place."

As we followed my mother inside, I caught Zayne shooting Cam a warning glance that said more clearly than words: Remember our agreement. PG only.

The familiar scents of the beach house – salt air, sunscreen, and my mother's perpetual pot of seafood gumbo – washed over me as we stepped inside. The main living area was my favorite room in the house: weathered hardwood floors, overstuffed furniture in shades of blue and white, and walls adorned with family photos and beachy art. Through the large windows, I could see the afternoon sun casting golden light across the deck and the sugar-white sand beyond.

"Everyone else will be here tomorrow," my mother explained as she led us toward the staircase. "Drake and Serena are driving down from the Tampa airport, and the cousins won't arrive until Saturday morning."

"Wait, Drake and Serena?" I stopped, surprised. "They're coming together?"

My brother Drake had dated Serena Ruiz on and off throughout high school and college, but their relationship had ended definitively (or so I thought) when he was drafted by San Jose and she took a job in Miami.

"Oh, didn't I tell you?" My mother's attempt at innocence was painfully transparent. "They reconnected at Christmas. I always knew they'd find their way back to each other."

Her meaningful glance between Cam and me wasn't subtle. *Great.* Now she was mentally planning a *double* wedding.

"You've got that 'my mother is matchmaking again' look," Cam murmured close to my ear as we ascended the stairs.

"How could you possibly know that look?" I whispered back.

"I've been studying your expressions for three years," he replied, his breath warm against my skin. "I know all your looks."

Something fluttered in my chest at his words, a sensation I promptly squashed. This was exactly the kind of emotional quicksand I needed to avoid.

"And here we are!" My mother announced, throwing open a door at the end of the upstairs hallway with a flourish worthy of an HGTV host. "Your old room, though I think you'll find it's had quite the transformation."

Transformation was an understatement.

My childhood bedroom, once a shrine of hockey memorabilia, dance trophies, and boy bands, had been completely reimagined as what could only be described as a honeymoon suite. Gone was the sleepover-ready trundle bed and mismatched furniture of my youth, replaced by a king-sized four-poster draped with gauzy white fabric. The walls had been painted a soft, oceanic blue, and the windows now featured billowing curtains that caught the sea breeze. A plush white rug covered much of the hardwood floor, and there were – I counted in mounting horror – no fewer than seventeen scented candles strategically placed around the room.

"Mom," I managed through a suddenly dry throat. "What did you do?"

"Just a little updating," she replied, beaming with pride. "I've been wanting to redo this room for ages, and when you told us about your engagement, I thought, what better time?"

I couldn't look at Cam. I didn't dare. The thought of sharing that massive bed with him for the next three nights made my pulse race in a way that had nothing to do with panic and everything to do with the way he'd looked at me outside my hotel room door in Vegas.

"It's beautiful, Mrs. Decker," Cam said, his voice remarkably steady. "You have a real eye for design."

My mother practically glowed under his praise. "Call me Diana, please. And you haven't even seen the best part."

She crossed to a door I hadn't noticed and opened it to reveal an entirely new en-suite bathroom complete with a claw-foot tub large enough for two and a shower with far too many jets.

"We had this added last year," she explained. "Originally it was going to be a reading nook, but I convinced your father another full bathroom made more sense. And now I'm so glad we did! Much more privacy for you two lovebirds."

I was going to die. Right here, right now, of acute embarrassment.

"It's perfect," Cam assured her, placing a hand at the small of my back in what appeared to be a gesture of affection but felt more like he was physically holding me from bolting out the door. "Thank you for going to so much trouble."

"No trouble at all for my future son-in-law," my mother replied warmly. "Now, I'll let you two get settled. Dinner's at seven, but come down whenever you're ready for drinks on the deck. Your father's making his famous mojitos."

"Thanks mom."

With a conspiratorial wink that made me want to sink through the floor, she left, closing the door behind her.

The moment her footsteps faded, I collapsed face-first onto the bed with a groan.

"Kill me now."

"Aw, it's not that bad," Cam said, though I could hear the amusement in his voice.

"Not that bad?" I rolled over to glare at him. "My mother has created a sex nest, Cam. A fully-equipped love shack. There are massage oils on the nightstand."

He glanced over and his eyebrows shot up. "Flavored?"

"I will end you."

He laughed, dropping his duffel bag by the closet and surveying the room with an expression that hovered somewhere between amusement and admiration. "Your mom really committed to the bit. I respect that."

"She will have a venue picked out in 24 hours," I said, sitting up as I pressed my palms to my forehead. "Mark my words. Did you see the bridal magazines on the coffee table downstairs? *So* subtle."

"Yeah, well, some parents get excited about this stuff." There was something wistful in his tone that made me look up sharply. "It's nice that they care so much."

Right. Cam's parents had never been the enthusiastic, involved type. His mother, though he loved her, wasn't able to attend his games most of the time. His last step-dad had attended exactly one of his NHL games – and spent most of it on his phone.

"I'm sorry," I said softly. "I shouldn't complain. It's just... a lot."

"Hey." He sat beside me on the bed, the mattress groaning a bit under his weight. "I get it. There's pressure when they care this much. Different kind of pressure than when they don't, but still pressure."

I nodded, strangely comforted by his understanding. For all our differences, Cam had always been able to read situations, and people, with remarkable clarity. It was what made him so valuable on the ice.

"So," he said after a moment, "sleeping arrangements?"

Reality crashed back in. We were sharing a room. A very romantic, very intimate room with exactly one bed. In my childhood home. With my entire family within earshot.

"I can take the floor," he offered when I didn't immediately respond.

"Don't be ridiculous. That bed is big enough for four people. We're adults. We can share." I was aiming for nonchalant but feared I missed by a mile. "We just need, uh, boundaries."

"Boundaries," he repeated, looking amused. "Like what? A pillow wall down the middle?"

"If necessary."

"Would it help if I promised to keep my hands to myself?" He raised them in mock surrender. "Scout's honor."

"Were you ever actually a Scout?"

"No, but I look good in a uniform, I know how to start a fire, and I did once help an old lady cross the street. Isn't that basically the whole gig?"

Despite everything, I found myself laughing. "Fine. We share the bed. But fully clothed."

"Fully clothed," he agreed, though his eyes held a mischievous glint that made my stomach flip. "Though I should warn you, I get hot when I sleep."

"That's not a boundary-respecting statement, Murphy."

"I just mean I might need to lose the shirt at some point."

"And I just mean I might need to smother you with a pillow."

He grinned, unbothered by my threat. "You know, for someone who's supposedly engaged to me, you seem awfully resistant to witnessing my bare torso. It's a good torso, Lana. *Men's Health* did a whole feature on it. So did *Pop Sugar*."

"Yes, I'm aware." The words slipped out before I could stop them.

His eyebrows shot up. "Are you now? Been admiring my *Men's Health* spread, Decker?"

Heat crept into my cheeks. "It was research. For work."

"Uh-huh." He looked entirely too pleased with himself. "Very *thorough* research, I'm sure."

"Shut up and unpack," I grumbled, standing to grab my suitcase. "I need to change before dinner."

"Need any help with that?" he called as I escaped into the bathroom with my bag.

"Boundaries, Murphy!"

His laughter followed me, warm and rich, and I couldn't help but crack a smile as I closed the door.

Twenty minutes later, changed into a casual sundress and with my hair freshly brushed, I emerged to find Cam standing by the bay window that overlooked the Gulf. He'd changed too, into khaki shorts and a light blue button-down that made his sun-kissed skin glow. Barefoot with his sleeves rolled up to reveal strong forearms, he looked relaxed, at home – and entirely too appealing.

He turned as I approached, and something in his expression – a flash of genuine appreciation – made my breath catch.

"You look nice," he said simply.

"Thanks. You too." I gestured to his outfit. "No tie? Didn't want to go full beach formal?"

"I save formal for family gatherings involving at least two aunts and a disappointed grandfather." He tapped his temple. "Strategic dressing. Always leave room for improvement."

"Smart. My dad respects a man who dresses appropriately for the occasion."

"What about you? What do you respect in a man?" The question was casual, but his eyes held mine with unexpected intensity.

I swallowed, aware of how close we were standing, how easily I could reach out and touch him if I wanted to. And I did want to, which was the problem.

"Honesty," I said finally. "I respect honesty."

Something flickered across his face (Regret? Guilt?) before he masked it with a smile. "Then I should *honestly* tell you that you look beautiful. And I'm *honestly* looking forward to having a drink before we face the full Decker interrogation."

The moment passed, and I let out a breath I hadn't realized I was holding. "Lead the way, fiancé."

Downstairs, we found my parents and Zayne on the deck, relaxing in Adirondack chairs as the late afternoon sun painted the sky with streaks of pink and gold. My father was indeed making his famous mojitos, crushing mint leaves with practiced precision.

"There they are!" my mother called, waving us over. "Frank, pour them some drinks! They need fortification before the rest of the clan descends tomorrow."

My father nodded, resuming his methodical muddling. "Have a seat. How was the drive?"

"Smooth," Cam replied, selecting the chair next to my father, a choice I was absolutely certain wasn't accidental. He was making an effort. "Beautiful coastline. I see why your family has kept this place for generations."

My father grunted approvingly. "Been in Diana's family since the fifties. My father-in-law won it in a poker game, or so the story goes."

"It was not a poker game," my mother corrected with a fond eye roll. "It was a gentleman's agreement. A handshake between friends."

"Over poker," my father insisted.

My mother waved away the distinction. "The important thing is that it's been our family sanctuary ever since. We've had every major celebration here."

"And a few major arguments," Zayne muttered.

"Every family has those," Cam said diplomatically, accepting the mojito my father handed him. "Thank you, sir."

"Frank," my father corrected, offering me the second drink. "Sir makes me feel ancient."

"You are ancient," I teased, settling into a chair. The familiar banter was soothing, grounding me despite the surreal nature of the situation.

My father narrowed his eyes on me. "Watch it, or I'll break out the photo albums from your awkward braces phase."

"You wouldn't dare."

"Oh, I'd pay to see those," Cam said, eyes twinkling. "Seriously, I'm prepared to write a check to the charity of your choosing right now."

I kicked his ankle under the table. "Traitor."

He caught my foot between his, holding it hostage with a mischievous grin that made my heart stutter. The casual contact sent warmth spreading up my leg, and I found myself intensely aware of the pressure of his foot against mine.

"Honey, I've been meaning to ask," my mother said, her tone deceptively casual. "Have you two started thinking about wedding colors yet? I was going through some ideas, just preliminary thoughts, of course, and I found this soft seafoam palette that would be perfect for a beach ceremony."

I nearly choked on my mojito. "Mom, we haven't even... "

"Blue," Cam interrupted smoothly. "Blues and silvers, right, babe?"

My head snapped toward him. What was he doing?

He continued, his voice steady. "Blues reflect the ocean, which is meaningful since we live in St. Pete and spend so much time by the water. We both love the beach. And silver would complement Lana's ring so perfectly."

I stared at him, genuinely speechless. We had never discussed wedding colors. We had never discussed a wedding at all, because there wasn't going to be one. Yet here he was, answering with such confidence, such specific detail – as if we'd had long, long conversations about our future together.

"Exactly right," my mother beamed. "Oh, that's just perfect! The blue would bring out your eyes, Cam, and Lana has always looked lovely in silver. See, Frank? I told you he was a keeper. Most men wouldn't care about details like that."

My father made a noncommittal noise, but I caught the slight approval in his gaze as it shifted between Cam and me.

"What about a date?" my mother pressed, clearly encouraged. "I know it's still early, but venues book up so quickly these days."

"June?" Cam replied without missing a beat. "After the playoffs. That way we could take a proper honeymoon during the off-season."

I kicked him again, harder this time. He squeezed my foot in response, his expression innocently bland.

"Early summer is perfect," my mother agreed. "May can be unpredictable, but June is lovely. What about the 15th? That's when your father and I were married."

"Mom," I finally managed, finding my voice. "We're still figuring things out. Can we just enjoy being engaged for a like five minutes before we start planning the whole wedding?"

My mother looked momentarily crestfallen, but my father came to the rescue. "Diana darling, let them breathe. They just got here."

"Of course, of course." She waved a hand, recovering quickly. "I'm just excited. My only daughter, engaged to such a wonderful young man. It's a lot for a mother's heart."

"Well, we're not in any rush," I said, hoping to stem the tide of wedding planning. "We have plenty of time to figure out the details."

"Of course you do," my mother agreed, though her expression said otherwise. "Now, tell me how you proposed, Cam. Lana hasn't shared the details yet."

I braced myself, genuinely curious how Cam would navigate this minefield.

"Well," Cam began, setting down his drink. "It wasn't exactly planned."

I watched him, fascinated despite myself. His expression had softened, a small smile playing at the corners of his mouth as if he were recalling an actual cherished memory.

"We were at the beach one evening after a particularly tough week at work," he continued. "One of those days where it felt like everything that could go wrong, did. Lana was stressed, so I suggested we take a walk by the water to clear our heads."

He glanced at me, his eyes warm. "Well, she was standing there with the sunset behind her, with that adorably frustrated yet determined face, like she always does when she's tackling a tough problem, and I just... knew."

My heart was pounding so hard I was certain everyone could hear it.

"I didn't have anything planned to say," Cam admitted with a self-deprecating laugh that sounded remarkably genuine. "I just blurted out, 'Marry me.' Not even a question... more of a realization. Like it was the most obvious thing in the world."

"And what did you say?" my mother asked, turning to me with rapt attention.

I swallowed hard, thrown completely off-balance by the emotion in Cam's voice, the vivid detail of his fabricated memory.

"I said..." My voice faltered, then steadied as I realized where this was going. "I said, 'Are you serious right now?'"

Cam's eyes locked with mine, and something passed between us – an electric current of understanding, of shared deception that somehow felt more intimate than it should.

"And I said, 'I've never been more serious about anything in my life,'" he finished softly.

For a moment, the deck was silent except for the distant sound of waves against the shore. My mother dabbed at her eyes with a napkin.

"That's beautiful," she said with a sniff. "So romantic."

Zayne made a slight gagging noise, breaking the spell. "If you guys are done with the Hallmark moment, I'm starving. Is dinner happening or what?"

"It's almost ready," my mother assured him, rising from her chair. "Frank, will you check on the grill? Zayne, help me with the salad. Lana, honey, why don't you give Cam a quick tour of the property before we eat?"

The dismissal was transparent – my mother clearly wanted to give us some alone time, but I was grateful for the escape.

"Sure," I agreed, standing and motioning for Cam to follow. "Come on, I'll show you the beach and the boat dock."

As we descended the steps from the deck to the sandy path leading to the water, I finally exhaled.

"That was... creative," I said when we were out of earshot.

Cam slipped his hands into his pockets, looking uncharacteristically sheepish. "Too much?"

"The sunset? The spontaneous proposal? The wedding colors we apparently discussed?"

"I figured we should have our story straight," he said with a shrug. "And it seemed believable. You do get that determined look when you're working through a problem."

I stopped walking, turning to face him. "How do you know that?"

His eyes met mine, steady and unnervingly perceptive. "I notice things."

The admission sent a flutter through my chest that I tried desperately to ignore.

"Well, next time, maybe give me a heads-up before you start waxing poetic about our nonexistent engagement story," I said, resuming our walk. "I felt like I was being ambushed."

"Sorry," he said, not sounding particularly sorry. "I stuck to the rules. I didn't actually lie. You were on a beach with me after a tough week. Your silhouette was great against the sunset. And you were frustrated and problem-solving. And you did look beautiful."

I stopped in the middle of the wooden boardwalk and stared at him. "Wait, what? When?"

"That sponsors' dinner at Clearwater Beach last summer," he said simply. "The one where Crawford showed up drunk and insulted the mayor's husband. You were putting out fires all night, and afterward, you were standing at the edge of the water looking like you wanted to scream. I brought you a glass of champagne."

I remembered that night. I'd spent hours doing damage control after our second goaltender had too much to drink and asked the mayor's husband "So, how's it feel to be the *second most important person* in your own house?" After I hustled him out of there and sent him home in a Towncar, Cam appeared just as I was contemplating throwing myself into the Gulf, handing me a full glass of champagne with a sympathetic smile.

"You remember that?"

"Of course I remember. You'd kicked off your heels and had your toes in the sand. Your hair was coming down – right about here." He reached out, his fingers hovering just above the nape of my neck where a few strands had escaped my updo that night. "You looked beautiful. Exhausted, but beautiful."

My breath caught at the unexpected tenderness in his voice. For a moment, we just stood there, the air between us charged with something I didn't dare name.

"This isn't a game, Cam."

"Isn't it? Just a different kind of performance, with different stakes." He paused as we reached the small private dock that extended into the calm waters of the bay. "Besides, your mother was thrilled. Did you see her face?"

I had, and that was part of the problem. My mother's undisguised joy made the deception feel that much worse.

"I don't like deceiving them," I admitted, leaning against the weathered railing. The setting sun cast long golden fingers across the water, painting everything in warm light. "My parents think this is real. They're making plans, Mom's gonna lose her mind when this comes crashing down."

"I know," Cam said, his voice softening. "But we'll handle it. Once the deal is signed, we'll find a way to let them down gently."

"And how exactly do we do that? 'Sorry, Mom and Dad, turns out we were just pretending to be in love for a sneaker contract'?"

Cam winced. "When you put it that way, it does sound kind of terrible."

"Because it *is* terrible. This whole situation is..." I trailed off, the weight of our deception settling on my shoulders like a physical burden. "Terrible.

Cam moved closer, his arm brushing mine as he leaned on the railing beside me. "Hey," he said gently. "I'm sorry. I didn't mean to make this harder for you. I know your family means everything to you."

I looked up at him, surprised by the genuine contrition in his voice. The setting sun gilded his profile, turning his hair to burnished gold and softening the sharp angles of his face. He looked... different here, away from the rink and the cameras. More real somehow.

"Why does this come so easily to you?" The question tumbled out before I could stop it. "The whole... pretending thing. It's like you're not even acting."

Cam was quiet for a moment, his eyes on the horizon where the sky met the sea in a blaze of orange and pink. "Maybe because part of me isn't."

My heart stumbled over itself, but Cam continued before I could process what he was saying.

"I didn't have anything like this growing up," he said, gesturing toward the house, the dock, the entire scene. "No constant. We moved a lot, different apartments, different schools. Different step-parents."

The vulnerability in his voice caught me off guard. Cam rarely talked about his childhood, and I'd only gleaned bits and pieces over the years.

"That must have been hard," I said softly.

He shrugged, his casual demeanor returning like a shield sliding into place. "It taught me to adapt. New situations, new people – I got really good at reading the room."

"Is that what you're doing now? Reading the room?"

His eyes found mine, steady and unexpectedly sincere. "With you? No. I'm just being me."

"Lana! Cam! Dinner's ready!"

The moment shattered like glass, and I stepped back, breaking the strange intimacy that had settled around us.

"We should go," I said, my voice sounding odd to my own ears.

Cam nodded, but as I turned to head back up the path, he caught my hand, his fingers warm against mine.

"Lana," he said, his voice low. "For what it's worth, I meant what I said earlier. About respecting honesty."

I looked up at him, confused. "What do you mean?"

"I'll try to give you more warning before I start improvising," he said with a small smile. "Scout's honor. For real this time."

Despite everything, I found myself smiling back. "Come on, fake fiancé. Let's go feed that bear you call a stomach."

His answering laugh was warm and genuine. As we walked back to the house hand in hand, for appearances, I told myself firmly, I couldn't shake the feeling that something fundamental had shifted between us, something that had nothing to do with our carefully constructed charade and everything to do with the man beside me.

Dinner was a surprisingly relaxed affair. My mother had prepared her famous seafood feast: grilled snapper, garlic shrimp, crab cakes, and an array of fresh sides. The conversation flowed as easily as the wine my father kept pouring.

To my relief, wedding talk was kept to a minimum, though my mother did occasionally drop not-so-subtle hints about her preference for outdoor ceremonies and her collection of family heirloom tablecloths that would be "perfect for a rehearsal dinner."

What surprised me most was how naturally Cam fit into our family dynamic. He asked my father thoughtful questions about his coaching career, traded good-natured barbs with Zayne about their last practice scrimmage, and repeatedly complimented my mother's cooking with such genuine enthusiasm that she was practically glowing.

"So, Cam," my father said as we lingered over dessert. Key lime pie, another Decker family tradition. "Lana tells me you've got a big endorsement deal in the works."

I tensed slightly. This was dangerous territory.

"Potentially," Cam acknowledged with practiced casualness. "Nothing's finalized yet, but it's looking promising."

"Redline, right? They make good gear. My knee brace is Redline."

"That's the one," Cam confirmed. "They're expanding their hockey line, looking for a new face."

My father nodded thoughtfully. "Smart choice on their part. You've had a solid few seasons."

The casual compliment from Frank Decker – notoriously stingy with praise – was like receiving the hockey equivalent of a knighthood. I could spot it immediately by the slight widening of Cam's eyes that he recognized the significance.

"Thank you, sir – Frank," he corrected himself. "That means a lot, coming from you."

My father waved away the gratitude with characteristic gruffness. "Just stating facts. You could be stronger off the puck, though. You could definitely hustle more on the back check."

"Dad," I began with a warning look, but Cam was already nodding.

"You're right," he agreed readily. "Rocco's been chirping me about it all season."

My father's eyebrows rose slightly. He'd clearly expected pushback, not immediate acceptance. "Good. Too many young players these days get defensive about criticism."

"No point in that," Cam said with a shrug. "You don't improve by ignoring your weaknesses."

Something that might have been respect flickered across my father's face. "Well said."

My mother, sensing an opportunity to steer the conversation away from hockey, jumped in. "Speaking of improvement, Cam, did Lana tell you about the family photo session tomorrow? We're doing it right on the beach at sunset."

"Family photo session?" I repeated, instantly suspicious. "No, I did not tell him because this is the first I'm hearing of it."

"Just a casual thing," my mother assured me. "Auntie Margaret's friend Connie is the photographer, and she's doing it as a favor. Nothing fancy, just some nice shots of everyone together while we're all here."

"And by 'everyone,' you mean..."

"The whole family," she confirmed brightly. "Your aunts, uncles, cousins, everyone! It's been a year since we've had everyone in one place for photos."

I groaned internally. The last Decker family photo session had devolved into chaos when Uncle Pete had too many beers and decided to go for a spontaneous swim – fully clothed – halfway through the shoot.

"That sounds great," Cam said, because of course he did. Mr. Perfect Fiancé, never missing an opportunity to score points with my mother. What surprised me was how genuinely happy he looked at the prospect.

"Wonderful!" she beamed. "I've laid out some options for coordinating outfits in the guest bedroom. Nothing too matchy-matchy, just complementary colors. Blues and whites, mostly."

I shot Cam a pointed look. This was his fault for mentioning blue as our wedding color.

"Of course," my mother continued, "I thought Lana might wear this lovely sundress with the blue flowers... it's hanging in your closet, honey. And Cam, if you have anything in a similar shade, that would be perfect."

"I think I packed something that might work," Cam replied, the picture of cooperation. "I love blue on Lana."

"Excellent!" My mother clapped her hands together. "And while we're on the subject of photography, I was wondering if you two had given any thought to engagement photos? My friend Marjorie's daughter just had the most beautiful shots taken at the Selby Botanical Gardens, or there's always Bayfront Park– "

"Diana." My father's voice, while gentle, carried an unmistakable note of warning. "They haven't even finished their dessert."

"You're right, you're right," she conceded, though I could tell it was killing her to drop the subject. "Plenty of time for all that. More pie, anyone?"

As conversation shifted to safer topics, I felt Cam's hand find mine under the table, giving it a reassuring squeeze. The gesture was small but anchoring, reminding me that at least I wasn't facing this charade alone.

By the time we'd finished dinner and helped clear the dishes, over my mother's pride and protests, the day's travel and emotional rollercoaster had finally caught up with me. A wave of exhaustion hit so suddenly that I had to stifle a yawn behind my hand.

"I think we should call it a night," Cam said, noticing immediately. "It's been a long day."

"Of course, of course," my mother agreed. "You must be tired from the drive. And the inquisition." She winked at Cam conspiratorially. "We'll see you in the morning – breakfast is at eight-thirty, but don't feel like you have to be punctual."

The knowing smile that accompanied this statement made me want to sink through the floor again. I managed a quick goodnight to everyone before escaping upstairs, Cam following close behind.

Back in my transformed bedroom – which looked even more romantic with the setting sun casting a golden glow through the gauzy curtains – I let out a long, slow breath.

"Well, we survived dinner," I said, kicking off my sandals.

"Your dad likes me." Cam sounded genuinely pleased as he leaned against the dresser, arms crossed.

"He tolerates you," I corrected, though secretly I had been surprised by my father's relative warmth. "But yes, you did okay."

"Just okay? I believe he said I've had 'solid seasons.' Coming from Frank Decker, that's practically a sonnet."

I laughed despite myself. "Fine. You charmed everyone. Even my Dad, which makes you the first boyfriend in history, real or imagined, to do so. Happy?"

"Getting there," he said with a grin that made my cheeks warm. "I still have the rest of the weekend to win over Uncle Pete and convince your grandmother I'm astrologically suitable."

The easy confidence in his voice made me pause. He was treating this whole situation with such... comfort. Like meeting my family, playing the doting fiancé, navigating the complex dynamics of the Deckers was all perfectly natural to him.

"Why are you so good at this?" I asked before I could stop myself.

Cam tilted his head, studying me. "At what?"

"This." I gestured vaguely between us. "The whole... pretending thing. It's like it's second nature to you."

Something flickered across his expression – a shadow of something serious beneath the easy charm – before he shrugged. "I told you, I had to adapt a lot growing up. New homes, new schools, new family configurations. You learn to read the room, figure out what people want, what will make them comfortable."

The admission carried a weight that made my heart ache a little. I'd known Cam had a complicated childhood, but I'd never fully considered what that might have meant for him emotionally, constantly having to figure out how to fit in, how to be accepted.

"That sounds exhausting," I said softly.

"It can be." He met my gaze, suddenly serious. "But this doesn't feel like that."

"No?"

He shook his head slowly. "No. This feels..."

The word hung in the air between us, unspoken. Real? Right? Dangerous territory, either way.

"We should get some sleep," I said quickly, breaking the moment. "Tomorrow's going to be a long day of family interrogation and coordinated photoshoots."

"Ooh, my favorite," Cam nodded, accepting the change of subject with grace. "Right. You want first shower?"

"You go ahead," I said, needing a moment alone to regain my equilibrium.

It took us some fanagling to work out a nighttime routine that didn't involve bumping into each other in the overly romantic bathroom or changing clothes in awkward proximity. By the time we were both ready for bed – me in silk pajama shorts and a tank top, Cam in athletic shorts and a well-worn Slashers T-shirt – the buzzy tension had built to an almost unbearable level.

We stood on opposite sides of the king-sized bed, staring at it like it might bite.

"So," Cam said, breaking the silence. "How are we doing this? Left side, right side? Pillow wall down the middle?"

"I usually sleep on the right," I admitted.

"Left it is, then." He pulled back the covers on his side. "And I was just kidding about the pillow wall, but if you want one..."

"I think we can manage without." I slipped under the covers on my side, careful to stay firmly in my half of the bed. "Just... stay on your side."

"Yes, ma'am." He climbed in beside me, the mattress dipping slightly under his weight. "Though I should warn you, I've been told I sometimes sleep-cuddle."

I shot him a look. "Sleep-cuddle?"

"It's a real condition. Very serious. Medical journals are baffled."

"If you sleep-cuddle me, I will knee you in a place that will end your hockey career."

He laughed, the sound rich and warm in the quiet room. "Noted. Though you might want to reconsider. I've been told I'm an excellent big spoon."

I tried not to think about what that would feel like – his strong arms around me, his chest pressed against my back, his breath warm on my neck. The mental image alone sent a shiver through my body.

"Goodnight, Cam," I said firmly, reaching over to turn off the bedside lamp.

"Goodnight, Lana," he replied, his voice softening in the darkness.

I lay rigidly on my back, acutely aware of his presence just inches away. The sound of his breathing, the subtle shifts of his body, the faint scent of his soap – all of it seemed magnified in the darkness. This was a terrible idea. There was no way I was going to get any sleep like this.

"Lana?" His voice was quiet in the darkness, startling me from my thoughts.

"Hmm?"

"Thank you for bringing me here. I know this isn't easy for you."

The sincerity in his voice caught me off guard. "It's fine. It's just a weekend."

"Still. I know you hate lying to your family. And having me in your space... in your bed..." He paused. "I appreciate you doing this."

I swallowed hard, grateful for the darkness that hid my expression. "It's just business, right? For the deal."

There was a beat of silence before he replied, "Right. The deal."

Were we still talking about the same thing?

"Well, goodnight then," I said again, turning onto my side, facing away from him.

"Sweet dreams, Cupcake Queen."

I smiled into my pillow despite myself. With the gentle sound of waves through the open window and Cam's steady breathing beside me, I drifted off to sleep far more easily than I would have thought possible.

I woke hours later in the dark, momentarily disoriented in the unfamiliar room. Suddenly, I registered the warm weight of an arm draped around my waist, the solid heat of a body curled against my back.

Cam.

Somehow in the night, we'd migrated toward each other. His chest was pressed against my back, his arm wrapped securely around me, his breath warm against my neck. Sleep-cuddler, indeed.

I should move away. I should wake him up. I should reestablish the boundaries I'd been so insistent on earlier.

Instead, I found myself relaxing into his embrace, my body responding to his proximity with a kind of quiet recognition. It felt safe. It felt familiar. It felt...right.

That last thought jolted me fully awake like a myoclonic jerk. Nothing about this situation was right. This was Cam Murphy. My colleague, my fake fiancé, the man who had once known me more intimately than anyone and then disappeared without a word.

So why did his arms around me feel like coming home?

I gently extricated myself from his embrace, careful not to wake him, and slipped out of bed. The clock on the nightstand read 3:17 AM – too early to start the day, but sleep now seemed impossible.

I moved to the window seat, pulling my knees up to my chest as I gazed out at the moonlit beach. The Gulf stretched before me, a vast expanse of silver under the night sky, constant and unchanging as it had been throughout my childhood. How many nights had I sat in this same spot, dreaming of the future, convinced I knew exactly where my life was headed?

Nowhere in those dreams had there been a Cam Murphy – infuriating, charming, complicated Cam, who made me feel things I'd spent years convincing myself I didn't want to feel.

A slight noise made me turn. Cam had shifted in his sleep, his arm now outstretched across the empty space where I'd been, as if reaching for me even in sleep. The moonlight illuminated his features, softening them in a way that made him look younger, more vulnerable.

There were so many versions of Cam Murphy. The confident, cocky player that fans saw on the ice. The charming playboy I'd helped create for the media. The attentive "fiancé" who'd impressed my parents tonight. But this version, this unguarded, sleeping man reaching across empty sheets, felt like the most real of all.

My chest tightened with an emotion I couldn't, *wouldn't* name.

This was the problem with pretending. The lines got blurry. Reality and fiction began to blend until you couldn't tell where one ended and the other began. And that was dangerous, especially when your heart was involved.

Because the truth, the terrifying, undeniable truth I'd been running from since the moment Cam had asked me to be his fake fiancée, was that there was still an annoying, too-dumb-for-her-own-good part of me that didn't want this to be fake at all.

I turned back to the window, watching the gentle ebb and flow of the tide, trying to calm the storm of emotions inside me. Morning would come soon enough, bringing with it another day of pretending, another day of navigating the dangerous watersbetween what was and what would never be.

But for now, in the quiet hours before sunrise, I allowed myself the luxury of watching Cam Murphy sleep in my childhood bedroom, wondering if in some alternate universe, this all might have been real.

Chapter 9

W armth. That was the first sensation that registered as I drifted toward conscious-ness. A solid, comforting warmth pressed against my back, radiating through my thin tank top and settling deep in my bones. For a moment, I kept my eyes closed, savoring the sensation and the hazy, dreamlike quality of those first seconds of wakefulness.

Then reality crashed in.

That wasn't just any warmth. That was Cam Murphy's body wrapped around mine, one arm draped heavily across my waist, his breathing deep and even against the back of my neck. Once again during the night, we'd gravitated toward each other like magnets, and now we were full-on spooning in my childhood bedroom, his long legs tangled with mine and his long fingers splayed possessively across my abdomen.

I should move. I should extricate myself carefully and pretend this never happened. That would be the professional thing to do.

But I didn't move.

Instead, I found myself hyper-aware of every point of contact between us: his chest solid against my back, his knees tucked behind mine, the light scratch of stubble where his jaw rested against my shoulder. The soft cotton of his t-shirt against my bare skin. His breath stirred the fine hairs at my nape, sending whispers of electricity down my spine with each exhale.

And most surprising of all – my own reluctance to break the connection.

A strange, unbidden emotion welled up inside me: relief. Relief that he was still here. Relief that I hadn't woken up alone in a cold bed with nothing but the memory of his touch. Relief that, unlike ten years ago, Cam Murphy hadn't disappeared before dawn.

The ridiculous irrationality of that feeling jerked me fully awake. Of course he hadn't disappeared. Where would he go? We were in my parents' beach house, pretending to be engaged. It wasn't like he had a choice.

Still, the relief lingered, a soft counterpoint to the hammering of my heart.

Behind me, Cam stirred, his arm tightening briefly around my waist in a reflexive gesture that sent a cascade of tingles across my skin. His hand slid up to rest just beneath the curve of my breast, and I held my breath, wondering if he'd wake up and realize our compromising position. How would he react? Would he pull away? Make a joke? Or would he...

"Morning," he murmured, his voice sleep-rough and low, vibrating against my shoulder blade.

So much for pretending to be asleep.

"Morning," I replied, aiming for casual and missing by about a mile. My voice came out embarrassingly breathy.

Neither of us moved. The moment balanced on a knife's edge – intimate, charged, dangerous.

"Sleep okay?" he asked, still not relinquishing his hold. If anything, his thumb began aimlessly tracing random figures against my hip, as if he wasn't even aware he was doing it – each lazy swirl sending fresh sparks along my nerve endings.

"Fine," I managed. "You?"

"Best night of sleep I've had in months," he said, and I could hear the smile in his voice. "You're very, uh, cuddly."

That broke the spell. I twisted away from him, sitting up abruptly, instantly missing his warmth even as I tried to look affronted. "We agreed to boundaries, Murphy."

He propped himself up on one elbow, looking unfairly attractive with his hair rumpled and his eyes still heavy with sleep. The morning sun filtering through the gauzy curtains cast him in a golden glow that emphasized the planes of his face and the undeniably bawdy stubble along his jawline, that every cell in my body was begging him to rough up. The sheets pooled at his waist, revealing the worn Slashers t-shirt that had ridden up to expose a stripe of tanned skin and the faint trail of golden-brown hair disappearing beneath the waistband of his shorts.

I dragged my gaze away, annoyed at my body's instant, visceral response.

"Pretty sure you're the one who migrated into my territory," he teased, gesturing to the obvious depression on his side of the mattress where I'd clearly been nestled. "I was just being accommodating. You know, like any good houseguest would."

Heat crept up my neck. "I did not migrate."

"You did. You practically burrowed into me like a little heat-seeking missile." His grin widened, transforming his face into something almost boyish. "Don't worry, I didn't mind. You're cute when you're unconscious."

"I'm not... " I sputtered, then caught the teasing gleam in his eye. He was deliberately trying to rile me up, and damn it, it was working. "You're impossible."

"Impossibly comfy, according to your sleep self." He stretched languidly, giving me an unwanted glimpse of his abs as his shirt rode up further. "Your sleep self is very wise."

I grabbed a pillow and smacked him with it. "My sleep self is clearly delusional and not to be trusted."

He caught the pillow easily, laughing. "Let the record show that you're the one who broke the pillow DMZ. This was an act of aggression, Decker."

"This is... " A knock at the door cut me off mid-retort.

"Lana? Cam? Are you awake?" My mother's voice filtered through the door. "Breakfast is ready, and Connie is arriving in an hour for the photos!"

I groaned, letting my head fall forward. "We're up, Mom! Be down in fifteen!"

"No rush!" she called back, though the tone of her voice definitely implied *rush*. I could practically hear her vibrating with excitement through the door.

When her footsteps receded, I looked up to find Cam watching me with amusement dancing in his eyes. "Family photo day," he said. "Your favorite."

"How did you know it was my favorite?" I asked dryly, swinging my legs over the side of the bed.

"Because you've been radiating dread since your mom mentioned it last night," he replied, sitting up and running a hand through his mussed hair. "Don't worry, I clean up nice for pictures."

"I'm not worried about how you'll look," I said truthfully. Cam Murphy photographed like a model. It was part of what made him such a marketing asset. I'd seen hundreds of photos of him across every type of media, and not once, *not once*, had he ever taken a bad picture. It was like, impossible. The camera loved his golden god bone structure almost as much as female hockey fans did. "No. *I'm* worried about my extended family interrogating you for the next two hours while we all pretend not to be sweating to death in coordinated outfits."

"You underestimate my charm," he said confidently, stretching his arms overhead in a way that showcased the sculpted muscles of his shoulders. "I'll have them eating out of my hand."

"You've never met my Aunt Margaret," I warned, forcing myself not to stare. "She once made my cousin's boyfriend cry by asking about his five-year plan."

"I have a five-year plan," Cam said, standing and running a hand through his sleep-tousled hair. "Win more Cups, perfect my wrist shot, make you admit I'm the best fiancé in the league, fake or otherwise."

"That's not a plan. That's a wish list."

"Semantics." He headed for the bathroom, pausing at the door. "You want first shower?"

The mental image of Cam in the shower, water sluicing down his broad shoulders, soap bubbles trailing across his sculpted torso, down his...flashed through my mind. I shoved it away forcefully, cursing my overactive imagination.

"No, go ahead," I said quickly.

His eyes lingered on my face for a moment, as if he could read my thoughts. Then he grinned, slow and knowing. "Don't worry," he said. "I'll save you some hot water."

As the bathroom door closed behind him, I flopped back onto the bed with a groan. The sheets still held his warmth and the faint scent of his body. I inhaled deeply before I could stop myself, then immediately sat up, disgusted with my own weakness.

This was going to be a very long weekend.

By the time we made it downstairs, the house was already humming with activity. My mother was in full hostess mode, balancing coffee refills with outfit coordination duties, while my father maintained his usual position of strategic retreat: newspaper open at the kitchen table, pretending to be engrossed in sports scores rather than family chaos.

"There you are!" My mother brightened when she spotted us. "Coffee? Pancakes? Aunt Margaret and Uncle Pete just arrived, and Drake called to say he and Serena are about twenty minutes out."

"Coffee," I said. "Lots of it."

"Thank you. Same for me," Cam agreed. "And pancakes sound amazing, Mrs. Decker."

"Diana," my mother reminded him, sliding a mug of coffee into his hand. "Or mom. You'll be family soon."

"You look lovely and relaxed this morning," Cam said smoothly. "Must be all this salt air."

"Oh, stop it." My mother actually blushed, swatting him with a dish towel. "Frank, aren't you going to say good morning to the lovebirds?"

My father lowered his newspaper just enough to peer at us over the top. "Morning, lovebirds" he grunted, eyes lingering on Cam's choice of a Slashers t-shirt and athletic shorts. Clearly not photo-ready attire. "Sleep well?"

"Like a rock," Cam replied, either missing or ignoring the subtle judgment in my father's tone. "Best sleep I've had in months."

I choked on my coffee, remembering his identical words upstairs. My mother beamed.

"That's wonderful," she said. "I always sleep better at the beach too. Oh, Cam, I laid out some options for you to wear for the photos. Nothing too formal, just a nice button-down that would complement Lana's dress. They're in the yellow guest room – Zayne can show you."

I shot him a look that clearly said don't even try, resistance was futile. Even my dad had learned long ago that when Diana Decker decided on a color scheme for a family photo, you just smiled and nodded and found something in your closet that matched. For all his gruff dominance on the ice and in his coaching career, Frank Decker had never once won a battle against his wife's aesthetic vision.

"Of course," Cam said with a gracious nod. "I'm in your capable hands, Diana."

"Oh, these are just options in case you need them. Zayne and Frank have plenty of clothes here that might fit you if you didn't bring the right shade of blue." She turned to me. "Lana, honey, I pressed your dress. It's hanging in your closet."

"Thanks, Mom," I said, cheerfully resigning myself to the outfit she'd chosen. "I saw it this morning. Super cute." She beamed. Although she was an immovable force when it came to wardrobe coordination, she had impeccable taste, at least.

Zayne appeared in the doorway, already dressed in the exact shade of light blue shirt that was hanging in my closet. "Reinforcements have arrived," he announced. "Aunt Margaret's already asking when we're starting the mimosas."

"Eleven," my mother said firmly. "Not a minute before. We need lovely photos first."

"She says she brought her special champagne glasses," Zayne continued. "The ones that say 'But First, Champagne' in the fancy script."

My mother closed her eyes briefly, as if praying for patience. "Wonderful. Just what we need."

"Zayne, you know what to do."

Exactly how far would your mother go for perfect pictures?" whispered Cam. "Am I going to be helping Zayne move a body after lunch or something?"

I suppressed a smile. My Aunt Margaret's dedication to day drinking was legendary in the Decker family, matched only by her tendency to speak her mind with increasing bluntness as the day progressed. By dinner, she could be counted on to ask at least three wildly inappropriate personal questions and make at least one politically incorrect observation that would have my mother frantically changing the subject.

"No," I whispered back. "Zayne will just hide the glasses during the photo shoot, and then they'll magically reappear later in the afternoon."

"Oh, and Nana's here too," Zayne added with a pointed look at me. "She's already set up her astrology charts on the back deck and wants to know Cam's birthday. For cosmic alignment purposes. Obviously."

I groaned quietly. "I forgot she was coming this early."

Before I could process this unexpected revelation, a voice called from the deck, "Is that my Lana I hear? Bring that fiancé of yours out here so I can read his chart!"

"Here we go," I muttered. "Remember, whatever she says, just smile and nod."

"I've faced NHL defenders, Lana. I think I can handle your grandmother." Cam's hand settled at the small of my back as we made our way to the deck, a brief touch that made my knees wobble every single time. So unfair.

Nana Decker sat at the picnic table, a collection of charts, crystals, and books spread out before her. At seventy-eight, she was still a formidable presence, with the same steel-gray eyes as my father and a crown of silver hair piled into an elegant updo. Today she wore a flowing caftan in shades of purple and teal, with multiple strands of beads around her neck and no fewer than six rings adorning her fingers.

"There's my girl!" she exclaimed, rising to embrace me. She smelled of jasmine and patchouli, a scent that instantly transported me back to childhood summers. She held me at arm's length, studying my face with sharp eyes. "You're glowing, darling. Love looks good on you."

"Thanks, Nana," I said, accepting her assessment with a smile. "This is Cam."

Nana turned her full attention to Cam, who stood beside me with an easy smile that didn't quite hide his curiosity. She circled him slowly, like a jeweler appraising a particularly interesting gem.

"Strong aura," she declared. "Vibrant blue with purple flecks. Very unusual." She stopped in front of him, taking his hands in hers and turning them palm up. "Interesting life line. Split here, then rejoins. *Oh*, look," she cooed, "a major life change that brought you back to your true path." Her eyes flicked to me. "Or your true person."

Cam's smile had shifted from polite to genuinely intrigued. "What does that mean?"

"It means destiny has its hooks in you, young man," Nana said sagely. "Now, when exactly were you born? I need day, month, year, and time."

"August 12th, 1994, at 2:17 AM," Cam replied promptly.

Nana's eyebrows shot up. "You know your birth time? Most men have to call their mothers."

"Good memory," Cam said with a shrug. "Although I *did* call my mother yesterday... but just to check in."

"Hmm." Nana eyed him suspiciously before turning to her charts. "Let's see what the stars have to say about you two."

For the next fifteen minutes, I watched in a mixture of amusement and mortification as my grandmother calculated compatibility charts, consulted ephemeris tables, and made pronouncements about our "cosmic connection." Cam played along gamely, asking questions and listening intently as my grandmother spoke.

"Leo sun, Sagittarius rising, with that Gemini moon," Nana mused, tapping a pencil against her charts. "Fire and air. Passionate, adventurous, quick-witted... hmmm... potentially restless." She glanced at me. "Good match for your Capricorn stability, darling. You ground him, and he brings spontaneity to your life."

"So we're compatible?" Cam asked, catching my eye with a smile that made my stomach flutter unmanageably.

"Oh, very," Nana assured him. "Your Venus aligns beautifully with Lana's Mars – powerful physical attraction. And your Mercury conjunct her Jupiter indicates deep intellectual connection and growth."

I felt heat rising in my cheeks. Trust Nana to jump straight to "physical attraction" within minutes of meeting my supposed fiancé.

"Nana, you're killing me here."

"But most interesting," she continued, oblivious to my embarrassment, "is this Pluto aspect. Transformative connection. Not just any romance... a life-changing bond." She looked up, her eyes unexpectedly serious. "Most people search lifetimes for the kind of alignment you two have. The stars don't lie, my dears."

Something shifted in the air between us: a weight, a possibility, a question none of us had voiced.

Cam cleared his throat. "Well, that explains a lot," he said lightly, though I noticed his hand had sought mine, fingers intertwining as if seeking an anchor. "I've always felt drawn to Lana."

Nana nodded approvingly. "As it should be. Now, when are you planning the wedding? We'll need to choose an auspicious date."

"We haven't set a date yet," I said quickly. "Still enjoying the present moment."

"Well, don't wait too long," Nana advised. "Next summer has some excellent celestial alignments for marriage. June especially. Venus will be in Cancer, perfect for home and family foundations."

I felt rather than saw Cam's eyes on me, a tangible weight that made my skin prickle with awareness. "We'll keep that in mind," he said, his voice carrying a warmth that seemed to wrap around me like a soft blanket.

"Come find me later," Nana told Cam. "I'll do a more detailed reading for you both. The universe has so much to say about your journey together!"

As we made our escape back to the kitchen, Cam leaned close. "I like her," he murmured. "She's very sure about us."

"She's sure about everyone's cosmic destiny," I whispered back. "Last year she told Drake he should move to Tibet and study with the monks."

"Still," Cam's eyes held mine, something playful but also searching in their depths. "Venus aligned with Mars. That explains a lot, doesn't it?"

I rolled my eyes, ignoring the flutter in my chest. "Don't tell me you actually believe in that stuff."

He shrugged, an enigmatic smile playing at the corners of his mouth. "I believe there are forces in the universe we don't fully understand. Like why I can't seem to stop thinking about you, even when I should."

My heart flip-flopped wildly at what he'd said, but before I could formulate a response to that bombshell, my mother called from inside, "Lana! Cam! Time to get ready for photos!"

"Saved by the bell," I muttered, grateful for the interruption. "Go find your cosmic blue shirt. I need to get changed."

His low laugh followed me up the stairs.

The family photoshoot was every bit as chaotic as usual. My entire extended family descended on the beach house like a hurricane, filling every corner with noise and motion and opinions – lots and lots of opinions.

Aunt Margaret immediately cornered Cam, champagne flute already in hand despite my mother's eleven o'clock rule, and began a rapid-fire interrogation about his "intentions." Uncle Pete argued with my father about the best spot on the beach for the photos, even though neither one of them would ultimately have a say. My cousin Nora's three kids, all under the age of eight, rampaged through the house like the tornadoes that aways accompany hurricanes, while her husband Ben trailed behind them with an exhausted and apologetic expression.

Meanwhile, Drake and Serena arrived in a cloud of noticeable sexual tension that made me both happy for them and yearn for a genuine connection of my own. They couldn't seem to stop touching: his hand on her back, her fingers brushing his arm, casual contact that spoke volumes about their reconnection. I caught Drake looking at her with such naked adoration while she chatted with my mom that I almost didn't recognize my usually reserved brother.

Through it all, Cam remained remarkably composed. He fielded Aunt Margaret's increasingly personal questions with grace ("Yes, I see children in the future. No, not before the wedding. Yes, I've met her parents; we're standing in their house right now."), won over Uncle Pete by asking about his fishing boat, and, most impressively, managed to corral Nora's children into a game that somehow left them clean, largely stationary, and completely entranced.

"How are you doing this?" I whispered as I watched him demonstrate a complicated hand-clapping game to six-year-old Emma, who gazed at him with undisguised adoration. "They're usually climbing the walls by now."

Cam shrugged, not missing a beat in the clapping sequence. "Kids are easy. They just want someone to pay attention to them."

There was something in his tone, a hint of hard-earned wisdom, that made me tilt my head and study him closer. "You're good with them."

"I coach youth hockey in the off-season," he said, high-fiving Emma as she successfully completed the pattern. "Kids this age are my specialty. Old enough to follow instructions, young enough to still think I'm cool."

I blinked, genuinely surprised. "You coach? I didn't know that. Although to be fair, I also didn't know that you were cool." Teasingly, I elbowed him in the ribs.

"Har har. Mini-Mites, four to eight-year-olds," he said, his attention still on Emma as she attempted a more complicated pattern. "Two years now at the community rink in St. Pete."

"But that's a volunteer program," I said slowly, trying to reconcile this information with the Cam Murphy image I'd helped create. "I've been scheduling your charity appearances for three years. Why didn't this ever come up?"

He glanced up, something unreadable flickering in his eyes. "There's a lot you don't know about me, Lana."

Before I could respond, my mother clapped her hands for attention. "Everyone! Connie is here. Let's get organized! Family beach photos first, then we'll do smaller family groupings."

What followed was the controlled chaos of herding twenty Decker family members onto the beach and into aesthetically pleasing arrangements. Connie, a cheerful woman with bright red lipstick and an impressive array of camera equipment, seemed unfazed by my mother's exacting standards, directing us with gentle but firm instructions.

"Now the engaged couple in the center," she called after capturing several large group shots. "Parents and siblings around them."

My mother practically glowed as she positioned herself next to me, while my father stood beside Cam with what almost passed for a smile. Drake and Serena, who couldn't keep their hands off each other for more than thirty seconds, stood to our left, with Zayne completing the family circle on the right. Nana insisted on standing directly behind us, claiming the "energy flow" was best there. Which...of course it was.

"Cam, put your arm around Lana's waist," Connie directed. "Lana, lean into him a bit more. That's it."

Cam's arm settled around me, heavy and secure, drawing me against his side. I tensed instinctively, then forced myself to relax, to play the part of the blissfully engaged girlfriend. To my surprise, it wasn't difficult at all.. Cam's body now felt familiar, even after only one night of sharing a bed. My own treacherous body recognized his, molding against him as if we'd been doing this for years instead of fumbling through a charade that had started mere weeks ago.

"Perfect!" Connie exclaimed. "Now, Cam, look at Lana like she's the most precious thing in your world."

I expected him to ham it up, to assume some exaggerated expression of adoration that would make me roll my eyes. Instead, when I glanced up, I found him already looking at me with a softness in his eyes that made my breath catch. There was no performance in that look, or if there was, it was the most convincing acting I'd ever witnessed.

And the Oscar goes to...

"Beautiful," Connie murmured, snapping away. "The camera loves you two."

For the next hour, we moved through a series of poses, each seemingly designed to increase the physical contact between Cam and me. Hands linked, his arm around my shoulders, my head tucked against his chest. At one point, he stood behind me, arms wrapped around my waist, chin resting lightly on my shoulder as we faced the Gulf.

The combination of his solid presence, the heat of the Florida sun, and the constant sea breeze created a sensory cocoon that made it surprisingly easy to melt into him. Or melt period because it was like 8,000 degrees outside. The steady rhythm of his heartbeat against my back created a hypnotic cadence that threatened to lull me into a dangerous comfort.

"Whisper something that will make her laugh," Connie suggested.

His breath tickled my ear. "Your aunt just asked me if I'm planning to get a tattoo of your name. I told her I already have one, but it's not in a location I can show in a family photo."

A startled laugh escaped me, genuine and unforced. "You did *not*."

"I did. She nearly choked on her mimosa." His lips brushed against my temple, a touch so light it could have been accidental. "You have the best laugh, you know that?"

Something warm unfurled in my chest at his words, a dangerous tendril of pleasure that had nothing to do with our fake engagement and everything to do with the man holding me.

"Alright, just a few more," Connie announced. "Let's get some with just the couple. Everyone else can take a break."

As my family retreated to the deck, leaving Cam and me alone with the photographer, I felt suddenly exposed. Without the buffer of relatives around us, the pretense felt more intimate, more real.

"Let's try some walking shots," Connie suggested. "Just stroll along the water's edge, talking naturally. Pretend I'm not even here."

Cam took my hand, lacing his fingers through mine as we began walking along the shoreline. The sun was high now, its light dancing across the gentle waves, and a soft breeze carried the scent of salt and sunscreen. Tiny sandpipers darted along the wet sand ahead of us, leaving delicate footprints that disappeared with each incoming wave.

"You okay?" he asked quietly as we walked. "You seem tense."

I was – but not for the reasons he probably thought. I was tense because of how easy this all felt. How right. How real. How my hand fit perfectly in his, as if our fingers had been designed to interlock.

"I'm fine," I said. "Just... a lot of... togetherness."

"We can take a break after this," he offered. "I'm sure your family would understand if we needed some time alone."

The suggestion was practical, a respite from the constant performance, but something in his tone made me glance up sharply. His expression was carefully neutral, yet I sensed an undercurrent I couldn't quite name.

"Spin her around!" Connie called from behind us. "Like you're dancing on the beach!"

Cam raised an eyebrow. "May I have this dance?"

Before I could respond, he twirled me gently, then pulled me back against him, one hand settling at the small of my back, the other still holding mine. We swayed together for a moment, not quite dancing but not quite standing still either, the warm sand shifting beneath our bare feet. His eyes never left mine, and I found myself caught in their blue depths like a surfer in a riptide. Beautiful and dangerous.

"You look really pretty today," he said softly. "That dress... the color suits you."

The simple compliment shouldn't have affected me so deeply, but I felt the warmth of a blush spreading across my cheeks. The dress was nothing special, just a simple blue sundress with tiny white flowers scattered across the fabric, but the way he looked at me made me feel as though I was wearing couture.

"Thank you," I managed. "You don't look so bad yourself."

He grinned. "High praise from Lana Decker."

"Don't let it go to your head."

"Too late." His expression sobered slightly. "Your family is great, you know. They really love you."

The observation caught me off guard. "They're... a lot. But yeah, they do."

"You're lucky," he said simply.

There it was again. That flicker of something deeper, a glimpse behind the confident facade he showed the world. I kept thinking about what he'd told me on the dock yesterday, about never having a constant place growing up, about constantly learning to adapt to new situations and new people. How different his childhood must have been from mine, with its revolving cast of step-parents and new homes, compared to the fierce, stable, even if sometimes overwhelming, love of the Decker family.

"Perfect!" Connie called, breaking the moment. "I think we've got some beautiful shots. Let's do a few more by the dunes before we lose this light."

The photoshoot continued for another thirty minutes, but my mind kept returning to that brief, unguarded moment. To the way Cam had said "You're lucky" without a trace of resentment, just a quiet acknowledgment of something precious.

By the time Connie declared the session complete and began packing up her equipment, I felt emotionally drained. Something had shifted between Cam and me, something subtle but undeniable, and I wasn't sure what to do about it.

"That wasn't so bad, was it?" my mother asked as we rejoined the family on the deck. Mimosas were flowing freely now, and Aunt Margaret had commandeered the Bluetooth speaker to play what she called her "beach party playlist": an eclectic mix of Jimmy Buffett, Bob Marley, and inexplicably, Pitbull.

"It was fine," I said, accepting the glass of water my father pressed into my hand. "Connie seemed to get some good shots."

"You two photographed beautifully together," my mother said with satisfaction. "There's something about the way you look at each other. It just translates so well on camera."

I took a long sip of water, avoiding her knowing gaze. "We're just good at posing; all that media training."

"Hmm," she said, unconvinced. "Well, lunch is ready whenever you're hungry. We've got a seafood spread set up inside."

As the afternoon unfolded, I found myself watching Cam more closely, noticing things I'd somehow missed despite working with him for years. The way his smile started in his eyes before it reached his mouth. How he remembered everyone's name after a single introduction. The genuine interest he showed in my cousin Nora's husband's boring tech job, drawing the man out until he was actually animated and engaging. (Nora always claimed he was, but this was the first time we'd actually seen it first hand.)

But most of all, I noticed how seamlessly Cam fit into the chaotic tapestry of my family. He traded fishing stories with Uncle Pete, enthusiastically discussed a "Mexico Week" debacle on the *Great British Bake-Off* with Aunt Margaret until she declared him "a man of impeccable taste, unlike that last boy Lana brought around," and even managed to engage my typically monosyllabic father in a lengthy conversation about defensive strategies that had Dad actually gesturing enthusiastically with the salt and pepper shakers. Nana kept shooting me significant looks whenever Cam answered a question, mouthing "Venus-Mars" with exaggerated winks.

"Your fiancé is quite the charmer," Serena observed, sidling up to me as I watched Cam demonstrate a hockey stick-handling move to Drake using a plastic spoon and a lime. "When did you two finally get together? Drake said you've known each other for a few years."

I gave her the same abbreviated story I'd told my mother, watching her face for signs of suspicion. But Serena just smiled knowingly.

"Sometimes the best ones are right in front of us the whole time," she said, glancing at Drake with unmistakable affection.

"You two seem happy," I said, genuinely pleased for them. Drake had been devastated when they broke up after college, though he'd tried to hide it behind his usual stoic demeanor. Typical of the Decker men.

"We are," Serena confirmed. "Different this time. More honest." She twisted a strand of dark hair around her finger, a habit I remembered from our college days. "We wasted so much time pretending we didn't want the same things."

"And now?" I prompted.

She smiled, and the happiness radiating from her was almost blinding. "Now we're both finally being honest with ourselves and each other about what we want. No more pretending."

Her words hit uncomfortably close to home, though not in the way she intended. Cam and I weren't pretending we didn't want the same things. We were pretending we wanted things we didn't. Or at least, that's what I'd been telling myself.

"I'm happy for you," I said, meaning it. "Drake deserves someone who sees past the Decker name and the hockey legacy."

"So do you," Serena said pointedly. "And it looks like you found him."

Before I could formulate a response, Drake called Serena over to settle a debate about the best place on Lido Key for lobster rolls, (answer: the snack bar on Lido Beach) and I was left alone with her words echoing in my mind.

"You know what we really need..." Aunt Margaret winked conspiratorially at Cam, devilishly swirling her mimosa in the glass...

Cam immediately grinned and the two of them began cracking up before they could even get the punchline out, yelling in unison, "GUAKY-MOLO!", before exploding into riotous laughter.

It hadn't even been a full 24 hours and Cam already had an inside joke with my Aunt Margaret.

"What are your pet names for each other?" my mother asked, her eyes gleaming with curiosity as she sipped her mimosa across the outdoor breakfast table. "I always think they say so much about a couple."

I froze mid-chew, my potato salad suddenly tasteless in my mouth. Pet names were something we had explicitly avoided discussing in our fake relationship planning session. I shot a panicked glance at Cam, who sat beside me radiating casual confidence.

Without missing a beat, Cam leaned forward with an easy smile. "Well, I call her Cupcake Queen because she loves these lavender cupcakes from Sweet Caroline's downtown. She practically goes into a trance when she eats them. It's adorable."

My mother clasped her hands together, delighted. "Oh, that's precious! What about you, sweetheart? What do you call Cam?"

All eyes turned to me. I felt heat creeping up my neck as my mind went completely blank. What would I call Cam if we were really together? Honey? Baby? Sweetheart? All too generic and unconvincing.

"Um, I..." I stammered, feeling Zayne's suspicious gaze boring into me from across the table.

Cam slipped his arm around my shoulders, his thumb rubbing reassuringly against my skin. Completely useless, as Cam's touch had literally *never* helped my ability to think clearly.

"She's shy about it," he said, his voice warm with affection. "It's cute."

That only intensified my mother's curiosity. "Oh, now you have to tell us!"

Cornered and desperate, I blurted out the only thing that came to mind – the ridiculous name I'd mockingly threatened him with during our planning session.

"Puck Daddy," I admitted, my face burning. "I call him Puck Daddy."

There was a split second of silence before my father let out a roar of laughter, followed by my aunt and uncle. My mother's eyes widened before she joined in.

Zayne rolled his eyes so hard I thought they might get stuck. "Jesus Christ," he muttered, stabbing at his potato salad.

"Did she just say Fu..." inquired Aunt Margaret. My mother gasped in faux outrage and swatted Aunt Margaret with her napkin.

"Puck Daddy?" my younger cousin Emma repeated, giggling. "Like hockey?"

"Exactly like hockey," Cam confirmed, looking entirely too pleased with the situation. He leaned over and pressed a kiss to my temple, whispering, "Nice save, Cupcake Queen."

"I love it!" my mother declared between fits of laughter.

I caught Cam's eye as my family kept giggling. His smile was genuine, his eyes twinkling with mischief. And I couldn't help but smile back, despite being absolutely mortified.

The afternoon mellowed into evening, the sun beginning its slow descent toward the horizon, painting the sky in increasingly vivid shades of pink and gold. Gradually, the extended family began to disperse – Nora and Ben leaving first with their exhausted children, followed by Aunt Margaret and Uncle Pete, who had dinner reservations at a restaurant down the Key. Nana insisted on hugging Cam tightly before she left, whispering something in his ear that made his eyes widen before he smiled at her with genuine warmth.

"We'll be back tomorrow for the bonfire," Aunt Margaret promised, kissing my cheek. "Can't wait to hear more about this whirlwind romance." She winked at Cam. "I've got more questions for you, young man."

"Looking forward to it," Cam replied with a grin that made my aunt giggle like a schoolgirl.

I helped my mom put dinner on the table: A huge pot jambalaya with spicy shrimp, warm corn bread and a giant spinach salad. My dad, brothers, and Cam made quick work of the meal as usual — everyone laughing and chatting animatedly.

As we finished dinner and the house quieted, I found myself drawn to the beach, seeking a moment of solitude after the social marathon of the day. I slipped off my sandals at the edge of the dunes, relishing the feel of cool white sand between my toes as I carefully stepped around a sea turtle's nest marked with wooden stakes and yellow tape, and made my way down toward the water's edge.

The Gulf was calm, barely a ripple disturbing its surface as it reflected the kaleidoscope of the sunset. I stopped where the sand met the water, letting the gentle waves lap at my feet, and took a deep breath of salt-tinged air.

"Room for one more?"

I turned to find Cam standing a few feet away, his hands in the pockets of his shorts, the breeze ruffling his hair. His linen shirt billowed in the breeze, revealing a tantalizing glimpse of tanned skin beneath. It was terribly unfair that he was so hot. And kind. With the fiery sunset illuminating his face, he looked like something out of a travel magazine: the quintessential beach dream come to life.

"It's a free beach," I said, though my heart sped up at his presence. "How'd you escape the Decker inquisition?"

"Your brother rescued me," he said, moving to stand beside me. "Zayne challenged Drake to a round of beach volleyball. I think it was partly to save me and partly to show off for Serena."

I smiled, picturing it. "Some things never change."

We stood in companionable silence for a moment, watching as the sun continued its descent, the sky deepening from pink to a rich, vivid orange that reflected off the water in shimmering ribbons of gold.

"Thank you," I said finally. "For today. For being so... good with my family."

He shrugged, but I could tell he was pleased. "They're easy to like. Zayne's always been the closest thing I've ever had to a brother," he paused. I'm really hoping that's still true after all of this."

"Still. It can be overwhelming. The Decker clan en masse is a lot."

"I liked it," he said simply. "The chaos, the teasing, the way everyone just... belongs. It's nice."

There it was again. That glimpse of vulnerability, quickly masked but unmistakable.

"You know," I said slowly, "you belong too. Not just here, but with the team. With the guys."

He glanced at me, surprised. "I know that."

"Do you? Because sometimes it seems like you're still... adapting. Still trying to fit in, even after all these years."

He was silent for a long moment, his gaze returning to the horizon. "Survival instinct, I guess," he said finally. "When the ground is constantly shifting under your feet as a kid, you learn to become whoever you need to be in the moment. After a while, it's second nature. But sometimes it can feel like you never really get to be yourself."

The admission lodged in my chest, a tender ache for the boy he must have been. Always having to adjust, always watching for clues about how to belong to the latest iteration of his own family.

"You don't have to do that with me," I said softly. "I like the real Cam."

His eyes found mine, intense and searching. "Do you even know who that is?"

The question was weighted with more meaning than I was prepared to face. Because the truth was, I wasn't sure I did know the real Cam. At least not fully. I'd spent so much time filling in the blanks in my own mind after that night in Boston so many years ago, and then crafting an image of him for public consumption so vivid I believed it myself, that I'd really never *properly* looked below the surface.

"I'm starting to," I said honestly.

A small smile curved his lips. "Better late than never, I guess."

The sun was nearly gone now, just a sliver of fiery pink on the horizon, the sky deepening to purple above us. A solitary gull flew overhead, its cry echoing across the water as it banked toward the distant pier.

"It's beautiful here," Cam murmured, his gaze following the bird's flight. "Peaceful. I see why your family has held onto this place for so long."

"It's my favorite spot in the world," I admitted. "No matter how crazy life gets, I always feel calm here."

"Even with me disrupting your calm?" he asked, a teasing note in his voice.

I looked up at him, really looked, taking in the relaxed set of his shoulders, the softening around his eyes, the way the fading light gilded his profile with burnished gold.

"You're not disrupting anything," I said softly. "You fit here."

His eyes met mine, and something electric passed between us – a recognition, a possibility, a bridge spanning the careful distance we'd maintained. He took a half step closer, close enough that I could feel the warmth radiating from his body, smell the subtle notes of his cologne mingling with salt air..

"Lana," he said, my name little more than a breath. He raised his hand, gently brushing a strand of hair from my face, his fingertips grazing my cheek. "You have sand..."

The touch was brief, but it sent shivers racing down my body, cheeks flushed, nipples hardening, goosebumps rising on my arms despite the lingering warmth of the day. His hand lingered, cupping my face with a tenderness that made my heart stutter. Time seemed to slow, the space between us charged with something fragile and dangerous and inevitable.

He leaned in, his eyes never leaving mine, giving me every opportunity to pull away. But I didn't. I couldn't. Some magnetic force held me in place, tilting my face up to his, my breath catching his in anticipation. The universe suddenly narrowed to just us: his face inches from mine, the warm brush of his breath against my lips, the roar of blood in my ears drowning out even the sound of the waves.

His lips hovered a breath away from mine "Is this okay?" he murmured, his voice rough with a want that mirrored the ache building in my own chest.

Reality crashed back with jarring suddenness. *What was I doing?* This wasn't part of the plan. This wasn't pretending for an audience. We were *alone* on the beach, no cameras, no family watching. Just us. Just real.

I stepped back abruptly, breaking the connection, a sudden emptiness filling the space Cam had filled just seconds before. "We should head back," I said, my voice sounding strained even to my own ears. "It's getting dark."

Confusion flickered across his face, followed by something that might have been hurt before he masked it with a careful neutrality. "Right," he said. "Of course."

The walk back to the house was silent, a new tension strung between us like high-voltage wire. I kept my arms wrapped tightly around myself, as if I could physically hold in the riot of emotions threatening to spill over. Cam maintained a respectful distance, hands in his pockets, eyes focused ahead.

I'd almost let him kiss me. Worse, *I had wanted him to*. Not for show, but for me. Because standing on that beach with Cam Murphy, bathed in the golden light of sunset, I'd felt something dangerously close to real.

I couldn't do it again. I'd spent ten years trying to get over him after he'd walked away the first time, and I didn't have it in me to survive another Cam-shaped hole being torn through my heart when this charade inevitably ended. When the photo ops were completed, the contract signed, and the cameras stopped rolling, he'd move on to his next conquest, professional or otherwise. This connection between us would vanish into thin air, as if it had been nothing but a mirage. And I'd be left picking up the pieces of my professional reputation and my bruised heart, once again wondering if what had felt so true, so real to me had been completely one-sided – if I'd imagined the spark in his eyes when he looked at me, manufactured the electricity in his touch to satisfy some pathetic fantasy that had never quite died. The image I'd created of Cam was so powerful, so magnetic, it had even worked on me.

The moon was rising as we reached the deck, casting long silver shadows across the weathered boards. Inside, I could see my family gathered around the table, laughter spilling out through the open windows along with the warm glow of lights. Normal. Safe. *Real.*

Cam paused at the bottom of the steps. "Lana... I'm sorry, I..."

I shook my head, cutting him off before he could say whatever truth or lie was about to leave his lips. "Let's just get through this weekend, okay? Keep things simple."

He studied me for a long moment, then nodded once, his expression unreadable in the gathering darkness. "If that's what you want."

It wasn't what I wanted. Not even close. What I *wanted* was for Cam to take me in his arms on the beach and kiss me so hard I lost the ability to make good decisions. But it was what I *needed* if I was going to survive this with my heart intact.

I climbed the steps without looking back, steeling myself to rejoin my family and pretend that everything was fine. That I hadn't just come dangerously close to crossing a line that would change everything.

That I wasn't already wondering what Cam's lips would have felt like against mine, ten years after I'd first tasted them and spent every night since trying to forget.

Chapter 10

The walk back to the beach house after our almost-kiss was excruciating. Cam and I walked to the house in silence, the only sound between us the soft thud of our footsteps on weathered wood and the distant rhythm of waves against the shore.

I'd nearly let him kiss me. Worse – I'd wanted him to. For one reckless moment on that moonlit beach, my body had remembered what it felt like to be close to Cam Murphy, and wanted more. My lips still tingled with the phantom sensation of a kiss that never happened. My skin burned where he had touched my cheek.

Now, as we approached the sliding glass doors that led back to the warm glow of family dinner, I tried to compose myself. To slip back into the armor of professionalism I'd been attempting and miserably failing to maintain since we'd arrived. But my hands were trembling slightly, and my heart refused to settle into its normal rhythm.

"Ready?" Cam asked, his voice low and careful, hand hovering near my lower back but not quite touching – a habit he'd developed over the last few days that somehow felt more intimate than actual contact. His eyes searched mine, and I wondered if he could see all the chaos swirling behind them.

I nodded, not trusting my voice, and plastered on what I hoped was a convincing smile as we stepped inside.

The family dinner table was exactly as we'd left it – my parents and brothers deep in conversation, Serena laughing at something Drake had said, plates of half-eaten key lime pie scattered across the table. For a surreal moment, it felt as if time had frozen while Cam and I had been on the beach, as if our almost-kiss existed in some parallel dimension that hadn't affected the normal flow of the evening at all.

"There they are!" my mother exclaimed, glancing up with a beaming smile. "We were starting to wonder if you two had decided to take a late swim."

"Just needed some air," I said, sliding into my empty seat and reaching for my abandoned wineglass with fingers that weren't quite steady. "It's a beautiful night."

"Gorgeous," Cam agreed, settling beside me with easy grace. "The Gulf is like glass tonight."

His voice betrayed nothing of what had almost happened between us. The almost-kiss, the charged moment, the question hanging in the air between us when I'd stepped away. He was the picture of relaxed contentment, smiling as my father launched into a story about a fishing trip gone wrong years ago.

Only I noticed the way his knuckles whitened slightly where he gripped his water glass, the slight tension in his shoulders as he leaned back in his chair. And I caught the flash of something unreadable in his eyes when they briefly met mine across the table.

And Zayne, apparently. My brother was watching us with narrowed eyes, his gaze flicking between Cam and me with suspicious precision. When our eyes met, he raised one eyebrow in silent question. I took a large gulp of wine, avoiding his scrutiny.

"Did you show Cam the boathouse?" Drake asked me, seemingly oblivious to the undercurrents below the table.

"Not yet," I said, grateful for the distraction. "Maybe tomorrow."

"If the weather holds, we could take the boat out," my father suggested, passing a plate of cookies that no one really needed after the key lime pie. "Show Cam some of our favorite fishing spots."

"That would be great," Cam replied with genuine enthusiasm. "I haven't been fishing in years."

"You'll love it," Drake said. "Dad knows all the secret spots where the redfish hide."

"It's settled then," my mother said happily. "Fishing tomorrow, bonfire tomorrow night. The rest of the family is coming back for s'mores and ghost stories."

"Decker tradition," Drake explained to Serena, his hand finding hers on the table. "Dad tells the same three ghost stories every year, and Mom pretends to be scared even though she's heard them at least thirty times."

"They get scarier with age," my father protested good-naturedly, winking at my mother.

The conversation flowed around me, but I remained hyperaware of Cam beside me – the scent of him mingling with salt air, the casual brush of his arm against mine when he reached for his water glass, the warmth of his thigh inches from my own beneath the table. Every small contact sent a jolt through me, keeping me on edge. Memories of the beach kept flashing through my mind – the look in his eyes as he'd leaned toward me, the gentle touch of his fingers on my face, the way my heart had raced in anticipation.

At one point, he reached for the salt at the same moment I did, our fingers colliding. The brief contact sent a shock up my arm, and I jerked back as if burned. Zayne's eyes narrowed further.

My mother, bless her, seemed to attribute my distraction to romantic bliss. "You two look so happy together," she said, beaming at us over her wineglass. "Don't they, Frank?"

My father grunted what might have been agreement, though his eyes held a hint of skepticism as they moved between Cam and me.

"Young love," my mother sighed. "It reminds me of us, darling. Remember how we couldn't keep our hands off each other?"

"Mom!" Drake and Zayne protested in unison, while I felt heat creep up my neck.

Once dinner finally ended, dishes were done, and leftovers put away, I seized the opportunity to escape.

"I think I'll turn in," I announced, stifling an exaggerated yawn. "It's been a long day."

"Me too," Cam said immediately. "Those beach photos wore me out."

I shot him a look, he didn't have to follow me upstairs right away, but it was too late to object without seeming odd. So we found ourselves making goodnight rounds to my family, enduring my mother's knowing smile and Zayne's suspicious glare as we headed upstairs together.

The bedroom door closing behind us felt like a thunderclap in the sudden silence.

With the door closed and the pretense temporarily suspended, the air between us felt charged with unspoken words and the echo of our almost-kiss on the beach. The room suddenly seemed much smaller than it had this morning.

"Well," I said briskly, moving toward my suitcase, needing something to do with my hands. "I'm going to get ready for bed."

Cam nodded, running a hand through his hair, mussing the golden strands. "Sure. You take the bathroom first."

I grabbed my toiletry bag and pajamas, then locked myself in the bathroom, leaning heavily against the door. Staring at my reflection in the mirror, I hardly recognized myself. Cheeks flushed, eyes too bright, hair slightly tousled from the sea breeze. I looked... affected. Undone.

My fingers drifted to my lips involuntarily, tracing where Cam's mouth would have touched mine if I hadn't pulled away. What would it have felt like? Would it have been like that night in college – hungry, desperate, consuming? Or something softer, deeper, more dangerous?

I rinsed off in the shower and took my time with my nighttime routine, brushing my teeth methodically, washing my face, applying moisturizer in slow, careful circles. Anything to delay facing Cam again. I changed into my silk pajama shorts and matching camisole, a practical choice for Florida's humid nights that now felt dangerously revealing.

When I finally emerged, Cam was standing by the window, staring out at the ocean, still fully dressed. His profile was bathed in silver moonlight, casting half his face in shadow while illuminating the sharp line of his jaw, the curve of his mouth, the muscular line of his shoulders and back. He turned at the sound of the door, and something flickered in his expression as he took in my appearance: a momentary darkening of his eyes that made my breath catch.

"All yours," I said, my voice sounding strangely formal to my own ears.

He cleared his throat. "Thanks. I'll be quick."

The door closed behind him, and I let out a breath I hadn't realized I'd been holding. I moved to the bed, pulling back the covers and sliding in on my side. The sheets were cool against my bare legs, and I pulled the comforter up to my chest, staring at the canopy above me, listening to the muffled sounds of water running in the bathroom.

True to his word, Cam spent less time in the bathroom than I had. I heard the shower run for just a few minutes, probably a quick rinse to get any remaining sand off. When he emerged in a fresh t-shirt and athletic shorts, I was lying stiffly on my back, pretending to be absorbed in a text on my phone. I snuck a glance at him – his hair was damp at the temples, his face freshly washed, and the scent of toothpaste and soap followed him across the room. Something about seeing him like this – clean, rumpled, domestic – made my chest ache.

He slid into bed beside me, careful to maintain the invisible boundary down the middle of the bed. I set my phone on the nightstand, every part of my body acutely aware of his proximity. He reached over and turned off the bedside lamp, plunging the room into darkness broken only by strips of moonlight sneaking through the gauzy curtains.

"Goodnight," I said quietly.

"Night," he replied.

Silence fell between us, thick and complicated. I lay perfectly still, listening to the sound of his breathing, feeling the warmth radiating from his body even across the careful space between us. Outside, waves crashed rhythmically against the shore, a soothing counterpoint to my restless thoughts. A ceiling fan whirred softly overhead, stirring the air and making the gauzy bed canopy flutter like a ghost.

Sleep was impossible. My mind kept replaying the beach scene on an endless loop. The moonlight on the water, the warmth in Cam's eyes, the way my heart had pounded as he'd leaned toward me. The words he'd whispered, "Is this okay?" still echoed in my ears.

What would have happened if I hadn't pulled away? If I'd let myself have that moment, consequences be damned?

I shifted again slightly, trying to get comfortable, trying to quiet my racing thoughts.

"Can't sleep?" Cam's voice came softly through the darkness.

I sighed. "No."

"Me either."

More silence, but different now – acknowledged, shared. I could hear the distant sound of the AC unit, the music of the occasional night bird, the eternal rhythm of the waves.

"Do you want to talk about it?" he asked after a moment.

"Talk about what?" I hedged, though we both knew exactly what he meant.

I could practically hear him smile in the darkness. "The weather. The fascinating economic state of the NHL. Why your Aunt Margaret owns seventeen pairs of the exact same sandals in different colors."

Despite myself, I laughed softly. "How do you know about Aunt Margaret's sandals?"

"She told me. In great detail. Something about the company discontinuing her favorite style, so she bought out their remaining stock in every color. She seemed very proud of her foresight."

"That sounds like Aunt Margaret."

"She also told me you went through a phase where you only wore purple. For an entire year."

I groaned. "I was seven! Why is she telling you these things?"

"Because that's what families do," he said, his voice warming. "They embarrass you in front of people and tell stories you'd rather forget and show baby pictures where you're naked in a bathtub."

"Oh dear dawg. Did she show you bathtub pictures?" I demanded, horrified.

"Not yet, " he teased. "But there's always tomorrow."

I rolled onto my side to face him, though I could barely make out his profile in the darkness. "If you see a single naked baby picture of me, Murphy, our deal is off."

He chuckled, a low rumble that I could feel through the mattress. "No deal. Those pictures are actually my primary motivation for this whole fake engagement. Besides, I want to see what our imaginary children will look like."

The easy banter settled something in me, eased the tight knot of tension that had been coiled in my chest since the beach. The darkness made everything feel intimate, cushioned, safe. As if the words we spoke here couldn't follow us into daylight.

"Your family is amazing, you know," he said after a moment, his voice shifting to something more serious. "I didn't really know it could be like this."

"They're... they're pretty great."

"They love you. Really love you. Not because of what you do or who you know or what you can give them. Just because you're you." There was a wistfulness in his voice that made my heart twist. "That's rare."

I thought about what I knew of Cam's family, which wasn't much, despite working with him for years. He had a complicated relationship with his mother and father. A collection of step-parents that seemed to rotate every few years. But the details were fuzzy, the full picture unclear.

"What was your family like?" I asked. "Growing up, I mean."

He was quiet for so long I thought he might not answer. When he finally spoke, his voice was softer, lacking its usual bravado.

"Chaotic. Unpredictable. Always changing." He shifted slightly, the sheets rustling. "My mom remarried three times before I graduated high school. My dad, four times. I had different bedrooms in different houses almost every year. Christmas looked different each year: new traditions, new step-siblings, new rules. By the time I was ten, I'd learned to sleep with my hockey gear in my room so I wouldn't forget it when we moved again."

The image of a young Cam, clutching his gear like a security blanket in an ever-changing series of bedrooms, made my throat tighten.

"You learn not to get too attached," he continued, "because that stepmom who makes the good brownies, or the stepdad who helped you with your algebra homework might just disappear one day and never call again. My third stepdad taught me to ride a bike, took me fishing every weekend for a year. Then one day, my mom tells me they're splitting up, and I never saw him again. Like, poof!" He paused. "I was eight."

"That sounds hard," I said quietly, wanting to reach for him in the darkness but holding back.

"You adapt," he said simply, though I could hear the cost of that adaptation in his voice. "You figure out how to fit in, how to be what each new family needs. What will make the new step-parent like you, what will keep the peace."

Something in his tone made my chest ache. I thought about what he'd said on the dock about learning to read rooms, to adjust to new situations. It hadn't just been about making small talk or navigating social events. It was about survival.

"Is that why hockey was so important to you?" I asked. "Something stable?"

"Yeah." The admission came easily in the darkness. "The rink was always the same. The rules never changed. I knew exactly what was expected of me. It was, uh, predictable. Safe." He shifted again. "When everything else in your life keeps changing – your home, your family, your school – you hold onto the things that stay the same. For me, that was hockey. No matter where we moved, I could find a rink, find a team."

I'd never thought of hockey that way; as a refuge. For me, it had always been about the game we all love, family, about belonging to the Decker dynasty. I wondered what it might have been like to find the sport on my own, to choose it rather than inherit it.

"That's why the team means so much to me," he continued, his voice deepening with emotion. "The guys, coaches, even staff." It's the closest thing I've ever had to a real family. People who are actually sticking around, who want me to be there, not as someone who has to be crowbarred into their new life plan."

"Even Zayne?" I teased gently, trying to lighten the moment.

"Especially Zayne," he said seriously. "He was the first person I met my freshman year at BU. He's constant. Solid. When everything else was shifting, Zayne was just Zayne. Same in the dorms as he was on the ice as he was in class. Never pretended to be something he wasn't, never expected me to be anything but myself."

His voice softened, became reflective. "I'd never had that before, someone who didn't change depending on the circumstance. He's always Zayne. Loyal, steady, Zayne."

I felt a sudden surge of affection for my stoic, grumpy brother. For all his flaws and overprotectiveness, Zayne *did* have a steadiness to him that I'd always taken for granted. I'd never considered how that quality might have appeared to someone like Cam, whose life had been defined by instability.

"We're lucky to have him," I said softly. "Even when he's being an overprotective pain in the ass."

Cam laughed quietly. "He loves you. He just wants to protect you."

"I know." I paused, then added, "He's not about to murder you in your sleep for coming within five feet of me, is he?"

"Nah. He's more the broad-daylight murder type. Witnesses, consequences... he's not afraid."

I snort-laughed, then sobered. "How bad was it? Moving around so much?"

"On the positive, it taught me to adapt. To read people, adjust, become what was needed. But... yeah. Never feeling like you belong anywhere, like you have a home base? It wears on you. Especially as a kid." His voice had taken on a reflective quality I'd rarely heard from him. "Some days, even now, I'll wake up and not remember which house I'm in. Just for a second. Disoriented until I remember it's *my* place, and I never have to move unless I want to."

He paused, and I could hear him swallow in the darkness. "That night in college, with you... that was only the second time I felt like maybe I could just be me. Not whoever I needed to be to keep the peace or fit in. Just... Cam."

My breath caught at the unexpected pivot. We'd been carefully avoiding any direct mention of that night for years, dancing around it with practiced precision. Now here it was, suddenly looming large between us in the darkened room.

"I didn't think you remembered that night," I said carefully, my heart suddenly pounding so loudly I was sure he could hear it.

His laugh was soft, disbelieving. "Lana. How could I forget?"

The simple question was loaded with implication. My pulse skittered wildly, and I was grateful for the darkness that concealed my expression.

"You left," I said finally, the words coming out before I could stop them. "You didn't even say goodbye. You never called."

He was silent for a long moment, and I could sense him gathering his thoughts in the darkness. "I know."

"I woke up, and you were just... gone." The memory still stung, even after all these years and I felt my eyes burning. *Do. Not. Cry.* I breathed slowly to manage my emotions so Cam wouldn't hear. "I felt so stupid. I thought we had this... connection. This amazing night. And then you disappeared like it meant nothing."

"It didn't mean nothing," he said quietly, intensely. "It meant everything."

"Then why did you leave?" The question I'd wanted to ask for ten years finally escaped, hanging between us.

"It's complicated."

"That's not an answer."

He sighed, a long exhale that seemed to carry the weight of a decade. "No, it's not."

I waited, but he didn't elaborate. The silence stretched between us, taut with unspoken words. Outside, the waves continued their eternal conversation with the shore, indifferent to our human struggles.

I was not dropping this. I'd waited ten years to have this conversation.

"Do you know what the worst part was?" I finally said, my voice barely above a whisper. "Not that you left. But that I didn't see it coming. It felt like we'd found something real, and it turned out to be nothing." I swallowed hard against the lump forming in my throat. "I laid there like an idiot, waiting for you to come back, making up excuses – maybe you went to get coffee, maybe you had an early class. But you never came back."

I could hear the embarrassing tremor in my voice but couldn't seem to stop the words that had been locked inside for too long. "It made me doubt myself. My judgment. Like I couldn't tell the difference between what was genuine and what wasn't. Like I'd imagined the entire connection."

"Lana – "

"Ever since then, I've been so careful. So determined not to be fooled again. And now here we are, pretending to be engaged, sleeping in the same bed, playing this elaborate game where it's getting harder and harder to tell what's real and what's for show, and I just – " I broke off, horrified to feel tears threatening again, betraying my vulnerability. I blinked rapidly in the darkness, willing them away.

"Hey," Cam said softly, and I felt his hand find mine on top of the covers, his fingers wrapping gently around mine. "This isn't like that."

His palm was warm against the back of my hand, sending a current of awareness up my arm.

"Isn't it?" I whispered, absolutely *hating* the vulnerability in my voice.

He was quiet for a moment, his thumb continuing its gentle path across my skin. The simple touch anchored me in the darkness, a physical connection to match the emotional one we were tiptoeing around.

"I wanted to stay," he finally said, his voice so low I had to strain to hear him. "That night in college. I wanted to stay more than anything."

The raw honesty in his voice made something catch in my chest. "Then why didn't you?"

I felt, rather than saw, him shake his head in the darkness. "I can't... it was complicated."

A wave of frustration swept through me, and I tried to pull my hand away. His fingers tightened, not letting go. "That's cryptic and unhelpful."

"I know." His fingers intertwined with mine, holding on when I would have retreated. "I'm sorry. I just... I need you to know that it wasn't because of you. It wasn't because what we had wasn't real. It wasn't because I didn't care."

The earnestness in his voice was almost painful to hear. He moved closer, just a few inches, but I could feel the heat of him now, the mattress dipping slightly with his weight.

"I've regretted leaving a thousand times," he continued, his voice rough with emotion. "I've replayed that night in my head more times than I can count. I've wondered what might have happened if I'd stayed, if we'd had a chance to see where things could go."

I lay there in the darkness, trying to process his words. They didn't make sense – if he'd wanted to stay, why hadn't he? If it had meant something to him, why had he never mentioned it in all the years since? Why was he being so evasive now?

"I don't understand," I said finally.

"I know," he repeated, squeezing my hand. "And I'm sorry for that. I'm sorry I left. I'm sorry I hurt you."

The apology was unexpectedly affecting. I'd locked the memory away, pretended it didn't matter, convinced myself it was just a college hookup gone wrong. To hear Cam recognize the hurt he'd caused made something inside me crack open.

"I've spent ten years trying not to think about that night," I admitted. "Trying to forget how it felt. How *you* made me feel."

His breath caught audibly, and his hand tightened around mine. "How did I make you feel?" The question was hesitant, almost vulnerable, as if he was bracing himself for the answer. But the darkness gave us both cover, a veil of protection.

I closed my eyes, letting myself remember. The way we'd talked for hours. The walk back to my dorm, stars overhead, our shoulders bumping as we laughed. The kiss that had started gentle and quickly blazed out of control. The way he'd looked at me as we'd undressed each other, like I was something rare and cherished.

"Like I was the only person in the world who mattered," I said softly. "Like you saw me, really saw me. Not as Frank Decker's daughter or Zayne's sister or a back door into some hockey dynasty. Just... me."

The truth of it settled over me as I spoke. That was what had been so intoxicating about that night: the feeling of being truly seen, of connecting on a million different levels with someone who wasn't looking at me through the lens of my family name or reputation.

"I did see you," Cam said quietly, his voice thick with emotion. "I still do."

He shifted again, his free hand finding my face in the darkness, fingertips ghosting along my jaw with exquisite gentleness. The touch was so unexpected, so tender, that I couldn't have pulled away if I'd wanted to.

"That night with you," he continued, his voice low and intimate, "it was different from anything I'd ever experienced. It wasn't just physical. It was... everything. The way you looked at me. The way you listened. The way you laughed. I'd never felt so known."

I didn't know what to say. It felt too big, too laden with meaning I had no idea how to examine. I was acutely aware of his hand still holding mine, his other hand now resting lightly on my cheek, the heat of him so close in the darkness. My pulse was roaring in my ears, and I was sure he must feel it.

We lay in silence for what felt like a long time, the tension between us electric and fragile. His thumb traced the curve of my cheekbone, a touch so light it was barely there, but it sent tremors through me.

"I should let you sleep," he finally said, though he didn't move away, didn't release my hand.

"Yeah," I agreed, my voice barely above a whisper. "Big day tomorrow. Fishing and ghost stories."

"Can't wait," he murmured, and I could hear the smile in his voice.

Slowly, reluctantly, his hand slipped away from my face. He gave my hand a gentle squeeze before finally letting go, and I immediately missed the warmth of his touch. I rolled onto my other side, facing away from him, trying to process the conversation and what it meant.

Cam had wanted to stay that night. He'd seen me, really seen me, and whatever had made him leave, it apparently hadn't been a lack of interest or connection. The thought was both comforting and confusing, leaving me with more questions than answers.

Behind me, I felt Cam settle into his pillow, heard his breathing gradually deepen and slow. But sleep eluded me, my mind replaying our conversation on an endless loop as the night stretched on. The weight of ten years of wondering, of hurt, of what-ifs felt both heavier and lighter now, transformed by his words but not erased.

It was hours later that I finally drifted off with Cam's words echoing in my mind.

"I wanted to stay more than anything."

After our midnight conversation, my mind refused to quiet down, replaying Cam's words over and over.

What did that even mean? Why had he said it now, ten years too late? And if it *was* actually true, *why didn't he?*

I'd finally drifted off sometime after 3 AM, **and** awoke again to the sensation of warmth against my back and something heavy draped across my waist. For a moment, I kept my eyes closed, savoring the comfort of it. Then reality filtered in, and I realized that I was once again wrapped in Cam Murphy's arms.

Sometime during our brief sleep, we'd gravitated toward each other once again, and now we were spooning in the middle of the bed, my back pressed against his bare chest, his arm wrapped securely around me. His breath was warm against the back of my neck, steady with sleep. It was warmer than usual in the room, which explained why Cam's t-shirt was balled up at the end of the bed.

Sunlight cast the room in a soft golden glow. Outside, I could hear the first chorus of birds greeting the day against the distant sound of the waves.

I should move. I should carefully extract myself and retreat to my side of the bed before he woke up and things got awkward again. That's what a professional would do, what someone maintaining appropriate boundaries would do.

Instead, I found myself lying perfectly still, allowing myself to absorb the feeling of being held by him. His arm was heavy and warm across my waist, his body solid and reassuring behind mine. The steady rhythm of his heartbeat against my back was hypnotic, soothing. His leg was tangled with mine, his bare foot resting against my calf. It felt... right. Safe. Like coming home after a long journey.

And that was terrifying. Okay, comfy but terrifying.

Whatever this strange intimacy was that had developed between us, it couldn't, shouldn't, last beyond the next few weeks. This wasn't real; it was a temporary arrangement, a business deal with an expiration date.

But my treacherous body didn't seem to care about that distinction. It responded to Cam's proximity with a humming awareness that belied all my mental arguments.

Could it?

Behind me, Cam stirred as he drifted toward wakefulness. I felt the exact moment he became fully conscious. His body stiffened slightly, his breathing changed, and for a heartbeat I thought he would pull away.

He didn't.

"Morning," he mumbled, his voice rough with sleep, vibrating against my shoulder blade.

"Morning," I replied, my own voice surprisingly steady given the circumstances.

Neither of us moved. The moment stretched between us, fraught with possibility and danger.

"Did you sleep okay?" he asked, his breath warm against the nape of my neck. He shifted his weight but still made no move to release me from his embrace. If anything, he seemed to settle in more comfortably, his fingers lazily tracing the edge of my camisole where it had ridden up, sending tiny tingles across my skin.

"I was awake for a while," I admitted, fighting to keep my voice even despite the havoc his touch was wreaking. "My mind wouldn't quiet down after... everything."

"Mine either," he said softly, his breath warm against my shoulder. "But it was worth it. Talking like that."

There was something different in his tone this morning; a quiet vulnerability that made my chest tighten. Yesterday had been playful, teasing. Today felt weighted with the revelations of our midnight conversation.

"Lana," he began, his voice serious in a way that made my pulse quicken. His hand splayed across my abdomen, warm and solid. "About last night... "

Before I could respond or he could continue, a knock sounded at the bedroom door, sharp and insistent.

"Lana? Cam?" My mother's voice filtered through the wood. "Rise and shine! Everybody decent?"

"Hey Mom," I called back, aching to hear what Cam had been about to say. He quickly pulled on a t-shirt, and I yelled through the door, "Yeah, we're decent."

"Up and at 'em, lovebirds! You're on breakfast duty!"

Cam's arm loosened around me, and I took the opportunity to sit up, putting some much-needed distance between us. He propped himself up on one elbow, watching me with an expression I couldn't quite decipher. Part amusement, part frustration, part something deeper and more dangerous.

"Another day of our magical fake engagement," he whispered lightly, though his eyes remained serious, searching mine. "Ready for it?"

I nodded, barely trusting my voice, but definitely not trusting my morning breath. After our midnight conversation, after waking up in his arms for the second morning in a row, with his confession about that night ten years ago still echoing in my mind, I was less sure than ever about what was real and what was pretend.

Other than the fear that this would all go terribly, terribly wrong. That felt *very* real.

Chapter 11

I groaned, pulling the pillow over my head. "Mom, it's vacation. Why are we up at the crack of dawn?"

"It's hardly dawn, sweetie. And everyone will be hungry after their morning walks. I've already got coffee brewing."

Beside me, Cam was already sitting up, looking frustratingly alert for someone who'd been up half the night talking about feelings. "Morning, Diana," he said. "We'll be down in ten."

"Perfect! I've left out all the pancake ingredients. The kids have been asking for chocolate chip ones."

When the door closed behind her, I emerged from under my pillow cocoon. "How are you so chipper? We barely slept."

Cam stretched, revealing ab muscles I definitely wasn't staring at. "Hockey schedules. I can function on basically no sleep." He glanced at me and grinned. "Plus, thanks to my aforementioned childhood, I can pretty much sleep anywhere."

"That's what got us into this mess," I quipped.

"Haha, smartass. You, on the other hand, look like you've been hit by the Zamboni."

"Wow. Just the compliment every girl wants to hear first thing in the morning." I sat up, running a hand through my tangled hair. "Next you'll tell me my morning breath smells like a locker room."

"Actually, I was going to say your grumpy morning face is cute, but if you prefer the Zamboni comparison..."

I threw my pillow at him, which he caught effortlessly. "Let's just get this over with. Fair warning: I'm useless before coffee."

"Noted. I'll protect the general public from your pre-caffeinated wrath. Rise and shine."

Twenty minutes later, showered and marginally more alert, I made my way downstairs to find Cam already in the kitchen, casually wearing a hot pink apron emblazoned with KISS THE COOK over his t-shirt and shorts, signature funky socks on his feet. He studied the ingredients my mother had left out with the focused intensity I'd seen him use when watching game tapes.

"Looking pretty serious there, Murphy," I said, heading straight for the coffee maker.

"I'm just planning my approach," he replied, measuring flour with surprising precision. "Your mom mentioned she was hoping for blueberry pancakes, but I'm thinking we could do a mixed berry situation. Maybe add some lemon zest."

I paused mid-pour. "Since when are you a pancake connoisseur?"

"I may have binged an entire season of Crime Scene Kitchen last week." He shot me a grin over his shoulder. "Plus, pancakes are basically just a simplified version of cake, and I happen to be excellent with cake."

"Wait. You bake?" I asked, genuinely surprised. This was a side of Cam I'd never seen before.

"Don't sound so shocked," he said, cracking eggs into a bowl with practiced ease. "A man needs hobbies that don't involve getting checked into boards. Baking is... therapeutic."

I leaned against the counter, watching as he whisked the batter with confident strokes. "The Slashers' notorious enforcer finds solace in cupcakes?"

"Mostly cupcakes, yes," he admitted without a hint of embarrassment. "But I'm branching out. My cheesecake game is coming along nicely."

I sipped my coffee, oddly charmed by this revelation. "So what you're telling me is that beneath that NHL superstar exterior beats the flambéed heart of a *Great British Bake-Off* contestant?"

"Guilty as charged." He measured vanilla extract, adding it to the mix. "Though I'd appreciate it if you kept that information within these four walls. I have a reputation to maintain."

"Your secret's safe with me," I promised, moving beside him to add some sugar to my coffee. "Though I'll reserve judgment until I taste these pancakes."

"Ye of little faith... Play your cards right, Decker, and I might even make you my famous espresso chocolate cupcakes." He bumped my hip lightly with his. "I don't like to brag, but they've been known to trigger spontaneous marriage proposals."

He moved to the sink, rinsing the strawberries under cool water. The sleeves of his well-worn Violent Femmes t-shirt stretched across his biceps as he worked, outlining every curve of muscle beneath the thin cotton. I tried not to stare at the way his shoulders flexed with each movement, or how the fabric clung to the planes of his back. Not that I noticed. Not at all.

For the next fifteen minutes, we worked in companionable silence, Cam mixing batter while I washed and cut the rest of the fruit. It was oddly domestic, this morning routine, and I found myself sneaking glances at him – the furrow of concentration between his brows as he flipped the pancakes, the way he hummed something under his breath, the easy confidence of his movements despite being in unfamiliar territory.

"You're staring," he said without looking up.

"I'm supervising," I corrected, turning back to my fruit salad. "Making sure America's favorite hockey player doesn't set the grill on fire."

"America's favorite hockey player, huh? I'm keeping that quote for my next contract negotiation. Hey Zayne!" he yelled.

"Shh," I playfully covered his mouth with my palm. "Don't let it go to your head."

"Too late." He grinned, sliding the cutting board of fruit toward me. "What's next, boss?"

I was about to answer when the patter of small feet announced the arrival of Nora's kids, followed closely by my aunt Margaret, uncle Pete, and Nora herself, all in various states of post-morning-walk dishevelment.

"Pancakes!" Six-year-old Emma squealed, her eyes lighting up at the sight of the chocolate chips waiting to be added to the batter.

"Are those dinosaurs on your socks?" Her eight-year-old brother Tyler dropped to his knees to get a better look at Cam's feet.

I glanced down, noticing for the first time Cam's incredibly mismatched socks – one bright green with cartoon dinosaurs on skateboards, the other purple with what appeared to be tacos wearing sombreros.

"Sure are," Cam said, lifting one foot to give Tyler a better view. "These are my special breakfast-making socks. I think the saddest part about dinosaurs going extinct is that they weren't around when we invented pancakes."

"That's so cool!" Emma was instantly at his side, examining the socks with total fascination. "Can I have dinosaur socks?"

"Every person should have at least one pair of dinosaur socks," Cam said solemnly. "It's practically a rule."

"Mom, did you hear that? I need dinosaur socks!" Emma tugged at Nora's sleeve.

"I heard," Nora said, giving Cam an amused look. "Thanks for that."

"Sorry," he whispered, not looking sorry at all.

"Do you have other funny socks?" Tyler asked, still crouched near Cam's feet.

"At home? About 60 pairs. It's kind of my thing."

"Only 60?" I interrupted, genuinely surprised. "You probably get at least that many in a week from all your fans."

"I keep a few, but most of those I donate to The Spring."

"The domestic violence shelter?"

"Yeah, socks and underwear are some of the items survivors need most when they escape."

"What about all the *underwear* your fans send you?" I whispered, as a tiny tinge of jealously bubbled to the surface, "Do you donate those too?"

He grinned and winked me conspiratorially, "No, but we definitely should. I'm not the only player on the team who gets a steady supply."

I rolled my eyes in response. "I can't decide if that's completely gross or fulfilling a critical need in our community."

"Can't it be both?" he laughed.

"How long have you been collecting socks?" Tyler asked.

"Since always," Cam replied, looking equally surprised by my surprise. "I wear a different pair for every game. It's my one rebellion against the dress code." He winked at me playfully.

"So, you're like the James Dean of knitted footwear," I laughed. "I had no idea you were such a bad boy."

Something flashed in his eyes before he shrugged. "There's a lot you don't know about me, Decker."

There was that phrase again, the same one he'd used yesterday during the photoshoot. It bothered me more than it should have, the reminder of how superficial my knowledge of him might actually be, despite the years of working together.

"All my socks have stories," he continued, the excitement in his voice nearly matching Tyler's as he showed off his mismatched feet. "These dinosaur ones were from a kid at Children's Hospital. The tacos I found at a gas station in Winnipeg when we were stuck there during a blizzard."

Something about the care with which he preserved these tiny mementos made my chest tighten. It wasn't just the silliness of them; it was the history, the sentimentality behind each pair.

"Uncle Cam has the best socks!" Tyler announced to the room at large, apparently having appointed himself Cam's newest fan. "He has sixty pairs!"

"Uncle Cam?" I mouthed at Cam, who had the grace to look slightly abashed.

"It just kind of...happened last night," he whispered. "I didn't want to correct them."

"Uncle Cam," my aunt Margaret echoed, sipping her coffee with a knowing smile. "Has a nice ring to it, don't you think?"

I felt heat creep up my neck and turned back to the stove, focusing intently on the griddle. "Who wants the first batch of pancakes?"

"Me!" chorused the kids.

"I hope you two slept well," my aunt continued, ignoring my obvious attempt to change the subject. "That mattress in Lana's room can be a bit... cozy."

"We slept fine, thank you," I said quickly.

"More than fine," Cam added with a wink that made my aunt chortle delightedly. "Though we did stay up pretty late talking."

"Talking," my aunt repeated skeptically. "Is that what they call it these days?"

"Aunt Margaret," I hissed, glancing meaningfully at the children.

"Oh, they're not paying attention," she waved dismissively. "They're completely obsessed with Cam's socks. Smart strategy, by the way," she added to Cam. "Children are excellent judges of character. Win them over, and you've won half the battle."

"No strategy," Cam said. "I just like kids. And weird socks."

There was something so genuine in his tone that I paused in my pancake pouring to look at him. He'd crouched down again to let Emma examine his dinosaur sock more closely, his expression warm and open. Cam had always been good with the junior fans at team events, but this was different – more natural, less performative. I'd assumed his ease with children yesterday had been part of our charade, but watching him now, I realized it was simply *him*.

"Come on, shortstop," he said to Emma, scooping her up and settling her on a kitchen stool. "You can be my official taste tester."

"What about me?" Tyler asked.

"You can be assistant chef. Here," Cam grabbed a whisk and handed it to Tyler. "Stir this while your aunt Lana pours."

The kitchen quickly filled with more family members; Zayne and Drake stumbling in looking for coffee, my parents returning from their walk, Nana taking her usual place at the head of the table. Before long, we had an assembly line going with me manning the griddle, Cam and Tyler mixing more batter, and Emma solemnly reporting on the quality of each pancake batch.

"I didn't know NHL superstars could burn toast," Zayne commented dryly as Cam scraped a blackened piece into the trash.

"I have many talents," Cam replied airily. "Toast isn't one of them. Or eggs. Or bacon. I'm more of a dessert guy."

"That's why he needs me," I said without thinking, then froze when I realized how couple-y it sounded. "I mean – for the bacon. Obviously."

Cam caught my eye over Zayne's shoulder and smiled, a small, private thing that made my stomach flip. "Obviously," he agreed. "I'd be lost without you."

The simple statement, delivered with such quiet sincerity, sent an unexpected warmth blooming through my chest. It was part of the act, I reminded myself firmly. All for show. Which at this rate, I needed to remind myself every twelve seconds.

My father, who had been quietly observing from the corner with his coffee, finally spoke up. "So, Cam, are you ready for our fishing trip today? Tide's best around noon."

"Looking forward to it, sir," Cam replied, his tone shifting to something more respectful. "Been years since I've been deep-sea fishing."

"Frank," my father corrected. "And it's not really deep-sea, just the bay. But we might catch some decent redfish if we're lucky."

I watched the exchange carefully. My father wasn't an easy man to read, and his approval didn't come quickly. But something in the way he nodded at Cam seemed... accepting. Almost *warm*. He was going to be so pissed at me when this is ober.

"Drake's packing the cooler," Dad continued. "Zayne's on bait duty. You and I'll handle the rods."

"Got it," Cam said, and I could tell he was pleased to be assigned a role. To be included. Something about their easy exchange made my throat tighten unexpectedly.

As the morning progressed, the line between pretending and reality became increasingly blurred. We moved around each other in the kitchen with surprising ease, anticipating each other's needs, passing utensils without having to ask, laughing at inside jokes. When I absent-mindedly tucked a strand of hair behind my ear with flour-covered fingers, Cam reached over and brushed the white streak from my cheek gently. When he confessed he'd never made bacon except in the microwave, I showed him the crispy magic of my mother's cast-iron pan.

It felt... comfortable. Natural. Domestic in a way that was both terrifying and exhilarating.

"You two make quite the team," my mother observed, watching us work. "I've never seen Lana so patient in the kitchen."

"I'm just trying not to mess up her system," Cam replied with a self-deprecating grin.

"He's teachable," I allowed, handing him the spatula. "Here, check the eggs. Dad likes his over soft, Zayne and Drake like theirs over hard, so you'll have to take them out of the pan in stages."

"Are you sure you want to trust me with such responsibility?"

"You've been watching me do it for half an hour. Time to see if you've learned anything."

He took the spatula with exaggerated care, positioning himself at the griddle like he was about to take a penalty shot. His tongue poked slightly out of the corner of his mouth in concentration, and I bit back a smile at how adorably serious he looked.

"Just slide it underneath, *gently*, and flip it over. Try not to break the yolk," I instructed, fighting the urge to put my hand over his.

He nodded, focused intently on the fried egg as if it were the puck in a championship game. With surprising delicacy for a man known for his power on the ice, he gently slid the spatula under the egg and executed a perfect flip, revealing the golden-brown bottom of the egg, yolk miraculously intact.

"Yes!" He pumped his fist in triumph, turning to me with such boyish delight that I couldn't help but laugh. "Did you see that? Perfect flip!"

"Very impressive," I agreed, strangely proud of his small victory. "You may have a future in breakfast cuisine after all."

"I had a good teacher." His eyes held mine, warm and genuine..

The kitchen suddenly felt too warm, too small. Too domestic.

"I need to grab more syrup from the pantry," I said abruptly, needing a moment alone to collect myself. "Keep an eye on those pancakes."

The walk-in pantry was blissfully cool and dim, a respite from the chaos of the kitchen and the confusing swirl of emotions Cam's presence evoked. I leaned against the shelf, taking a deep breath. What was happening to me? I'd been so determined to keep this arrangement strictly professional, to maintain the walls I'd carefully built around my heart. But with each passing hour, those walls seemed to be crumbling, revealing the vulnerable part of me I'd sealed away ten years ago.

"Lana?"

I startled at the sound of Cam's voice as he appeared in the pantry doorway, his tall frame blocking most of the light from the kitchen.

"If you burn the pancakes..."

"Did you find the syrup?" he asked, stepping inside and letting the door swing partially closed behind him. The space immediately felt smaller, the air between us charged with something I wasn't ready to name. Outside, I could hear the clatter of dishes and the rise and fall of conversation, but in here, with the door nearly shut, we might as well have been miles away.

"I was just looking," I said, turning to scan the shelves, hyperaware of his presence behind me.

"Need help reaching something?"

"I'm not that short, Murphy."

"No, but the top shelves in here are ridiculous. I even have to stretch." As if to demonstrate, he moved closer, reaching past me for a jar on the top shelf, his chest brushing against my back.

The contact, brief as it was, sent a jolt through my system. I turned instinctively, meaning to step aside, but somehow that just brought us face to face, mere inches apart in the narrow confines of the pantry. In the dim light, his eyes were darker, the blue deepened to something like midnight. His breath, warm and coffee-scented, mingled with mine.

"Sorry," he murmured, not sounding sorry at all. "Didn't mean to crowd you."

But he didn't move away, and I found that I didn't want him to. In the dim light filtering through the partially open door, his eyes were dark, intent, focused entirely on me.

"Cam," I whispered, still undecided if it was a warning or an invitation.

His hand came up slowly, giving me every opportunity to pull away, before his fingers brushed a strand of hair from my face with exquisite gentleness. "You still had some flour," he said softly, though we both knew there was no flour there.

"Thanks," I managed, my voice barely audible.

His fingers lingered, tracing the curve of my cheek with a touch so light it was almost reverent. I should step back. I should make a joke, break the tension, maintain the professional boundaries I'd insisted upon. But I remained frozen, caught in his gaze, my heart thundering against my ribcage. The shelf pressed into my back, cool metal against warm skin, grounding me when everything else felt like it was spinning out of control.

"What are we doing, Lana?" he asked, his voice low and serious.

"We're..." My throat felt dry, the words sticking. "We're making breakfast."

"That's not what I mean, and you know it." His thumb brushed across my lower lip, sending a cascade of shivers down my spine. "What's happening between us? Is this still pretend?"

The question hung in the air, weighted with all the things we hadn't said, all the history between us, all the possibilities stretching out before us.

"I don't... " I started, but was interrupted by the pantry door swinging fully open.

"Are you two looking for the syrup or making out?" Zayne's eyes narrowed as he took in our proximity, Cam's hand still hovering near my face.

"Looking for syrup," I said quickly, stepping away from Cam as if I'd been burned. "Top shelf." I gestured vaguely upward, desperate to explain our closeness.

"Right," Zayne said, clearly unconvinced. "Well, the kids are getting restless, and Mom's asking what's taking so long."

"We'll be right there," Cam said, his voice remarkably steady given what had almost just happened. "That top shelf is pretty high."

Zayne looked between us for another long moment, then nodded curtly. "Don't take too long. People are hungry." He pushed the pantry door wide open as he departed, a not-so-subtle hint.

"Lana," Cam began once Zayne was out of earshot.

"We should get back," I interrupted, unable to meet his eyes. "Like Zayne said, everyone's waiting."

"We need to talk about this."

"There's nothing to talk about." I finally looked at him, steeling myself against the hurt in his eyes. "This is pretend, remember? That's what we agreed to."

Without waiting for his response, I grabbed the syrup and fled the pantry, my cheeks burning and my heart racing. I could feel Cam's eyes on me as I returned to the kitchen, could sense his frustration and confusion at my retreat. But I couldn't, wouldn't, let myself go down that road again. Not with Cam. Not when I already knew the ending.

I pasted on a smile as I rejoined the family, pouring syrup for the kids with forced cheer, avoiding Cam's gaze as he emerged from the pantry a few seconds behind me. When breakfast was finally served, I deliberately sat next to Nana instead of in the empty seat beside Cam, ignoring his wounded expression.

"The stars are aligning in interesting ways today," Nana announced, studying me over her coffee cup. "Particularly for you, dear. Venus and Mars in perfect harmony."

"That's nice, Nana," I said absently, focusing on my pancakes to avoid looking at Cam.

"Passion and truth," she continued. "A powerful combination. Cosmic alignment speaks of revealing what's hidden, bringing truth to light."

"Pancakes are delicious, Lana," my aunt Margaret interrupted, mercifully changing the subject. "Now, about wedding plans – have you thought about colors yet? Lana's ring could be inspiring."

"Sapphires in the engagement ring," Nana nodded sagely. "I saw it in my vision." *Great*, now my grandmother was psychic too.

"Leave them alone, all of you," Zayne grumbled, giving me a look that was part suspicion, part concern. "They're still getting used to the idea themselves."

"Thank you, Zayne," I said, grateful for the intervention despite knowing his motives weren't entirely altruistic.

"I don't mind," Cam spoke up, finally meeting my eyes across the table. There was something challenging in his gaze, a quiet determination that made my pulse quicken. "I'm all in, whatever Lana wants."

The double meaning in his words wasn't lost on me, and I looked away quickly, afraid of what he might see in my eyes if I held his gaze too long.

Drake caught my eye from across the table and raised an eyebrow. Unlike Zayne, who wore his suspicion like armor, Drake had always been more perceptive, less reactionary. "You okay?" he mouthed silently.

I nodded, forcing a smile. He didn't look convinced, but thankfully didn't press the issue.

The rest of breakfast passed in a blur of conversation and laughter, with me participating just enough to avoid suspicion while my mind replayed what had happened in the pantry on an endless loop. Cam's touch. His question. The raw honesty in his eyes.

What are we doing, Lana?

I wished I knew.

As the family dispersed to prepare for the day's beach activities, Cam caught my arm gently as we were clearing plates.

"We need to talk about this," he said quietly, his voice serious. "About what's happening between us."

I pulled my arm away, ignoring the hurt that flashed across his face. "There's nothing to talk about." The words felt like a lie even as I spoke them, a weak defense against a truth I couldn't bring myself to acknowledge. "Go have some fun with the boys," I smiled brightly.

Through the kitchen window, I watched as my father and brothers gathered fishing gear on the deck. Cam opened the slider and stepped outside. He moved with easy grace, laughing at something Drake said, helping my father untangle a fishing line. They moved around him naturally, making space for him in their circle. He fit so perfectly into the tableau of Decker men that for a moment, it stole my breath.

A sharp pain bloomed in my chest – part longing, part fear. I pressed my palm flat against my sternum as if I could physically hold back the unwanted feelings. This was dangerous, this softening toward him. This was exactly how I'd been hurt before.

And yet, watching him through the window, the sunlight catching in his hair, his smile so genuine as he listened to my father's instructions, I couldn't stop the treacherous thought that whispered through my mind: What if it *could* be real this time?

Chapter 12

After breakfast, I'd headed back upstairs to take a nap, and apparently I needed one because I zonked out in about 3 minutes.

By the time I'd showered and dressed in a simple sundress over my swimsuit, the men had departed, leaving the beach house blissfully quiet. Or at least, as quiet as it could be with my mother, Nana, Aunt Margaret and the kids still in residence.

I found them by the pool, already settled with a pitcher of mimosas. My mother reclined on a lounge chair in an elegant cover-up, large sunhat shading her face. Nana had arranged her crystals in a semicircle around her chair, and Aunt Margaret sat with her feet in the water, the pink pair of those infamous sandals lined up neatly beside her.

"There she is!" Aunt Margaret called, raising her mimosa glass. "We were wondering when you'd join us. Cam said to let you sleep in."

"Did he now?" I replied, trying to ignore the little flutter in my chest at the thought of Cam being considerate of my rest. I ignored the further implication: that they had discussed me, that Cam had seen me sleeping, that we were truly acting like a couple in all the little ways that mattered. "When did they leave?"

"About an hour ago," my mother said, passing me a mimosa. "Your father was eager to get out before the tide changed. They took some sandwiches with them, so they probably won't be back until late afternoon."

I settled into the empty lounge chair, grateful for the momentary reprieve from Cam's presence. Not that he was doing anything wrong, quite the opposite. He was being charming, attentive, thoughtful. Basically perfect. And that was the problem. The sweeter he was, the harder it became to remember this was all an act.

"So," Aunt Margaret began, swirling her mimosa with that mischievous glint in her eye that spelled trouble, "now that the men are gone, you can tell us the real story. How did you and Cam finally get together? After all these years of working together, what changed?"

I took a fortifying sip of mimosa, trying to say something true that also fit within our agreed-upon story. The last thing I wanted to do was lie to my family. "It just happened naturally. One day I looked at him and saw him differently."

"Mmm-hmm," Aunt Margaret looked unconvinced, her eyebrow arching skeptically. "Was alcohol involved? Because that man is delicious, and if you waited years to jump on that, you either have the willpower of a saint or the observational skills of a turnip."

"Margaret!" my mother chided, though I could see she was fighting a smile.

"What? I'm just saying what we're all thinking." She shrugged unapologetically.

"What is the real Cam like?" my mother asked, her voice softer, genuinely curious. "Behind all the charm and hockey talent?"

The question caught me off guard. What was the real Cam like? Not the carefully crafted heartthrob image we'd built for marketing purposes. Not the performance he was putting on for my family. The real Cam.

"He's..." I paused, surprised by how easily the words came. "He's thoughtful. Observant. He notices things about people that others miss. He remembers little details, like how everyone takes their coffee or which kids like which pancake shapes. He's funny and warm and makes everyone around him feel included."

I realized I was smiling as I spoke, my voice taking on a warmth that wasn't practiced. "He's this confident jock on the ice, but he's actually kind of a homebody. And he's surprisingly vulnerable sometimes."

The three women exchanged a look I couldn't quite interpret.

"Mmm-hmm," Aunt Margaret teased, "Look who's blushing like a teenager talking about her first crush..."

My hand flew to my cheek, which did indeed feel warm. "It's just the sun," I protested.

"Darling," my mother said gently, "it's wonderful to see you so happy. Cam is clearly good for you – you just light up when he's around. And your dad likes him. Who knew that was even possible in our lifetimes?"

"*And* he can't take his eyes off of you," Aunt Margaret added with a wink. "That man looks at you like you hung the moon and stars."

"I don't know about that," I said, attempting to brush it off while ignoring the little thrill her words sent through me.

"He's so good with the kids. They were climbing all over him this morning like he was a jungle gym. No pressure, darling, and all in your own time – but he'll certainly make a wonderful father someday." My mother smiled affectionately and patted me on the leg. "And Oh! Those blue eyes!"

I couldn't tell if my mother was just suddenly overwhelmed by the thought of Cam's striking blue eyes or already imagining her future grandchildren. And endorphins be damned, I couldn't stop myself from swooning a little when I recalled Cam hamming it up with the kids this weekend, "I think so too."

"Look, she's blushing again," teased Aunt Margaret.

"Connection like that isn't something you can fake," Nana pronounced with the confidence of one who had consulted the cosmos and found them in agreement. "I saw it in his aura the moment you two walked in. Blue with purple flecks. Very rare. Very powerful bond."

"Purple means passion and spiritual awakening," Aunt Margaret supplied helpfully.

"I thought it meant royalty," my mother chimed in.

"In crystal energy, it's transformation," Nana corrected them both with a dismissive wave. "And in Cam's aura, surrounding Lana, it means he's found his soul's match."

I nearly choked on my coffee. "Nana, please. Let's not get carried away with auras and soul matches. We're just... dating." Even I could hear how weak that sounded, given the giant sea-colored sapphire on my finger, glinting in the sun.

"The stars don't lie, dear," Nana said firmly, peering at me over her reading glasses. "I dug a little deeper into your charts again this morning while you were sleeping. Pluto is activating your seventh house: the house of partnerships. Major transformation is coming. By the next full moon, everything will be different."

"Different how?" I asked, unable to stop myself. If I could have rolled my own eyes at myself right that moment, I would have. *What was happening to me? Looking for horoscope confirmation that Cam and I have a future? Am I completely out of my lust-addled mind?*

Nana's eyes took on that misty, faraway look that always preceded her most dramatic pronouncements. "The walls you've built will come down. What began as pretense will become truth. The heart cannot be fooled for long, dear one."

An uncomfortable silence fell as her words settled over us. I fidgeted with my mimosa flute, unsure how to respond. Did she know? Had she somehow intuited that our engagement was fake? Or was this just more of Nana's typical mystical generalizations that could apply to anyone?

"Well," my mother finally said brightly, "enough serious talk. Who wants another mimosa?"

"Me!" I said, draining my glass and grateful for the distraction.

As my mother poured, the conversation mercifully shifted to lighter topics: Aunt Margaret's cruise plans, my cousin Nora's daughter starting kindergarten, the outrageous price of the beachfront property down the shore that had just sold. I let their chatter wash over me, contributing enough to seem engaged while my mind continued to circle around Nana's words and my own confusing feelings.

By the time we'd finished the pitcher of mimosas and relocated to the kitchen for a late lunch, I was no closer to sorting out the tangle of emotions in my chest. One thing was becoming clear, though: somehow I'd ended up talking about Cam all morning like I'd completely fallen for him, not just for show. And that felt like the opening salvo of the biggest crisis I'd ever manage.

The men returned mid-afternoon with sunburned faces, the smell of fish and salt clinging to their clothes, and the boisterous, masculine energy that always accompanied a successful fishing trip. My father led the procession, proudly carrying a cooler that presumably contained their catch, with Drake, Zayne, and Cam following behind, each laden with gear.

"Ladies!" my father called as they trooped up to the deck where we'd relocated to enjoy the sea breeze. "Hope you're hungry for the freshest redfish you've ever tasted!"

"Did you save any fish for the rest of the Gulf?" my mother asked dryly, eyeing the catch.

"Wait till you see what Cam caught," Drake said, clapping Cam on the shoulder with obvious respect. "Biggest one of the day. Dad's still salty about it."

"Beginner's luck," my father grumbled, though the pride in his voice belied his words. "Though I'll admit, the boy's got a natural feel for when to set the hook."

Cam looked like a different person than the polished NHL star the public knew. His face was slightly sunburned across the nose and cheeks, his hair tousled by the sea breeze, and his t-shirt bore the stains of a day spent hauling in fish. But his eyes were bright with excitement, and his smile – a real, unrehearsed grin – was infectious.

"How was it?" I asked, rising to help them with the gear.

"Incredible," Cam said, his enthusiasm genuine as he set down the tackle box. "Your dad knows all the best spots. I've never seen fish that size so close to shore."

"Tell her about the osprey," Drake prompted, grinning.

Cam laughed. "We were trolling around this little mangrove island, and this massive osprey swoops down about twenty feet from the boat, hits the water like a missile, and comes up with a fish nearly as big as him. Then..." his hands animated the story, eyes lighting up, "Frank hands me his binoculars and points to this tree, and there's a whole nest with babies. The osprey flew the fish home, and we watched the whole feeding frenzy. It was amazing."

My father actually preened a bit at his enthusiasm. "Been watching that same osprey family for three summers now," he said. "They always come back to the same spot."

"Like your dad was saying, they're nature's greatest comeback story... they were almost wiped out fifty years ago and now they're thriving." Cam's respect for my father's knowledge was evident. "He knows this coastline like he designed it himself."

"You're a natural, though," my father replied, in what might have been the most complimentary tone I'd ever heard him use with anyone outside the family. "Good instincts. Patience. Most young guys today want instant results. You understood the waiting game. That's rare."

I watched this exchange with a sense of wonder. (And also a great deal of amusement at Dad's determination of the sub-par fishing chops of "young guys today.") My father, a man who had scared off more of my potential boyfriends than I could count with his gruff demeanor and impossibly high standards, was practically gushing over Cam. And Cam, for his part, was basking in my father's approval without seeming to try too hard for it.

They continued to unpack the gear, trading stories and good-natured ribbing. I helped, half-listening to their animated recounting of the day's catches while watching how naturally Cam had integrated himself into the Decker male dynamic. Even Zayne was relaxed around him, laughing at something Cam said about a seagull that had tried to steal their bait.

"You're staring," Drake murmured as he passed behind me, fishing rods in hand.

"I'm not," I protested automatically.

"You are. It's cute. He keeps looking for you too, when you're not watching." Drake's voice held no judgment, just quiet observation. "It's nice to see you happy, Lana. Real happy, not just your *everything is under control* face."

Drake could always see right through me.

Before I could respond, he'd moved on to help my father clean the fish, leaving me with his words echoing in my ears. Was I that transparent? And was Cam really looking for me when I wasn't watching?

As if on cue, Cam glanced over at me from where he was helping Zayne rinse some equipment. Our eyes met, and he smiled – not the practiced, camera-ready grin he used for public appearances, but something smaller, more private. A smile just for me. My heart thrummed in my chest and I was struck by a sudden and inexplicable desire to run towards him at full speed and just jump into his arms.

This was bad. This was very, very bad. Very very.

Cam stepped towards the patio, reaching for the hem of his t-shirt with casual grace. In one fluid motion, he pulled it over his head, revealing the sculpted perfection of his torso. *Holy pectorals, Batman.* Tanned skin stretched over defined muscle, the sharp cut of his abs, the broad planes of his chest. I nearly choked on my iced tea.

He tossed the shirt casually over his shoulder, completely oblivious to my sudden inability to form coherent thoughts. The midday sun caught the droplets of sweat along his collarbone, making his skin gleam like burnished gold. As he bent to lift the cooler, muscles rippling across his back, I forced myself to take a sip of my drink, suddenly parched in a way that had nothing to do with the blazing sun.

My gaze traced the lean lines of his waist, the trail of golden-brown hair that disappeared beneath the waistband of his shorts, and suddenly heat pooled low in my bikini bottoms. This was ridiculous. I'd seen hockey players shirtless a thousand times. Cam even more than that, since I kept booking him for magazine spreads where that was a major component. But something about Cam, the easy confidence in his movements, the playful smile that crinkled the corners of his eyes, made my heart race like I was sixteen again.

Zayne chose that moment to sprint across the deck, snatching Cam's discarded shirt as he ran past. With a mischievous grin so unlike my usually serious brother, he dove into the pool, surfacing with a triumphant whoop.

"Come and get it, Murphy!" he taunted, waving the soggy shirt like a flag.

Cam's eyes narrowed playfully. "Oh, it's like that, Decker?" Without hesitation, he charged toward the pool and launched himself into a perfect dive that sent a wave of water cascading over the edge, drenching several nearby chairs and eliciting delighted screams from the kids.

For a moment, there was just churning water and bubbles. Then both men surfaced, wrestling and laughing like overgrown boys. Cam dunked Zayne under, emerging victorious with his soaked shirt held high above his head like the Stanley Cup.

"And the Hitman takes the championship!" he crowed, water streaming down his chest as he hauled himself out of the pool in one powerful movement. The kids cheered excitedly and rushed to give him high-fives.

I tried, and failed miserably, not to stare as he stood there, water beading on his perfectly defined chest and abs, shorts clinging to powerful thighs. Rivulets traced paths down his skin that my fingers itched to follow. His hair was slicked back, droplets clinging to his long lashes, and that mischevious grin made something molten and dangerous coil through me.

What would it be like to press my palms against that chest? To feel his heart hammer beneath my hands? To trace the defined muscles of his abdomen with my lips, tasting chlorine and salt and him? The thought sent a shiver through me, despite the heat.

I forced myself to look away, suddenly very interested in the pattern of my napkin. Because watching Cameron Murphy, dripping wet and half-naked, his eyes dancing with delight as he triumphantly wrung out his t-shirt, was the kryptonite to my willpower.

In that moment, with Cam sun-kissed and relaxed, fitting so seamlessly into my family that it seemed he'd always been there, I wanted nothing more in the world than for this to be real.

God, I was cooked.

After the fish were cleaned and prepped for dinner, the whole family migrated to the beach. Emma and Tyler immediately began clamoring for sandcastles. Being the pushover that I was when it came to my little cousins, I found myself drafted into a full-scale sandcastle competition.

"Teams of four!" Emma declared with the absolute, unshakable, authority of a six-year-old. "Me and Tyler and Auntie Lana and Uncle Cam against everyone else!"

I glanced at Cam, expecting him to politely find a way out of this. Instead, he was already crouched down, helping Tyler gather buckets and shovels from the beach toy stash.

"Sounds perfect," he said, high-fiving Emma. "We're definitely going to win."

"You know this is a losing battle, right?" I whispered to him as we walked down to the wet sand where the best castle-building would happen. "Drake and Zayne take these competitions way too seriously. They once built a scale replica of Hogwarts complete with working drawbridge."

"Ah, but they don't have Emma and Tyler's creative vision," Cam replied, completely unfazed. "Plus, I happen to be an expert sandcastle architect."

"Is there anything you're not surprisingly good at?" I asked, only half-joking.

"Toast," he replied immediately. "Also folding fitted sheets. And remembering to water plants. Actually, I'm pretty terrible at most domestic things."

I laughed, surprised by his candid admission. "Good to know you're not actually perfect."

"Far from it," he said, his tone shifting to something more serious. "But I'm trying to be better." His eyes met mine, and there was such earnestness in them that I had to look away.

"At toast-making?" I joked, deflecting the sudden intensity.

"Obviously that's first priority on the list," he replied with a soft smile. "I'm a work in progress."

Something in his expression made my heart stutter, but before I could respond, Emma tugged on my hand.

"Auntie Lana, help me dig the moat!"

For the next hour, we worked on our sandcastle, which evolved from a traditional turret design into what Emma called a "fairy princess dragon castle" (complete with a seashell dragon guarding the entrance). Cam turned out to be surprisingly skilled at intricate sand sculpture, carefully crafting detailed windows and a spiral staircase that had Emma squealing with delight.

"Where'd you learn to do that?" I asked as he carved perfect little battlements along the top of a tower.

"YouTube," he admitted with a boyish grin. "I went through a phase last off-season where I couldn't sleep. Watched a lot of random tutorials."

"Insomnia YouTube rabbit holes. The things I'm learning about you this weekend..."

"Just wait till I show you my origami skills," he teased. "I make a mean paper crane."

We worked well together, anticipating each other's needs without having to ask – Cam steadying the bucket as I packed it with wet sand, me smoothing the walls as he carefully removed the mold, both of us encouraging the children's increasingly fantastical additions. It felt easy. Natural. Like we'd been building sandcastles together for years.

"You guys are the best team," Emma declared, patting a lopsided turret into place. "Way better than Uncle Drake and Uncle Zayne. They always argue."

"That's because Cam and I have lots of practice working together," I explained, helping her position a shell.

"Because you're in love?" she asked innocently.

I fumbled the shell, dropping it into the moat. Cam smoothly retrieved it and handed it back to Emma.

"Because we're a good team," he said simply, his eyes finding mine over Emma's head. "Sometimes you just click with someone, and everything works better."

"Like LEGOs!" Tyler piped up from where he was decorating the drawbridge.

"Exactly like LEGOs," Cam agreed solemnly. "The pieces fit together perfectly."

I ducked my head, focusing intently on shaping the sand, hyper-aware of the double meaning in his words and the soft look he'd given me.

At one point, I was struggling to add a tower that kept collapsing under its own weight. Cam moved behind me, his chest warm against my back as he reached around to help stabilize the structure.

"Like this," he said softly, his breath tickling my ear. "We need to pack it tighter at the base."

His hands covered mine, guiding my movements as we formed the sand. Every cell in my body was aware of his proximity, the solid warmth of his bare chest against my bare back, the scent of sun and salt and something, I don't know, like uniquely him. Time seemed to slow, the sounds of the beach fading as my focus narrowed to the points where our bodies connected.

Deep breath.

"Perfect," he murmured as the tower finally held. He didn't pull away immediately, and I didn't move either, caught in a moment that felt both peaceful and charged with unspoken possibility.

A pointed throat-clearing broke the spell. I looked up to find Zayne watching us, his expression a complicated mix of suspicion and concern. Cam stepped back, turning his attention to Tyler's request for help with the drawbridge, but the moment lingered like a drunk at closing time.

When Emma and Tyler ran off to collect more shells for decoration, Zayne approached, ostensibly to check on our progress.

"Looking good," he said, nodding at our creation. "Kiddos seem to be having fun."

"They're great," Cam replied. "Emma's got a real eye for design."

Zayne nodded, then fixed me with a look that immediately set off warning bells. "Lana, can you help me grab more water?"

It was obviously a pretext, but I couldn't refuse without making a scene. I followed him to the water's edge, where he filled one of the buckets while keeping his voice low.

"Subtle, buddy." I teased.

"You're not faking anymore, are you?"

The directness of his question caught me off guard. "What are you talking about?" I stalled.

"Don't bullshit me, Lana." His voice was tight, controlled, but I could hear the concern underneath. "I've known you your entire life. This thing with Cam; it's not just for show." His eyes, so like our father's, missed nothing. "The way you're looking at him – that's real. And the way he looks at you... well, I've never seen him look at anyone like that, and I've known the dude a helluva long time."

"We're just playing our parts," I insisted, though the words sounded hollow even to my own ears. "We have to be convincing."

"Convincing? From where I'm sitting, it looks like you're falling for him. Hard." His concern was palpable. "And I don't want to see you get hurt when this charade ends."

"I'm a big girl, Zayne. I know what I'm doing." The lie tasted bitter on my tongue.

"Do you?" He studied me for a long moment, then shook his head. "Just... be careful, okay? The line between pretending and real feelings gets blurry fast."

"I'm aware of that," I said, more sharply than I intended. "I don't need you to protect me."

"Maybe not. But I'm your brother. It's kind of in the job description." His expression softened slightly. "And for what it's worth, I love Cam. Always have. But this situation, it's so complicated. I don't want you to get hurt."

I couldn't argue with that. Complicated didn't even begin to cover it.

"We'd better get back," I said, nodding toward the sandcastle where Cam was helping Tyler position a flag made of driftwood and a leaf.

Zayne nodded, but as I turned to go, he caught my arm. "Lana. I'm here. Whatever happens. Just remember that. Always. Family first.."

The simple sincerity in his voice caught me off guard. Beneath all his gruff protectiveness, Zayne had always been my steadiest ally. I nodded, my throat suddenly tight with emotion.

"I know. Thanks. Best big brother ever. Don't tell Drake."

"Drake! Lana just told me I'm her favorite!" he yelled.

"Lana, tell Zayne he's hallucinating and I'm your favorite," Drake yelled back.

"You're both my favorite," I grinned at my brothers.

I remained at the water's edge a moment longer after Zayne walked away to rib Drake, letting the gentle waves lap at my feet as I tried to steady my breathing. Was I really so transparent? If Zayne could see through me so easily, who else could? Uh, probably everybody.

More importantly, was he right? Or were Cam and I just trapped in some strange feedback loop of our own making? We'd start pretending our engagement was real, which made it start feeling real, which convinced my family it was absolutely real, which only reinforced to both of us how real it seemed... and around and around we went, like skaters tracing endless infinity loops on ice.

Was I falling for Cam *for real*? Or was my brain just completely unable to recognize the difference between reality and my own spin? Was Cam falling for me? The possibilities were both exhilarating and distressing, like that breathless moment in double overtime when the puck slides toward an undefended net – victory and heartbreak balanced precariously on the edge of a blade, everything you've worked for hanging in a suspended moment while the crowd holds its collective breath and time stretches like taffy, knowing the game could end in glory or devastation in one final second

As the afternoon waned, I escaped for some solitude, needing space to think. I found a quiet spot a little way down the beach and sat on the sand, watching the sun begin its slow descent toward the horizon. The Gulf stretched before me, a vast expanse of blue-green dotted with the distant silhouettes of boats returning to shore. The rhythmic sound of waves against the sand had always calmed me, even as a child.

I wasn't entirely surprised when I heard footsteps approaching. Some part of me had expected – or, *okay*, even hoped – that Cam would seek me out.

"Okay if I join you?" he asked, his voice carrying over the sound of the waves.

I gestured to the sand beside me, drawing my knees up to my chest.

He settled next to me, close enough that I could feel his warmth but not quite touching. For a while, we sat in surprisingly comfortable silence, watching the sky slowly transform from blue to a palette of pinks and golds. The fading sunlight caught in his hair, turning the golden-brown strands into a halo of fire. It highlighted the strong line of his jaw, the fan of lashes against his cheek when he briefly closed his eyes to feel the sea breeze.

"Your family is so easy to be with," he said finally, opening his eyes to gaze at the horizon. "Today was..." He paused, seeming to search for the right word. "Special."

"They like you," I said, drawing patterns in the sand with my finger. "Especially my dad. I've never seen him warm up to someone thoroughly."

"I like them too." His voice was soft, reflective. "It's easy to see where you get your strength. Your humor. That *anything for the team* loyalty."

I glanced at him, finding his gaze already on me, tender and intent in a way that made my heart stutter.

"Can I ask you something?" he said.

"Depends on what it is."

"Why haven't you ever settled down? For real, I mean." His question was gentle but direct. "You're smart, beautiful, successful... you could have anyone you wanted. You *can*."

The question caught me off guard. It wasn't something I discussed often, even with close friends. But there was something about this moment – the fading light, the sound of waves, the strange intimacy we'd been cultivating to pull off this ruse – that made honesty feel safe.

"I guess it's been a very long time since I met someone who seemed worth the risk," I said slowly. "Someone who made me feel like I could be completely myself, without performing or pretending. Someone who saw me – not just Frank Decker's daughter, or Zayne & Drake's sister, or the team publicist, or potential hockey royalty trophy bride. Plus, I work about a million hours a week, so unless I decided to marry somebody who works at the arena, I'd never see them except on alternate Tuesdays from 3 - 3:15."

"I can make that happen," Cam teased lightly. I happen to know a guy who works at the arena who'd be perfect for you..."

"Is it Marv, the Zamboni guy?" I retorted, "Because I'm pretty sure he's already married."

"It's not Marv..." he said under his breath.

I paused, gathering my thoughts. "And after what happened in college..."

"With me," he said quietly, his gaze dropping to the sand between us.

I nodded, unable to look at him. "With you. It made me doubt my own judgment. Made me wonder if I could really trust what I felt, or if I was just... projecting what I *wanted* to see."

He was quiet for a moment, his eyes on the horizon where the sun was now a half-circle of fiery orange. "I'm sorry. I never meant for..." He paused. "I understand that better than you might think."

"You do?"

He nodded, running his hands through his hair in a gesture I'd come to recognize as a sign he was deeply uncomfortable but trying to be honest.

"Remember yesterday when I said I learned to be whoever I needed to be to fit in. New step-parent? Figure out what they want and become that version of myself. New school? Watch the popular kids and mimic them until I belonged. It became second nature." He picked up a handful of sand, letting it sift through his fingers. "Even with women. I'd figure out what they wanted – the charming player, the strong silent type, the ambitious go-getter – and I'd become that. For a night, for a week, however long it lasted."

"And that worked for you?" I asked softly.

He shrugged, his eyes still on the sand trickling through his fingers. "It was easier than being rejected for who I really was. But after a while... it gets lonely, being someone else all the time."

"Is that what you're doing now?" I asked gingerly, attempting to glean more information without him feeling like I was judging him.

I watched his profile, struck by the vulnerability in his expression. This wasn't the confident NHL star or even the charming houseguest who'd won over my family. This was Cam stripped down to his essence: uncertain, honest, real.

"No," he murmured. "That night in college," he continued, his voice dropping lower, "with you... that was different. I didn't feel like I was performing. I was just me. And you. It was just instantly, effortlessly easy to be together." He finally looked at me, his eyes reflecting the gold of the setting sun. "It scared the hell out of me."

My breath caught in my throat at his admission. "Why?"

"Because it meant something. It was real. And in my experience, things that feel real at the beginning were usually just performative until the inevitable blowout and stepparent replacement." He set the remaining sand down, brushing his palm clean against his shorts. "When you're used to keeping people at a distance, real connection feels like... I don't know, like suddenly playing without pads or a helmet. Exposed. Vulnerable. Scary as hell."

The picture he painted hit me *soooo* close to home – the professional in me always analyzing, always planning, always armored against personal attachment. Maybe that was what was making our fake fiancée performance *feel* so real now. "I can relate," I responded quietly.

"I didn't know how to handle it back then," he continued. "I didn't know how to be that vulnerable with someone and survive. Now I wonder if I've been playing it safe ever since. Hockey's so much more straightforward than this." He gestured vaguely between us. "On the ice, I know exactly what I'm doing. Off the ice, with you. I feel like a rookie, like, *all the time.*"

His honesty disarmed me completely. "Cam – "

"No one after you ever came close, Lana," he said, holding my gaze with an intensity that made it impossible to look away, like he *needed* to get it all out before I stopped him or he lost his nerve. "I don't know how to want anyone else. I've tried. For ten years, I've tried."

The air between us seemed to crackle with electricity. His words hung there, raw and honest. I didn't know how to respond, how to process what he was telling me. Did he mean it? Or was this just another persona he was trying on, the secretly devoted fake fiancé?

But the vulnerability in his eyes, the slight tremor in his voice – those didn't look faked. At all.

I realized I was suddenly leaning toward him, drawn by an invisible force I couldn't resist. He moved too, closing the distance between us inch by inch. His hand came up to cup my cheek, so gently it was as if he feared I might break. Or run. I could feel his breath, warm against my lips, could see the flecks of darker blue in his eyes, the slight crease between his brows as he gazed at me with undisguised longing.

"Lana! Cam!" My mother's voice pierced the moment. "Dinner's ready!"

I jerked back, heart pounding as if I'd been caught doing something illicit. In a way, I had been. Not the almost-kiss – that would have been perfectly in character for our fake engagement – but the real feelings building behind it.

"I guess we should..." I gestured vaguely toward the house.

"Yeah." Cam didn't move for a moment, his eyes still holding mine. I didn't move either. Then he smiled – a small, rueful thing. "To be continued?"

It sounded like both a question, but we both knew at that moment it was a promise.

After a spectacular redfish dinner, my father announced it was time for the traditional Decker family bonfire and ghost stories. The fire pit on the deck was lit, chairs arranged in a circle around it, and the supply of s'mores ingredients was set out within easy reach. As darkness fell completely, we gathered around the crackling fire, enjoying the slight chill of the evening sea breeze.

My father took his usual position as storyteller, beginning with the tale of the phantom lighthouse that had supposedly led ships to their doom a century ago. It was a story I'd heard at least thirty times, but there was something comforting about the familiar cadence of his voice, the predictable gasps from the children at the scariest parts, and my mother's exaggerated reactions that fooled no one but had practically become part of the story themselves.

I sat beside Cam on an Adirondack loveseat designed for two, a light blanket draped over both of us. The firelight cast flickering shadows across his face, highlighting his high cheekbones, the sun-plumped fullness of his lips, the sparkle in his eyes. Under the blanket, his hand found mine, fingers intertwining with a gentleness that contrasted with the strength I knew those hands possessed.

Should I pull away? That would be the smart, self-protective thing to do. Instead, I found myself curling my fingers around his, savoring the warmth and security of his touch.

Dad moved on to his second story, a local legend about a ghostly fisherman who appeared only during summer storms. Cam's thumb began tracing soft slow shapes on the inside of my wrist, sending shivers up my arm. I glanced at him, but his attention appeared to be on my father's story. Only the slight quirk of his mouth told me he was fully aware of the effect he was having on me. And by "effect" I mean I was about two minutes away from dragging him upstairs and clawing off his t-shirt.

Two could play that game. I shifted slightly, ostensibly to get more comfortable, allowing my leg to press against his under the blanket. I felt rather than heard his sharp intake of breath, saw the momentary widening of his eyes before he regained his composure.

The ghost stories continued, but I was barely listening. My attention had narrowed to the warm press of Cam's thigh against mine, the charged space between our bodies.

It was as if we were engaged in our own private conversation beneath the blanket while outwardly participating in the family gathering.

As the final story wound down and the younger children's eyes began to droop, I found myself relaxing into Cam's side, my head resting against his shoulder as naturally as if I'd been doing it for years. His arm came around me, protective and secure, and I let myself sink into the warmth of him.

"Tired?" he murmured against my hair, his voice low enough that only I could hear.

"Mmm," I confirmed, too comfortable to form actual words. I knew I should probably sit up, maintain some distance, but exhaustion, Cam's comfortable embrace, and the hypnotic effect of the firelight were eroding my defenses.

Around us, the family began the process of winding down the evening. Uncle Pete carried a sleeping Emma inside, followed by Nora with a drowsy Tyler. Aunt Margaret and my mother began gathering empty mugs and plates. My father tended to the fire, closing the cover on the fire pit. Drake and Serena slipped away hand in hand, heading for a moonlit walk on the beach. None of them seemed to find anything unusual about Cam and me curled together under our blanket, the picture of contented lovers.

"Are you two still planning to head back to St. Pete tonight, or in the morning?" my mother asked as she collected our empty mugs. "It's getting late, and that drive can be dangerous when you're tired."

I opened my mouth to confirm our plans to leave tonight, to put some safe distance between us and this bubble of domestic fantasy, but Cam spoke first.

"What do you think, Lana? I'm happy to drive whenever you want, but your mom's right about the late-night drive."

He was giving me the choice, I realized. Letting me decide whether to extend this fantasy for one more night or return to reality.

"Maybe we should stay," I heard myself say. "Leave first thing in the morning."

"Perfect," my mother beamed.

As she moved away to continue tidying, Cam's arm tightened slightly around me. "You sure?"

I nodded, not trusting myself to speak. I wasn't ready for this weekend to end. For our shared bed and comfortable mornings to become history. For the professional wall between us to go back up. I wanted one more night of pretending, of being held by him, of falling asleep to the sound of his breathing.

"We should probably go in soon," I said, making no move to get up.

"Probably," Cam agreed, his fingertips brushing against my shoulder through the blanket. "Especially if we're getting an early start tomorrow."

In the flickering light of the dying fire, with the sound of waves in the background and the stars emerging in the darkening sky, I allowed myself to imagine, just for a moment, that this was real. That Cam and I were actually engaged, actually planning a future together. That I could have *this*, his warmth, his strength, his quiet understanding, every night for the rest of my life.

The thought should have been a warning shot for me. Instead, it filled me with a longing so acute it was almost painful.

"What are you thinking?" Cam asked, his voice barely above a whisper.

I hesitated, unwilling to voice the dangerous thoughts swirling in my mind. "Just that... this is nice," I said finally.

"It is," he agreed, his arm tightening slightly around me. "It really is."

We sat in silence a moment longer, watching the embers glow in the dying fire. Then, with obvious reluctance, Cam began to shift.

"We should get some rest," he said, though he made no move to release my hand. "Early start tomorrow if we want to beat the traffic off the key and on the Skyway bridge."

As we made our way inside, climbing the stairs to our shared room in companionable silence, I felt a bittersweet ache in my chest. Tomorrow we'd leave this bubble, return to our real lives, our professional relationship, our carefully maintained boundaries. But tonight? Tonight I still had Cam, and one more change to wake up in his arms..

Inside our room, the moonlight streamed through the window. Cam moved to his duffel bag, pulling out a t-shirt and shorts to sleep in.

"You can have the bathroom first," he offered, his voice soft in the dim light.

"Thanks," I nodded, gathering my things and slipping into the en-suite. As I went through my nightly routine – a quick shower to rinse off any remaining sand, washing my face, brushing my teeth, changing into the silk shorts and camisole that had become my standard sleeping attire for the weekend – I tried not to think about how much I would miss this tomorrow. The easy domesticity. The sound of his quiet breathing as he fell asleep. Waking up spooning with a super hot pro hockey player who has *clearly* never missed a workout. Like, ever.

When I emerged, Cam had turned down the bed and was standing by the window, gazing out at the moonlit Gulf. He turned as I approached, his expression softening as he took me in.

"Your turn," I said, gesturing to the bathroom.

He nodded, but paused before passing me. "Lana," he said softly, uncertain. "Today was..."

"I know," I replied, saving him from having to find the words. Because I did know. Today had been perfect and dangerous and wonderful and overwhelming all at once.

The bathroom door closed behind him, and I slid between the cool sheets. My body was tired, but my mind raced, replaying every moment of the day. Every touch, every smile, every word that might mean something real beneath our pretense.

I heard the shower start from behind the bathroom door, and an unsolicited image crept into my thoughts: Cam, just steps away, water cascading down his broad shoulders, soap sliding over the defined muscles of his chest and lower... I squeezed my eyes shut, trying to banish the mental picture. I mean, not like *straining myself* to ignore it or anything. But this was precisely the kind of dangerous territory I should probably avoid if I were being smart. The soft sounds of water running, knowing he was so close yet so untouchable, made heat bloom across my skin.

I shifted restlessly, remembering how it had felt ten years ago to trace those muscles with my mouth, to feel his skin against mine. *What would happen if I just got up, opened that door, and joined him?* The thought sent a jolt of electricity through me that settled low between my legs and elsewhere.

The shower faucet squeaked quietly as Cam turned off the water, and for the life of me, I couldn't decide if I'd just missed a catastrophe or the opportunity of a lifetime.

When Cam returned, his hair was damp, his face freshly washed. He moved with quiet grace through the moonlit room, the low light casting shadows that accentuated the cut of his jaw, the breadth of his shoulders beneath his thin t-shirt.

My eyes tracked his movement, taking in the way his shorts hung low on his hips, the tantalizing glimpse of defined abdominal muscles as he stretched slightly before slipping into bed beside me. I ached to touch his skin, impossibly warm in the moonlight, and I felt a deep, visceral pull toward him that I struggled to ignore.

He caught me staring and the corner of his mouth lifted in a small, knowing smile that made my pulse quicken. Still, he carefully maintained that invisible boundary down the middle of the mattress, though the heat in his eyes suggested he was just as aware of me as I was of him.

For a long moment, we both lay there in silence, staring up at the gauzy canopy above us. I could feel the warmth radiating from his body, could smell the clean scent of soap and toothpaste, could sense the same tension vibrating through him that was coursing through me.

"Being here with you, with your family," he said quietly to the darkness, "makes me long for something I didn't even imagine was possible."

His words were vulnerable and raw. I turned my head to look at him, finding his profile silver-edged in the moonlight. He wasn't looking at me, but at the ceiling, as if it was easier to admit such things without eye contact, even in the dark

"What's that?" I asked, my voice barely above a whisper.

He was quiet for so long I thought he might not answer. Then, so softly I almost didn't hear it: "Belonging. Not just fitting in temporarily. Actually belonging somewhere. *With* someone."

The simple honesty of his admission – free of any charm or deflection – made my heart ache. I understood exactly what he meant. Despite my large, loving family, despite my professional success, I'd often felt like I was playing a role rather than fully belonging. The Decker daughter. The team publicist. The professional woman who had it all together. The gatekeeper for the far more interesting and important Frank, Drake, and Zayne Decker.

This weekend, pretending with Cam, somehow felt more authentic than most of my real relationships. What did that say about me? About us?

I reached across the space between us, finding his hand in the darkness. His fingers immediately closed around mine, warm and solid.

"Me too," I admitted, the words barely audible even to my own ears.

I felt him shift beside me, turning to face me though I kept my eyes fixed on the ceiling, afraid of what he might see in my expression.

"Hey Lana...".

"Should we sleep?" I whispered, still not looking at him, still not fully ready to face what was happening between us. "Early start tomorrow. You've got practice tomorrow and we've got our season opener on Tuesday."

"Probably," he agreed, though he didn't release my hand. "Goodnight, Lana."

"Goodnight, Cam."

Neither of us moved away. Our hands remained linked in the dark, a bridge across the careful distance we maintained. Eventually, the steady rhythm of his breathing and the warmth of his hand in mine lulled me toward sleep.

As I drifted off, I allowed myself one final, dangerous thought: What if this didn't have to end? What if, somehow, we could make this real?

Tomorrow would bring reality crashing back. Tomorrow I'd have to face the consequences of my growing feelings. Tomorrow I'd remember all the reasons this was impossible.

But tonight... Tonight I would hold his hand in the darkness and pretend, just for a few more hours, that this fairy tale could have a happy ending.

Chapter 13

I'd been awake for several minutes, but I hadn't moved, reluctant to disturb the man sleeping beside me.

Cam lay on his stomach, one arm tucked beneath his pillow, the other stretched across the space between us. The sheet had slipped down to his waist during the night, revealing the broad expanse of his back – all sculpted muscle and smooth skin, interrupted only by a small scar near his left shoulder blade. *Funny, he was wearing a t-shirt when we went to sleep,* I remembered. I glanced around the bed, taking great care not to move or shift my weight, until I saw it, scrunched into a gray ball at the foot of the bed. He must have gotten too warm overnight again. His face was turned toward me, relaxed in sleep in a way it rarely was in waking hours. Long eyelashes fanned against his cheeks, his usual cocky grin softened into something sweeter, more vulnerable.

I allowed myself the luxury of looking at him, really looking, while he couldn't catch me staring. The strong line of his jaw was covered in golden-brown stubble. The slight furrow between his brows remained even in sleep, as if he was puzzling through some hockey strategy in his dreams. The curve of his bicep, the definition in his shoulders that revealed countless hours of training.

God, he was beautiful. The kind of beautiful that made my breath catch and my fingers itch to trace the contours of his sleeping form. I wondered what it would be like to wake up to this sight every morning, to reach across and run my palm along the warm skin of his back, to feel those muscles flex beneath my touch.

My smutty Cam thoughts were going to be the ruin of me.

I carefully slipped from the bed. This was dangerous territory. In less than two hours, we'd be back in St. Pete, back to our professional roles and carefully maintained boundaries. Whatever this strange, liminal space had been between us this weekend, it wasn't real life.

I padded to the bathroom, closing the door softly behind me. As I got dressed, I tried to mentally shift gears, preparing myself for the transition back to work mode. Monday meant a full slate of meetings, media requests to sort through, and preparations for Tuesday's season opener. I needed to be Lana Decker, capable PR director, not this softer version of myself who'd spent the weekend pretending to be in love with Cam Murphy and finding the "faking it" part a whole lot harder than the "madly in love" part.

When I emerged from the bathroom forty minutes later, I'd armored myself as best I could. My hair fell in soft waves around my shoulders, my makeup was subtle but flawless, and I'd chosen a structured teal sundress that happened to match the sapphire on my finger. The espadrille slides added three inches to my height, making my legs look longer, giving me the confidence boost I desperately needed.

Cam was awake now, sitting on the edge of the bed in just his shorts, hair adorably mussed from sleep. He looked up as I entered, and the appreciation that flashed in his eyes sent a flutter through my stomach.

"Wow," he said simply, his gaze traveling from my face down to my legs and back again with unhurried admiration. "You look... incredible."

I smoothed a nonexistent wrinkle from my dress, secretly pleased by his reaction. "Thanks. Early start, remember? We've got practice and meetings."

He nodded, smoothing his disheveled hair with his fingers. "Right. Reality calls."

The word hung between us – reality. As if this weekend had been something else entirely, a shared fantasy we'd both temporarily inhabited.

"Bathroom's all yours," I said, turning away from the intensity in his eyes. "I'll finish packing."

We moved around each other with surprising ease as we prepared to leave, a domesticity that felt both alien and familiar. I folded my clothes with perhaps more precision than necessary, trying not to think about how Cam's toiletries had mingled with mine on the bathroom counter, how his hoodie was draped over the chair next to my cardigan.

"Ready?" he asked, surveying the room one last time.

I nodded, knowing as soon as we walked out this door, the spell would begin to break. The knowledge sat like a stone at the bottom of my stomach.

Downstairs, my parents had gathered for a farewell breakfast. My mother fussed over us, pressing a bag of extra muffins into my hands for the road. My father actually hugged Cam – not the brief, manly clasp he usually offered, but a real, actual embrace.

What in the world?

"You'll come back for Thanksgiving?" my mother asked us, her eyes hopeful as she squeezed my hands. "Both of you, of course."

"We'll have to see, Mom," I said, glancing at Cam. "You know the schedule gets pretty crazy during the season."

"That I do. At least for Christmas, then," she insisted. "We can do some wedding planning."

I felt Cam stiffen slightly beside me, but his smile never faltered. "We'd love to, Diana," he said warmly. "But we'll have to check the schedule."

"Don't forget what we talked about on the breakaway," my father said to Cam, clapping him on the shoulder. "You're drifting a bit low in the defensive zone — trust your D and center and support the puck by getting to the boards and staying in your lane to take the breakout pass. If you stay high between the circles and the blue line, you've a better chance of slipping behind the D on the breakout. Work with Rocco on that."

"Already texted him," Cam replied. "Said he'd run me through some drills this afternoon."

My father nodded approvingly. "Good man."

"Shame Zayne had to rush back last night," my mother said, walking us to the door. "But I suppose he wanted to avoid the Monday morning traffic."

"Smart move," Cam agreed. "The Skyway can be a mess around rush hour."

"Text me so I know you've arrived safely," my mother instructed, hugging me tightly. "And Cam," she turned to him with a warm smile, " take care of our girl."

"Always," he promised, and something in his tone made my insides all warm and gooey.

We made our final goodbyes, and as we pulled away from the house, I watched it recede in the side mirror until it disappeared around a bend in the road. The bubble was bursting, one molecule at a time.

"Your mom thinks I'm good for you," Cam observed after we'd driven in silence for a few minutes.

"My mom thinks everyone should be happily married with 2.5 children and a golden retriever."

"Not a golden retriever person?" he asked, changing lanes smoothly as we approached the causeway to the mainland.

"I'm more of a rescue mutt person," I replied. "Something with a big personality that doesn't shed too much."

"Noted," he said with a small smile, as if filing away this information for future reference.

"When did you text Coach Rocco?" I asked, genuinely curious. "I didn't see you on your phone much this weekend."

"This morning when you were in the shower," he replied. "Your dad gave me some great pointers. Said he's noticed the same issue since college."

"That sounds like Dad. He probably has a file on every player's technical weaknesses going back to peewee."

Cam laughed. "Probably. But he's not wrong. If I can work through that before Tuesday's opener, we'll have a better shot against Montreal."

I studied his profile as he drove, the tiny dimple in his chin, the focused set of his eyes on the road ahead. For all his playboy reputation, Cam was deadly serious about hockey. It was one of the things I'd always respected about him, even when I was determined to keep my distance.

"Your family's amazing," he said as we crossed the bridge to the mainland. "I mean, Zayne's said that a million times over the years... but seriously, Lana. I can see why you're so close to them."

"They liked you," I replied, glancing over at him and then burying my head in my hands. "Ohmygod, my mom and all the wedding stuff." I laughed. "She's out of control."

He laughed, but there was a strange note in it... almost wistful. "Your dad actually offered to take me fishing again next time we have a few days off."

"Really?" I raised my eyebrows. This was profound. "Frank Decker extending a fishing invitation is practically a formal adoption ceremony."

"Yeah?" Cam looked genuinely pleased. "I haven't been fishing since I was a kid. One of my stepfathers used to take me, but then he stopped after he and my mom..."

"You hardly ever talk about your family, thanks for sharing this weekend," I said.

He shrugged. "Not much more to tell. Mom is still in Minnesota, my dad is somewhere in Arizona with fiancée number six or maybe seven, I think? I stopped counting once I left home. We're not exactly the Deckers."

The casual way he dismissed his own family squeezed something in my chest. Before I could respond, he changed the subject.

"So, what's on your agenda this week? How many disasters do I need to create to keep you busy?"

I rolled my eyes, grateful for the lighter tone. "Please, no disasters. I'm still dealing with Nick Fosse's accidental livestream from that club in Ybor City."

"Hey, at least you've trained us well. He kept his clothes on the *whole* time."

"Small miracles," I laughed. "I've got the usual Monday chaos. Planning for the community skating event on Thursday, finalizing media credentials for the opener, media training with the new trade, Axel Blackwood about his post-game interviews." I gave Cam a sideways glance. "You know he only gives one-word answers, right?"

"That's because he hates the spotlight," Cam replied. "Always has. Give him a box of caps to sign for kids, he'll stay for hours. Put a microphone in his face, he transforms into a monosyllabic hockey robot."

"Well, this hockey robot needs to be more articulate if we want national coverage on how happy he was to be traded to the Slashers."

"Good luck with that. I'm not sure 'happy' is in his wheelhouse."

"Yeah, he has a bit of a reputation," I said.

"He's a hell of a player. Always had some challenges off the ice, though."

"Yeah, I've been warned. What about you?" I asked. "Besides working with Rocco?

"Early skate, film review, probably get my ass handed to me by Dr. Peters for that hip flexor thing again."

"From a fight you didn't need to get into," I reminded him. "Pre-season games aren't worth a strained hip, Cam."

"Asshole cross-checked Zayne from behind," Cam said simply, as if that explained everything. And in a way, it did. Cam's loyalty, especially to teammates, was absolute and unwavering.

"And don't forget the meeting with Redline on Thursday!!!!" I did a little happy dance for Cam in the passenger seat, and my voice went up about three octaves when I mentioned the sneaker meeting.

He laughed. "How could I?"

As we approached the Sunshine Skyway Bridge, I leaned forward slightly in my seat. On a clear day, the drive across the massive yellow cable-stayed bridge was one of my favorites in Florida – a spectacular view of Tampa Bay stretching to the horizon, the funny excitement of rising 200 feet above the sparkling water. Like a slow-moving roller coaster.

"Wow," Cam said, slowing as we joined the line of cars preparing to cross. "This traffic is worse than usual."

I checked the time on my phone. "Almost 8:00. This is pretty bad, even for rush hour. I wonder what's going on..."

"Might be an accident," he concluded, peering ahead. "I think I see flashing lights."

As we inched onto the bridge, an official-looking orange sign confirmed his theory: "ACCIDENT AHEAD. SINGLE LANE. EXPECT DELAYS."

"Great," I sighed. "We're going to be late."

"Could you please text Rocco and let him know we're stuck in traffic on the bridge," Cam asked. "He'll let Sully know. I don't want to get fined for being late to practice, especially not with the Redline deal hanging in the balance."

"Already on it," I said, fingers flying across my phone. "You've never been late to practice, have you?"

"How do you know that?" He looked at me inquisitively.

"I know all," I tease. "I literally get reports on everything you guys do because I have to know everything, all the time so I don't look like a deer in headlights when some reporter decides to surprise me with a question about somebody's secret baby or whether that hamstring injury is going to sideline so-and-so for the rest of the season, or, or, or..."

Cam raised his eyebrows for comic effect, "Who's got a secret baby?"

I rolled my eyes at him, "You're terrible."

"Well, yes, but I've only been late to practice once in my life since I started peewee hockey and I don't have a secret baby."

"Once?"

"Yeah," he answered, eyes on the road. "I was late to practice once, back in college."

I couldn't help but wonder, but I didn't dare ask.

Traffic crawled forward at an agonizing pace, stopping completely for long stretches before lurching forward a few car lengths. By the time we reached the steep incline of the bridge, dark clouds had begun gathering in the distance, the air taking on that charged, electric quality that precedes Florida storms.

"Looks like we're in for some weather," Cam observed, nodding toward the horizon where gray clouds billowed like smoke.

I watched the clouds with growing unease. The Sunshine Skyway was beautiful on clear days, but its exposed position over the bay made it vulnerable to sudden weather shifts, particularly high winds. As we climbed higher, I could see whitecaps forming on the water below, the palm trees along the fishing pier bending in the strengthening breeze.

By the time we'd crept to the apex of the bridge, the highest point, 200 feet above the bay with nothing but steel cables and engineering between us and the churning water, traffic had stopped completely. We sat immobile, the first fat raindrops beginning to splatter against the windshield as the wind audibly picked up around us.

I gripped the edge of my seat, trying to appear casual, but when a particularly strong gust rocked the car slightly, I couldn't suppress a small gasp. The bridge was designed to sway in high winds (a safety feature, not a flaw) but the sensation of movement while suspended so high above the water sent a spike of adrenaline through my system.

"You okay?" Cam asked, his eyes concerned.

"Fine," I said automatically, then reconsidered. "Actually, no. I hate being stopped up here. Especially in weather."

He nodded, not dismissing my fear or trying to reason me out of it. "It should clear up soon."

As if in direct contradiction, the sky darkened further, and a flash of lightning illuminated the clouds. The rain intensified into a torrential downpour, drumming on the roof of the car, and the wind howled around us, causing the bridge to sway perceptibly.

"The whole structure is designed to flex with the wind," Cam offered. "I think it's rated for a Cat 3 or 4."

Any Floridian who plans to survive the increasingly intense hurricane season each year must basically become an amateur meteorologist. One of the hazards of living in the Sunshine State, among others.

"That's not as reassuring as you think," I replied through gritted teeth as another gust rocked Cam's sports car. My heart hammered in my chest, and I found myself taking short, shallow breaths.

Cam reached across the center console and took my hand, his palm warm against my suddenly clammy fingers. "You're okay," he said firmly. "We're okay."

I nodded, unable to speak as another powerful gust buffeted the car.

"Breathe with me," he instructed, his voice calm and steady. "In for four counts, hold for seven, out for eight."

I stared at him, surprised. "Since when do you know breathing exercises?"

A small, self-deprecating smile crossed his face. "I had panic attacks when I was a kid. Not many people know that."

This revelation, this unexpected vulnerability from Cam of all people, momentarily distracted me from my fear. "You did?"

He nodded, still holding my hand. "Started after my parents' first divorce. Got worse during high school. Better now, but..." He shrugged. "I've learned some techniques."

I couldn't reconcile all this new information with the Cam I *thought* I knew: the carefree, confident Hitman who seemed to skate through life as effortlessly as he skated on ice.

"Breathe with me," he said again, and this time I followed, matching the steady rhythm he set. In for four... hold for seven... out for eight. Again and again until the vice grip of panic around my chest loosened slightly.

"Talk to me," I said, needing further distraction as the wind howled around us, the bridge creaking beneath our tires. "Tell me something else I don't know about you."

He thought for a moment, "I usually sleep with the TV on," he said finally. "Always have a game or a baking show or a documentary playing."

"Why?"

"Um...I used to have a hard time settling down to sleep, thanks to the musical chairs of all my parents' different houses when I was a kid. Too many weird sounds. And then later when I played on traveling teams, and now sleeping in different hotels all the time when we travel for games... I can get too many thoughts when it's quiet. TV drowns them out."

"Oh no! You should have told me," I said apologetically. "I would have turned the TV on for you at the beach house."

Cam grinned suddenly and winked at me, charisma radiating on full blast. "Thanks, but I already had *plenty* to distract me, Cupcake Queen."

"I alphabetize my spices," I offered in return. "And my books. And my nail polish."

He grinned. "That tracks."

"What's that supposed to mean?"

"You like order. Control." There was no judgment in his tone, just observation. "Makes sense, given everything."

"Everything?" I echoed.

He gestured vaguely with his free hand. "Family legacy. Brothers in the spotlight. Always having to prove yourself."

The accuracy of this assessment, from someone I'd never really discussed it with, took me by surprise. The car rocked again in the wind, but my anxiety had dialed back from acute to merely uncomfortable.

"What was it like?" he asked after a moment. "Growing up in the Decker dynasty?"

I'd been asked variations of this question a hundred times by reporters, but something about Cam's genuine curiosity made me want to give a real answer, not the polished sound bite I usually offered.

"Complicated," I said finally. "I love my parents and my brothers obviously; they're my favorite people in the universe. The "anything for the team" mentality was sometimes hard to deal with. The dynasty part – I'm *so* proud of my family's accomplishments. I loved the games, being part of the community, always being around hockey. But also..."

"Never quite feeling like you belonged?" he suggested quietly.

I looked at him intensely, trying to puzzle out how he saw so much. "Yes. Exactly. How did you know?"

He shrugged, eyes on the stationary traffic ahead. "Recognized something familiar, I guess. Different circumstances, same feeling."

The bridge swayed beneath us, but I barely noticed now, caught in the current of this unexpected conversation. "Tell me," I said.

Cam was silent for so long I thought he might not answer. Then he sighed, his fingers still intertwined with mine.

"The family stuff. I've made some pretty bad choices in my life, sacrificed some things I shouldn't have, just trying to feel like I belonged."

The raw honesty in his voice made my throat tighten. It struck me again how similar we were – I wasn't the only one who'd been hiding behind a professional mask all these years. Suddenly, I wanted nothing more than to just *hug* him.

"I get that," I said softly. "Different version of the same thing. Frank Decker's daughter. Drake and Zayne's little sister. The team's PR director. Never just... Lana."

He fully turned to me then, his blue eyes serious. "I'm looking at you right now, and I don't see anything *but* Lana. Just so you know."

Something fluttered in my chest, a dangerous, fragile thing I wasn't ready to name. Outside, the rain had intensified to sheets of water cascading down the windshield, the wail of the wind creating a cocoon around our stillness.

In the enclosed space of the car, with rain drumming on the roof and the bridge swaying beneath us, something shifted between us, revealing vulnerable spaces beneath. I was acutely aware of how close we were, how his hand still held mine, how his eyes had darkened to the color of the storm-tossed waters below us.

He leaned forward slightly, gaze dropping to my lips, and I didn't pull away. My heart hammered against my ribs, anticipation coiling tight within me. This wasn't for show. There were no cameras, no audience, nothing and no one to perform for. Just us, suspended above the world.

His free hand came up to brush a strand of hair from my face, his touch feather-light. "Lana," he murmured.

I couldn't speak, couldn't think, could only nod almost imperceptibly as he closed the distance between us. I felt his breath, warm against my lips, his masculine scent filling my senses. My eyes drifted closed, and my mind emptied of everything but just this moment, just this man.

A horn blast fractured the moment. In front of us, traffic had begun to move, drivers impatient to be off the bridge as the storm intensified. Cam pulled back, his expression unreadable as he released my hand and put the car in drive.

"Shit. Looks like we're moving," he said, his voice strained.

The descent from the bridge was steep and quick, the car picking up speed as we passed the wreck and followed the flow of traffic down toward solid ground. As we descended, I felt reality crashing back in. The weekend was over, we were heading back to work, to colleagues, to the carefully constructed fiction of our engagement that increasingly felt like everything but fiction.

The silence between us wasn't uncomfortable, exactly, but it was heavy with things unsaid. As we reached the mainland and the road flattened out, sheets of rain now falling in earnest around us, Cam finally spoke.

"I should probably take you straight to the rink, if it's okay," he said, glancing at the clock on the dashboard. "It's already 8:30, and with this rain, we won't make it back to your place and then to practice on time."

"Right," I agreed, my voice sounding strangely normal given the turmoil inside me. "I have that media training with Blackwood at eleven anyway."

He nodded, adjusting the wipers as the rain intensified. "Back to the grind."

"Back to reality," I echoed, my voice laced with dread.

As we pulled into the training facility parking lot, I felt an irrational urge to ask him to keep driving – to take us anywhere but here, where we'd have to resume our professional roles and pretend the weekend hadn't changed something fundamental between us.

Cam found a spot near the staff entrance and cut the engine, the sudden silence filling the car. Rain pounded on the roof as we sat there for a moment, neither making a move to get out.

"I'll grab the bags," he said finally.

"You don't have to... "

"I want to," he interrupted, his eyes meeting mine briefly before he pushed open his door and stepped out into the downpour.

I watched as he retrieved my luggage from the trunk, hunching his shoulders against the rain. He was soaked within seconds, his t-shirt clinging to his torso, outlining every muscle, his hair plastered to his forehead. When he opened my door, holding my bags in one hand and offering me the other, I didn't hesitate to take it, letting him pull me from the car into the storm.

We ran for the entrance, laughing despite ourselves as the rain drenched us completely. Inside, we stood dripping on the mat, water pooling around our feet.

"Well," I said, pushing wet hair from my face, "that was refreshing."

Cam grinned, raindrops clinging to his eyelashes. "Nothing like a brisk shower to start the day."

For a moment, we just looked at each other – wet, disheveled, and somehow more honest than we'd been in years. Then the double doors to the training area opened, and Logan appeared, already in his practice gear.

"There you are," he said, eyeing us curiously. "Sully's looking for you, Cam. Team meeting in ten." His gaze traveled from Cam's soaked form to mine, a knowing smile playing at his lips. "Welcome back, lovebirds. Good weekend?"

"The best," Cam replied, his eyes never leaving my face.

"Great," Logan said, already turning back toward the locker room. "Hurry up, Hitman. Sully's in a mood. Something about Montreal's new defensive scheme — it's a modified neutral zone trap with a left wing lock component. He's concerned that it's going to stop our breakouts from the zone if they clog up lanes and intercept passes. It's gonna be carry, dump, and chase."

"I'd better go," Cam said quietly once Logan had disappeared. He set my bag down next to me, hesitating. "Lana... "

"We'll talk later," I promised, though I wasn't sure what there was to say, what came next in this uncharted territory we'd wandered into.

He nodded, then impulsively leaned forward and pressed a kiss to my cheek, his lips warm against my rain-chilled skin. "Later," he agreed, and then he was gone, striding toward the locker room, leaving me standing alone in the lobby, water dripping from my hair and my carefully chosen teal dress clinging to my skin.

I touched my cheek where his lips had been, the warmth of his kiss lingering. For years, I'd maintained careful professional boundaries, kept my heart guarded after that one night in college. But now those walls were crumbling, and I wasn't at all certain I wanted to rebuild them.

Like the storm raging outside, something had shifted between Cam and me – powerful, unpredictable, and impossible to ignore. I'd come back from Siesta Key with more than just sand in my luggage and a fake engagement ring on my finger. I'd returned with the unsteady realization that what had started as pretend was rapidly becoming the most real thing in my life.

And I had absolutely no idea what to do about it.

Chapter 14

I spent most of Monday morning pretending to work. In reality, I was staring out my office window at the practice rink below, where the team was running drills for tomorrow's season opener against Montreal. My laptop screen displayed the media release draft I'd been "editing" for the past hour, cursor blinking accusingly at the same spot where I'd stopped typing forty-five minutes ago.

The media notes for tomorrow's game against Montreal sat half-finished beside three page-marked player interview transcripts I needed to approve. The social media content calendar remained woefully incomplete, and I still hadn't confirmed the pregame broadcast schedule with ESPN. I was falling behind, badly, and yet I couldn't tear my eyes away from the ice. From *Cam*.

The Slashers training facility had been designed with efficiency in mind. My second-floor office overlooked the practice ice, theoretically so I could monitor media presence during practices. Today, however, I was monitoring only one player.

Cam skated with fluid grace, his movements precise and powerful as he ran through Coach Michaels' new offensive zone entries. His jersey, practice gray with the number 22, clung to his broad shoulders as he accelerated, executing a perfect cross-over before cutting sharply between Zayne and Blackwood. He feathered a tape-to-tape pass to Logan at the far post that Montreal's defense would never see coming tomorrow night. Even from this distance, I could see the concentration etched on his face, the complete absorption in the moment that made him so mesmerizing on the ice.

I caught myself absently twirling the sapphire ring on my finger like a super fancy security blanket. The stunning stone caught the fluorescent lighting overhead, sending oceany glitters across the wall where our Stanley Cup team photo hung.

I could take it off. There was no one here to see, no one to convince. The charade wasn't necessary within these walls, where Coach Sully and Coach Rocco knew the truth. And yet...

Below, Cam executed a perfect toe-drag around my brother, earning a good-natured slash across his shin guards from Zayne, before flipping the puck top-shelf past Fosse's glove. As his teammates tapped their sticks against the ice in appreciation, he looked up toward my window, as if he knew I'd been watching all along.

Our eyes met across the distance, and he raised his stick slightly in acknowledgment, a small smile playing at the corners of his mouth. My heart fluttered traitorously against my ribs, the same way it had on the Skyway Bridge this morning when he'd leaned across the center console, his eyes darkening as they dropped to my lips.

This was out of hand.

With determined effort, I swiveled my chair away from the window and refocused on my laptop. The media release for tomorrow's season opener wasn't going to write itself, and I had a mountain of media requests to sort through before tomorrow afternoon's player availability session.

I managed to write two solid paragraphs before my gaze drifted back to the window.

Fuck it. I just wanted to watch him play.

"Get it together, Lana," I muttered to myself, rubbing my temples. Whatever had happened, or almost happened, between Cam and me at the beach house and on the bridge needed to stay firmly in the past. We had a job to do, a sneaker deal to secure. We needed to stay absolutely focused on the goal at hand. Three more days until the deal meeting.

So why couldn't I stop thinking about the way his eyes had darkened when he'd leaned toward me in the car? Or how perfectly our bodies had fit together when we'd awakened spooning at the beach house? Or the strange intimacy of our midnight conversations, when he'd confessed that no one after me had ever come close?

With a frustrated sigh, I pulled the ring off my finger and set it on the desk beside my keyboard. Out of sight, out of mind. FOCUS.

Five minutes later, I was staring at the ring again.

I picked it up, flipping it in my palm. The platinum setting was substantial but elegant, the ocean-deep sapphire multifaceted and mesmerizing, almost exactly the color of Cam's eyes when he smiled. Had he chosen it for that reason? Or was I reading too much into an expensive prop most likely selected by his agent?

Before I could stop myself, I slid it back onto my finger. *Just for consistency*, I told myself. In case someone from the training staff came by. It would look strange if I suddenly wasn't wearing it. People would talk.

The justifications sounded weak even to my own ears.

My phone buzzed with a text from Mitch in the marketing department, asking about player availability for All Childrens' Hospital visit request. I welcomed the distraction, diving into coordination logistics with perhaps more enthusiasm than necessary. When my office phone rang a few minutes later, I answered without checking the caller ID, grateful for the interruption from my own thoughts.

"Lana Decker," I answered, professional tone firmly in place.

"Ms. Decker? This is Latisha Brown from Redline Athletics. I'm calling to follow up on the paperwork for Mr. Murphy's endorsement deal."

My pulse quickened. Redline.

"Of course, Ms. Brown. How can I help?"

"Just wanted to confirm we're still on track for Thursday's announcement and signing ceremony? Our CEO and creative director will be flying in specifically for the occasion."

"Absolutely," I assured her, pulling up the relevant document on my computer. "Cam's schedule is cleared for Thursday morning. We've arranged the private room at Bayside for the signing and lunch afterward, as requested."

"Excellent. And we've seen the, er, development in Mr. Murphy's personal life. The company is quite pleased with this new direction. The marketing department is already considering family-oriented campaign concepts for next year... perhaps involving both of you?"

I swallowed hard, guilt twisting in my stomach. "That's, uh, wonderful to hear."

"Will you be joining us on Thursday as well?" There was a note of curiosity in her voice. "As Mr. Murphy's fiancée, you're more than welcome to attend. We'd love to get to know the woman who's tamed hockey's most eligible bachelor."

The word 'fiancée' hit me like a slapshot. It was one thing to imply the relationship; it was another to hear it stated so matter-of-factly by an industry professional who was basing multi-million dollar decisions on our deception. Guilt flooded my body. This was a whole lot easier to swallow in the abstract. Or far away from reality at the beach house.

"Thank you for the invitation," I said carefully. "I'll need to check my schedule, but I appreciate the inclusion."

After finalizing a few more details and ending the call, I sat back in my chair, unsettled. What had started as a quick image fix had grown tentacles, extending into areas of our lives we hadn't anticipated. First my family, now Redline specifically mentioning "family campaigns." How far would this charade have to go before the deal was signed and secure?

And then what?

It's fine, I told myself. Cam was no troublemaker or man-tramp. He'd be an incredible spokesperson for Redline. The "fiance Cam" persona was more him than the hockey heartbreaker image I'd concocted for him anyway.

The thought of unwinding it all, of removing this ring and stepping back into my purely professional relationship with Cam, created an unexpected hollow sensation in my chest. Which was ridiculous. This was exactly what we'd planned from the beginning. Get the deal signed, then stage a quiet, amicable split after an appropriate interval.

Simple. Clean. Professional.

So why did my throat tighten at the thought?

A knock at my door provided welcome relief from my self-imposed spiral of questions. I quickly composed myself, expecting one of my team with the media credentials for tomorrow's game.

Instead, Coco stood in my doorway, a practice bag tucked under one arm and a bright smile on her face. Her auburn hair was pulled back in a neat ponytail that emphasized her high cheekbones and striking green eyes. She wore a Tampa Bay Skating Club jacket over sleek athletic leggings, her Olympic figure skater physique evident even in casual clothes. Versus me, skinny because I was constantly too busy to eat, and who got all my exercise by circling the skating arena in stilettos 500 times a day.

"Hey! Have I caught you at a bad time?" she asked, taking in what must have been my slightly frazzled appearance.

"No, not at all. Come in," I said, genuinely pleased to see her. "Logan's looking good today."

"He's been more stressed than usual over the season opener, so I thought I'd swing by to see if I could help settle him down a bit. Like he did for me at Nationals. I'm his lucky charm, it's kind of our thing."

"You two are the cutest."

Coco set her practice bag near the door before dropping gracefully into one of the sleek chairs facing my desk. Up close, I could see the fine dusting of freckles across her nose.

"I've got conditioning with my trainer this afternoon, but Logan mentioned he had a short practice, so I thought I'd surprise him for lunch." She smiled, a slight blush coloring her cheeks. "Plus, I wanted to give him a little "congrats" gift in person for the award. He was so nervous about that speech."

"He did great," I said sincerely. "And it was sweet how he thanked you and Poppy first."

"Yeah, well, he knows who really runs the show," she joked, though the pride in her voice was unmistakable. "Speaking of awards night, I think you and Cam broke the internet. That dress was absolute fire, by the way. And that ring..." Her eyes flickered to my hand. "Wow."

I instinctively touched the sapphire, warmth creeping up my neck. "Thanks. It was a fun night."

"Mmm-hmm." She tilted her head, studying me with those perceptive green eyes. "So, how are things going with hockey's most eligible bachelor? Or I guess he's not really eligible anymore, is he?" There was gentle humor in her tone, but something knowing in her gaze made me shift uncomfortably.

"Fine. Good. It's..." I trailed off, my usual smooth PR deflections failing me. This was Coco, after all – Logan's girlfriend, an Olympic athlete, and probably the only woman in my social circle who understood the unique pressures of the intersection of professional sports and media. "It's complicated," I finished lamely.

"I bet," she said with a sympathetic nod. "Must be weird having your relationship so public all of a sudden. Trust me, I get it. When Logan and I first started dating, I felt like every move we made was being analyzed by the entire hockey community. The entire figure skating community. The entire universe..."

I nodded, grateful for her understanding but also acutely aware that her relationship with Logan was genuine, while mine with Cam was... what, exactly? The lines were blurring more each day.

A commotion on the ice drew our attention to the window. Logan had apparently scored on a drill, and the players were celebrating with exaggerated cheers and stick taps. Cam was in the middle of it, laughing as he gave Logan a congratulatory head tap with his gloved hand.

"Look at them," Coco remarked fondly. "They're basically overgrown children,"

I found myself smiling, my gaze fixed on Cam as he lined up for the next drill. "They really are."

"Hey, where are you sitting tomorrow night?"

"Probably in the WAGs box unless I get a better offer."

"Want to sit with me in the VIP box? I've got the Redline folks coming in, and the food will be better."

"I'm in," Coco said casually. "So...how was the family beach weekend? Logan mentioned you guys drove back this morning and got caught in that mess on the Skyway."

"It was..." I hesitated, searching for a neutral descriptor. "Interesting."

Coco raised an eyebrow. "That's PR-speak for 'total disaster' or 'completely amazing but I don't want to admit it.' Which one?"

I laughed despite myself. "Neither. Both. It was just... not what I expected."

"In what way?"

I glanced toward my office door, which stood slightly ajar. Rising from my desk, I crossed the room and closed it softly before returning to my seat.

"Can I tell you something in confidence?" I asked, lowering my voice.

Coco's expression turned serious. "Uh, yes."

"Like, *I signed an NDA and this could wreck my career* confidence?"

"Always," she said.

I took a deep breath, suddenly desperate to confide in someone who might understand. "The engagement isn't real. It just looks real. It's a PR move to help Cam secure the Redline deal."

To her credit, Coco didn't look particularly shocked. She merely nodded thoughtfully. "I had a feeling."

"What? How?" I asked, surprised.

She shrugged, her eyes kind but knowing. "First, Logan is constantly saying you and Cam would be perfect together if you would only get out of your own way, and I happen to know Cam's had a massive crush on you for a while."

"How long is a while?"

"Um, forever. Let's just say that in real life, the *Hitman* is more of a *one-hit wonder*," she smiled. "At least when it comes to love. He has it bad for you."

"No, he..."

"Also, something about the timing seemed awfully convenient. Plus, Logan mentioned it happened *very* suddenly. And..." She gave me a meaningful look. "You've spent the last year I've known you pretending Cam Murphy doesn't exist except when you have to manage his image. Or when you've had more than one margarita. Like at our party last summer."

"That's not true," I protested automatically. "We work together all the time."

"Uh-huh. And you maintain about fifty feet of professional distance at all times." She leaned forward, her expression turning gentle. "So what changed? Why agree to fake an entire relationship? That's a pretty extreme PR strategy, even for the Hitman."

I sighed, running a hand through my hair. "Redline was ready to walk away just days before the announcement. His agent suggested a PR relationship to rehabilitate his image."

"And he asked you?" Coco looked intrigued. "Out of all the women in Tampa who would literally lie down in traffic for a chance with Cam Murphy, he asked his team publicist? The woman who, as far as I can tell, has spent years perfecting the art of professional disinterest around him?"

Put that way, it did sound strange. "It made sense for the optics," I explained. "I know how to handle the media, I understand the hockey world, and I'm..." I faltered.

"You're what?" Coco prompted.

"Safe," I finished. "I'm a safe choice. No messy emotional complications."

Coco's skeptical expression was almost comical. "Right. And how's that working out for you?"

"What do you mean?"

"Lana," she said patiently, "you've been staring out that window at Cam every time there's a break in our conversation. And you haven't stopped fidgeting with that ring since I walked in."

Caught, I self-consciously placed both hands flat on my desk. "It's just – it's become a habit."

"Mmm-hmm." She didn't sound convinced. "So tell me about the beach trip with your family. How was that?"

"Complicated," I admitted. "My parents think it's real. So does the rest of my family. Only Zayne knows the truth."

"And sharing a room with Cam? How was that?" Her tone was light, but her eyes were astute.

I felt heat rise to my cheeks, remembering how I'd woken up with his arm draped over me, his chest pressed against my back, his breath warm against my neck. "Fine. Professional. We maintained boundaries."

"Right." Coco nodded slowly, a knowing smile playing at her lips. "And nothing happened that made you question those boundaries? Not even once?"

The memory of Cam's arms around me as we'd fallen asleep, the intensity in his eyes as he'd nearly kissed me on the bridge, the way my heart had raced when he'd confessed that no one after me had ever come close – all of it rushed through me in a wave of confusion.

"It's complicated," I repeated, feeling suddenly defensive.

"When did it stop being fake for you?" Coco asked quietly.

I stared at her, caught off guard by the directness of the question. "I – what? It's still fake."

"Is it, though?" She tilted her head, studying me. "Because from here, it looks like something real is happening. Maybe something that's been brewing for a while."

"That's..." I started to deny it, but the words stuck in my throat. With sudden clarity, I realized I didn't want to lie to Coco. Maybe I needed someone to talk to, someone who might understand the complex emotions swirling inside me. "I don't know what's happening," I admitted finally. "It's all getting... muddled."

"Let me guess," she said gently. "You're starting to have genuine feelings, or maybe acknowledging feelings that were already there. But you're terrified of what happens when this *arrangement* inevitably ends."

I looked at her, startled by her accuracy. "Are you secretly a therapist?"

She laughed. "No. But I did spend the better part of a season fighting my feelings for a certain hockey captain because I was convinced it would be a disaster. Sound familiar?"

I sighed, slumping back in my chair. "Maybe. A little."

"Tell me something," Coco said, her voice softening. "What was it like with your family?"

The question caught me off guard. "What do you mean?"

"I mean, how did it feel to see him interacting with your parents, your brothers... seeing him in your childhood home, or swimming with your nieces and nephews?"

Images flashed through my mind: Cam laughing with my father over fishing stories, helping my mother carry groceries from the car, getting soaked in an impromptu pool wrestling match with Zayne, his patient hands executing Emma's creative vision as we built a sandcastle tower. The warm glow in my chest at seeing him fit so seamlessly into my world, as if he'd always belonged there.

"It felt..." I swallowed hard, surprised by the emotion welling in my throat. "It felt right. Like he'd always been there."

Coco nodded, as if I'd confirmed something she already knew. "And what about the ring? The first time you put it on, what did you think?"

I glanced down at the sapphire. "I thought it was beautiful. Too beautiful for a PR stunt, honestly. I figured it was a loaner from his agent."

"Did you ask?"

"No," I admitted. "I didn't want to know."

"Because if it was real, that would mean something," she replied. "Or if it wasn't real, that would mean something too."

I nodded, not trusting myself to speak.

"This isn't fake anymore. You know that, right?" Coco's direct statement hit like a punch to the gut.

"I can't..." I shook my head. "There's so much riding on this. The Redline deal is worth millions to Cam and would be huge for the team. My professional reputation. My relationship with Zayne. My family's expectations now that they think we're engaged." I gestured helplessly. "It's all too complicated."

"Maybe what's really at stake isn't your job or the deal," Coco suggested. "Maybe what's at stake is your heart, and that's what's really scaring you."

I opened my mouth to argue, then closed it again. Was she right? Was I hiding behind professional concerns to avoid confronting my real fears?

"Here's a scary question," Coco said, leaning forward. "What happens after the deal is signed? When the PR stunt has served its purpose? Have you two even talked about that?"

We hadn't, not really. The plan had been vague – maintain the appearance of a relationship for a respectable period, then stage an amicable, private breakup. Simple in theory, but the thought now made my chest ache.

"Sort of," I admitted. "We've been more... living in the moment."

"Most fake relationships have a clear end date," Coco observed. "At least, according to all my favorite Priscilla Oliveras romances. Yours seems to be getting more entangled, not less."

Before I could formulate a response, a commotion from below indicated practice was wrapping up. I glanced out the window to see the players exiting the ice, Cam among them. As if sensing my gaze, he looked up toward my office, our eyes meeting across the distance. Even from here, I could see his smile, a private one meant just for me. My heart performed a completely unprofessional somersault in my chest.

Coco, who had turned to follow my gaze, let out a soft laugh. "Yeah, that's what I thought." She stood, gathering her bag. "Look, I'm not saying it's simple. But from someone who nearly talked herself out of the best thing that ever happened to her – don't let fear of the unknown stop you from exploring something real."

"It's not that simple," I protested weakly.

"It never is," she agreed. With a small wave, she slipped out the door, leaving me alone with thoughts I'd been trying very hard to avoid.

I sat in silence for several long minutes, turning over Coco's words in my mind. *This isn't fake anymore. You know that, right?* The simple statement had cracked open something I'd been desperately trying to keep contained.

My phone buzzed with a text message.

> CAM: Dinner tonight? Need to strategize about tomorrow's practice media availability.

I stared at the message, reading between the lines. "Strategize." Right. We both knew that was just an excuse to spend more time together. A professional pretext that would allow us to maintain the fiction that this was still just about work.

Part of me – the rational, professional part – knew I should suggest a quick call instead. Set firmer boundaries. Keep things strictly business.

But another part – the part that couldn't stop remembering how it felt to wake up in his arms, to feel his thumb tracing circles on my palm under the blanket during the bonfire, to see the vulnerability in his eyes as he told me no one else had ever come close – wanted nothing more than to say yes.

I glanced again at the ring on my finger, at the way the sapphire caught the light. This wasn't fake anymore.

Maybe it never was.

With a deep breath, I typed my reply:

> ME: 7 PM. And don't get any bright ideas about breaking curfew the night before our season opener.

His response came almost immediately:

> ⊠ + ⊠

I smiled at the screen like an idiot.

Setting my phone down, I turned back to my computer, determined to at least attempt productivity for the rest of the afternoon. But Coco's words echoed in my mind, impossible to silence:

Maybe what's really at stake is your heart.

Chapter 15

The mirror didn't lie. I had changed outfits three times, finally settling on a sleek, pencil skirt and silk shell in Slashers teal with a fitted black blazer. Professional, yet feminine. My makeup was flawless – smoky eyes, subtle contour, a sheer gloss that made my lips look fuller. I'd even spent twenty minutes curling my hair into perfect waves, a far cry from my usual sleek ponytail for games.

"This is ridiculous," I muttered to my reflection as I fastened small diamond studs to my ears. "You're the PR director, not a trophy girlfriend."

But as I slipped the sapphire ring onto my finger, I couldn't deny the truth any longer. I wasn't dressing for the cameras or the Redline executives. I was dressing *for Cam*.

I bit my lip, studying my reflection. Did he even notice these things? Did he care how I looked? The memory of his appreciative gaze when I'd worn that blue sundress at the beach house suggested he did. The thought sent a flutter through my stomach that I refused to analyze.

My phone buzzed on the counter.

> CAM: Ready to watch me embarrass Montreal tonight, Cupcake Queen?

I felt a treacherous smile spread across my face as I typed back.

> ME: Don't jinx it. And yes, I expect nothing less than total domination. Redline execs will be watching from box 3.

> CAM: Roger that. Hitting the ice extra hard for you tonight.

> ME: For Redline, you mean.

His response came almost immediately.

I set my phone down, warmth spreading through my chest. With one last glance in the mirror, I grabbed my tablet and headed out. Tonight was crucial, not just for the team, but for Cam's Redline deal. The executives would be watching his performance closely, evaluating whether their multimillion-dollar investment in hockey's reformed heartthrob would be worthwhile.

And here I was, the architect of this entire charade, wearing his ring and trying desperately not to reveal how real my feelings had become.

Ninety minutes before puck drop, I stood in the media control room, watching the clock tick down as my to-do list remained stubbornly unfinished. The energy in the arena was already building, a special electricity unique to season openers. This year felt different, though. More significant. More personal.

"Hey, boss." Katie, my assistant, appeared in the doorway, tablet in hand. "ESPN wants to know if they can get an exclusive with Cam after the game, regardless of the outcome."

"Tell them he's scheduled for the standard post-game press conference only," I replied, straightening my blazer. "No exclusives tonight. I need to keep the Redline people happy, which means equal access for all media."

"Got it. Also, Coach Sully wants to confirm you've briefed the newbs on media protocol."

I nodded. "Blackwood and Petrovich are both clear on the talking points. And make sure everyone sticks to the 'no comment' line about the Ottawa trade rumors." If I got two whole words out of Blackwood tonight I'd consider it a win.

The overhead speaker crackled. "Media check commencing in five minutes."

Right. *Work*. The thing I was supposed to be focusing on.

As Katie hurried off, I took a deep breath, squaring my shoulders. I could do this. I was Lana Decker, youngest PR Director in the league. I'd built my career on maintaining composure in high-pressure situations.

So why did the thought of seeing Cam in action tonight make my heart race like I was sixteen again?

An hour later, I stood in the executive suite, supervising the final preparations. The catering staff arranged elegant platters of hors d'oeuvres while bartenders stocked premium spirits. Every detail was meticulously planned, from the branded napkins to the overflowing gift bags filled with Slashers merch.

"Lana, sweetheart!" My mother's voice carried across the suite like a bell.

I turned to find my parents entering, my mother radiant in a custom-tailored teal dress with subtle black Slashers accents, my father looking distinguished in his gray blazer and the Slashers tie Zayne had given him when he got drafted.

"Mom? Dad? I thought you were watching from Marcus's box tonight." I hurried over to embrace them, genuinely surprised to see them in the VIP area instead of the GM's box.

"We were," my father explained, his eyes crinkling with amusement, "but your mother insisted we be moved to this box instead."

"I told Marcus we needed to support Cameron with these sneaker people," my mother said, waving her hand excitedly. "And besides, we wanted to sit with you."

"You mean you wanted to meddle," I corrected with a knowing smile.

My mother patted my cheek. "I prefer to call it 'supportive participation.' You know we'd never miss Zayne's season opener, sweetheart. This year we just have two reasons to celebrate."

I felt a headache forming behind my eyes. "Mom, please don't call him Cameron. And please, please don't mention the wedding to the Redline executives. This deal is really important to Cam and the team."

My mother gave me a knowing smile. "I'm not going to embarrass you, Lana. I'm just here to support my future son-in-law. And your brother, of course."

Before I could spiral further, Coco breezed in, looking effortlessly chic in fitted jeans and a stylish Slashers jersey knotted at her waist, her auburn hair pulled back in a sleek ponytail.

"Diana! Frank! What a lovely surprise," she exclaimed, embracing my parents warmly. She turned to me with a grin that held a hint of mischief. "Quite the family affair tonight, huh?"

"Apparently." I forced a smile, mentally rearranging my plans for the evening. With my parents here, the pressure to maintain our "engagement" performance had just doubled. The sapphire ring on my finger suddenly felt a whole lot heavier.

"You look amazing," Coco whispered, linking her arm through mine as we walked toward the window. "That's not your usual game-day outfit."

"Just trying to make a good impression on the Redline people," I replied automatically.

"Mmm-hmm," she hummed skeptically. "And the extra mascara and that lipstick you only wear on dates has nothing to do with a certain number 22?"

I felt heat rise to my cheeks but was saved from responding when Coco gasped, pointing to the ice below.

Through the floor-to-ceiling windows, I could see the arena slowly filling with fans. The energy was palpable, even from inside the box. On the ice below, players had begun to emerge for warm-ups, their skates cutting crisp patterns across the fresh surface.

My eyes automatically found Cam, unmistakable even from this distance. He moved with fluid grace, his tall frame powerful yet agile as he worked through his pre-game routine. The way he handled the puck, like an extension of himself, was mesmerizing. Each stride showcased the athletic perfection of his body, the result of countless hours of training and natural talent.

God, I could watch him play all night.

As if sensing my gaze, he glanced up toward the executive boxes. Even from this distance, I felt the intensity of his eyes as our gazes locked briefly before he returned to his drills.

"He looks ready," my father commented, coming to stand beside me. "Focused."

"He's been working on that adjustment you guys talked about at the beach house," I replied automatically. "Said it made a big difference."

My father nodded with approval, almost imperceptibly to the untrained eye, which was Frank Decker's way of showing he was impressed. "Good. It'll create more shooting lanes, against Montreal's defensive system."

The suite began to fill with executives, media partners, and VIP guests. "Knock 'em dead, sweetheart," my dad whispered with a kiss to my temple. I slipped into professional mode, making introductions and ensuring everything ran smoothly.

"Mr. and Mrs. Decker, may I introduce James Whitley and Vanessa Cheng from Redline Athletics," I said smoothly, leading my parents toward the executives. "They're here discussing a potential partnership with Cam."

"Wonderful to meet you," my mother said warmly, extending her hand with the elegance of a woman who'd spent decades in hockey's social circles. "We're so excited about Cameron's opportunity. He was just telling us about it at our beach house last weekend."

Two seconds, and my mom had already inserted herself into the mix.

I managed not to wince as Vanessa's eyebrows raised slightly. "Cam spent the weekend with the Deckers, did he? How lovely."

"Frank Decker," my father said, extending his hand. "Former Minnesota North Stars, now just a retired old man who likes to give unsolicited advice to his kids."

"Frank Decker?" James Whitley's expression shifted from polite interest to genuine excitement. "*The* Frank Decker? Stanley Cup winner, Hall of Fame inductee? What an honor!"

"That's ancient history," my father demurred, though I knew he was always pleased by the recognition.

"Hardly! Your defensive strategies revolutionized the game. And now your son, following in your footsteps. That's quite a legacy."

"Both my sons," my father corrected. "Drake's an assistant coach for San Jose. And my daughter here is making her own mark in hockey, just in a different arena."

I felt a rush of warmth at my father's pride, even as the conversation shifted to the upcoming game. Throughout it all, part of my attention remained fixed on the ice below, where Cam was preparing to take center stage.

My parents were hockey royalty – Frank Decker, Hall of Fame player and coach, and Diana, longtime presence in hockey charity circles. Their embrace of Cam as a future in-law would only strengthen his new image.

At the same time, a wave of guilt washed over me. I'd dragged my family into this charade. If the truth ever came out, it wouldn't just be my reputation on the line, but theirs as well. The Decker name had always stood for integrity in hockey. What would happen to that legacy if the world discovered their only daughter had orchestrated a fake engagement for a sponsorship deal?

How would they feel when they found out I'd lied to them?

The guilt was squeezing me like a vice.

The opening face-off set the tone immediately: fast, physical, and fierce. Montreal came out aggressive, challenging the Slashers at every turn. Ten minutes in, they drew first blood with a slick wrist shot that sailed past our goaltender Fosse's glove.

The crowd tensed collectively, but I felt a strange calm. This was when Cam was at his best: when challenged, when pushed. I'd seen it enough times to know what was coming.

Sure enough, with just under two minutes left in the first period, Cam intercepted a sloppy pass at center ice. What happened next was pure artistry. He accelerated past one defender, deked around a second, and then – employing the exact correction my father had suggested – cut back sharply to evade the third. The Montreal goalie didn't stand a chance as Cam flicked the puck top shelf, lighting the lamp and bringing the crowd to their feet.

"That's my boy!" my mother shouted, clapping wildly. "Go Cameron!"

I cheered loudly and exchanged a meaningful glance with my father. "Looks like you were right about that adjustment."

My father nodded, clearly impressed. "Quick study. He's implemented it perfectly."

The Redline executives exchanged pleased glances. I maintained my professional composure, but inside, a fierce pride bloomed. The sapphire on my finger caught the light as I applauded, and I noticed Vanessa Cheng's eyes tracking it with interest.

"Quite a stunning ring," she commented during a lull in play. "Unique. Like your relationship, I imagine."

I smiled, running my thumb over the ring's band. "Cam has always had excellent taste."

Next to me, Coco suppressed a smirk. "Lana looks at that ring at least fifty times a day," she added helpfully. "I caught her admiring it in the ladies' room mirror earlier."

I shot her a warning look, but the Redline executives seemed charmed by this particular insight into our relationship.

The second period began with renewed intensity. Montreal, stung by the late equalizer, came out hitting harder, playing with an edge that bordered on dirty. Midway through, their defenseman delivered a vicious cross-check to Zayne's back, sending my brother crashing face-first into the boards.

My mother inhaled sharply, and the crowd roared in outrage as Zayne lay motionless for a heart-stopping moment. I tensed, half-rising from my seat, my professional detachment momentarily forgotten as fear clutched my heart. My mother gripped my father's arm, her knuckles white.

Suddenly Cam was there, dropping his gloves, spinning the Montreal player around to face him. The fight was controlled, precise – not the wild brawl typical of hockey enforcers, but the measured response of a protector. Four quick punches, and it was over.

Cam stood over the fallen player, said something only the ice-level mics could pick up, then skated to the penalty box with dignified fury.

"Now that's a gentleman's fight," my father commented approvingly.

"That's why they call him 'The Hitman,'" James remarked. "Precise. Effective." He glanced at me. "Loyal."

I nodded, watching with relief as Zayne slowly got to his feet, waving off the trainer. My brother skated past the penalty box, exchanging a nod with Cam. An acknowledgment between warriors.

My parents let out a simultaneous sigh of relief.

"He'd do the same for any teammate," I said automatically, the PR director speaking.

"Perhaps," Vanessa replied with a knowing smile. "But one gets the sense there was something personal about that response."

She wasn't wrong. I'd seen Cam defend teammates before, but there was something different about the controlled rage in his movements when he'd seen Zayne go down. It sent a shiver through me that wasn't *entirely* professional – but there was something undeniably sexy about a man willing to pummel a guy to defend someone he cared about. The reaction I felt was primal.

The momentum shifted palpably after that. The Slashers, energized by Cam's defense of Zayne, played with renewed purpose. When Cam emerged from the penalty box, the crowd erupted, and he responded by immediately stealing the puck and setting up a play that led to Logan scoring, putting the Slashers ahead 2-1.

As the second period wound down, Cam struck again. It was a classic Hitman goal, brutal in its efficiency. He muscled past a defender, maintained possession despite a hook that should have been called, and buried the puck with such force that the net rippled violently. 3-1 Slashers.

"Your man is on fire tonight," Coco whispered, nudging me gently. "I wonder what got into him..."

"He's always had the skill," I replied softly. "But he seems... a bit different tonight. More focused."

"Hmmmm...I wonder why," she said with a knowing smile, her eyes dropping pointedly to the ring on my finger.

I found myself unwittingly cataloging every move Cam made on the ice. The power in his stride. The deft handling of the puck. The way his jersey stretched across his shoulders when he leaned into a shot. The intensity of his expression when he battled for position.

It was impossible not to notice the sheer athleticism of his body, the effortless strength that commanded attention.

And it was also becoming increasingly difficult to ignore how that athleticism was affecting me. The professional distance I'd always maintained when watching games was crumbling, replaced by a visceral awareness of Cam as a *man* – powerful, dominating, completely in his element. I crossed my legs, trying to ignore the heat building low in my body each time he executed a particularly impressive play. Or grinned at his teammates. Or, you know, skated around wearing his uniform.

The third period unfolded like a coronation. The Slashers dominated, skating circles around an increasingly frustrated Montreal team. With less than five minutes remaining, it happened – the moment that would soon flood social media and sports highlight reels.

Cam collected the puck behind the Slashers' net, then began an end-to-end rush that defied description. He weaved through defenders as if they were standing still, his speed and control otherworldly. At the blue line, he executed a spin move that left Montreal's star defenseman completely flat-footed. Then, with a single, fluid motion, he flipped the puck into the top corner of the net, completing his hat trick in spectacular fashion.

The arena erupted. Hats rained down onto the ice as the crowd paid tribute to the achievement. The Slashers bench emptied, players piling onto the ice and surrounding Cam in a celebratory huddle.

And then, at the height of the chaos, Cam broke free from his teammates and looked directly up to our box. Past the executives, past the media, his eyes found mine with laser precision. Even from this distance, the intensity of his gaze was palpable. He raised his stick slightly – a subtle, private salute.

"Oh my," my mother whispered beside me. "That was for you, sweetheart."

I felt heat rush to my cheeks as I tried to maintain my composure. Around me, the suite had erupted in applause, the Redline executives looking positively gleeful at their star prospect's performance. But all I could focus on was the lingering sensation of Cam's eyes locked with mine, the wordless communication that had passed between us.

Coco leaned over, speaking low enough that only I could hear. "Nothing fake about that."

I didn't answer. I couldn't. Because she was exactly right.

The final horn sounded with a decisive 5-1 Slashers victory. Zayne had scored an empty net goal in the final seconds, sealing their win with an exclamation point. As the crowd began to disperse and the executives exchanged enthusiastic handshakes, I excused myself to handle the post-game media coordination.

In the bustling corridor outside the locker rooms, I directed traffic – ensuring photographers got their shots, reporters found their assigned positions, and the team's messaging remained consistent. All the while, a steady stream of updates flowed to my phone: social media metrics, press requests, congratulatory messages from league officials.

"Ms. Decker!" A reporter from ESPN waved me over. "Any comment on Murphy's stellar performance tonight? Three goals and a fight – talk about a statement game."

"The team played exceptionally well," I replied, falling back on PR autopilot. "Cam exemplified the Slashers' commitment to each other and to winning hockey games. That's what the organization is all about."

I moved on quickly, not wanting to linger on the subject of Cam any longer than necessary. Through the nearby monitors, I could see the post-game interviews beginning. Logan spoke first, captain's responsibility, praising the team's collective effort. Then Zayne, stoic as ever, discussing defensive adjustments and the physicality of the game.

Finally, Cam took the microphone, still flushed with exertion, hair damp with sweat, his eyes bright with the unique high that comes from complete and total athletic dominance. He fielded standard questions about the hat trick, the fight, and the team's performance. And then:

"Cam, that was possibly your strongest season opener ever. You seem to be playing with a new level of focus this year. What's changed?"

A small, reflective smile crossed his face. The camera lingered on him, capturing every nuance of his expression as he considered his answer.

"I've got someone in my corner this year who's changed everything," he said simply. "Makes me want to be better. Play better. Be worthy of the faith they've put in me."

The reporter pressed, clearly sensing a story. "A new coach? Training regimen?"

Cam just smiled enigmatically. "Some things are private. But they know who they are."

I froze, my heart hammering against my ribs. Around me, staff members exchanged curious glances, looking in my direction with speculative expressions. I kept my face carefully neutral, but inside, emotions crashed like the waves against our seawall.

On the monitor, I saw Zayne approach Cam as the interviews concluded. They stood on the ice, now nearly empty except for a few lingering staff members. The camera caught them in profile from behind: Zayne's intense expression, Cam's earnest response. I couldn't hear what they were saying over the noise in the corridor, but the serious set of both their faces suggested it was significant.

Their conversation appeared deep and meaningful, Cam's hand gesturing occasionally to emphasize a point while Zayne listened intently. After a moment, Zayne's posture seemed to relax slightly. The camera captured them exchanging what appeared to be a meaningful fist bump followed by the typical hockey guy half-hug, both men's expressions hidden from view. Whatever had passed between them clearly held significance.

Before I could ponder it further, my phone buzzed with a text from Cam.

> CAM: Still need to hit the shower. Wait for me? We should leave together – good optics for Redline.

I hesitated, then replied:

> ME: I'll meet you in the box. Don't rush. Told my parents we'd join them for a quick celebration drink with the Redline people. Great game tonight.

I paused, then added:

> ME: Seriously impressive. Hat tricks look good on you.

His response came quickly:

> CAM: Just wait till you see what else looks good on me. Or off me.

I felt heat rise to my cheeks and quickly locked my phone screen as a staff member approached with questions about tomorrow's media availability. *Professional.* I needed to be professional. But the undercurrent of anticipation flowing through me felt anything but.

Forty-five minutes later, I sat at my desk, reviewing post-game media coverage while trying not to obsessively check the time. I'd changed from my formal blazer into a more casual sweater I kept in my office for late nights, smoothed my hair, and touched up my makeup – all while telling myself these actions were unrelated to Cam's imminent arrival.

A soft knock on my door made my pulse jump.

"Come in," I called, feigning absorption in my computer screen.

Cam entered, freshly showered and changed into a tailored smoke gray suit that fit perfectly across his broad shoulders, and everywhere else for that matter. His hair was still damp, curling slightly at the ends, and his face glowed with the lingering effects of athletic triumph. He carried his practice bag over his shoulder, usual sneakers replaced with dress shoes.

"Hey," he said, his voice low and warm. "Sorry to keep you waiting."

I looked up, trying to project casual professionalism. "No problem. Congratulations on the hat trick."

"Thanks." He set his bag down and leaned against my desk, close enough that I could feel the heat of exertion still radiating off of him. "Did the Redline people seem happy?"

"Ecstatic," I confirmed, swiveling slightly in my chair to put minimal distance between us before my body betrayed me. "Your performance tonight couldn't have been better timed. The fight defending Zayne was particularly appreciated: shows your loyalty and team-first mentality."

His expression shifted subtly. "That wasn't for Redline."

Our eyes locked, and the atmosphere in the office seemed to thicken. I swallowed hard.

"Well, it made an impression regardless," I said lightly, breaking eye contact to gather my things. "Ready to go? My parents and the Redline execs are waiting for us."

"Of course." His eyes crinkled at the corners. "Your mom already texted me. Twice."

I groaned. "I *swear* I did not give her your number. She has her ways. I'm sorry. She's a bit... *enthusiastic* about all this."

"I like it," he said simply. "Makes me feel like I belong somewhere."

The candid admission caught me off guard. Before I could respond, he straightened and offered me his hand.

"Shall we, Cupcake Queen? Best to give the lingering media what they want."

I took his hand, trying to ignore how perfectly our fingers interlaced. "Right. For the optics."

His thumb brushed over my knuckles. "Right. The optics."

We walked through the arena corridors hand in hand, nodding to staff members and lingering reporters. The energy between us felt electric, charged with something I couldn't – or wouldn't – name.

Back in the VIP suite, a small celebration was already underway. My parents, the Redline executives, and a few team officials mingled over drinks. My mother beamed when she spotted us, hurrying over to embrace Cam with unabashed enthusiasm.

"Three goals! What a performance!" she exclaimed. "We're so proud of you, Cameron."

I watched as Cam's expression softened, his smile genuine as he accepted her praise. Something gooey tugged at my heart – he wasn't just playing a part anymore. He was soaking in the Decker family warmth like a man who'd been cold for too long. I suddenly realized just how much it meant to him to have my parents there, supporting him. A strange mixture of guilt and tenderness washed over me.

"Couldn't have done it without Frank's advice," he replied, nodding toward my father. "That adjustment made all the difference."

My father clasped Cam's shoulder, his expression pleased. "You implemented it perfectly. Textbook execution."

I watched the interaction with growing awareness. All the things my parents had said about Cam at the beach house were true. He was a generational talent, as my father claimed. He was great with kids, as my mother had observed. He did love fishing with my brother and father. He fit into our family as if he'd always been there.

And my family had fully embraced him, rallying around to support him with the Redline executives. I felt a swell of pride at how easily they'd accepted him, how naturally they treated him as one of our own. This was a Decker first.

James Whitley approached, champagne flute in hand. "Mr. Murphy, spectacular performance tonight. Exactly the kind of presence Redline is looking to associate with."

"Please, call me Cam," he replied easily, his arm sliding around my waist in a gesture that felt both possessive and protective. "And I appreciate your support. I'm looking forward to our meeting on Thursday."

"As are we," Vanessa added, her eyes moving between Cam and me with undisguised interest. "And perhaps Ms. Decker will join us as well?"

I forced a professional smile. "I'll be coordinating the media aspects, of course."

"Of course," she said smoothly. "But we'd also value your perspective as someone... personally invested in Cam's future."

I felt Cam's hand tighten slightly at my waist, "Everything's better when Lana's around."

James agreed, raising his glass. "To tonight's hat trick... and to many more victories ahead."

We all clinked glasses, the moment picture-perfect for our carefully constructed narrative. But as the conversation continued around us, Cam's hand never left my waist, his thumb tracing some unknown pattern against my hip through the fabric of my dress. Each touch sent electricity skittering across my skin, making it increasingly difficult to focus on the business discussion.

My mother sidled up to Cam, linking her arm through his free one and leaning in conspiratorially. "We've got them right where we want them," she whispered, though not quite quietly enough that I couldn't hear.

Cam's surprised laugh was genuine, his eyes crinkling with warmth as he squeezed her hand affectionately. "Diana Decker, master strategist. I'm not surprised."

My mother preened, clearly delighted by his response. "Well, we take care of our own, dear. Always have."

The casual inclusion in "our own" wasn't lost on Cam. I could see it in the way his expression softened, in the subtle straightening of his shoulders. He seemed like he belonged here, with my family, in a way that had nothing to do with our arrangement and everything to do with who he was.

The realization left me breathless.

After about twenty minutes of obligatory socializing, during which Cam's hand found seemingly endless excuses to touch me – my waist, my lower back, my elbow, even a quick brush of his fingers against mine as he handed me a fresh drink – he smoothly made our excuses.

"I hate to cut this short," he said, the perfect blend of apologetic and exhausted athlete, "but it's been a very long day, and we have an early practice tomorrow."

I hate to cut the night short, I thought to myself, *but I can't wait one more second to rip this man's clothes off...*

My mother hugged us both goodbye, whispering something in Cam's ear that made him laugh. My father shook his hand firmly, promising to call with more observations from the game. The Redline executives seemed thoroughly charmed by the entire Decker family dynamic and Cam's place within it.

We made our exit, hand in hand, through the main concourse where a few lingering fans and media personnel snapped photos. Perfect optics indeed.

But once we reached his car in the darkness of the executive parking area, something shifted. The air between us crackled with tension as he unlocked my door, his body close enough that I could feel the heat radiating from him. Our eyes met, and suddenly the last shreds of pretense fell away.

"Lana," he said, my name a low rumble that sent electricity shooting through my body like a downed power line.

Suddenly I was breathless. "Puck Daddy."

He grinned, a slow, predatory smile that made my heart race. He stepped closer, caging me against the car, one hand braced beside my head, the other settling on my hip. His touch was firm, possessive, and sent a jolt of desire through me. "Tell me to stop," he whispered, his face inches from mine. "Tell me this is all just for show."

I couldn't. I didn't want to. Instead, I reached up, my fingers threading through his still-damp hair, and pulled his mouth to mine.

The kiss was explosive, ten long years and the last few weeks of pent-up tension finally breaking. His lips moved against mine with hungry precision, demanding and giving in equal measure. I matched him eagerly, my body arching into his, desperate for more contact. Desperate to feel every part of his body against every part of mine. His hand slid from my hip to the small of my back, pressing me closer until I could feel every hard plane of his athletic body against the soft curves of mine.

"Tell me," he whispered.

"I don't want you to stop," I whispered back. *Ever*, I didn't say. But I was thinking it.

He lifted me effortlessly onto the hood of the car, his hands strong and sure as they supported my weight. I wrapped my legs around him, pulling him closer, desperate to feel every inch of him against me. His hands moved to my thighs, sending shivers of pleasure coursing through me.

"Tell me you want this too," he said, his breath hot on my skin.

I looked into his eyes, seeing the man I'd known for a decade come into sharp focus. The man I'd been trying to deny, trying to push away, for fear of how much he could hurt me. But in that moment, all fear was eclipsed by the sheer, overwhelming need to be with him.

"I want this too," I whispered, my voice shaking with the weight of the admission. "I want you."

His lips curved into a slow smile, one that promised everything I'd been longing for without even realizing it. He leaned in, his mouth finding mine again, this time with a gentleness that was almost reverent. It was as if he was savoring the moment, drawing out every sensation, every whispered promise.

His tongue teased the seam of my lips, and I opened for him, letting him deepen the kiss. He tasted like champagne and desire, a heady combination that made me dizzy with need. My hands roamed over his broad shoulders, down his powerful back, feeling the muscles shift beneath my touch. He growled low in his throat, a sound of pure masculine satisfaction that had me trembling with anticipation.

When we finally broke apart, both breathing hard, his eyes had darkened to the deep blue of a stormy ocean. He looked at me like he wanted to devour me, like I was the only thing that mattered in the world. It was intense, overwhelming. And I couldn't look away.

"My place," he growled, his voice rough with desire. "Now."

My knees buckled.

Chapter 16

The drive from the arena felt eternal, the streets blurring past my window as Cam drove, his hand resting on my leg, his thumb brushing against the hem of my dress, like it was the gate of a castle he was intent on breaching. Each touch sent electricity through my body, rendering me incapable of focusing on anything except the heat of his palm against my thigh and the lingering taste of his lips on mine.

We pulled up to a red light at a deserted intersection, and Cam turned to me, his blue eyes dark with desire. The streetlights cast a soft glow on his face, highlighting the angles of his jaw, the stubble that I desperately wanted to feel against my skin. *Everywhere* on my skin. The car was filled with a charged silence, the air thick with anticipation.

"Lana," he whispered, his voice low and gravelly, sending shivers throughout my body. His gaze locked onto mine, and in that moment, I knew there was no turning back. This wasn't a game, wasn't a charade. This was real, raw, and undeniable. I felt it in every bone in my body and I could see it all over his face.

Without thinking, I reached out, my fingers tangling in his hair, and pulled him towards me. Our lips met in a fiery collision, a desperate clash of need and longing. His mouth moved against mine with an intensity that left me breathless, his tongue teasing my lips, demanding entry. I opened up to him, matching his hunger with my own.

His hands were everywhere, tracing the line of my jaw, sliding down my neck, and resting on my waist. The heat of his touch seared through the fabric of my dress, setting my skin on fire. I grasped at him, moving awkwardly around the center console, desperate to feel every inch of the hard planes of his body against the soft ones of mine.

The world outside the car blurred into insignificance. All that mattered was the feel of his lips on mine, the slide of his hands over my body, the electric current running between us.

"Cam," I whispered against his mouth, my voice shaking with need. The first word of a confession – of everything I'd been too terrified to admit.

He growled low in his throat, the sound vibrating through me, sending a wave of desire crashing through my body. His hands shifted, one sliding up to cup my breast, the other moving to my lower back, pressing me closer. I arched into him, a soft moan escaping my lips as his thumb brushed the thin fabric over the sensitive peak of my nipple. I felt them tighten with want under his fingertip, and my body's reaction to his touch elicited a low groan from Cam, "I..."

The car behind us blared its horn, startling us both.

"Oh shit," Cam said. We burst into laughter as he pulled away, his eyes dark and wild, his breath coming in short, ragged bursts. I knew my own eyes mirrored his, filled with the same raw desire, the same uncontrollable need.

"Home," he said, slamming his foot on the gas. The car roared to life, speeding through the empty streets.

Every touch, every glance was charged with electricity. His fingers sending jolts of pleasure up my leg with every slow, deliberate movement. I wanted more. He wanted more. I leaned over, my lips brushing against the line of his jaw, tasting the salt of his skin, feeling the rough stubble against my sensitive lips. Wanting to feel him everywhere, in every way.

"I've wanted this for so long," he said quietly, eyes fixed on the road. "You have no idea."

But I did. Because I'd wanted it too. I'd been fighting it for years, hiding behind professionalism and old wounds and the fear of being hurt again. Tonight, watching him on the ice, seeing the raw power and skill as he dominated the game, his easy rapport with my family, Coco's spot-on assessment of what I'd been too afraid to admit to even myself – shifted something inside me. The careful walls I'd built to protect my heart had finally crumbled completely.

When we stopped at another light, I leaned over and pressed my lips to the sensitive spot just below his ear. His sharp intake of breath was deeply satisfying.

"Not fair," he growled, his knuckles whitening on the steering wheel. "I'm trying to get us home in one piece."

"Then drive faster," I whispered against his skin.

By the time we pulled into his long, curving driveway, we were both desperate, our bodies shaking with need.

He was out of the car in an instant, opening my door and pulling me into his arms. He closed the door behind me and instantly pressed me against the passenger door, the cool metal against my back contrasting with the heat that radiated from his body. His eyes locked onto mine with an intensity that stole my breath away. It was as if every cell in my body was drawn to him, and I couldn't look away even if I wanted to. His hand slipped from my hip, traveling slowly up my body, tracing a path that left a trail of fire in its wake. When his thumb brushed over my bottom lip, I couldn't help but let out a soft gasp.

Everything about this moment felt magnified – the pounding of my heart, the electricity in the air, the way his fingers lingered on my cheek. It was more than just attraction; it was a desperate, overwhelming need that had been building since the moment we met a decade ago. His other hand pressed against my lower back, pulling me closer until there was no space left between us. I could feel every hard line of his body, every muscle taut with the same urgency that pulsed through me.

Our breaths mingled, each ragged inhale and exhale a testament to the desire we'd been holding back for so long. His eyes, darkened with lust, never left mine as he leaned in closer, his lips hovered just above mine. The anticipation was almost painful, a sweet torture that I both craved and feared. When he finally pressed his lips to mine again, it was explosive – a release of all the pent-up tension that had been simmering between us.

His kiss was demanding, hungry, and I met it with equal fervor. Our bodies pressed together, I couldn't get enough of him – the taste of his lips, the feel of his hands, the urgency in his touch.

Suddenly, he scooped me up in his strong arms and carried me to his front door like I was weightless. Like some insanely sexy warrior throwing me over his shoulder to take me home and ravish me. I wrapped my arms around his neck, feeling the corded muscles beneath his skin.

My heart pounded against my ribs, and I could feel his breath hot on my cheek as he whispered, "I've wanted you for so long." The urgency in his voice sent a shock of desire through me, and I tightened my grip on him, pressing myself against his chest. His lips found mine in a fierce, hungry kiss that promised everything. We couldn't get inside fast enough; the need between us was palpable, a fire that had been smoldering for years was now burning out of control.

His fingers fumbled slightly with the keys – a small, humanizing detail that made my heart squeeze. Cam Murphy, hockey heartthrob and NHL superstar, was *nervous*.

Finally, the lock clicked and he swung the door open wide. We tumbled inside, our bodies entwined, our hearts pounding in sync.

"Baby," he whispered, his voice filled with a reverence that made my heart ache. His hands cupped my face, his thumbs brushing gently over my cheeks. "Tell me you want this. Tell me you want me."

I looked into his eyes, seeing the reflection of my own desire, my own longing. "I want this," I whispered, my voice steady and sure. "I want you, Cam." A thought I'd never admit bubbled up out of nowhere: *I've always wanted you.*

A slow smile spread across his face, and he leaned down, capturing my lips in another searing kiss. "Would you like a drink, or a tour, or a..." he asked, gently setting me down.

"Bed," I whispered breathlessly, my hand still grasping his.

"Or bed," he grinned.

We stumbled up the stairs. We couldn't wait, couldn't slow down. Every touch, every kiss was a claim on the other.

We made our way into Cam's bedroom, a wild, delicious chaos of limbs and laughter. His hands roamed over my body with a desperate hunger, and I responded in kind, my fingers tracing the hard lines of his muscles, feeling the heat of his skin through the fabric of his dress shirt.

Cam's lips found mine again, drawing me in with the heat and urgency between us. I surrendered to the sensation, letting everything else fade away. There was only us, only this moment, only the overwhelming need that pulsed through our bodies.

His hands slipped under the hem of my dress, pushing it up and over my head. I raised my arms, helping him, and then I was bared before him, clad only in my black lace bra and panties. He pulled back slightly, his eyes traveling over my body with such naked appreciation that I felt beautiful, powerful, desired in a way I never had before.

"Beautiful," he murmured, his voice thick with emotion. "You're so fucking beautiful, Lana."

I reached for him, my fingers fumbling awkwardly at the hem of his shirt. He covered my hands with his own, helping me, and then his shirt was gone, tossed aside, leaving him bare-chested and breathtakingly, unattainably gorgeous.

I couldn't help but stare and give a few seconds of reverence for the fact that I was essentially living out the fantasy of thousands, probably hundreds of thousands, of Cam's fans who would gladly pawn all their worldly possessions for a chance to be where I was right now.

And it would be totally worth it.

His torso was a masterpiece of athletic perfection, all defined muscle and golden skin, marred only by the scars and fading bruises that were the badges of his profession.

I reached out, tracing the bruise that bloomed along his ribs – likely from the fight defending Zayne earlier. "Does it hurt?" I asked softly.

His eyes, hooded with desire, held mine. "Not enough to matter," he replied, his voice rough with need.

I leaned forward, pressing my lips to the bruise in a feather-light kiss. His breath hitched, and his hand came up to tangle in my hair.

Cam faced me, his expression suddenly uncertain again. "I've thought about having you here so many times," he admitted softly. "But the reality of you being here with me... it's better than anything I imagined."

The vulnerability in his voice undid me. I stepped forward, placing my hands on his bare chest, feeling his heart thundering beneath my palm. "Show me," I whispered. "Show me what you've imagined."

Suddenly, he grinned like it was Christmas morning. "You asked for it, Cupcake Queen. But just so you know, I have a *vivid* imagination."

"Do you now?" I laughed with flirty anticipation.

He kissed me deeply, hungrily, his hands roaming my body with newfound urgency. I reached for his belt, my fingers fumbling slightly with the buckle. He covered my hand with his own, helping me, his touch warm and strong. As he stepped out of his suit pants, kicking them aside, my breath hitched. His black boxer briefs did little to hide his arousal, which was fine by me. My gaze slid over his body, taking in every chiseled line, every hard muscle. The sight of him, all powerful, masculine perfection, sent a rush of heat through me that rushed straight to my panties, already hot and damp with desire.

Slowly, I let my hands glide up his chest, feeling the ridges of his abs, the firmness of his pecs. His skin was warm under my touch, his heart pounding beneath my palm. I leaned in, pressing a soft kiss to his chest, feeling the warmth of his skin, the heady, pure testosterone scent of him.

His hands found my waist, pulling me closer, his fingers splaying across my lower back. The touch sent a shiver of pleasure through me, my body responding to his like a lens focused on the sun. His lips met mine, our kiss deepening into a dance of urgent need and pent-up desire.

My hands traveled lower, tracing the waistband of his boxer briefs, feeling the curve of his hips. His cock strained against the fabric, thick and hard, a promise of what was to come. A low moan escaped my lips as I imagined him inside me, filling me, claiming me.

I hooked my fingers into the waistband, feeling the heat of his skin against mine. His hands tightened on my waist, his breath ragged against my lips. "You have no idea what you're doing to me, Lana," he whispered.

I looked down at his cock and rolled my eyes dramatically. "Well, I do have *some* idea…"

He laughed, and with a final tug, I pulled his boxer briefs down, revealing him fully. His cock was magnificent – long, thick, and perfectly proportioned. The sight sent a wave of intense desire through me, my muscles clenching in anticipation. I reached out, wrapping my hand around him, feeling the silkiness of his skin, his rock-hard erection, the heat of his arousal.

His breath caught, his hips rocking forward slightly as he pressed into my touch. His eyes found mine again, and there was a raw vulnerability in them that I'd never seen before. It undid something deep inside me, a final barrier crumbling away.

He reached behind me and tenderly unclasped my bra, letting it slip off my shoulders and fall to the floor.

I gasped as the cool night air hit my skin, my body reacting to the sudden exposure. His eyes darkened with desire as he took in the sight of me, his gaze lingering on the swell of my breasts, the curve of my waist.

"You're so beautiful," he whispered, his voice rough with intensity.

I watched the hunger in his gaze as his eyes roamed over my breasts. Cam leaned down and took one nipple into his mouth, swirling his tongue around it until it hardened into a tight peak. I gasped, arching into him, as he moved to the other nipple, giving it the same teasing attention.

I was wet, so wet, and I could feel the moisture pooling between my legs. I wanted him to touch me there, to feel how much I wanted him. As if reading my mind, he trailed his hand down my stomach, his fingers dipping beneath the waistband of my panties.

He groaned when he felt how wet I was, his fingers sliding through my folds, spreading the moisture. "You're so hot, Lana. Is this all for me?" He found my clit and circled it gently, making me gasp and writhe against him. I was so close, so close to the edge.

I moaned my response and he stepped back to take me in, his eyes roaming over every inch of me.

We stood there for a moment, him naked, me nearly naked, the air between us charged with anticipation. Then Cam closed the distance, his hands sliding into my hair, down my back, as he kissed me deeply. The feeling of his skin against mine was electrifying – all heat and strength and barely contained desire.

He walked me backward until my legs hit the edge of the bed, then gently lowered me onto the mattress, following me down. His body covered mine, his weight deliciously heavy, his hardness pressing against my sex. Our breaths mingled, our hearts synced in a rhythm that felt like the pulse of the universe itself. His lips trailed from my mouth to my jaw, then down the column of my throat, each kiss more intoxicating than the last.

"I want you so much," he murmured against my collarbone. "I've dreamed about this... about you... for so long."

His words, the reverence in his touch, made my heart ache. This wasn't just physical attraction. This was something deeper, something that had been building between us for years. Cam's hands and mouth explored my body with exquisite attention, foraging a trail of kisses down my throat, each whisper of contact sending tingles like tiny fireworks inside my body. I arched into him, my body desperate for more, every nerve ending alive and sparking with need. His strong hands roamed my back, pressing me even closer, as if he could fuse us together through sheer force of will.

"Mmmm, Lana" he murmured against my skin, his voice ragged with desire. The sound of my name on his lips was a secret incantation, unlocking depths of longing I hadn't known existed. I couldn't help but let out a soft moan, the primal sound torn from the depths of me.

His mouth found mine again, greedy and insistent. My fingers threaded through his hair, pulling him closer, deeper into the kiss. It was too much and not enough, a clash of sensations that left me reeling. I could taste the salt of his skin, the lingering hint of the champagne we'd shared earlier. It was a heady mix that made me feel drunk on sensation.

His thumb traced the line of my jaw, sending electricity skittering across my skin. I gasped as his teeth grazed my earlobe, a sharp contrast to the gentle sweep of his fingers. My whole body was a symphony of contradictions, each touch pushing me closer to the edge, each moment driving me to crave more.

I reached for his cock, but he gently pushed my hand away. "Lie back," he instructed, "and let me worship you like the goddess you are."

Naked Cam was bossy. And I was absolutely here for it.

I complied, my heart racing as I stretched out beneath him. Cam leaned over me, his eyes locked onto mine as he began to trail kisses down my neck, each touch sending shivers of anticipation through my body. His hands, strong and purposeful, roamed over my skin, making me arch into his touch. When he reached my breasts, he paused, taking a moment to admire them before dipping his head to capture one nipple between his lips.

His tongue was hot and insistent as he teased and swirled around my peaked nipple. The sensation shot directly to my core, making me gasp and writhe beneath him. He moved to the other breast, giving it equal attention, drawing out moan after moan from deep within me as my desire grew more intense.

"It's always been you, Lana," he murmured against my skin, his breath hot and sensuous. "You like that?" he asked as his hands continued their exploration, sliding over my stomach and down to my hips. Lava pooled between my legs, the slick wetness growing as he expertly built the tension within me.

"Yes," I moaned.

He moved down, trailing kisses over every inch of my skin as if it were sacred ground. When he finally reached the apex of my thighs, he paused, looking up at me with a wicked grin. "I want to taste you, I want my mouth all over your beautiful pussy. I want to feel you come on my tongue," he said, his voice low and husky. "Is that what you want too?"

I could only nod, my breath coming in quick, desperate pants. He dipped his head between my legs, his tongue pressing against my panties, already soaked through with the want of him. I gasped, feeling every nerve ending spark with anticipation. Cam's fingers hooked under the delicate black lace, slowly pulling it down, the cool air hitting my skin making me shiver. His breath was hot against my inner thigh, every movement slow, deliberate, sensual. He gently peeled my panties off completely, his eyes never leaving mine, the intensity of his gaze sending shockwaves of desire through me.

I was splayed out for him, fully naked except for the mermaid sapphire ring.

He raised an eyebrow at me. "I love what you're wearing." I was just about to respond with some smartass comment when he dipped his head between my thighs again.

I nearly came undone at the first touch of his tongue against my clit. He licked and sucked, drawing out a cry from me as pleasure coursed through my body. His fingers joined the dance, sliding inside me, curling and stroking in a rhythm that matched the movements of his tongue.

Oh my god.

The sensation was overwhelming, and I found myself gripping the sheets, my hips lifting off the bed as I chased the promise of release. But just as I was about to explode, he pulled back, his mouth moving back to my breasts. I groaned in frustration, my body arching towards him, begging for more.

"Cam, please don't stop. I'm almost..."

He chuckled, the sound muffled against my skin. "Not yet, Cupcake Queen," he whispered, his hands, and more importantly, his tongue, moving back to my nipples, pinching and teasing them until I was a writhing mess of need.

"Cam, please," I begged, my voice ragged with desire. "I need you..."

His tongue flicked at my nipples, driving me wild with anticipation. "Say that again."

"I need you."

"That's more like it," he said, obligingly, slowly moving his mouth back down to my pussy. This time, he took his sweet time, licking and sucking in long, drawn-out strokes that had me clawing at the sheets. He relished that I was on the edge and completely under his control. He bit down gently on my clit, the pleasure-pain sending shockwaves through my body. I felt like I was losing my mind, the heat building and building until I was sure I would combust.

"Please..." I pleaded, every nerve on fire.

And then, finally, he gave me what I was begging for. He slid two fingers back inside me, curling them in just the right way as his mouth worked magic on my clit. The pressure built and built and built until it was too much, and I shattered, my orgasm exploding through me like a supernova. I cried out his name, my body convulsing with the force of my release.

As I came down from the high, Cam moved back up my body, his eyes never leaving mine. He kissed me softly, letting me taste myself on his lips. "I adore you," he whispered, his voice filled with awe and satisfaction. "You're beautiful. A goddess."

"And you're some kind of sex god," I laughed. "Holy smokes." My body still trembled with the aftershocks of my orgasm. I had never felt so completely worshiped, so utterly consumed by pleasure. No one had ever made me feel like he did. Only Cam. Always Cam.

Spent, I nuzzled his neck, slowly making my way to his lips. We snuggled in the afterglow as I panted to catch my breath. Every brief shift or movement hit me with more aftershocks.

"So," I said sweetly. "Can I suck your cock?"

Cam let out a low groan, his eyes darkening with desire. "You have no idea how many of my smuttiest dreams have started with you saying that," he laughed softly, but there was a raw edge to his voice that made my heart beat faster.

I trailed kisses down his chest, exploring every ridge and valley of his muscles with my lips and tongue. His skin was warm and smooth under my touch, the masculine scent of him – sex and salt and fucking unfiltered, Grade A virility – making my head spin. I could feel his heart pounding beneath my fingertips as I kissed down his stomach, tracing the lines of his abs before gripping his cock firmly.

His cock was like granite after someone had left a hot pan on it. It throbbed in my hand, warm to the touch. He inhaled sharply, his hips tightening in response to my touch. I looked up at him, meeting his gaze as I began to stroke him slowly, marveling at the way his body responded to mine. His eyes were hooded, his lips parted, and every muscle in his body seemed to tense with anticipation.

Leaning down, I flicked my tongue against the head of his cock, tasting the salty bead of precome that had gathered there. He let out a strangled groan, his hands fisting the sheets as I took him into my mouth, swirling my tongue around his head before taking him deeper.

His breath came in ragged gasps as I worked him with my mouth and hand, the sounds of his pleasure spurring me on. It seemed impossible, but I could feel him getting even harder, his body coiling with tension as I brought him closer and closer to the edge. His fingers threaded through my hair, guiding me gently, the touch both controlling and tender.

"Fuck, Lana," he growled, his voice rough with need. "You're going to make me come."

I hummed around him, the vibrations making him buck his hips upward. His grip on my hair tightened, and I could feel the pulse of his cock against my tongue. He was so close, his entire body trembling with the effort to hold back.

"Stop," he rasped, gently pulling me away. "I want to be inside you when I come."

I released him with a soft pop, watching as he caught his breath, his chest heaving with each inhale. As I kissed my way back up to his face, he slid an arm under me, reversing our positions in one smooth motion. Suddenly, he was on top of me, his strong body pressing me into the mattress. The weight of him on top of me was absolutely fucking delicious.

Our mouths met in a fierce kiss, the taste of him still lingering on my lips. The taste of me still lingering on his. His hands roamed over my body, caressing every curve and dip, making me gasp with pleasure.

He broke the kiss, trailing his lips down my neck, nipping and sucking at the sensitive skin there. I arched into him, my body aching with desire, every nerve ending alive and sparking with anticipation.

"Please, Cam," I whispered, my voice barely more than a breath.

He looked down at me, his eyes filled with an intensity that stole my breath away. Without a word, he shifted his hips, his cock brushing against my entrance. I ached with need, my body opening up for him, yearning for the connection.

And then he was inside me, filling me completely. I gasped at the sensation, my eyes fluttering closed as waves of pleasure washed over me. He began to move, slow at first, then faster, each thrust sending waves of ecstasy through my body.

"Okay?" he whispered, his control visibly tenuous.

"More than okay," I breathed, wrapping my legs around his waist to draw him deeper. "Don't stop."

What followed was unlike anything I'd experienced before. It wasn't just the physical pleasure – though that was undeniable, Cam's athletic body moving with a precision and strength that left me breathless. It was the connection between us, the way he watched my face as if memorizing every expression, the way he seemed to know exactly what I needed before I did.

Our breaths mingled, our bodies slick with sweat, as we moved together, lost in the rhythm of our lovemaking. Every touch, every kiss, every whispered word felt deeper and more profound than anything I'd ever experienced.

As the pleasure built inside me again, I clung to him, my nails digging into his back, my legs tightening around his waist. When I finally exploded beneath him, crying out his name, he followed soon after, his face buried in my neck, his body tensing as he spilled into me, my name a ragged chant. We clung to each other, our bodies trembling with our release, our breath uneven and raw.

When the world finally came back into focus, I opened my eyes to find Cam looking down at me, a tender smile on his lips. He brushed a strand of hair from my face, his thumb tracing the curve of my cheek.

"I've wanted this for so long," he whispered against my ear, his lips brushing against mine with each word. "*You.* I've wanted *you*. Only you."

The admission was gasoline thrown on kindling. Every part of me ached to be closer to him. I pulled back just enough to meet his gaze, seeing the raw desire in his eyes. There was no pretense now, or carefully crafted images. Just the two of us, stripped bare and exposed in a way that was both terrifying and exhilarating.

We lay entwined, our bodies slick with sweat, our breaths coming in ragged gasps. His hand found mine, his fingers interlacing with mine as if to say, *Here. I have you. I'm not letting go.*

"This is my favorite outfit on you," he teased.

"Oh, naked?" I laughed. "You just want me to run around all day naked as a jaybird?"

"Not *all* day," he teased, bringing my hand to his lips. "You're not naked, you're wearing this." He lightly kissed the sapphire ring before curling my hand and his against his heart.

"Well," I said, "the engagement may be fake, but the orgasms definitely aren't. Cam Murphy, you put the dirty in dirty blond." He laughed, a deep rumbling laugh, and buried his face in my hair.

As we lay tangled together, my head on his chest, I listened to his heartbeat gradually slow. His fingers moved in their usual lazy patterns on my bare back. I felt more content, more at peace, than I could remember feeling in years.

"That was..." I began, then trailed off, unable to find adequate words.

"Yeah," he agreed, pressing a kiss to the top of my head. "It really was." He leaned in, his forehead touching mine, his breath mingling with mine in a dance as intimate as any we'd shared. "I don't want to lose this," he whispered. "I don't want to lose you."

My heart swelled with emotion, the words a balm to the wounds of the past, to the fears that had haunted me for so long. "I don't want to lose you either," I said, my voice barely more than a whisper.

Moonlight bounced off the bay and streamed through the large windows casting long shadows across the decimated bed. For the first time as I looked around the masculine, tastefully decorated suite, I noticed the photos on the walls – not family portraits, but images of Cam and his teammates, snapshots of a life lived on and off the ice. There was a picture of him and Zayne in their college days, arms slung around each other, grinning widely. One of Cam and Coach Rocco goofing around at a charity golf game. Another showed the entire Slashers team celebrating their Stanley Cup win, Cam and Logan front and center, holding the trophy high.

But it was the photo of Cam with my father that caught my eye. It was a candid shot, probably taken during a practice session back at Boston University. My dad was standing on the ice, arms crossed, deep in conversation with Cam and Zayne. The three of them looked so serious, so focused, so... right. Like they belonged together. Like they were family.

The realization hit me like a slapshot. *This* was Cam's family – not blood relations or step-parents, but the team, the players, the coaches. The people who had been there for him, who had supported him, who had made him the man he was today.

We lay in comfortable silence for a while, just breathing together, skin to skin. I traced the tattoo on his ribs – a small, simple design I'd never noticed in team photos.

"What does it mean?" I asked, fingertips outlining the geometric pattern.

He was quiet for a moment. "It's a Norse protection symbol. I got it after my first really bad concussion my rookie year. The doctors weren't sure if I'd play again."

I raised my head to look at him, surprised. "I didn't know it was that serious."

"Not many people did." His fingers continued their gentle exploration of my back. "I was terrified. Hockey was... everything. The thought of losing it..." He shook his head slightly. "Anyway, I got the tattoo as a kind of talisman. Stupid, maybe, but it helped."

"It's not stupid," I said softly, pressing my lips to the symbol. "We all need something to believe in. Also, it's kinda hot."

He laughed as his arms tightened around me. "What do you believe in, Lana?"

The question caught me off guard. "I believe in hard work," I said after a moment. "In family. In the game." I hesitated, then added quietly, "I'm still working on believing in myself sometimes."

He shifted, rolling us so we were face to face on the pillow, his hand coming up to cup my cheek. "You should. You're extraordinary."

The sincerity in his eyes made my throat tight. "Cam..." I kissed him, pouring everything I felt but couldn't yet say into it. He responded immediately, his arms wrapping around me, pulling me flush against him once more.

This time was different – slower, deeper, more deliberate. Where our first encounter had been about finally giving in to years of pent-up desire, this was about connection, about seeing and being seen. His hands mapped my body with reverent attention, his eyes never leaving mine as we moved together.

When we finally lay spent in each other's arms again, the night had deepened around us. Cam pulled the covers over us, tucking me against his side, his arm a comforting weight around my shoulders.

"Stay," he murmured against my hair, his voice thick with approaching sleep. "Stay with me tonight."

I nodded, already drifting off, feeling safer and more content than I had in years. "I'm not going anywhere," I whispered back, meaning it more than he knew.

As sleep claimed me, my last conscious thought was that this, being held in Cam's arms, feeling his heartbeat steady beneath my cheek, felt like coming home. And once again, I allowed myself to hope that maybe, just maybe, I could have this. Have him. For real.

And so we lay there, in the quiet of the night, our bodies tangled together, our hearts beating in sync. The world outside could wait. For now, we were enough. We were everything.

Chapter 17

I blinked slowly, momentarily disoriented by the unfamiliar surroundings – the artful black and white hockey photographs on the wall, the stack of well-worn novels on the nightstand, the surprisingly soft throw blanket tangled around my legs.

Cam's arm draped possessively over my waist, his chest pressed against my back, his steady breathing tickling my neck – and everything from last night came rushing back in tender, delicious waves of memories.

The game. The car. His mouth on mine. His whispered confessions in the darkness.

I smiled into the pillow, a giddy happiness bubbling through me like expensive champagne. We'd finally given in to what had been building between us for weeks – years, really. My body still hummed with the lingering aftermath of his touch, his kisses, the way he'd whispered my name when he'd moved inside me. And the best fucking orgasms, *plural*, of my life.

Like, *call a press conference* amazing...

A brief flash of memory – Cam's face above mine, his eyes locked on mine as we moved together, the reverence in his expression making my heart clench – sent a renewed shiver of pleasure through me.

I shifted slightly to look at him. In sleep, his handsome features appeared younger, more vulnerable, relaxed in a way they rarely were in public. His golden-brown hair was adorably mussed against the white pillowcase, his stubble glinting in the morning light, those unfairly long eyelashes casting shadows on his cheeks. One arm was tucked under his head, the other still wrapped around me, as if he was afraid I might disappear.

And he was mine. At least, I thought he was. We hadn't exactly defined what came next, but after last night – the raw honesty, the intense connection, the way he'd held me afterward – it felt like we'd finally crossed some invisible threshold. We'd moved beyond pretending, beyond old hurts, beyond the carefully constructed boundaries of our fake engagement.

For the first time in longer than I cared to admit, I felt hopeful. Open. Maybe we really could make this work for real. The thought made my heart flutter against my ribs.

My phone buzzed on the nightstand, disrupting the peaceful moment. I gently extricated myself from Cam's arm, careful not to wake him, and reached for it.

It was a text from Marcus, the team's GM:

> MARCUS: Emergency meeting. 9:30 AM. My office. Critical to have all senior management present.

I frowned at the screen, the glow of contentment dimming slightly. It was already 7:45, and I needed to get home to shower and change before heading to the office. Whatever the emergency was, I was not showing up to work in last night's clothes.

For a moment, I contemplated waking Cam. But he'd played his heart out last night: the hat trick, the fight defending Zayne, the intense hours we'd spent tangled together afterward. Pro hockey players needed their recovery time. Besides, he looked so peaceful sleeping.

Instead, I slipped quietly from the bed, gathering my scattered clothes from where they'd been hastily discarded across his bedroom floor. In his bathroom, all gleaming marble and glass, I splashed water on my face and attempted to tame my wild hair, which pretty much screamed "thoroughly ravished." I couldn't help but grin at my reflection. The woman staring back at me looked different somehow; eyes brighter, cheeks flushed, lips slightly swollen from Cam's kisses. And satisfied. Holy shit, that woman looked satisfied.

I looked happy. I looked like a woman who had finally stopped running from what she wanted.

Back in the bedroom, Cam had shifted to his stomach but was still sleeping soundly, the sheet draped low across his hips, revealing the muscled expanse of his back. The sight of him, vulnerable, peaceful, *mine*, made my chest tighten with something that felt... like...love.

I scribbled a quick note on the back of a receipt I found in my purse:

Morning, Hitman. Emergency meeting at the office called me away. Last night was... spectacular. Text me when you wake up. −CQ

I hesitated, then added a small heart before placing it on my pillow where he'd see it when he woke.

Leaning down, I pressed a feather-light kiss to his temple, breathing in the warm scent of him one more time before heading downstairs. His house was tastefully masculine, and surprisingly tidy, with floor-to-ceiling windows that showcased the stunning waterfront view.

I stood in the kitchen as I waited for my Lyft, as my eye spotted something unusual on the kitchen island: a bag of cake flour, sugar, two types of vanilla, piping bags, lavender, and a stack of whimsical cupcake liners.

My ride approached, and I headed outside. As the Lyft pulled away from Cam's Davis Island home, I couldn't stop myself from grinning like a lunatic. Whatever came next, something fundamental had shifted between us. For once, I wasn't overthinking or second-guessing. I was simply letting myself feel the happiness bubbling through me.

And for the first time in ten years, I allowed myself to want Cam Murphy without reservation or fear.

At home, I rushed through my morning routine, showering away the delicious evidence of last night's activities and changing into a sleek magenta blazer and matching pencil skirt – my power suit for whatever emergency awaited. As I applied my makeup, covering the light mark Cam had left on my collarbone, I found myself humming, occasionally breaking into a full smile at the memory of his hands, his mouth, the way he'd looked at me as if I were the only woman in the world.

"You are in such big trouble, Decker," I murmured to my reflection, unable to wipe the smile from my face.

My phone chimed with a text from Coco:

COCO: DETAILS. NOW.

I laughed, typing back:

ME: I plead the fifth.

Her response was immediate:

COCO: Coward. Your car was still in the parking lot when I got to practice at 5:30 this morning, but your office was dark. I

Instagram clip? I frowned, but had no time to investigate. Whatever social media drama was brewing would have to wait. I was already cutting it close for the meeting.

As I slipped on my heels, I caught sight of myself in the full-length mirror. I looked composed, professional, but there was something different in my eyes, a softness I usually kept carefully hidden. I wondered if everyone would be able to tell what had happened just by looking at me. Coco certainly had. There was no hiding from that girl.

The thought didn't panic me like it would have a few weeks ago. Maybe it was time to stop hiding. Maybe what Cam and I had, whatever it was becoming, deserved to be real, publicly *and* privately.

I absently twisted the sapphire ring on my finger, watching how it caught the light. It was funny, it no longer felt like a prop. For once, the future seemed full of hopeful possibilities instead of carefully managed risks.

The Slashers' administrative offices were unusually quiet when I arrived, though I noticed several curious glances from staff members as I made my way through the corridors. A few offered knowing smiles or raised eyebrows, making me wonder if my attempt to look professional and unaffected was failing miserably.

Katie, my assistant, was already at her desk, eyebrows rising with obvious interest as I approached. Her eyes widened slightly as she took in my appearance – perhaps noting the extra care I'd taken with my makeup or the lingering flush on my cheeks.

"Good morning," I said, trying to sound normal, professional. "Any idea what this emergency meeting is about?"

"No idea," she replied, handing me a stack of message slips. "But social media is blowing up. Have you seen it?"

"Seen what?" I asked, distracted by the messages. Three from ESPN, two from Sports Illustrated, and at least a dozen from various other media outlets, all wanting comments or interviews with Cam.

Katie looked surprised. "The clip from after last night's game? It's everywhere." She pulled out her phone, tapping rapidly before handing it to me. "Here."

It was a TMZ Sports post, its headline screaming:

CAM "THE HITMAN" MURPHY DECLARES HIS LOVE: "IT'S ALWAYS BEEN HER"

Below was a video clip that appeared to have been taken from behind Cam and Zayne as they stood on the nearly empty ice after the post-game interviews. The camera angle suggested it was shot by someone on the maintenance crew, capturing what the subjects clearly thought was a private conversation.

My heart hammered against my ribs as I pressed play.

Zayne's face was serious, intense in that particular way I recognized as full protective-brother mode. Though we couldn't hear their exact words over the ambient arena noise, the body language told the story clearly. Zayne pointed at Cam's chest, saying something with clear emotional intensity.

And then Cam – shoulders squared, stance solid – was speaking, his passion evident even from the back angle. The clip had been enhanced with caption overlays:

"I didn't pursue her 10 years ago when we were seniors and she was a junior at BU because of my respect for you and because I love you, man, we're brothers...and I would never risk our friendship...but it's ruined me for anyone else. It's always been her. She's the only one."

The video captured Zayne's surprised expression, then back to Cam, his voice now audible:

"I'm sorry I didn't tell you at the time. I didn't know how."

The clip ended with Zayne's reluctant nod and what appeared to be a grudging hug between the two men.

I stared at the screen, my heart in my throat, heat flooding my face. He'd told Zayne. He'd told him the truth – not just about our past, but about his feelings. After ten years of silence, of respecting Zayne's "hands off my sister" rule, Cam had finally claimed what he wanted.

Me.

I handed the phone back to Katie, trying to compose myself. "I... hadn't seen that."

Her eyes widened with disbelief. "Seriously? It's got like two million views already. TikTok is losing its mind."

"I've been a little preoccupied," I grinned, grateful when my office phone rang, saving me from further explanation.

"I'll bet," she nodded with a knowing smile. "I think I want to be you when I grow up."

I retreated to my office, closing the door behind me. For a moment I just stood there, processing. Cam's words replayed in my mind: *It's always been her. She's the only one.* The genuine emotion in his voice, the way he'd stood up to Zayne. It was everything I hadn't known I needed to hear.

My fingers unconsciously found the sapphire ring, twisting it around my finger.

A knock at my door interrupted my thoughts.

"Lana?" Katie peeked in. "Sorry. They're ready for you in the conference room."

I nodded, smoothing my skirt and squaring my shoulders. Whatever this emergency was, I could handle it. Especially today. Today, I could handle anything.

The conference room fell silent as I entered. Around the polished table sat Marcus Thompson, our general manager; Coach Sully; Coach Rocco; and Ryan Keller, Cam's agent – slick and sharp as always in his tailored suit.

And there, at the far end, was Cam himself.

Wait, what was this?

My stride faltered slightly at the sight of him. He'd clearly just rolled out of bed and he looked Sunday morning sexy in dark gray shorts and a well-worn Regrettes t-shirt. Hot AF. Our eyes met, and for a brief second I saw the same warmth from last night, a flicker of heat that made my pulse quicken before either of us had said a word.

But something was off. His expression was guarded, his posture tense. A flicker of unease ran through me, cooling the warmth that had been building to a crescendo since last night.

"Lana, thanks for joining us," Marcus said, gesturing to an empty chair, conspicuously not next to Cam's. "We've got some developments to discuss."

I took my seat, setting my tablet in front of me like a shield. "What's going on?"

Cam glanced at Ryan, who leaned forward, all business. Ryan's perfectly whitened teeth flashed in a practiced smile.

"First, the good news: Redline has confirmed they're proceeding with Cam's endorsement deal. The signing is set for Thursday as planned."

Everyone around the table clapped and cheered, and relief washed through me. Our plan had worked. Cam would get his multi-million dollar deal, and the Slashers would benefit from the association. Mission accomplished.

"That's excellent," I said, allowing myself a small smile in Cam's direction. He nodded but didn't return the smile, his jaw tight.

The unease in my stomach intensified, a cold weight settling there. *What was going on?*

"However," Ryan continued, his voice taking on the careful cadence of a man delivering complicated news, "there's been another development."

Marcus cleared his throat, leaning forward slightly. "Following last night's performance, the Cup win, the Redline deal, Montreal has expressed serious interest in acquiring Cam in a trade and sign deal. Montreal has presented an offer that is... well, unprecedented."

The room seemed to tilt slightly beneath me. Montreal. One of our biggest rivals, a storied franchise with deep pockets and a rabid fanbase. And they wanted Cam.

I felt the blood drain from my face, my fingers suddenly cold. My mind raced, attempting to process the implications. Cam in Montreal. Cam leaving the Slashers. Leaving St. Pete.

Leaving *me*.

"As you all know," Marcus continued, his tone measured as he avoided looking directly at me, "Cam's contract with us expires at the end of this season. We'd certainly love to keep him, but after winning the Cup last season, we're going to have major challenges with the salary cap next year. This might be the way to solve that problem."

I struggled to maintain my professional composure, my mind spinning with questions. Had Cam known about this last night? As we'd made love for hours, as he'd whispered tender words against my skin, had he already been planning his exit strategy?

The thought made me feel physically ill, a wave of nausea rising in my throat.

"The timing is complex," Ryan continued, oblivious to my internal turmoil. "With the Redline announcement coming Thursday, we need to coordinate how we handle this news. Montreal's eager to start negotiations immediately."

My gaze fixed on Cam, who was studying the table intently, jaw tight, a muscle working in his cheek. He wouldn't look at me.

The meeting continued, details washing over me in a blur. PR strategies. Timing considerations. Team realignment. The potential fan reaction. I nodded in all the right places, made appropriate notes, asked professional questions – all while feeling like I was being waterboarded in my own bathtub.

"Cam's got a no-trade clause in his contract, so obviously he'll need to approve any potential trade," Ryan explained, gesturing expansively. "But I think we all know that the Slashers will never be in as strong a position as you are today to get, well, pretty much anything you want in exchange for Cam. First round draft picks for a decade. A Brinks truck full of cash. The moon."

He chuckled at his own joke. No one joined him.

"And obviously those negotiations are between you and Hughes, Marcus," Ryan continued, unperturbed, "but I think Cam and I can rest assured that Montreal will lay out the red carpet for him and give him the deal of a lifetime. A career-making deal worthy of a superstar talent like the Hitman."

My chest felt tight, making it hard to breathe. Everything I'd worried about from the beginning was coming true. The situation had become too real, too complicated. I'd dropped my defenses, allowed myself to hope, to feel... and now I was facing the same heartbreak all over again. Fucking deja vu.

"Plus," Ryan added helpfully, leaning toward me with a conspiratorial smile, "this lets you two break off your fake engagement earlier than planned – everybody knows long distance relationships never work out. Win-Win!"

"Win-win," I echoed, disconnected.

I felt Cam's eyes on me finally, but I couldn't bring myself to look at him. I focused on my tablet, jotting notes I would never read, my handwriting increasingly shaky.

Coach Sully cleared his throat. "Let's not get ahead of ourselves. No decisions have been made."

"Of course, of course," Ryan backtracked smoothly. "Just laying out all the angles."

As the meeting wound down, I became acutely aware of the sapphire ring on my finger. What had felt like a promise just hours ago now felt like a fucking mockery. I twisted it absently, the weight suddenly uncomfortable.

Marcus turned to me, his expression serious. "Lana, did you know about this?"

The question hung in the air. Five pairs of eyes turned to me, including Cam's – blue and intense, pleading for understanding. The silence stretched, tense and expectant.

I straightened my shoulders, finding my professional mask. "Nope," I said, my voice cool and controlled. "Because I'm his fake fiancée, not his real one."

The words landed like ice, and I saw Cam flinch as if I'd slapped him. Good. Let him feel a fraction of the hurt coursing through me.

And never let it be said that Frank Decker's daughter doesn't know how to deliver a body check.

"Right," Marcus said after an awkward pause, exchanging a quick glance with Coach Sully. "Well, everyone, let's maintain a media blackout on this for at least 48 hours while we figure out next steps. Agreed?"

Murmurs of assent sounded around the table. I gathered my notes with trembling hands, not meeting anyone's eyes, especially not Cam's. I could feel his gaze burning into me, but I refused to look up.

Coach Rocco, who'd been silent throughout the meeting, gave my shoulder a gentle squeeze as he passed behind my chair. A small gesture of solidarity that nearly broke my composure.

"Lana," Marcus added as everyone began to disperse, "we'll need a comprehensive PR strategy for both scenarios: Cam staying or Cam going. Can you have something to me by tomorrow afternoon?"

Professional. I needed to be professional. "Of course."

As quickly as dignity would allow, I exited the conference room, making a beeline for my office. I just needed to be alone, to process, to breathe through the tightness in my chest that threatened to suffocate me.

Once inside, I closed the door and leaned against it, finally allowing my professional mask to slip. The morning's happiness felt like a cruel joke now, a brief glimpse of something I desperately wanted but couldn't have. I blinked rapidly, fighting back tears that burned behind my eyes.

Cam Murphy. *Again*.

I looked down at the sapphire on my finger, the deep blue stone catching the light. Yanking it off, I placed it in the center of my desk, where it gleamed accusingly at me. I never should have agreed to the whole fake fiancée insanity. *What was I even thinking?*

I'd barely had time to collect myself when the door opened again. I hadn't even heard the knock.

Cam stood in the doorway, tension radiating from every line of his body. "Lana," he said quietly, "we need to talk."

"Oh? About what, exactly?" I turned to face him, arms crossed protectively over my chest, using anger as a shield against the hurt threatening to overwhelm me. "Your exciting new future in Montreal? Or the fact that you kept me in the dark while I was making a complete fool of myself?"

He stepped inside, closing the door behind him. "It's not like that. I only found out this morning, literally fifteen minutes before the meeting. Marcus called me as I was about to get into the shower, and Ryan was already in town for last night's opener and the Redline meeting."

"Convenient timing." The bitterness in my voice surprised even me. I moved behind my desk, putting the furniture between us like a barrier.

"I couldn't tell you about it – "

"Because of confidentiality, right?" I laughed, the sound hollow and brittle. "I get it. I'm just the PR director. Just the woman you spent the night with. Just the person who put her entire professional reputation, not to mention my family's legacy, on the line for you. But sure, whatever."

Cam's frustration was evident in the tightness of his shoulders, the set of his jaw. "You know how these things work, Lana. There are protocols, legalities. It's not my decision what gets disclosed when."

"But it is your decision whether to take the offer." The words hung between us, heavy with implication.

His eyes flickered to the ring sitting in the middle of my desk. "I haven't decided anything yet."

"Really?" My voice dripped with skepticism. "Because you know that offer is going to be life-changing money, Cam. The kind of offer players dream about. We faked a freaking engagement for a sneaker deal. Whatever Montreal's offering is going to make that look like peanuts." I paced to the window, needing distance from his presence, from his familiar scent that reminded me of being wrapped in his sheets. Wrapped up in *him*. "And Montreal: what a market to play in. Historic franchise, rabid fanbase, you'll be a media darling." *Thanks to me.*

My throat constricted painfully. "Plus, as Ryan so helpfully pointed out, it gives us the perfect excuse to end our charade. Mission accomplished, no broken engagement fallout, everyone wins."

Except me. I wouldn't win. I'd be left behind again, just like ten years ago.

He took a step toward me, his expression softening. "Lana, please. Can we just talk about what this means for us?"

"Us?" I turned to face him, anger and hurt finally breaking through my professional veneer. "Was there ever really an 'us,' Cam? Or was last night just... what? A pre-goodbye? A big game hook-up? A fantasy before reality sets in?"

"Last night was real," he said, voice low and intense. "Everything I said, everything I felt – it was all real." His eyes flickered again to the center of my desk, where my fake engagement ring now sat.

"Just like ten years ago? When you disappeared without a word?"

The parallel wasn't lost on him. His expression darkened with remembered pain. "That was different. You know why I left then."

"And now there's a new reason to go. Different city, same result." I wrapped my arms tighter around myself, trying to hold the pieces together.

"I haven't decided anything," he repeated, stepping closer. "I need time to think about what I want."

Something inside me snapped. My fear of being left behind *again*, of not being enough – it all crystallized into a vivid, sharp wound. "Well, don't let me factor into your decision. I wouldn't want to stand between hockey's golden boy and his payday."

Hurt flashed across his face, his eyes widening slightly. "That's not fair."

"Fair?" I laughed, the sound too close to a sob. "Was it fair to let me believe in something last night, knowing this bombshell was coming? Was it fair to tell Zayne you've always loved me when you're already considering a future 1500 miles away?"

"I didn't know about the offer when I talked to Zayne!" His voice rose slightly, frustration evident. "And I meant every word I said to him."

For a moment, I wanted to believe him. The raw emotion in his voice, the intensity in his eyes – it was everything I'd seen last night when he'd held me, when he'd whispered my name against my skin. But the timing was too painful, the similarities to our past too obvious.

"I told you, over and over again, to stick to the rules of our fake engagement," I hissed. "Not just for your protection, but for *mine*. But from the second your agent brought up this insane idea, you've been constantly coming at me like some overly-aggressive forechecker. And once again, I fell for your bullshit."

"Lana, wait..." Cam said, devastation in his eyes.

"You should go," I said, turning back to the window, unable to look at him anymore. The view of the practice rink below – where just yesterday I'd watched him skate, where just last night he'd scored that miraculous hat trick before taking me home, blurred through unshed tears. "You have a lot to think about, and I have PR strategies to develop for your imminent departure."

"Lana, please – " His voice caught, a rough edge to it that almost broke my resolve.

"Get out, Cam." My voice cracked slightly. "Just... please go."

The silence stretched between us, taut with emotions. Finally, I heard him move toward the door. I kept my back turned, afraid that if I looked at him, my fragile composure would shatter completely.

"This isn't over," he said quietly from the doorway. "And I'm not walking away this time, Lana. Not unless you tell me that's really what you want."

The door closed behind him with a soft click, leaving me alone with the shattered pieces of what had, just hours ago, felt like a brand new beginning.

I sank into my chair, the veneer of professionalism finally crumbling as tears spilled down my cheeks. My chest ached as if physically bruised, each breath painful. How could I have been so stupid? How could I have let myself believe, even for a moment, that Cam Murphy, *or anyone for that matter*, would ever choose me over hockey?

My gaze fell on the sapphire ring, glittering coldly in the center of my desk. I reached out, touching it with trembling fingers. For a brief twelve hours I'd allowed myself to imagine it was real – that everything whispered in the dark was more than just words.

History, it seemed, was determined to repeat itself. And this time, I had no one to blame but myself.

Chapter 18

I've always prided myself on maintaining control. In crisis management, being the calm in the storm is practically part of my job description. I'm Lana freakin' Decker, youngest PR director in the NHL, daughter of a hockey legend, professional problem solver.

But as I sat at my desk, staring blankly at my computer screen, control felt like a distant memory. My phone wouldn't stop buzzing with notifications, my inbox was overflowing, and my heart – well, that was another disaster entirely.

"Three more requests for comment on Cam potentially going to Montreal," Katie announced, placing a steaming cup of coffee on my desk. She gave me a concerned look. "I told them all 'no comment' for now."

"Good," I managed, grateful that at least my voice sounded steady. "Thank you."

She lingered in the doorway, clearly weighing whether to say something more. "Are you... okay? You seem..."

I pressed my fingertips against my temples, trying to ease the tension headache building there. Images of last night flashed unbidden: Cam's hands in my hair, his lips on my neck, the weight of him above me. The memory only sharpened the contrast with this morning's reality.

"Fine," I answered automatically, smoothing my blazer. "Just a lot happening today."

She shifted her weight, clearly debating whether to push. "You know, if you need anything, or someone to talk to..." She trailed off, the offer hanging in the air between us. "Or I could grab you a cupcake from downstairs? You look like you could use one."

The kindness nearly broke me. I swallowed hard, pressing my fingernails into my palm to maintain control. "Thanks, I really appreciate that. But right now, I need to focus on a strategy memo for Marcus." I gestured to my laptop. "Crazy busy day."

Katie nodded, unconvinced but professional enough not to push. "Well, you should probably know that Cam's confession to Zayne has officially gone supernova online." She pulled out her tablet and turned it to show me. "It's like, everywhere."

I forced myself to look at the screen, where a compilation of fan reactions to the now-infamous video filled the display. People had edited the video of Cam telling Zayne "It's always been her" with romantic music, slow motion, dreamy filters – transforming a private moment into public entertainment.

@HockeyHottiesDaily had posted: *Is anyone else DECEASED over Cam Murphy's declaration about Lana?? "It's always been her" I CANNOT BREATHE*

@Slashrr2232 said: *First rule of hockey, you don't mess with your teammate's sister*

@SlashersFanatic4Ever wrote: *If Montreal steals Cam from St. Pete after THAT video with Zayne, I'm throwing myself into Tampa Bay*

@PuckBunnyQueen's post had over 50,000 likes: *Let me get this straight: We find out Cam Murphy has been secretly pining for ONE woman for YEARS and now he might move to freaking CANADA?!*

And the comments just got worse from there:

OMG imagine being loved like that!! Lana is living everyone's dream!!

Bet Montreal's single ladies are already buying Hitman jerseys

Is it wrong that I kinda ship Cam with Zayne after that hug tho?

I closed my eyes briefly, a wave of nausea washing over me. "Thank you for the update," I said, taking the tablet and placing it face-down on my desk. "Can you hold my calls for the next couple of hours, and reschedule any non-essential meetings for later in the week please? Also, would you please confirm my cat sitter through the weekend? I'll be lucky to go home at all this week."

"Of course," Katie said, still hovering. "A couple more things: Coach Sully wants you at practice this afternoon. *Sports Illustrated* is sending a photographer for the 'Season Expectations' piece."

My stomach dropped so fast I felt momentarily dizzy. Practice. Where Cam would be. Where I'd have to stand on the sidelines, watching him skate in front of the press, pretending nothing had changed. Where everyone would see us together – or notably *not* together – after that viral video of his confession to Zayne.

"Thanks, okay, let's add that to the schedule." I managed, stealthily reaching for the ring from beneath the papers and slipping it back onto my finger. No matter how I felt, I still had a job to do.

"And Ryan Keller called. He said to tell you the Redline signing scheduled for tomorrow is being pushed to next week while they 'monitor the situation.' He'll call with details later."

There was only one explanation after Cam's performance last night: The trade rumors. Shit.

That was the final straw. The Redline deal – the entire reason for this fake engagement charade – was likely now in jeopardy because of the trade rumors. Everything we'd worked for, risked our reputations for, was hanging by a thread. *Fuck.*

After Katie left, I allowed myself exactly thirty seconds of panic. I put my head in my hands and took deep, shuddering breaths. Thirty seconds to feel the full weight of disappointment, betrayal, and heartache. Then I straightened my spine, smoothed my hair, and opened my laptop.

Professional Lana was reporting for duty.

I drafted press statements for every scenario: Cam staying, Cam leaving, the Redline deal proceeding, the Redline deal collapsing. I created talking points for Marcus, for Coach Sully, for the team owner. I worked methodically, efficiently, as if I were handling a crisis for any other player – not the man who had spent last night making love to me.

It felt like writing my own heartbreak into reality, formalizing the end before we'd even truly begun. I started typing anyway, my fingers stiff and reluctant on the keyboard.

If Cam leaves: Position as amicable separation benefiting both parties. Emphasize Cam's legacy with Slashers, focus on exciting new chapter for him. Slashers' best opportunity to become a powerhouse for decades to come. Redline partnership continues regardless of team. Break engagement quietly after announcement, citing long-distance challenges.

The words blurred as I typed them. I blinked hard, my throat tightening again. I forced myself back into PR Director mode. This was my job: to manage public perception, to craft the narratives, to control the story. Even when the story was crushing me.

If Cam stays: Celebrate loyalty to team, position as commitment to bringing another Cup to St. Pete. Emphasize connection to community, teammates. Engagement continues as planned through Redline launch, reassess after...

I stopped typing, cursor hovering. Reassess after what? After the fake engagement had served its purpose? After we'd both gotten what we wanted professionally?

But what about what I wanted personally?

I closed my eyes, remembering how it felt to wake up in his bed this morning, feeling his warmth against my back, his arm draped possessively over my waist. For those few blissful moments, I'd allowed myself to want more... to imagine a future where the ring wasn't just for show, where the loving glances weren't just performance.

The memory stung like salt in an open wound.

My phone vibrated with an incoming text from Cam. The fourth since I kicked him out of my office an hour ago.

CAM: Lana, please. We need to talk.

I turned my phone face down and continued working.

The rink buzzed with activity when I arrived downstairs. Players were already on the ice, running drills under Coach Sully's watchful eye.

The familiar sounds of hockey practice – skates cutting ice, pucks hitting boards, coaches barking instructions – usually centered me. Today, they set my teeth on edge as I stood in the observation area above the rink, pretending to review media schedules for the upcoming road trip while actually avoiding looking at the ice.

At #22, specifically.

Cam was below, going through drills with brutal intensity, his movements more aggressive than usual. Even from this distance, I could see the tightness in his shoulders, the extra force behind each shot. He was playing angry.

Because of me? Because of Montreal? Both?

"Wow, he looks like he's trying to murder the ice," came Coco's voice from beside me.

"Coco!" I startled, not hearing her approach.

She leaned against the railing next to me, watching both the practice below and my expression with equal sharpness. "So, you want to tell me what happened? Because last I checked, you two were sneaking kisses after the game, and now he's trying to shatter the plexiglass with his death stare."

"It's complicated, and I'm not allowed to talk about it," I mumbled, eyes fixed on my tablet. My fingers unconsciously twisted the engagement ring, a new nervous habit I couldn't seem to break.

"Does it begin with 'M' and end with 'ontreal?'"

I sighed, finally looking up at my friend. "There are no secrets in hockey. Yeah, they made us a trade offer. A massive one, apparently."

Coco's eyes widened. "Shit."

"Yep."

"And you found out after..." She trailed off, but her meaning was clear.

I nodded, my throat tight. "Surprise!" I said weakly. "Yeah. This morning."

"Ouch." She winced in sympathy. "But he just found out too, right? That's what Logan said."

"That's what he claims." I couldn't keep the bitterness from my voice. I shrugged, trying for casual and missing by a mile. "I dunno, he wouldn't even look me in the eye during the meeting, which feels suspicious. It doesn't really matter. This was always temporary, right? The so-called engagement has served its purpose – the Redline deal is basically done. Unless the trade rumors kill it."

"You're full of it."

I blinked at her blunt response. "Excuse me?"

"You heard me." Coco crossed her arms, unmoved by my PR director glare. "This stopped being fake weeks ago, and we both know it. The question is, are you going to throw away something real because you're scared?"

"I'm not scared," I protested, my shoulders tensing. "I'm realistic. He's probably going to Montreal, Coco. It's... fine. Just business."

Coco's eyebrow arched elegantly. "I saw you two at the awards show. In the box with your folks. I saw your face when he scored that hat trick. That wasn't just business, Lana."

The memory of last night – watching Cam dominate the ice, the electricity between us afterward, his strong hands on my body, his mouth on mine – threatened to overwhelm me. I dug my nails into my palm, trying to stay present.

"It doesn't matter," I said finally. "Montreal's offering the deal of a lifetime. And why wouldn't he take it? It's an incredible opportunity."

"Has he said he's taking it?" Coco asked.

"He says he hasn't decided," I admitted, smoothing my blazer. "But it's Cam. Hockey is everything to him."

Coco set her water bottle down, leaning forward. "Can I ask you something? And I want an honest answer."

I nodded warily.

"Are you mad that he might leave, or are you mad that history's repeating itself?"

The question hit me like a body check, knocking the air from my lungs. "I – what do you mean?"

"I mean, are you really upset about Montreal, or are you upset because once again, Cam might choose hockey over you? Just like in college?"

I stared at her, speechless for a moment. "Is there a difference?"

"A huge one," she said gently. "One's about circumstances. The other's about your worth."

The insight hit uncomfortably close to home. I twisted the ring on my finger, feeling exposed. "Maybe both," I admitted quietly. "I just... I opened up to him. I let myself believe we could have something real. And then, not even twelve hours later, I get ambushed in a meeting and find out he's considering moving across the continent."

"Did he know about the offer when you were together last night?" Coco asked.

"He says he didn't."

"And you don't believe him?"

I hesitated. Below us, Cam took a shot that went wide of the net, something he rarely did. Coach Sully shouted something, and Cam nodded sharply, his movements stiff with frustration.

"I want to," I said finally. "But the timing..." I trailed off. "I don't know. It feels like the universe is playing some cosmic joke on me. Like the second I let myself be vulnerable, everything falls apart."

Coco reached over and squeezed my shoulder. "Look, I don't know exactly what happened between you two last night, but whatever it was? It wasn't fake. He risked your brother's wrath by declaring his love for you. And we both know how that could have gone."

I thought about Cam's words from our confrontation earlier: *Last night was real. Everything I said, everything I felt – it was all real.* I wanted to believe him. Wanted it more than I'd allowed myself to want anything in years.

"Even if that's true," I said slowly, "it doesn't change the reality. He has a career-making opportunity. I have my job here. The timing is all wrong – yet again."

"Or maybe the timing is exactly right. Maybe this is your chance to break the pattern. To choose each other despite the circumstances."

"I can't go to Montreal. I'm the youngest PR Director in the league, one of only a handful of women to ever hold the job. Jack Donnelly has been in my position for fifteen years in Montreal, and plans to be buried below his desk so he can still run comms after he dies." I tried to laugh, but it came out hollow. "Besides, I can't ask Cam to give up an opportunity like this for me."

"Have you asked him what he wants?" Coco challenged.

"Not in so many words," I admitted. "But – "

"But you assumed," she finished. "Just like you've been assuming all along that what was between you wasn't real."

The observation stung. "I'm being realistic."

Coco laughed, the sound warm but exasperated. "Realistic? Lana, you've been in love with this man for ten years. There's nothing realistic about any of this. It's messy and complicated and painful – but that doesn't mean it's not real."

I opened my mouth to protest, but the words stuck in my throat. Had I? Been in love with him all this time?

My emotions hit me with such force that I had to grip the railing. All those years of keeping my distance, of telling myself I was over him – and here I was, still falling apart at the thought of losing him. Again.

Coco's expression softened. "Talk to him. Listen to him. Give him a chance to tell you what *he* wants before you decide it's not you."

I turned to face her, not bothering to hide the tears that had gathered in my eyes. "I don't know if I can. What if I open up and he still leaves? Or what if he stays and then resents me later because he turned down the opportunity of a lifetime?"

She wrapped an arm around my shoulders. "I know it's scary. But for what it's worth? That man is crazy about you. And I think you're crazy about him too."

"It's not that simple," I whispered.

"It never is," she agreed. "But sometimes, the messy, hard, complicated stuff? That's the stuff worth fighting for."

She hugged me tightly and I sank into her embrace, letting her comfort me as the walls I'd so carefully constructed around my heart continued to crumble, leaving me more exposed than I'd allowed myself in years.

I just didn't know if I had any fight left in me.

Before I could respond, my phone buzzed with a text from Marcus.

> MARCUS: Need statement for Redline delay ASAP. Meet now?

> ME: On my way.

"I have to go," I said, grateful for the excuse. "Media stuff."

I pulled away, my professional mask firmly in place like armor. Coco gave me a look that said she knew exactly what I was doing, but she didn't call me out. Instead, she squeezed my arm again.

"Just... don't make any decisions you can't take back, okay?"

The *Sports Illustrated* photographers arrived twenty minutes later, setting up along the glass, checking angles and light.

I nodded to them, keeping my expression neutral as I scanned the ice. The players had transitioned to scrimmage, and I couldn't help but notice that Logan kept putting himself between Cam and the other players, as if he was worried about what Cam might do. I'd never seen him play with such reckless aggression before.

"Miss Decker," one of the photographers called, breaking my trance, "where would you like us to set up for the team photo later?"

I forced my attention away from the ice. "The center logo would be best. I'll coordinate with Coach when they're done with drills."

As I spoke, I felt eyes on me. Looking up, I caught Cam watching me from the ice, his helmet under his arm, sweat glistening on his forehead. Our gazes locked for a moment, something unreadable passing across his face before I deliberately turned away, focusing on my tablet and pretending to check something important.

My heart hammered painfully against my ribs. This was ridiculous. I'd spent years maintaining professional distance from Cam. I could certainly do it again now. *While simultaneously pretending to be engaged to him.* Sure. Not a problem.

"Everything good?" Logan skated over to the boards near me, his captain's jersey standing out against the practice jerseys of the other players. His expression was carefully neutral, but his eyes, dark and perceptive, showed concern.

"Perfectly fine," I answered briskly, not meeting his gaze. "Looking forward to seeing the SI feature."

Logan glanced over his shoulder to where Cam was now taking shots on goal, his slap shots noticeably harder than usual. One ricocheted off the post with a metal clang that made several people jump. "Uh-huh," he said, unconvinced. "You know, if you two need to talk..."

"We don't," I cut him off, more sharply than I'd intended. I softened my tone. "It's being handled professionally."

Logan raised an eyebrow, leaning against the boards. "Professionally, huh? Is that why Cam just about took Blackwood's head off with that shot?" He leaned closer, lowering his voice. "Look, I don't know exactly what happened, but I know that look on your face."

"What look?" I asked defensively, straightening the collar of my blazer.

"The one that says you're five seconds from either crying or punching someone, but you're too professional to do either."

I blinked, surprised at his perception. "I'm fine, Logan."

He sighed. "You know, sometimes I think you and Cam are more alike than either of you realizes. Both of you put the team first, even when it's killing you inside."

The observation hit uncomfortably close to home. Before I could respond, Coach Sully blew his whistle, calling the players together. Logan gave me one last significant look before skating away.

I spent the next hour directing the photo shoot, positioning players, suggesting angles, all while maintaining a careful buffer zone between myself and Cam. If the photographers noticed the awkwardness, they didn't mention it. I felt Cam's eyes on me several times, but I refused to meet his gaze directly, focusing instead on my tablet or on other players.

When I had to speak to him, I kept my tone professionally detached. "Cam, can you move to the left a bit? We need to balance the shot."

He complied silently, his jaw tight. When his arm brushed against mine as he moved past me later, I stepped back as if burned, pretending to check something on my phone. The hurt that flashed across his face was quickly masked, but I caught it. It twisted in my chest like a knife.

Professional to the core, that was me. That was Cam.

After practice, I was gathering my things when a shadow fell across the bench where I'd been sitting.

"You're avoiding him," Zayne said, not a question but a statement. His practice jersey was dark with sweat, his hair damp beneath his backwards cap.

I looked at my brother, his dark eyes serious. "I'm working."

"Bullshit," he said quietly, sitting beside me. "I saw your face during the shoot. And I know Cam. Something happened."

"It's nothing," I said, standing to face him. "Just the reality of business."

Zayne studied me, his expression softening slightly. "Lana, if he hurt you – "

"He didn't," I interrupted, then corrected myself. "At least, not intentionally. It's complicated."

"Try me."

I glanced around, making sure we were alone. The last of the photographers were packing up their gear at the far end of the rink, and most of the players had headed to the locker room.

"We... got closer over the weekend," I admitted, my voice shaky. "I let myself believe maybe... and then I saw that clip where he told you... anyway, it doesn't matter now. There's an offer from Montreal, and – " I stopped, my voice cracking.

"And you think he's choosing hockey over you," Zayne finished, understanding dawning in his eyes.

The words stung with their accuracy. "This isn't college anymore. This is his career, his future. Probably a chance to be the highest-paid left wing in the league. And I would never ask him to give that up."

"Have you asked him what he wants?" Zayne challenged. "Because from what I can see, the guy's been a mess all through practice. Nearly knocked Logan flat with a cross-check during scrimmage. Broke a stick slamming it against the boards. That's not Cam being focused on a big career move – that's Cam when he's upset."

I twisted the sapphire ring on my finger, the reminder uncomfortable. "It doesn't matter what he wants," I said quietly. "Or what I want. The circumstances haven't changed. Hockey comes first. It always has."

Zayne sighed, looking suddenly tired. "You know, for someone so smart about everything else, you can be really dense about this. For what it's worth, and I can't believe I'm saying this, but... Cam isn't the same guy he was ten years ago. Maybe you should talk to him, Lana. Actually listen to what he has to say."

"I will," I lied. "When things settle down."

Zayne clearly didn't believe me, but he didn't push. Instead, he squeezed my shoulder gently and walked away, leaving me alone with thoughts I didn't want to face and a heart that felt too heavy for my chest.

By evening, I was emotionally exhausted but couldn't stop myself from scrolling through social media in my condo, a glass of wine in hand and my cats, Sid and Mario, purring beside me. The online frenzy had only intensified throughout the day.

Social media's trending topics included #HitmanHeartbreak, #MurphyMovingOn, and, most painfully, #LanaDeservesBetter.

Fan accounts had gone into overdrive analyzing every public interaction Cam and I had ever had. Someone had even created a montage set to James Arthur's *Say You Won't Let Go* that showed Cam looking at me at various events throughout the years, culminating with his declaration to Zayne.

But it was the Montreal speculation that truly twisted the knife:

Montreal ladies, prepare yourselves! The Hitman might be headed your way!

Who else is booking flights to Montreal for next season?

Poor Lana. Imagine finding your soulmate just to watch him move to another country...

And the worst: *Breaking: Sources say Cam Murphy already looking at penthouses in Montreal's Golden Square Mile. Moving on FAST.*

I knew I shouldn't believe anonymous "sources," but even the thought of Cam house-hunting in Montreal made me physically ill. I set my phone down and pulled Sid closer, burying my face in his orange fur.

"What am I going to do?" I whispered.

The answer, of course, was what I always did: my job. I would maintain my professionalism, help the team navigate this transition, and protect my heart by retreating behind my carefully constructed walls.

Team first. It was the only way I knew to survive.

The next morning, I was headed to a staff meeting when Cam appeared in the hallway, clearly waiting for me. My heart did that stupid lurch it always did at the sight of him, even now. He looked exhausted, dark circles under his eyes, his usual effortless charm replaced by tense determination.

"Lana," he said, moving like lightning to intercept me. "Got a minute?"

Every instinct screamed at me to flee, but there were too many people around. Running would create a scene, and if there was one thing Frank Decker's daughter didn't do, it was create public scenes.

"I'm on my way to a meeting," I said stiffly.

"It'll only take a minute." His blue eyes were pleading. "Please."

I glanced at my watch, then gave a short nod. "One minute."

He guided me a few steps away from the main traffic flow, his hand hovering near but not touching my elbow. Once we were relatively private, he took a deep breath.

"I haven't decided anything yet," he said quietly.

I maintained my professional mask with effort. "Whatever you decide, the team will support you, Cam. We all want what's best for your career."

Frustration flashed across his face. "That's not what I'm asking and you know it."

"Then what are you asking?" I kept my voice low, controlled.

"I'm asking if it matters to you what I decide." His eyes searched mine. "I'm asking if *we* matter to you."

The question pierced straight through my defenses, but I couldn't, *wouldn't*, let him see. "What matters is that you make the right choice for yourself."

"Goddammit, Lana," he muttered. "Can you stop being the PR Director for five seconds and just talk to me like a person? The real you?"

His intensity was drawing curious glances from passing staffers. I forced a pleasant, meaningless smile. "This isn't the time or place, Cam."

Before he could respond, I spotted an empty conference room. "In there," I said, nodding toward it.

Once inside with the door closed, I turned to face him, arms crossed protectively over my chest. "*What*? What do you want from me, Cam?"

"I want you to talk to me! I've been trying for two days!" His controlled frustration finally erupted. "You won't answer my calls, my texts – it's like the other night never happened."

"We slept together. It happens." I shrugged, the casual gesture costing me dearly. "It doesn't change anything."

"That's a load of crap," he said, echoing Coco's assessment from yesterday. "It changed everything and you know it."

I looked away, unable to meet the raw emotion in his eyes. "Maybe for you."

"Look me in the eye and tell me it meant nothing to you," he challenged, stepping closer. "Tell me you didn't feel what I felt."

My heart hammered painfully against my ribs. "What does it matter what I felt? You're leaving."

"I haven't decided that!"

"But you're considering it," I countered, finally letting some of my hurt show. "Which means you could go. Again. Just like before."

Understanding dawned in his eyes. "So this isn't about Montreal. This is about college."

I said nothing, my silence confirmation enough.

"Lana," he said softly, reaching for me. I stepped back. "That was different. I explained that already. I left because... "

"You didn't explain anything," I interrupted, my voice rising despite my efforts to control it. "You disappeared. And now there's another chance to leave. Different city, same result."

He took a step toward me, his expression a mixture of frustration and determination. "I'm trying to figure things out! But I can't do that if you won't even talk to me."

"What is there to talk about? This is an amazing opportunity. You should take it."

"What if I don't want to?" His voice dropped, heavy with meaning. "What if what I want is right here?"

The hope that flared in my chest was dangerous, painful. I smothered it immediately. "Don't."

"Don't what?"

"Don't make promises you won't keep."

He stepped closer again, close enough that I could feel the heat of his body, smell the faint traces of his cologne. "I'm not promising anything except that I want to figure this out. Together. If it's what you want too."

I could feel my resolve crumbling under the intensity of his gaze, the sincerity in his voice. It would be so easy to give in, to believe him, to let myself hope. But hope was dangerous. Hope could destroy me when he inevitably left.

"Do you want this to be real?" he asked, his voice barely above a whisper. "Us. Do you want us to be real?"

The question hung between us, loaded with possibility and terror. My heart screamed *YES*, but my self-preservation instinct kicked in hard. My fingers clutched at the engagement ring, twisting it anxiously.

"You don't get to ask that," I said, my voice brittle with unshed tears. "Not now. Not when you're this close to walking away again."

Pain flashed across his face, quickly followed by determination. "I'm not walking away, Lana. You're the one putting up walls."

"Because they're necessary!"

"No, they're not. They're just easier than taking a big shot." His voice softened. "I know you're scared. I am too. But what we have, what we *could* have – isn't it worth the risk?"

For one breathless moment, I wavered. The sincerity in his eyes, the warmth in his voice – it would be so easy to believe him.

But the memory of waking up alone ten years ago, of the humiliation and heartbreak that followed, was too powerful. And now everyone – the team, the fans, the media – would have front-row seats to my potential devastation.

"I can't," I whispered. "I can't do this. Not with you, Cam. I'm sorry."

Before he could respond, before I could change my mind, I walked out, leaving him standing alone in the conference room. Each step away from him felt like walking through quicksand, but I forced myself to keep moving.

I had survived Cam Murphy once before. I could do it again.

I had to.

Chapter 19

I arrived at the office earlier than usual, slipping through the quiet hallways like a ghost. The morning sun cast long shadows through the windows, illuminating dust particles dancing in the pale golden light. Most of the building was still dark, the familiar hum of fluorescent lights and ringing phones not yet filling the space.

Perfect. I could barricade myself in my office, bury myself in work, and maybe – just maybe – find a way to navigate this mess without completely falling apart. The dull throb of a tension headache had already settled behind my eyes, a physical manifestation of the emotional storm I was trying desperately to contain.

I rounded the corner to my office and stopped dead. Cam was already there, leaning against my door frame, arms crossed over his chest. The sight of him made my stomach drop. He looked as though he hadn't slept much either – dark circles under his eyes, hair slightly disheveled. Despite everything, he still managed to look unfairly handsome in worn jeans and a faded Nirvana t-shirt that stretched across his shoulders.

"Morning," he said quietly, his voice low and rough in the silent hallway.

I inhaled sharply, the scent of his familiar cologne making my heart clench painfully. I straightened my shoulders and walked past him, keys jingling as I unlocked my door. "I have nothing more to say to you, Cam."

"That's fine. You can listen."

I dropped my bag on my desk with more force than necessary, irritation flaring hot beneath my skin. "I have work to do. Important work that doesn't involve facilitating your career move to Montreal."

He followed me into the office, shutting the door behind him. The soft click of the latch felt oddly final, sealing us into our own private battlefield.

"I told you, I haven't decided about Montreal."

"And I told you, it doesn't matter." I busied myself with my laptop, the screen a blue shield between us. "We had a deal. The Redline contract is happening. Mission accomplished. You don't need me anymore."

"This isn't about Redline." His voice was low, insistent, almost desperate. "Lana, would you please just look at me?"

My fingers stilled on the keyboard. I could feel his eyes on me, a physical weight I couldn't ignore. Reluctantly, I raised my gaze to his. The raw emotion I saw there nearly undid me – pain, regret, longing.

"I need to explain something," he said. "About before. About us."

"There is no 'us,' Cam." My throat felt tight, the words sticking like sandpaper.

"There could be."

The words hung in the air between us, loaded with possibility and danger. Coffee from the break room drifted through the office, mingling with the scent of my floral perfume and his woody cologne – an unwelcome reminder of other mornings, other conversations.

"I can't do this right now." I pulled my gaze away, focusing on arranging items on my desk with meticulous precision. Pens aligned. Notepad squared. Control what you can control, Lana.

"When, then?" he pressed, taking a step closer. "Tonight? Tomorrow? Next week when I might be forced to make a decision about Montreal? When exactly are you planning to stop running from this?"

"I'm not running," I snapped, finally looking up at him again. "I'm being realistic. You run, remember? That's your thing."

His expression hardened, jaw tightening. "That's not fair."

"Isn't it? You've done it before."

Cam took a deep breath, visibly trying to maintain his composure. His hands flexed at his sides, a gesture I recognized from our days working together – he was fighting for control.

"That's exactly what I need to explain," he said more softly. "About that night. Ten years ago."

My heart stopped cold for a moment, then resumed at double speed, thudding so hard I was certain he could hear it. *Was this what a heart attack felt like?* I'd spent so many years trying not to think about that night, trying not to wonder what had gone wrong, what I'd done to make him leave without a word.

"Ancient history," I said dismissively, though my voice betrayed me with a slight tremor.

"Is it?" He stepped closer, his eyes searching mine. "Because I think it's still between us. I think it's always been between us."

I crossed my arms over my chest, creating a physical barrier between us. "What do you want from me, Cam?"

"I want you to stop pretending." His voice was low but intense, vibrating with emotion. "I want you to admit that what happened between us, what's happening between us now, is *real*."

"You don't get to decide what's real for me." My fingernails dug crescents into my palms.

"Fine." His jaw tightened. "Then tell me this: Do *you* want this to be real?"

The question struck me like a physical blow, making me step back until my legs hit the edge of my desk. Did I? Did I want to risk my heart, my career, my carefully constructed life for something that could disappear at any moment? For someone who had already left me once before?

"You don't get to ask that," I whispered, my voice catching. "Not now. Not when you're still considering leaving."

"Lana," he said quietly, "I think it's time I told you the truth about what happened that night."

And just like that, my mind catapulted back a decade, the present office fading as memories washed over me – the scent of falling snow, the taste of cheap beer, the feeling of finally being seen...

"When I realized who you were..."

"Zayne's sister," I said flatly.

He nodded, shoulders slumping slightly. "Zayne was my teammate, my best friend. One of my only real friends. And he had this one absolute rule... "

"Stay away from his sister," I finished, a dull ache spreading through my chest.

"Not just stay away. He made it clear to everyone on the team that if anyone so much as looked at you, we'd regret it." Cam's face darkened with the memory. "His exact words to a teammate who commented on seeing you at a game were 'My sister comes before hockey, and I will end anyone who touches her.' The guy had a black eye for a week. And I'm like 90% sure Zayne gave him a midweek refresher."

I remembered that incident. Zayne came home with bruised knuckles, refusing to tell me why he'd fought with his teammate. I'd been embarrassed and annoyed at his overprotectiveness, but I hadn't realized the extent of his threats.

"So what?" I challenged, a spark of anger cutting through the hurt. "You were afraid of my brother?"

"It wasn't that simple." Cam's voice was strained, his eyes pleading for understanding. "The team was... everything to me then. I told you my family was a disaster – my dad was on his fourth wife, my mom on her third husband, everyone too busy with their new lives and step-kids to care about mine. Hockey was all I had. Those guys were my brothers. My only *real* family."

Understanding began to dawn, unwelcome and painful. "And Zayne was part of that family," I said slowly.

"I don't know if I ever told you how alone I felt. For most of my life. He was my closest friend on the team, the closest thing I'd ever had to a brother. I couldn't..." He broke off, swallowing hard, "...I couldn't risk losing that. Not when my own family had shown me over and over that love doesn't last, that people leave when something better comes along. But teammates... teammates always have your back."

The pieces were finally falling into place. All these years, I'd thought he'd left because I wasn't enough: not pretty enough, not experienced enough, not interesting enough. But the truth was both better and worse: he'd left because of who I was. Because I was a Decker.

"You chose him," I said, the realization hitting me like a physical blow. "You chose my brother over me."

"I made the wrong choice," Cam said quietly, his voice thick with regret. "I know that now. I knew it then, too, if I'm being honest. But I was twenty-one and terrified of losing the only real family I'd ever known."

"So you just... what? Decided to pretend I didn't exist? That nothing had happened between us?"

"I thought it would be easier that way. A clean break." He stepped toward me, then stopped himself. "I told myself you'd forget about me, move on to someone who deserved you. Someone who wasn't breaking his best friend's trust." His voice cracked slightly. "I told myself I was doing the right thing, the honorable thing. But the truth is, I was a coward."

I stood frozen, struggling to process everything. Ten years of wondering, of hurt, of doubting myself – all because my brother had been too protective and Cam had been too afraid of losing his surrogate family to fight for what we *might* have had.

The office suddenly felt too small, too confined for the magnitude of emotions crashing through me. I moved to the window, needing space, air, distance to think.

"When I got drafted to the Slashers, and I found out you worked there – as the PR director, no less – I thought fate was playing some cosmic joke on me," Cam continued, his voice low. "I'd spent years trying to forget you, and suddenly you were there, every day. Beautiful, brilliant, and still completely off-limits."

"So you just continued pretending nothing had happened between us? For years?" I turned back to face him, incredulity sharpening my voice.

"What choice did I have?" he asked, frustration evident. "Zayne was still my teammate, still my best friend. And you clearly hated me. I figured you'd moved on long ago."

"I didn't hate you," I said quietly, wrapping my arms around myself. "I was confused. Hurt. You made me feel like I'd imagined everything between us."

My voice caught, and I turned away again, unable to face him as years of buried emotions threatened to overwhelm me. "Do you have any idea what that did to me? I was twenty years old. I thought I'd found something special with someone who actually saw me – not as Zayne's sister or Frank Decker's daughter, just... me. And then you were gone."

"Lana, I – "

"No." I held up a hand, silencing him. "Let me finish. After that night, I questioned everything. My judgment, my worth, what I could possibly offer someone. I convinced myself it was all in my head, that connection we had. And now you're telling me it was real? That you felt it too? But you threw it away because of some... what? Hockey bro code with my brother?" The second I said it, I knew it was cruel and unfair. Loyalty to my brother was not something I should be angry about. Ever. "Sorry, I didn't mean that. I'm...*hurt*."

Cam's face was etched with remorse. "It wasn't just some code. Zayne was like the only stable thing in my life. The BU team was the closest thing to a real family I'd ever had."

"And I wasn't worth fighting for. You barely knew me." The words escaped before I could stop them, raw and honest, coming straight from that wounded place I'd carried for a decade.

"You were worth everything," he said quietly, his blue eyes bright with emotion. "I just didn't realize what I'd given up until it was too late."

We stood there, the weight of a decade of misunderstandings and missed opportunities between us. The office was silent except for the distant hum of the air conditioning and the sound of our uneven breathing.

"When we started this whole engagement scenario," Cam continued, taking a cautious step toward me, "I thought maybe it was a second chance. A way to be near you, to finally show you who I really am. What you've always meant to me."

"And then Montreal happened," I said flatly.

He nodded, running a hand through his hair again. "The timing is... I know how it looks. But I swear to you, I didn't know about the offer when we were together the other night. Everything that happened between us was real, Lana. It's always been real for me."

I wanted to believe him. Part of me did. But another part, the part that had been protecting my heart for ten years, couldn't silence the voice whispering that history was repeating itself. That once again, when faced with a choice, Cam would leave.

"Even if that's true," I said, my voice steadier than I felt, "it doesn't change anything. You left once because hockey and my brother were more important than me, and honestly, I *completely* understand where you were coming from. And now you have an opportunity in Montreal that any player would kill for. It's just the fact that I understand *why* you made the decision you did, won't make it hurt any less for me if you leave." I met his eyes directly. "Tell me honestly, Cam. Can you look me in the eye and say you won't take it?"

He hesitated – just for a moment, but it was enough.

"That's what I thought," I said quietly.

"It's not that simple," he argued, desperation edging into his voice. "This is my career, my future. But that doesn't mean I don't want you in it."

"As what, exactly? The girlfriend waiting at home while you play in another country? The ex-fiancée who made a noble sacrifice for your career?" My laugh was bitter, brittle. "No thanks." I crossed my arms protectively. "I won't be second choice again, Cam."

"You were never second choice." His voice rose slightly, frustration evident. "Don't you get it? I've been in love with you for ten years. Ten years, Lana. Through girlfriends who never measured up, through seeing you every day at work, through forcing myself to keep my distance because I thought that's what you wanted."

The word "love" hit me like a physical blow, making my knees weak.

"That's not fair," I whispered, my voice barely audible. "You can't say that now. Not when everything's falling apart."

He stepped toward me, closing the distance between us. "When should I say it, then? When is the right time? Because I've been holding it back for a decade, and all it's done is cost us both."

There was something in his eyes, a raw vulnerability I'd only glimpsed in our most intimate moments. It made my chest ache with a longing so profound I could barely breathe.

"I told Zayne how I felt about you," he continued quietly. "I told him you're the only one. That it's always been you. I was ready to risk our friendship, his anger – everything – because I couldn't bear losing you again."

"And then Montreal called." I couldn't keep the bitterness from my voice.

His expression tightened. "Yes. Then Montreal called. With a trade deal that will probably set me up for life. But that doesn't change how I feel about you." He hesitated, then added softly, "And what if the Slashers are just another stepfamily that doesn't really want me? What if I give up everything for them, for this team, and they trade me anyway somewhere worse next year?"

The vulnerability in his admission made my heart twist. I understood his fear all too well – the fear of never truly belonging, of rejection.

I laughed, but there was no humor in it. "It doesn't have to change how you feel. That's the point, Cam. Your feelings didn't change ten years ago either, did they? You still left."

"I was a kid then!" His control finally snapped. "I made the wrong choice, and I've paid for it every day since."

"And what's your excuse now?" I challenged, angry tears threatening to spill. "We're not kids anymore. This is real life. Real choices. And once again, when it comes down to it, I'm not enough to make you stay."

He reached for me, but I stepped back, maintaining the distance between us. I couldn't let him touch me. If he did, if I felt the warmth of his hands, I might crumble completely.

"That's not fair," he said, voice tight with emotion. "I haven't made any decision about Montreal. I'm trying to figure it out. All I'm asking is for you to be part of that conversation."

"Why? So I can watch you talk yourself into leaving? So I can give you permission to go and ease your conscience? No thank you." I couldn't keep the hurt from bleeding through every word.

"So we can figure out what's possible together," he insisted, hands outstretched. "Long distance. Visits. Something. Anything. I'm not ready to give up on us, Lana."

"There is no *us*,'" I said, my voice breaking despite my best efforts. "There's just two people with really bad timing and a lot of history. We had one night ten years ago, the other night, and now we're in this mess. We're a two-night stand with a shit ton of baggage. That's all."

Even as I said the words, I knew they were a lie. There had always been an *us* – invisible, unacknowledged, but real. From that first night in college to now, something had connected us, always pulling us back into each other's orbit despite everything.

"You don't believe that," Cam said softly, his eyes never leaving mine. "I know you don't."

I turned away, unable to maintain my composure under his intense gaze. My fingers gripped the window sill, knuckles turning white. "It doesn't matter what I believe. What matters is what happens next. And history suggests that what happens next is you disappear. *Poof*."

"I want to stay." His voice was barely above a whisper, raw with emotion. "For you. With you."

"But you won't." I faced him again, forcing myself to speak the words that would end this once and for all. "You'll go to Montreal because it's the smart career move. And I'll stay here because this is where I belong. And in another ten years, maybe we'll finally stop wondering what might have been."

The finality in my voice seemed to hit him physically. He stepped back, his expression shifting from pleading to resignation.

"Is that really what you want?" he asked quietly. "To end this before we even give it a chance?"

"What I want," I said, struggling to keep my voice steady, "is to not be someone's consolation prize. I want to be someone's first choice. Their only choice."

"You are," he insisted, moving toward me once more. "Lana, you have been for ten years. Since that first night."

"Then prove it." The words escaped before I could stop them, a challenge I hadn't intended to issue.

Cam stared at me for a long moment, the weight of everything – our past, our present, our uncertain future – hanging between us. The morning sun had risen higher now, streaming through the window and illuminating the dust motes between us, a physical manifestation of all that remained unsaid.

"I need to go," I said finally, gathering my things with shaking hands. "I have a crisis management plan to finish. For your big move."

Pain flashed across his face. "Lana, don't – "

"Goodbye, Cam." I walked past him toward the door, every step an effort. "Take the Montreal offer. It's what you've worked for your whole career. You'd be stupid not to."

I paused at the door, not looking back. "Just don't expect me to wait around this time."

I walked out before he could respond, before I could change my mind. My vision blurred with tears as I made my way down the corridor, past curious glances from early-arriving coworkers.

I had survived losing Cam Murphy once before. Surely I could do it again.

Chapter 20

I'd had bad mornings before. The time my car was towed on the day of a major press conference. Waking up with the flu during the playoffs. Reading Zayne's name in trade rumors for three straight weeks during a slump a few years ago.

But this? This was catastrophic.

I was still reeling from my conversation with Cam and had just returned with a coffee when Katie's face appeared in my doorway, her expression grim. "Lana," she said, holding her tablet like it might burst into flames. "You need to see this. Now."

The headline from *HockeyInsider.com* glared up at me:

EXCLUSIVE: SLASHERS' STAR AND PR DIRECTOR CAUGHT IN FAKE EN-GAGEMENT SCANDAL

My stomach dropped through the floor. The coffee slipped from my hand, splashing across my heels and onto the carpet. I barely noticed the burning liquid as it seeped into my Maison Margiela stilettos.

Katie closed the door as I scrolled through the article, each paragraph more devastating than the last.

A source inside the St. Petersburg Slashers confirm that the much-publicized engagement between left winger Cameron "The Hitman" Murphy and team publicity director Lana Decker was fabricated as part of an elaborate scheme to secure Murphy a lucrative endorsement deal with Redline Athletics.

According to documents obtained exclusively by HockeyInsider, both Murphy and Deck-er signed non-disclosure agreements regarding their arrangement, which was designed to rehabilitate Murphy's well-known playboy image ahead of final negotiations with the sportswear giant.

They had a copy of the NDA. Someone had leaked our actual NDA. I felt sick.

The source confirms the relationship was entirely professional until recently, the insider noting, *"It was Lana's idea from the beginning. She created the playboy image for Cam, and then had to fix it when it backfired. The whole thing was a PR stunt."*

I kept reading, unable to look away from the devastation unfolding on the screen.

The revelation comes as Murphy is reportedly considering a trade offer from Montreal, raising questions about the timing of the engagement and its potential dissolution. Redline Athletics has not yet commented on how this development may affect their pending contract with Murphy, estimated to be worth over $5 million.

When reached for comment, the Slashers' front office declined to address specific allegations but stated that "personal matters between staff and players are handled internally."

My mind raced, trying to identify the source. Who had access to the NDA? Coach Sully, Coach Rocco, Marcus, Ryan Keller, legal... but why would any of them leak this? It made no sense.

"Who else has seen this?" I asked Katie, my PR brain calculating damage control scenarios while my personal life crumbled around me.

"It's everywhere," Katie said quietly, pulling up multiple tabs on her tablet. "ESPN picked it up. So did The Athletic. It's trending on TikTok. #FakeSlashers is the top hashtag in sports right now."

I scrolled through social media, each post like a knife to my gut.

@HockeyTalk79: So the Slashers PR director CREATED Cam Murphy as a player just to "fix" him later? That's some next-level manipulation. #FakeSlashers

@SlashersNation: I feel betrayed. We all bought into their love story. This is why you can't trust anything anymore. #FakeSlashers

@PuckPrincess24: @LanaDecker is a LIAR who used Cam for publicity. No wonder he's looking at Montreal. Get away from her, Cam! #FakeSlashers

I put the phone down, unable to take in any more. Numbly, I dabbed at my shoes with a wad of paper napkins.

"Just got a text from the GM's assistant. He called an emergency meeting in the conference room. Everyone's waiting," Katie said.

I grabbed my tablet and my coffee, taking a deep breath. Professional Lana needed to take over. I couldn't afford to be heartsick Lana right now.

"On my way," I said, squaring my shoulders. Crisis management 101: Acknowledge, Address, Advance. I'd navigated plenty of difficult scandals before, but nothing like this.

As we walked through the corridor, I noticed the stares. Staff members who normally greeted me cheerfully suddenly found reasons to look at their phones. A few whispered as I passed.

For over a decade, I had built my reputation in this organization. I'd started with the Slashers as a summer intern after my sophomore year of college. Ten plus years of integrity, hard work, and dedication. And in one morning, it was dissolving before my eyes.

The conference room felt like a war zone. Marcus, our GM, was at the head of the table, phone pressed to his ear. Coach Sully and Coach Rocco sat grim-faced to his right. Ryan Keller, Cam's agent, was pacing by the window, gesturing wildly during his own phone conversation.

And there was Cam, sitting alone at the far end of the table. Our eyes met briefly, his filled with apologies I couldn't accept right now.

I sat as far from him as possible.

"Redline is threatening to pull the entire deal," Ryan announced as he ended his call. "They're claiming potential brand damage. I've got a Zoom with their executive team in an hour."

Marcus hung up his own call. "I've just spoken with ownership. They're concerned, obviously, but they want to know our strategy before making any statements." He turned to me. "Lana, what are we looking at here?"

All eyes in the room turned to me. Despite the circumstances, they still expected me to fix this. It was both comforting and daunting.

"First, we need to identify the source of the leak," I said, falling back on training and experience. "Someone potentially breached the NDA, which gives us legal recourse. Second, we need coordinated messaging – from the team, from Cam, and from me. Third, we need to contact Redline directly and try to get ahead of their public statement."

Coach Sully nodded, "Who had access to the NDA?"

"Everyone in this room," I replied. "Plus legal."

"It obviously wasn't anyone here," Cam spoke up, his voice rough. "It had to be someone else."

"The only other people who knew the details are Logan and Zayne," I said. "And they wouldn't do this."

"Never," said Cam.

"Agreed," said Marcus. "But someone clearly did."

Coco knew too, but neither Cam nor I volunteered that information. She wouldn't betray us.

"Does anyone on your staff know?" Marcus asked me.

"No," I said. "They all assumed it was real."

"Well, you did a helluva job selling it," said Ryan. It sounded a lot more like an accusation than a compliment – rich coming from the certified genius who came up with this disaster-in-the-making in the first place.

I straightened in my chair, professional instincts taking over despite the emotional hurricane inside me. "We'll also need to correct some key misrepresentations in the reporting."

"Such as?" Coach Sully asked.

"For one, we never explicitly claimed to be engaged to the press," I pointed out. "We deliberately avoided using those terms in any official capacity. If you look at the NDA, the words 'engagement' and 'fiance' never appear – because I worded it that way intentionally."

"Why does that matter now?" Ryan asked, frustration evident in his voice.

"Because we haven't lied," I said firmly. "We've allowed assumptions, yes. We've been strategic with our presentation, absolutely. But we've never made false statements to the press or public."

"Will that distinction really help?" Marcus asked.

"It gives us solid ground to stand on," I explained. "And NDAs are standard practice in celebrity relationships – especially when they involve workplace dynamics. There's nothing inherently scandalous about having one."

"They're citing a source inside the Slashers organization," Marcus noted, reading from the article. "That could be anyone from coaching to equipment management to janitors."

My phone buzzed with an incoming call from *ESPN*. I silenced it, only to have it immediately start buzzing again with calls from *Sports Illustrated*, *The Athletic*, and several local stations.

"They're circling like sharks," Ryan muttered. "You need to make a statement before this gets worse."

I felt ill, watching my career disintegrate in real time. Everything I'd built, every barrier I'd broken as one of the few female PR directors in the league – all threatened because I'd crossed the line between professional and personal.

"We need to respond," I said, voice steadier than I felt. "I'll draft a statement for the organization refuting the unnamed source's claims..." Professional mode. Just focus on the job. "Cam, we should discuss what you want to say."

Cam nodded.

"Also, *HockeyInsider* was the original piece, and all the other outlets are running with their reporting so far. They're only quoting one source, which means they couldn't find confirmation. The NDA doesn't stand on its own without a source to tell the story – it looks like every other pro athlete's relationship NDA.

"What does that mean?" Marcus asked.

"If we can discredit the source in time, then the story dies," I say.

While I worked on the draft, my phone continued to light up with notifications. I couldn't help but glance at them.

@RedlineAthletics has officially put their deal with Cam Murphy "under review pending further information" #FakeSlashers

Sources say @LanaDecker masterminded the fake engagement to save Cam's deal after years of promoting his playboy image. Talk about creating a problem to solve it. #FakeSlashers

Montreal reportedly reconsidering trade offer for Murphy after character concerns raised by scandal. #FakeSlashers #NHL

The room felt suddenly airless. Not only was I watching my own reputation implode, but now I might be responsible for destroying Cam's career opportunities as well. The Redline deal. The Montreal trade. All potentially gone because of our fake fucking engagement.

While Marcus read, Katie appeared in the doorway. "More bad news," she said, apologetic. "The story's been picked up by non-sports outlets. *TMZ*, *People*, *Page Six*. They're framing it as 'Hockey's Fake Romance.'"

"Great," Ryan muttered. "Just great." Like he wasn't warned.

"Thanks, Katie," I said, as I thought about my hard-earned reputation and a decade of 70-hour weeks circling the drain.

"Lana," Marcus's voice broke through my spiral. "You okay?"

"Fine," I lied, passing him my tablet. "Draft statement for your review."

"Lana," Cam said suddenly, standing up. "Can I talk to you outside for a minute?"

Every instinct told me to refuse, to maintain professional distance. But all eyes were on us, so I nodded stiffly and followed him into the hallway.

Once the door closed behind us, Cam rubbed his forehead with his fingers, agitation evident in every movement. "I'm so sorry. This is... I never thought this would blow up like this."

"It's not your fault," I said automatically, though part of me wanted to blame him, to blame anyone but myself. "Someone violated the NDA, or there's a leak. We'll figure out who."

"That doesn't matter right now," he said, his blue eyes intense. "What matters is that you're bearing the brunt of this. The comments online, they're making it sound like you manipulated me, like you masterminded everything."

"Welcome to being a woman in sports management," I said, more bitterly than I'd intended. "No matter what happens, I'm either sleeping my way to the top or manipulating players for publicity. This time, it's both."

"It's not right." His voice was tight with anger. "I'm going to make a statement."

"We'll coordinate messaging – "

"No," he interrupted. "I'm going to tell the truth. That I asked for your help, that this was mutual, that if anyone's to blame, it's me."

I shook my head. "Cam, you can't. Redline is already wavering on the deal. Montreal might pull their offer. You can't risk your career for –"

"For what? For you?" He stepped closer. "Lana, this isn't just about the deal anymore. This is about your reputation. Your career."

"I'm the PR director. It's my job to take hits for the team, for the players."

"Not like this." His voice dropped, suddenly vulnerable. "Not when it's my fault. I'm the one who asked for the fake engagement. I'm the one who insisted on staying at your parents' place. I'm the one who..." he paused, swallowing hard. "I'm the one who took it too far."

The pain in his voice matched the ache in my chest. Even now, even after everything, part of me wanted to reach for him, to find comfort in his arms. But I couldn't. Not anymore.

"We both made choices," I said quietly. "Now we both have to live with the consequences. But your career, your future – that matters too."

"So does yours," he insisted.

"Let me just..."

"No," Cam interrupted, pulling out his phone as he headed back into the conference room. "I'm doing this now. My way."

"Cam, no – " I said, trailing behind him, "not without a strategy..."

But before anyone could stop him, he was dialing.

"Josh? Cam Murphy. I want to go on record about this relationship story. Exclusive. Right now."

He was calling Josh Winters, the most respected hockey journalist in the country. The one reporter everyone in the NHL trusted to tell the story straight. The one whose nationally-syndicated hockey podcast was streaming live. Right now. *Shit.*

"Cam," Ryan warned, "Think about Redline. Think about Montreal."

"Cam!" I pleaded. "Don't."

Cam's expression didn't waver. "Some things are more important."

There was a pause, and Cam took a deep breath.

His eyes found mine across the room. "I want to make a statement about the reports regarding my relationship with Lana Decker," he began, his voice clear and steady. "First, the facts: Yes, our *public* relationship began as part of an image rehabilitation strategy ahead of my Redline deal. That's true. What's false is the narrative that Lana Decker orchestrated this or manipulated anyone."

He continued, each word measured but tinged with emotion. "If anyone is at fault here, it's me. I approached Lana for help after my reputation, which I willingly participated in building, threatened a deal I wanted. I asked her to attend the NHL awards with me and play it up for the press. I pushed for it to continue even when she had reservations. Any criticism should be directed at me, not her."

I stared at him, stunned by his willingness to fall on his sword, potentially sacrificing millions in endorsements and a career-making trade.

"Furthermore," he added, "I don't know who *HockeyInsider*'s source is, but they were not present for any discussions about this arrangement and have no firsthand knowledge of how it came about. The so-called source's statements are speculative at best and malicious at worst."

There was a pause as Josh asked a follow-up question.

"Let's put it this way, Josh," Cam said confidently, "I'm professional hockey player at the center of a major trade negotiation, the Slashers are a Stanley Cup-winning team, and Lana Decker is the best PR Director in the NHL – do you really think they'd agree to let me start *any* relationship, even one with her, without the protection of an NDA?" Cam continued, a hint of protective outrage in his voice. "We work together. You think management and the coaching staff didn't have to sign off on this before Lana and I appeared in public together?"

Another pause as Cam listened intently to Josh's follow-up question.

"That's between Lana and me," Cam answered, his eyes never leaving mine across the room. "Our relationship plans are our business. But what I will say is that Lana Decker is the most professional, ethical person in this organization. She deserves better than to be dragged through the mud for doing her job and helping a player who asked for it."

I couldn't breathe. Couldn't move. Couldn't process that Cam was potentially setting fire to his own career to protect mine.

After a few more questions, Cam ended the call. The room fell silent.

"Well," Ryan Keller finally said, "that was either incredibly noble or incredibly stupid. Possibly both."

"It was the right thing to do," Cam replied simply.

"Thank you," I said gratefully, my eyes holding his a beat longer than I should have. "We'll schedule a formal press conference for Monday at 9 am," I said. "That gives us the weekend to track down the source and prepare our messaging."

"Monday?" Ryan protested. "The story will be completely out of control by then!"

"If we rush out half-cocked, we'll only make it worse," I countered. "Trust me on this. It's literally my job. We're playing Saturday in Boston, the team is traveling Friday and Sunday, so that gives us cover -- we're focusing on winning games, etc."

"Lana's right," Marcus affirmed, surprising me with his immediate support.

I nodded my thanks in his direction, "Going forward, no impromptu interviews. We are the Slashers and we do not employ a 'ready, fire, aim' approach to media communications. We make a plan and execute it."

"This looks good, Lana," Marcus said, pushing my tablet to Sully for review. "Coach, you want to take a look?"

Before he could respond, Marcus's phone rang. He answered, listened for a moment, then put it on speaker.

"You're on with the Slashers management team," he said.

"This is David Hughes, GM of the Montreal Canadiennes," came the response. "I'm calling about the trade discussions for Cam Murphy."

The room tensed. This was it. Montreal was pulling out. Everything was falling apart. Shit.

"In light of recent events," Hughes continued, "we wanted to express our continued interest in bringing Cam to Montreal. Any player with the integrity to stand up for a colleague the way he just did with Josh Winters is exactly the kind of leader we want in our organization."

My eyes widened. Well, that was... unexpected.

"We'd like to move forward with discussions as planned," Hughes finished. "Our offer stands."

After the call ended, Coach Sully stood up. "I'm scheduling a press conference for this afternoon," he announced. "Just a brief statement of support from the organization. Nothing detailed. We'll save that for Monday."

"Sully," I began, "maybe we should – "

"No," he cut me off, his expression determined. "We're not letting you swing in the wind, Lana. You're part of this team too." I nodded my head in thanks, speechless.

"Agreed," said Marcus.

Two hours later, I stood off to the side as Coach Sully addressed a small group of local media. Cameras flashed as reporters shouted questions, the atmosphere electric with scandal.

"The St. Petersburg Slashers organization stands firmly behind both Cam Murphy and Lana Decker," Sully stated, his gravelly voice commanding respect. "Ms. Decker has served this organization with distinction for ten years. Her integrity is beyond question."

He continued, his measured tone belying the anger I knew he felt. "We are investigating the source of confidential information that was shared without authorization, and we're gearing up to play in Boston on Saturday night. That is all we will say at this time, pending a full press conference on Monday morning at 9 am."

As the short press conference ended, I remained in the shadows, overwhelmed by the unexpected defense. I'd spent so long feeling like I had to prove I belonged in hockey, in this organization. And here they were, standing up for me when I needed it most.

By late afternoon, the tide was beginning to turn – at least partially. Clips of Josh Winters' podcast with Cam's statement were all over social media. Winters had written a story centered around Cam's statement, presenting a more balanced view than earlier reporting. Sports commentators were divided: some praising Cam's integrity, others continuing to question everyone involved in the "deception."

Redline Athletics issued a terse statement that they were "reevaluating the partnership in light of recent developments" but had made no final decisions.

In other words: still a complete disaster, just a slightly more nuanced one.

I spent the rest of the day in my office, drafting statements, fielding calls from friendly media contacts, and trying to salvage what I could of the situation. By seven p.m., I was emotionally and physically exhausted, staring blankly at my computer screen.

A soft knock at my door made me look up. Katie stood there, purse in hand.

"You should go home," she said gently. "There's nothing more you can do tonight."

I nodded, too tired to argue. "Thanks, Katie. For everything today."

"That's what I'm here for." She hesitated. "For what it's worth, the staff is on your side."

I managed a weak smile. "That means a lot."

After she left, I began gathering my things, wincing as I scrolled through yet more notifications on my phone. The hashtag #FireLanaDecker was gaining traction. Several sports blogs were calling me "the most hated woman in hockey right now." Wonderful.

Another knock, this one more hesitant. I looked up to see Cam standing in my doorway, his expression uncertain.

"Hey," he said softly.

"Hey."

An awkward silence stretched between us. There was so much to say, and yet I had no energy left to say any of it.

"I just wanted to check on you before I left," he finally said. "It's been... a day."

I laughed, the sound hollow and brittle. "That's one way to put it."

"Lana, I – "

"Don't," I cut him off, unable to bear whatever he was about to say. Apologies, explanations, regrets – none of it would change what had happened. "Please. I can't do this right now. I need to stay focused if I'm going to salvage this situation."

"You think I care about the damned sneakers? If this goes sideways, I lose my brother, my team..." he paused, "and the only woman I've ever loved."

My heart ached and tears stung my eyes, "I can't do this with you right now."

He nodded, understanding in his eyes. "Okay. But I meant what I told Josh. Every word."

I looked away, afraid of the hurricane of emotions threatening to sweep me away . "You shouldn't have done that. The Redline deal – "

"I don't care about the deal," he interrupted. "Not if it comes at the expense of your reputation."

"It's my job to protect your reputation, Cam. Not the other way around."

"Maybe I'm tired of everyone protecting me." He stepped further into the office, his voice low and intense. "Maybe I wanted to be the one who stood up for someone else. For you."

I was too exhausted for this conversation, too raw to navigate the complicated feelings his words stirred up. "Thank you for what you did today. But I think I need some time. Space."

He nodded, a flash of hurt crossing his face before he schooled his expression. "Of course. Whatever you need." He turned to go, then paused. "For what it's worth, I'd do it again. All of it. Even knowing how it would end."

After he left, I sat alone in my darkened office, surrounded by the wreckage of the day. My phone buzzed with a text from my mother:

> MOM: Saw the news. Call us when you can. We love you sweetheart.

Another from Coco:

> COCO: These assholes on Twitter don't know what they're talking about. You're a badass and everyone who actually knows you knows that.

And finally, from Zayne:

> ZAYNE: Coming over with pizza and bourbon in 30. No arguments.

My brother. Always the protector. The thought finally broke the dam of tears I'd been holding in all day.

I drove home in a daze, the weight of the day pressing down on me like a physical thing. As I climbed the stairs to my condo, all I could think about was crawling into bed and hiding from the world. But first, I needed to make a call.

Marcus answered on the second ring. "Lana. How are you holding up?"

"I've been better," I admitted. "Marcus, I just want you to know I won't be coming in tomorrow."

"Of course not. Take as much time as you need."

"Thanks, but it's not just for me," I explained. "The press will be camped outside the training facility. If I'm visibly present, it just adds oxygen and video to the story."

"Smart thinking, as always," he said. "Where will you go? The media might track you down at home."

I sighed, already dreading the conversations to come. "I'm going to my parents' in Siesta Key. The neighborhood has good security, and I think we both know no reporter is getting past Frank Decker."

He chuckled. "Good. Your family should be with you right now." His voice softened. "And Lana? This will pass. You've built up too much goodwill in this league for one scandal to define you."

"I hope you're right," I said, not entirely convinced. "Thank you, Marcus. For everything today."

"This organization stands behind you. Remember that."

After we hung up, I sank onto my couch, too numb even to cry. Sid, my orange tabby, jumped up beside me, butting his head against my hand for attention.

"At least you still like me," I murmured, scratching behind his ears.

Everything I'd feared had come to pass. My professional reputation was in tatters. The line between personal and professional had become hopelessly blurred. And Cam... Cam was both the cause of it all and the one person who'd stood up for me when it mattered most.

The irony wasn't lost on me: I, Lana Decker, supposed PR director extraordinaire, was now at the center of the biggest PR disaster in Slashers history. All because I'd broken my own cardinal rule: Never get personally involved with a player.

But as I stood there in my darkened bedroom, fighting back tears while I packed an overnight bag for Siesta Key, I couldn't bring myself to regret it entirely. Not the family weekend at the beach. Not the quiet conversations under the stars. Not the feeling of Cam's arms around me, his lips on mine, the way he'd looked at me as if I were the only woman in the world.

Real or fake, it had still been worth it.

The doorbell rang, and I cautiously checked the peephole before opening the door. Zayne stood on the doorstep, bearing a pizza and a bottle of Blanton's bourbon, my big brother's signature crisis management toolkit. No matter how complicated our lives became, he'd always been there for me. And I knew without a doubt he always would.

"Hey dork," he said sweetly.

And I burst into tears.

Chapter 21

The Skyway Bridge stretched before me like a metaphor for my life – a steep uphill climb followed by an inevitable, crushing descent.

I'd left St. Pete at dawn, unable to face another moment in my condo as my professional reputation burned to the ground in real time. My phone had buzzed incessantly until I'd finally silenced it, unable to stomach another notification about #FakeSlashers or another "insider" quote about how I was the evil mastermind behind Cam Murphy's moral corruption and career destruction.

The morning sky matched my mood perfectly. Heavy gray clouds threatening rain, the usually vibrant Gulf waters dull and choppy beneath the bridge. As I drove, memories of the last time I'd made this journey flashed through my mind: Cam beside me, his easy laughter filling the car, his hand finding mine across the center console when I got nervous about the height, the almost-kiss at the top of the bridge less than a week ago.

Now I was alone, the passenger seat occupied only by my hastily packed overnight bag and the crushing weight of humiliation.

The sapphire ring weighed down my finger, a constant reminder of what had been within my grasp for one life-changing night before it was all snatched away. A four-carat anchor I couldn't remove, just in case I was photographed by paparazzi. Even now, alone in my car, I had to maintain the façade that had already collapsed and threatened to bury me.

By the time I pulled into the shell-paved driveway of my parents' beach house, a light drizzle had started, droplets beading on my windshield like the tears I'd been fighting back for hours. I sat for a moment, engine off, gathering whatever fragments of composure I could find. The last thing I wanted was to fall apart the moment I saw my parents.

I'd texted them last night, a brief message saying I needed to get away for a day or two, and they'd responded with love and warmth, just like I knew they would.

> MOM: Home is always here for you, sweetheart. We're here if you need us.

No questions, no judgments. Just unconditional support I wasn't sure I deserved after lying to them and dragging our previously unblemished family name through the mud.

Before I could reach for my bag, the front door opened, and my parents appeared on the porch. My father, stoic as ever in his polo shirt and golf shorts, and my mother in her gardening clothes, a concerned smile on her face. They didn't rush toward me or bombard me with questions. They simply waited, giving me the space to approach in my own time.

I grabbed my bag and stepped out into the light rain, forcing a smile that felt brittle on my face.

"Hey," I said, climbing the steps to the porch. "Thanks for letting me crash here."

"You never need permission to come home, Lana," my mother said, pulling me into a hug that smelled of sea salt and her gardening herbs. "We're always happy to see you."

My father's embrace was briefer but no less genuine. "You look like you could use some coffee," he observed, his keen eyes taking in what I was sure were the dark circles under my eyes and the strain in my smile.

"Coffee would be great," I agreed, following them inside.

The house was exactly as it was a few days ago: the same comfy furniture, the same family photos lining the walls, the same scent of salt air and my mother's lavender candles. But everything felt different now. The happiness I'd felt here with Cam had been built on a foundation that was now crumbling beneath us.

My mother gestured toward the stairs, "Why don't you get settled while I make that coffee?"

I nodded gratefully, relieved for a moment alone to compose myself. As I climbed the familiar stairs, my hand trailing along the banister worn smooth by decades of Decker hands, I braced myself for what awaited me at the top.

My childhood bedroom – the same one Cam and I had shared just days ago. The room where we'd talked into the night, where I'd woken in his arms, where something that had started as pretense had begun to feel real.

I pushed open the door and was immediately assaulted by memories. The king-sized bed where Cam had slept beside me, his breathing a steady rhythm in the darkness. The window seat where I'd watched him sleep in the early morning light, confused by the tenderness that had welled up inside me. The gauzy curtains that had billowed in the sea breeze as we'd navigated the awkward morning-after of our midnight confessions.

I dropped my bag on the floor and sank onto the edge of the bed, finally allowing myself a moment of complete honesty. I missed him. Despite everything – Montreal, the scandal, the hurt – I missed Cam with an ache that permeated every part of my body.

Because I'd spent years building walls around my heart, years convincing myself that what I felt for Cam was nothing more than lingering resentment over a college hookup gone wrong. Years telling myself that men like Cameron Murphy – heartfelt, charming, gorgeous, universally adored – were exactly the kind I needed to avoid.

Yet here I was, heart shattered by the very man I'd sworn would never touch it again.

With a deep breath, I pulled out my laptop and opened it, determined to at least attempt to do some work. I had a crisis to manage, after all – even if I was at the center of it.

My mom brought me a mug of steaming coffee and set it on the edge of the small desk. "It will all be okay," she said, giving my shoulder a loving squeeze. "You'll see."

For the next hour, I drafted contingency plans, potential statements, and media strategies. I analyzed every angle of the scandal, every possible approach to damage control. I worked methodically, professionally, as if I were handling a crisis for someone else entirely.

And then, in a separate document, I began drafting my resignation letter.

To Marcus Thompson and the St. Petersburg Slashers Organization,

Please accept this letter as formal notification of my resignation from the position of Director of Public Relations, effective immediately.

In light of recent events, I believe it is in the best interest of the organization that I step down. My actions, regardless of intent, have created a situation that compromises both my professional credibility and the team's public image.

It has been my privilege to serve this organization.

I cried as I stared at the words on the screen, the cursor blinking accusingly at me. Was this really how my career with the Slashers would end? A decade of dedication, of breaking barriers, reduced to a scandal and a resignation letter?

But what choice did I have? The team couldn't keep me on after this. Not when #FireLanaDecker was trending on socials. Not when sports commentators were dissecting my "manipulation" of Cam for clicks and views. Not when my inbox was flooded with messages from other PR directors in the league, a mix of sympathy and, in rare cases, barely concealed schadenfreude.

My phone buzzed with a text, and I reluctantly checked it.

I smiled weakly at their loyalty, but couldn't bring myself to respond. What would I even say?

Thanks, but I've ruined my career, humiliated myself, and possibly lost the man I'm in love with – all because I couldn't admit how I really felt until it was too late.

Instead, I opened Instagram, TikTok, and X – a masochistic impulse I couldn't resist. The hashtag was still trending, the comments a mix of outrage, mockery, and armchair analysis of my professional ethics. I scrolled numbly, each tweet another punch to my already battered self-esteem.

@HockeyFanatic55: PR director creates fake love story to save a sponsorship deal? And we're supposed to believe anything from the Slashers organization now? #FakeSlashers

@PuckLife365: Ten years covering hockey and I've never seen anything this cynical. Fans deserve better than manufactured relationships. #FakeSlashers

@SlashersSuperFan: My daughter looked up to @LanaDecker as a woman succeeding in hockey. What lesson is she learning now? That lying is how women get ahead? Disgusted. #FakeSlashers

I closed the laptop with more force than necessary, unable to stomach any more. The resignation letter could wait. Everything could wait. Right now, I just needed to breathe without feeling like I was drowning.

A soft knock at the door interrupted my spiral. "Lana?" My mother's voice was gentle. "Lunch is ready if you're hungry. We're eating on the deck."

"I'll be right down," I called back, quickly wiping away the tears I hadn't realized kept falling. "Just finishing up something for work."

"Take your time, sweetheart."

I heard her footsteps retreat down the hallway, and I took a moment to compose myself, splashing cold water on my face in the bathroom and taking several deep breaths. I could do this. I could get through lunch with my parents without falling apart. I'd faced down hostile press conferences and locker rooms full of agitated hockey players. I could handle a family meal.

The deck was my mother's pride and joy – weathered wood whitewashed to a soft gray, decorated with potted plants and comfortable furniture that invited lingering. Usually, the view of the Gulf was enough to soothe any troubled mind, but today even the expanse of water stretching to the horizon couldn't calm the storm inside me.

My parents had set lunch at the small table in the corner, a simple spread of sandwiches, fruit, and iced tea. They both looked up as I approached, their smiles warm but cautious.

"There she is," my father said, pulling out a chair for me. "Just in time. Your mother made those crab salad sandwiches you like."

"Thanks, Mom," I said, settling into the seat. "It looks great."

An awkward silence fell as we began eating, the only sounds the clink of glasses and the distant cry of seagulls. I could feel my parents exchanging glances over my head, silently debating who would broach the subject first and how.

"The weather's supposed to clear up this afternoon," my mother finally offered. "Might be nice for a walk on the beach."

"Maybe," I said noncommittally, picking at my sandwich.

Another silence stretched between us.

"Zayne called," my father said suddenly, his voice carefully neutral. "Wanted to know if you'd arrived safely."

I looked up, surprised. "You talked to Zayne?"

My father nodded. "He's worried about you. Said you weren't answering your phone."

"I turned off notifications," I admitted. "It was... a lot."

My mother reached across the table, her hand covering mine. "We've seen the news, sweetheart. It looks like quite a mess."

The simple acknowledgment – and the complete lack of judgment in her tone – nearly undid me. I swallowed hard against the lump forming in my throat.

"It is," I managed. "It's pretty bad."

"Do you want to talk about it?" my father asked, his gruff voice gentler than usual.

I shook my head, not trusting myself to speak without breaking down completely. "Not yet. I'm still... processing."

They accepted this with nods, not pushing, and the conversation shifted to safer topics – my mother's garden, a fishing tournament my father was helping judge next month, mundane details of their daily lives that had nothing to do with hockey or scandals or broken hearts.

I tried to participate, to nod and smile in the right places, but I could feel myself fraying at the edges, the careful composure I'd maintained since arriving starting to unravel thread by thread. By the time lunch was finished, I was hanging on by the thinnest of margins.

"I think I'll go for that walk now," I said abruptly, standing up. "Clear my head a bit."

"Of course," my mother said, though concern flickered in her eyes. "Take all the time you need."

I made it as far as the steps leading down to the beach before the first sob escaped, a harsh sound that seemed to tear from somewhere deep inside me. I sank down onto the weathered wood, burying my face in my hands as the tears I'd been holding back finally broke free.

I cried for my career, for the reputation I'd spent years building, now in ruins. I cried for the team that had become my family, for the players and staff who might never look at me the same way again. I cried for Cam, for what might have been if we'd both been honest from the beginning. And I cried for myself, for the walls I'd built so high that I couldn't see over them until it was too late.

I don't know how long I sat there, shoulders shaking with silent sobs, before I felt a presence beside me. My father lowered himself onto the step, his knees cracking slightly with the movement, and simply sat in silence, offering the steady comfort of his presence without words.

After a while, my sobs subsided into hiccuping breaths. I wiped at my face with the back of my hand, embarrassed by the breakdown.

"I'm sorry," I mumbled. "I didn't mean to – "

"Don't apologize for your feelings, Lana," my father interrupted, his voice firm but kind. "Never apologize for that."

Coming from Frank Decker, a man known for his stoic demeanor both on and off the ice, the words hit with unexpected force. I looked at him, really looked, and saw not disappointment or judgment but deep concern and unconditional love.

"I've made such a mess, Dad," I whispered. "Everything I've worked for... it's all falling apart."

He was quiet for a moment, his gaze on the horizon. "Your mother and I think it might help if you came inside," he finally said. "There are some things we should talk about. As a family."

The gentle insistence in his tone left no room for argument. I nodded, allowing him to help me to my feet, and followed him back into the house, where my mother was waiting in the kitchen, a pot of fresh coffee brewing and a box of tissues already on the table.

The kitchen table. The heart of our family home. Where I'd first learned about hockey, where my brothers and I had done homework under our mother's watchful eye, where we'd celebrated victories and processed defeats. Where my father had taught us about the game using salt shakers as goals or players and an ancient red poker chip emblazoned with "Stardust Hotel" as the puck.

I sat down heavily, accepting the mug of coffee my mother placed before me, the familiar ritual somehow grounding in the midst of chaos.

"I don't know where to start," I admitted, my voice hoarse from crying.

"The beginning is usually good," my mother suggested gently, settling into the chair across from me. "Or wherever feels right to you."

I took a deep breath, then another, gathering the fragments of my courage. And then, haltingly at first but with increasing momentum, I told them everything.

About the night in college when Cam and I had first met, the connection that had seemed so real, the hurt when he'd disappeared without a word. About working with Cam these past years, maintaining a professional distance while nursing a private resentment. About the image we'd created for him: the playboy, the heartbreaker. And how it had come back to haunt us both when the Redline deal was at stake.

I told them about the fake engagement, the careful rules we'd established, the NDAs everyone had signed. About how coming here to Siesta Key with him blurred the boundaries we'd established, the feelings that had emerged despite my best efforts to keep them contained.

And finally, about the leak, the scandal, the public humiliation, and the trade offer that might take Cam to Montreal – away from the team, away from me.

"I know I should have told you the truth when we were here," I finished, staring into my now-cold coffee. "But we couldn't violate the NDA. I was afraid of disappointing you. Of you thinking I was unprofessional or... or desperate."

My mother reached across the table, her hand finding mine. "Oh, Lana, honey," she said softly. "We already knew."

I looked up, startled. "What?"

"Zayne told us," my father explained. "Last Sunday, before he left. Said he knew you'd tell us if you could, and he couldn't bear watching you two have to pretend anymore, not with family."

I blinked, trying to process this information. "Zayne told you? But he promised – "

"He didn't break your confidence lightly," my mother assured me. "But he said he'd never seen Cam look at anyone the way he looks at you. That his belief that the relationship wasn't real at first had actually helped him to see how right you two were for each other. He loves you both and was so worried about both of you getting hurt if the truth came to light before you figured out your feelings for each other."

Stupid, brilliant, overprotective Zayne.

"But if you knew it was fake," I said slowly, "why did you keep calling Cam your future son-in-law? Why did you come to opening night to support him with the Redline people?"

My mother smiled, a touch of mischief in her eyes. "Because we could see what you couldn't, sweetheart. That there was nothing fake about the way you two feel about each other. Also, don't forget...Nana proclaimed you're a perfect match."

"Mom..." I sighed.

"Cam's the most promising candidate you've ever brought home," my father interjected, his tone matter-of-fact. "Your mother and I have a good eye for these things. We recognize the real thing when we see it."

"This isn't the draft, Dad," I protested weakly. "You can't just scout my love life and declare a top pick."

"Watch me," he smiled with a hint of his trademark stubbornness. "Cam's my number one draft pick for Team Decker." His expression softened. "Lana, we've been watching you and Cam both mooning over each other when you thought nobody was looking since you and the boys were in college."

My mother finished his thought, "...even when you were pretending to ignore him. We just figured you two had finally gotten out of your own way."

"It doesn't take a hockey genius to see what's happening there," my father continued. "And I should know. I am one."

"Don't forget modest," my mother said, playfully pinching my dad's cheek.

Despite everything, a small laugh escaped me. My father's confidence had carried him through twenty NHL seasons and three Stanley Cups. It was both infuriating and comforting that he applied that same certainty to my love life.

"But the scandal," I said, sobering quickly. "You've seen the news, right? What they're saying about me? About us?"

"We've seen it," my mother confirmed, her expression darkening slightly. "Those vultures don't know the first thing about you or Cameron."

"I don't know. Maybe I should resign," I admitted, the words feeling like stones in my mouth. "Maybe I don't deserve this job in the first place. Maybe this is just... karma. For creating an image that wasn't real."

"Lana, stop." My father's voice was firm, the same tone he'd used when coaching his players through a slump. "You've always belonged in hockey. Not just because you're a Decker, but because you've got the sharpest mind in the sport."

I looked up, surprised by the vehemence in his voice. Frank Decker was notoriously stingy with praise, even with his own children. *Especially* with his own children.

"But..."

"No buts," he interrupted, leaning forward with the intensity he usually reserved for third-period playoff situations. "You think I don't know how hard you've worked? How many barriers you've broken? How many times you've had to prove yourself because of your gender or your last name?"

He tapped the table for emphasis, his knuckles hitting the wood with the same rhythm he used on the boards behind the bench. "I'm proud to pass the Decker torch to all my kids – not just to Zayne and Drake. You've always had the best instincts. Seeing all the possibilities, doing what's right for the team and the players, even when it costs you personally. That's what makes you *great* at your job."

My throat tightened with emotion. In all my years working in hockey, I'd never heard my father speak about my career with such pride.

"The Decker name in hockey isn't just about who can skate fastest or shoot hardest," he continued, his voice rough with emotion. "It's about understanding the game – all aspects of it. The strategy, the psychology, the business. And nobody gets that better than you do."

He reached across the table, his calloused hand covering mine in a rare gesture of physical affection. "You don't just belong in hockey, Lana. You're leading in hockey. And someday, maybe sooner than you think, I see you running the whole damn team."

The words landed like a slam drop – unexpected, powerful, knocking the air from my lungs. I'd always seen myself as an adjunct to the real action, the support staff behind the scenes. But my father was talking about me as if I were the future of the organization itself.

"You really believe that?" I asked, my voice small.

"I know it," he said with characteristic certainty. "Champions aren't made during the easy shifts – they're forged in the penalty kill after a five-minute major. This scandal is just your time in the box, Lana. The game isn't over; you're just waiting to get back on the ice and show everyone what you're made of."

My mother squeezed my other hand, her touch gentle but firm. "Your father's right." She shot him a fond look before turning back to me. "And there's something else we need to talk about, Lana."

I knew what was coming, and part of me wanted to flee the conversation. But I'd already laid my professional life bare; what was left but to confront the personal?

"Cam," I said softly.

"Cam," she agreed. "We know why you felt you couldn't tell us the truth about your arrangement. But I think the person you were really lying to was yourself."

I opened my mouth to protest, but she continued, her voice gentle but insistent.

"We've watched you light up every time Cam walks into a room. You're the only one who thought you were faking it." She smiled, a knowing look in her eyes. "Everyone else could see it – you two are meant to be together."

"But the trade..."

"Trade offers come and go," my father said with a dismissive wave. "Good ones get rejected all the time."

"And what if he takes it?" I asked, voicing the fear that had been gnawing at me since the meeting. "What if he leaves?"

"Then you'll face that challenge too," my mother said simply. "But not by running away or hiding how you feel. By facing it together."

The simple wisdom in her words struck a chord deep within me. I'd spent so long protecting myself, building walls, keeping my feelings locked away where they couldn't hurt me. And where had it gotten me? Alone, heartbroken, contemplating resignation from the job I loved.

"I'm scared," I admitted, the words barely audible. "I've never felt like this before. And if he leaves..."

"Then at least you'll know you were honest," my mother said. "With him and with yourself. That's all any of us can really do."

My father cleared his throat, looking slightly uncomfortable with the emotional turn of the conversation but determined to see it through. "You're a Decker," he said gruffly. "We don't back down from challenges. We face them head-on."

A memory surfaced – my father saying those exact words to me when I was twelve, nervous before my first public speaking competition. I'd won first place that day, surprising everyone but him. He'd simply nodded, as if he'd expected nothing less.

"What would you tell one of your players right now?" he asked, shifting into coaching mode. "If they came to you in this situation, what would you say?"

I considered the question, forcing myself to think as the PR director rather than the woman in the middle of the storm. "I'd tell them... that people are more forgiving than you expect. That one mistake doesn't define a career. That the best response to a setback is to come back stronger."

My father nodded approvingly. "Sounds like good advice to me."

For the first time in days, I felt something other than despair – a small spark of determination, of the fighting spirit that had carried me through countless challenges in my career. Maybe I couldn't control what happened with Cam or the scandal, but I could control how I responded to it.

"I'm not going to resign," I said, the decision crystallizing as I spoke the words. "I'm going to fight this. Fix it."

The pride in my parents' eyes was worth more than any championship ring.

"That's my girl," my father said, satisfaction evident in his voice.

My mother squeezed my hand. "And what about Cam?" she asked gently.

Did I love him? Yes, I could admit that now, at least to myself. But was love enough to overcome everything else – the scandal, the potential trade, the years of misunderstandings?

"I don't know," I answered honestly. "I need to figure out how to fix the PR disaster first. Then I'll figure out the Cam situation."

My father nodded, accepting this prioritization as sensible. My mother looked less convinced but didn't push.

"One step at a time," she agreed, setting a fresh mug of coffee before me. "But don't wait too long, Lana. Some opportunities don't come around twice. Well, thrice."

I knew she wasn't just talking about Cam now, but about life in general – about seizing chances, about being brave enough to reach for what you want.

After dinner, I retreated to my room, emotionally drained but somehow lighter than I'd been in the last 24 hours. The conversation with my parents had been a revelation in more ways than one: not just their support for my career, but their insight into my feelings for Cam, feelings I'd been denying even to myself.

I sat at the small desk by the window, looking out at the Gulf waters now turned silver in the moonlight. The storm had passed, leaving a clear night sky scattered with stars. It felt like an omen, though whether good or bad remained to be seen.

My laptop sat open before me, the resignation letter still on the screen, the cursor blinking at the end of a sentence I would never complete. With a decisive click, I deleted the entire document, watching with satisfaction as the words disappeared.

In their place, I opened a new document and began typing:

Crisis Management Plan

Step 1: Address the narrative head-on. No hiding, no deflecting.

Step 2: Correct factual inaccuracies in reporting, discredit source if found

Step 3: Acknowledge the arrangement without apology – NDAs are standard practice.

Step 4: Emphasize that no official statements claiming "engagement" were ever made.

Step 5: Focus on moving forward, not looking back.

It was just a start, but it felt good to be thinking strategically again, to be doing what I did best – managing difficult situations, crafting narratives, finding the path through the storm.

My phone rang, startling me out of my focus. I glanced at the screen, expecting another reporter or perhaps Marcus checking in. Instead, Coco's name flashed on the display.

I hesitated, my finger hovering over the answer button. Part of me wanted to continue avoiding the world, but Coco had been nothing but supportive, and I owed her at least the courtesy of picking up.

"Hey," I answered, my voice still rough from crying all afternoon.

"Lana," Coco's relief was audible. "Thank god. I've been worried sick about you."

"I'm okay," I said automatically, then amended, "Well, not okay, exactly, but... surviving."

"Where are you? Logan and I stopped by your place, but you weren't there."

"I'm at my parents' beach house in Siesta Key. I needed to... get away for a bit."

"Smart move," Coco said. "The press was camped outside the training facility all day." There was background noise on her end – announcements, the murmur of conversations. "Listen, I'm at the airport right now. The team flew out to Boston this morning, and I'm headed there with the other WAGs for tomorrow's game."

"Right. The Bruins." In the chaos of the scandal, I'd almost forgotten about the regular season schedule. "How's the team?"

There was a slight pause. "They're... processing. Most of them are just pissed about how you're being treated in the press. Logan's furious about the way that *HockeyInsider* article painted you as some kind of evil villain. The guys keep telling him they can't wait for the media blackout to be over so they can defend you."

I closed my eyes, a wave of gratitude washing over me. "Tell him thanks. Tell them all thanks."

"Actually," Coco continued, "that's part of why I'm calling. Trixie, Coach Sully's wife, has arranged for a private box for tomorrow's game. She wanted me to tell you that if you want to fly up to Boston, the WAGs will protect you in the box and keep the press away. She says, and I quote, 'Those vultures will have to go through all of us first.'"

I was momentarily speechless. Trixie Michaels was a formidable woman who took her role as the coach's wife and unofficial team mom seriously. The thought of her marshaling the players' wives and girlfriends into a defensive box around me was both touching and slightly terrifying.

"I... I don't know, Coco," I said finally. "I appreciate the offer, but I'm not sure I'm ready to face..."

"Just think about it," she interrupted gently. "The offer stands. We've got your back, Lana. All of us."

I swallowed against the sudden lump in my throat. "That's... thank you. I'll think about it."

There was a beat of silence before I gathered the courage to ask the question that had been burning in my mind. "How is he? Cam, I mean."

Coco sighed. "Honestly? He's all over the place. He didn't want to go home last night, stayed in our guest room. Logan said he's cycling between being livid about how you're being treated in the press, heartbroken over you, stressed about the Montreal trade, then back to anger again."

My heart clenched. "Was he... did he seem okay at practice today?"

"Define *okay*," Coco said dryly. "He was unfocused in the short practice this morning – missed passes, botched drills. Then he got into a shoving match with Hendricks over some comment about you. Logan had to physically separate them."

"Oh god," I murmured, pinching the bridge of my nose.

"Logan's worried about him," she admitted. "Says he's never seen Cam this distracted before a game. But he also says – " She broke off abruptly.

"What?" I pressed. "What does Logan say?"

She hesitated. "He says he's never seen Cam care about anyone or anything this much before. Not even hockey."

Her words stole my breath. I pressed my palm flat against my chest, as if I could somehow contain the ache blooming there.

I heard an announcement in the background. "They're calling my flight. But Lana?"

"Yes?"

"Whatever you decide about tomorrow, Boston or not, just know the team is behind you one hundred percent. No matter what *HockeyInsider* or those jerks on social media say."

"Thank you," I whispered, genuinely moved by her loyalty. "That means more than you know."

"Take care of yourself. And think about Boston," she added before hanging up.

I set the phone down, my mind spinning with this new information. Cam was struggling. The team was rallying. I had to find a way forward through this mess.

Outside, the waves continued their eternal conversation with the shore, a reminder that some things remained constant even as everything else changed. I'd always found comfort in that sound – the steady rhythm of water against sand, nature's own heartbeat.

Turning back to my laptop, I continued working on my plan with renewed determination. I was Lana Decker, PR director for the St. Petersburg Slashers, daughter of Frank Decker, sister to Zayne and Drake, and – for better or worse – the woman who had fallen hopelessly in love with Cameron Murphy.

I didn't know if I could fix everything that had broken between us. I didn't know if Cam would stay with the team or take the Montreal offer. I didn't even know if my career would survive this scandal intact.

But I did know one thing with absolute certainty: I wasn't giving up without a fight. Not on my career, not on the team, and maybe – if I could find the courage – not on Cam either.

Tomorrow, I would begin the work of rebuilding – my reputation, my career, and maybe, if I was brave enough, my heart.

And maybe, just maybe, I would go to Boston.

Chapter 22

I woke up to the Florida sunlight blasting me in the eyes. For the first time in days, I didn't immediately feel the crushing weight of humiliation pressing down on my chest. Instead, I felt something that had been missing since the scandal broke: determination.

My father's words echoed in my mind: *Champions aren't made during the easy shifts – they're forged in the penalty kill after a five-minute major.*

This was my penalty kill. And I sure as hell wasn't going to spend it hiding in Siesta Key.

I'd just finished showering when my phone rang. Coco's name flashed across the screen, and I answered while towel-drying my hair.

"Morning," I said, surprised by how steady my voice sounded.

"You sound better," Coco observed immediately.

"Better than yesterday. Had a good talk with my parents."

"Good." There was a pause. "So, listen. Trixie wanted me to remind you that the offer stands. If you want to come to Boston, we've got you covered."

I hesitated, my eyes drifting to the sapphire on my finger. Two weeks ago, I'd been determined to keep this fake engagement strictly professional. Now, after everything that had happened, I wasn't sure what was real anymore. Except one thing: I missed Cam. And I was tired of running.

"There's a flight at noon. I can text you the details..." Coco offered.

"Do that please," I said, already mentally packing. "I'll see if I can get on it."

By the time I hung up, I'd pulled out the small duffel bag I'd hastily packed when fleeing St. Pete, dumping its contents onto the bed. One professional outfit, two casual, toiletries, phone charger. What did you pack for a public reunion with your fake fiancé after a public scandal and possible trade bombshell?

I texted the team's travel coordinator with the flight information, and headed downstairs.

My parents were having coffee on the deck, the morning sun glinting off the Gulf waters, now calm after yesterday's storm.

"I'm going to Boston," I announced, setting my bag down and pouring myself a cup of coffee.

My mother looked surprised, but pleased. "For the game tonight?"

I nodded. "Coco says the WAGs have a plan to keep me away from the press. I'll stay at the team hotel, watch the game from their box, and fly back tomorrow."

My father studied me over the rim of his coffee mug. "You sure you're ready for that?"

"No," I admitted. "But I'm not hiding anymore." I need to face this – all of it. Including Cam."

A slow smile spread across my father's face. "That's my girl."

Frank Decker wasn't one for flowery sentiments or lengthy heart-to-hearts. But in those three words, I heard everything: his pride, his support, his absolute confidence that I was making the right choice.

My mother squeezed my hand. "What can we do?"

"I'll need to drive myself to the airport so I have my car when I get back," I said, mentally calculating the timing. "Can you help me find something warmer to wear? I don't have anything for Boston in October."

Twenty minutes later, I was wearing my mother's cashmere wrap and had a ticket booked on the noon flight to Boston. As I hugged my parents goodbye, my father held on a second longer than usual.

"Lana," he said, his voice gruff with emotion, "whatever happens in Boston, remember what I said. You belong in hockey. Not because you're my daughter, but because you've earned it."

I blinked back sudden tears and nodded against his shoulder. "Thanks, Dad."

"And tell Cam – " he hesitated, then shook his head with a small smile. "Never mind. You'll figure it out."

The drive to Tampa International gave me too much time to think. What was I doing? Flying across the country to surprise a man who might be leaving the team – leaving me – for Montreal? What would I even say to him? Sorry I ran away? Sorry I didn't trust you? Sorry I've been pushing you away for years because I've been afraid of my feelings since that night in college?

All of the above, probably.

The Tampa airport was mercifully free of journalists, though I kept my sunglasses on and a baseball cap pulled low just in case. As I settled into my window seat on the plane, I pulled out my phone to text Coco.

> ME: On the noon flight to Boston. Landing at 3:15.

Her reply was immediate.

> COCO: Yay! I'll have a car waiting for you under my name. Trixie's got everything arranged. We're staying at the Four Seasons with the team. She's put you in my room so no one sees your name on the hotel register.

> ME: Does Cam know I'm coming?

There was a longer pause before her response.

> COCO: No. Logan doesn't even know. Thought it might be better as a surprise. Less pressure on everyone.

> ME: Good call. Thanks for being such a good friend. See you soon.

I put my phone in airplane mode and leaned back, watching Florida disappear beneath the clouds. Three hours to Boston. Three hours to figure out what I was going to say to Cam when I saw him again.

The flight passed in a blur of half-formed speeches and aborted text drafts. None of them seemed right. How do you distill ten years of misunderstandings, weeks of pretending, and days of heartbreak into words that make sense?

By the time we landed at Logan International, I still had no idea.

The blast of cold air that hit me as I exited the terminal was a shock after Florida's perpetual warmth. I pulled my mother's wrap tighter around me, grateful for it but already regretting not bringing proper winter gear. Boston in October was a different planet from Siesta Key.

A sleek black SUV idled at the curb, with a small sign affixed to the passenger window that read "Coco Charmant."

I knocked lightly on the window, and the driver quickly stepped out to greet me.

"Car for Ms. Charmant? I'm Peter, with the Four Seasons."

"Thank you," I said, handing him my small overnight bag.

As we drove through Boston's narrow streets, memories surfaced from our time at Boston University, where all of this with Cam had first begun.

My father had brought me to the old Boston Garden when I was nine – my first road game. I remember being mesmerized by the history in those walls, the banners hanging from the rafters, the way my dad was treated like royalty even in an opposing team's arena. Hockey royalty transcended team colors, he'd told me. The respect was for the game first, the rivalry second.

I wondered if that same respect would extend to a PR director caught in a scandal of her own making. *Probably not.*

The Four Seasons Boston was elegant and discreet, its lobby mercifully free of hockey fans or media. The concierge directed me to a private elevator that would take me directly to the floor where the team was staying. "Ms. Charmant is expecting you," he said with a polite smile.

Coco was waiting when the elevator doors opened, practically bouncing with excitement. She pulled me into a fierce hug.

"You're here!" she exclaimed. "I was worried you'd chicken out."

"Me too," I admitted, returning her embrace. "Thanks for arranging everything."

"Oh, I can't take credit for that. It's all Trixie. She's gone full mama bear mode over this whole situation." Coco took my bag and led me down the hallway. "The team's at pre-game meetings right now, so the coast is clear. We have about an hour before Trixie wants us all to meet in her suite."

"All?" I asked, a new wave of anxiety washing over me.

Coco grinned. "The WAGs are very excited to meet you. Especially after everything that's happened."

"Great," I muttered. "Nothing like meeting your fake fiancé's teammates' wives and girlfriends in the middle of a PR disaster."

"They're on your side," Coco assured me, swiping her key card and opening the door to a spacious room with two queen beds. "Trust me. Trixie has declared you under WAG protection, and no one messes with Trixie."

I set my bag down and sank onto the edge of the bed. "I don't even know what I'm doing here, Coco. What am I supposed to say to Cam? *Sorry I freaked out and ran away after we slept together and then you dropped a trade bomb on me?*"

"Maybe start with 'hello' and see where it goes?" Coco suggested, sitting beside me. "Look, I'm not saying it's going to be easy. But you're here. That's a start."

I nodded, twisting the sapphire ring on my finger. "What is Logan saying about the Montreal offer?"

Coco said carefully. "Everybody knows now. It's been... tense."

Before I could ask more, there was a knock at the door. Coco jumped up to answer it, revealing a stunning woman in her early fifties with meticulously highlighted blonde hair and a Slashers-blue manicure that matched her silk blouse.

"There she is!" she exclaimed, sweeping into the room with the confidence of someone used to commanding attention. She headed straight for me, hands outstretched. "Lana, sweetheart. I'm so glad you're here. Sully's just been beside himself over all this mess."

I stood to greet her, momentarily overwhelmed by her perfume and presence. "Trixie, thank you for arranging all this. I really appreciate... "

"It's the least I could do." She grasped my hands in hers, her expression softening. "Sully told me everything. That poor excuse for a journalist who leaked your story should be thrown into the penalty box for life."

Despite everything, I found myself smiling at her indignation. Coach Sully was known for his stoic demeanor; Trixie was his opposite in every way. Kind of like my parents, the original grumpy-sunshine combo.

"Now," Trixie continued, giving my hands a final squeeze before releasing them, "we have a full WAG protection plan in place. You'll stay with us in the private box. No press, no photographers, no nosy fans. Just us girls supporting our men."

The fact that she included me in this collective, that she saw me as one of them despite the circumstances, brought an unexpected lump to my throat.

"Thank you," I managed.

"Of course, dear. Now come along, the others are waiting in my suite. We need to get you properly outfitted for tonight."

I glanced at Coco, who shrugged with a smile that said, *Just go with it.*

Trixie's suite was twice the size of ours and filled with women in various stages of game-day preparation. Some I recognized from team events or games: Shayna, the veteran defenseman's wife; Marcy DeLuca, always the life of the party, and others I'd only seen in passing. All conversation stopped when we entered. For a moment, I felt like I was back in high school, the new girl stepping into the cafeteria. Sure, I knew them all. Just not in this new context.

Then Shayna broke the silence. "There she is! Our PR queen!" She crossed the room to give me a warm hug. "We've been worried about you."

"It's been a rough couple of days," I admitted.

"Girl, we saw," Marcy said, raising a champagne flute. "Those assholes on Twitter or X or whatever they're calling it don't know what they're talking about. We're Team Lana all the way."

The knot in my chest loosened slightly as other women nodded in agreement. They'd seen the worst of the scandal, and they were still welcoming me with open arms.

"Now," Trixie said, clapping her hands to get everyone's attention, "we have a game to prepare for. Let's get Lana dolled up, and we need to go over the security plan."

What followed was a whirlwind of activity. Shayna produced a brand-new Slashers jersey – Cam's number, of course – that just *happened* to be in my size. Marcy, a former Miss Pennsylvania, insisted on doing my makeup ("Just enough to look good on camera if they spot you, honey"). Trixie outlined her elaborate CIA-level plan for getting me into and out of the arena without being noticed by the press.

It was overwhelming, this instant circle of protection and solidarity. These women barely knew me, yet they'd mobilized like an elite tactical unit to ensure my comfort and safety.

"You know," Shayna said as she helped me adjust the jersey, "your mom was the original WAG queen back in her day."

I looked at her in surprise. "She was?"

"Oh, honey, Diana Decker literally wrote the handbook," Trixie chimed in. "Not an actual book, mind you, but we all learned from watching her. The way she balanced family and the spotlight, protected you kids, supported Frank without losing herself. She was legendary."

I blinked, seeing my mother in a new light. I'd always known she was respected in hockey circles, but I'd never fully appreciated her role in this parallel universe of the sport. The thought that I might be following in her footsteps – not just as Frank Decker's daughter but as a woman navigating the complex world of hockey relationships – was strangely comforting.

"She is legendary," I nodded.

As game time approached, the energy in the suite shifted from social to focused. The veterans explained the rituals and superstitions to me:

- no one changed seats once the game started

- no one said the word "win" until the final buzzer

- Shayna always wore her husband's college ring on a chain

- Marcy had special game-day earrings.

I watched, fascinated by this parallel world of hockey that existed alongside the one I'd always known. My father had been a player and coach, my brothers were players, but I'd rarely been privy to this side of the sport: the wives and girlfriends who formed their own team off the ice.

"What about you?" Shayna asked, nodding at the sapphire on my finger. "Any superstitions yet?"

I hesitated. "I... I don't really have any. This is all new to me."

"The relationship or the WAG life?" Marcy asked bluntly.

"Both, I guess." It wasn't entirely true. My feelings for Cam were anything but new, but explaining the complexity of our situation wasn't something I was ready to do.

Trixie shot Marcy a warning look, but I appreciated the directness. No need to pretend with these women; they'd seen the headlines.

"You might need a quick refresher on your hockey history, Marcy," said Trixie, "Lana's mom is Diana Decker."

"OMG! I totally forgot!" laughed Marcy. "Too many pre-game cocktails, apparently. You'll be fine, Lana," she said, patting my arm reassuringly. "You learned from the best."

"Okay," Trixie said, checking her watch, "it's time. Cars are waiting downstairs. Remember the plan: we go in through the service entrance, straight to the elevator, directly to the box. No stopping, no talking to press."

The journey to TD Garden was a carefully choreographed operation. Two black SUVs, drivers who knew exactly where to go to avoid the main entrances, security personnel who guided us through service corridors and freight elevators. I felt like I was in a spy movie, being smuggled into enemy territory. If I'd been planning this PR maneuver for a player, I would have been impressed with myself.

The WAGs box was on a premium level, high above the ice but with clear sightlines to the action. Plush seats, a private bar, and waitstaff ready to bring anything we needed. Trixie directed the seating arrangements with military precision: me in the center, surrounded by her, Coco, Shayna, and Marcy, forming a sparkly human shield against prying eyes and press.

"Great," she declared once we were all settled. "Now we wait."

From a PR standpoint (which I couldn't seem to turn off, even when I wanted to), it occurred to me that the optics were spectacular. Even if the cameras did find me, I would be seen surrounded and supported by the player wives in a very exclusive clique – communicating "I'm not hiding, I'm right here front and center," without me actually being vulnerable or accessible to the press. It was kind of genius.

As the arena filled below us, I couldn't help scanning the crowd, looking for familiar faces from the media. Hockey journalists I'd worked with for years were now potential threats. What a difference a few days made.

The teams took the ice for warm-ups, and my heart stuttered when I spotted Cam. Even from this distance, I could see the tension in his shoulders, the mechanical way he went through his routine. He looked... off. Not the fluid, confident player I was used to watching.

"He's been like that since the story broke," Coco murmured beside me. "Logan says he's barely said two words since they arrived in Boston."

I twisted the ring on my finger, a twinge of guilt squeezing my chest. Had I done that to him? The confident, laughing man who'd shared a bed with me just days ago, reduced to this tense, silent shadow?

The first period was painful to watch. The Bruins came out aggressive, testing our goalie Nick Fosse early and often. Cam seemed a step behind every play, missing passes, losing puck battles he'd normally win easily. When Boston scored midway through the period, the home crowd erupted.

"It's okay," Shayna said, noticing my grimace. "First period is always rough in this building."

But the second period wasn't much better. Logan and Zayne were playing their hearts out, keeping the Slashers in the game with solid defense and a few good chances, but the team couldn't find the equalizer. Cam's frustration was visible in every line of his body: the way he slammed the bench door during line changes, the force behind his increasingly reckless checks.

"This isn't good," Coco muttered as Cam was called for a slashing penalty. "He's going to get himself thrown out at this rate."

I watched him skate to the penalty box, head down, and felt an ache deep in my chest. This wasn't the Cam I knew – the player who thrived under pressure, who played with joy even in the toughest games. I found myself leaning forward, wishing I could somehow catch his eye, let him know I was here.

The Slashers killed the penalty, but the momentum stayed with Boston. As the second period wound down, Morozov, a Bruins defenseman, checked Cam hard into the boards right below our box. We couldn't hear what was said, but suddenly Cam's head snapped up, and he shoved the player forcefully.

"Oh no," Shayna whispered.

The Bruins player said something else – something that made Cam's face contort with rage. In an instant, gloves were dropped, and Cam was throwing punches with a ferocity I'd never seen from him. The Boston player got in a few shots, but Cam was relentless, driving him back against the boards.

"Jeez. What did he say to him?" I asked, standing to see better.

Marcy, who was squinting through a pair of professional-grade binoculars, said, "Can't read lips from this angle, but..." She trailed off, lowering the binoculars to give me a knowing look. "If I had to guess, given recent headlines, he probably said something about you."

Other players converged, and suddenly it wasn't just Cam and the defenseman – it was a full-on brawl. Zayne was there in a flash, pulling a Bruins forward off Cam's back. Logan joined the fray, defending his teammates. A Bruins helmet skittered across the ice. Officials struggled to separate the players as the crowd roared its approval.

"What the hell happened?" I asked, still standing for a better view.

"Cam's been on edge since the whole scandal broke," Trixie explained, surprisingly calm as chaos unfolded below. "Sully says he's been taking everything personally. That boy down there is fighting for a lot more than just a hockey puck."

As the officials finally gained control of the situation, assessing penalties and sending players to the box, the Jumbotron began showing faces in the crowd, a standard way to keep fans entertained during delays.

I wasn't paying attention, too focused on trying to see if Cam was okay, until Marcy grabbed my arm.

"Lana," she hissed, "look up."

I raised my eyes to the massive screen hanging from the ceiling and felt my stomach drop. There I was, in full HD glory, wearing Cam's jersey, the sapphire ring clearly visible on my hand. The camera lingered, and a murmur went through the crowd as recognition dawned.

"Shit," I breathed, instinctively starting to shrink back.

"Take a breath, look right at me and nod like I just said something fascinating," Trixie advised, leaning in towards me. *"You're okay, what scandal?, no big deal, we're just supporting our team up here..."*

I did as instructed, forcing my features into a calm mask while my heart hammered against my ribs.

On the ice, the penalty boxes were being sorted. Cam, still breathing hard from the fight, had his back to the jumbotron. But as the crowd's murmur grew louder, he turned – and froze.

Even from this distance, I could see the exact moment he spotted me on the screen. His whole body went still, his eyes locked on my image. I couldn't look away, couldn't breathe, couldn't do anything but hold his gaze across the impossible distance between us. I gave up the pretense of calm and smiled directly at the camera, letting him see me – *really* see me.

The camera finally moved on to another section of fans, but the damage – or maybe the miracle – was done. Cam knew I was here.

"Well," Trixie said beside me, "that cat's out of the bag. That's fine, we've planned for this too."

I sank back into my seat, heart hammering. "So much for staying under the radar."

"Are you okay?" Coco asked, squeezing my hand.

"I don't know," I admitted. "I didn't exactly plan on announcing my presence via jumbotron, but I guess this saves me from having to figure out what to say to him first."

Shayna leaned in. "If it helps, Cam looked more awake in those five seconds than he has all game."

She wasn't wrong. When play resumed after the penalties were sorted (Cam got five minutes for fighting, offset by the Bruins player's five), something had changed. Cam's entire demeanor was different: focused, intense, present in a way he hadn't been all night.

"What did that Bruins player say to him?" I asked Coco again.

She raised an eyebrow. "My guess is he was talking shit about you." She cracked up, and suddenly I was too. "Wrong move, buddy..."

The third period started with the Slashers still down by one goal, but the energy on the ice had shifted. Cam came out of the penalty box like a man possessed, forechecking with ferocious intensity, winning puck battles, creating chances. Twice he nearly scored, only to be denied by brilliant saves from the Boston goaltender.

"That's more like it," Marcy said approvingly. "Looks like your boy just needed a little motivation."

The minutes ticked down, tension mounting with each Slashers rush. With five minutes left in regulation, Boston took a penalty for tripping Logan as he drove toward the net. Power play opportunity.

"Come on, come on," Coco muttered beside me, clutching my arm.

The Slashers' first power play unit took the ice: Logan at center, Miller at right wing, Cam at left wing, Zayne and Pietro back at the blue line at the points. They moved the puck with precision, looking for openings in Boston's penalty kill formation.

Logan won a face-off back to Miller who feinted a shot before sliding the puck to Pietro. Pietro found Cam on the left side, and Cam one-timed a rocket toward the net – only to have it blocked by a diving defenseman.

"So close!" Shayna groaned.

Boston cleared the puck, but the Slashers regrouped quickly. This time, Logan carried it into the zone himself, drawing two defenders before dropping it back to Zayne. Zayne fired a cross-ice pass to Cam, who was cutting toward the net.

In one fluid motion that seemed to happen in slow motion, Cam received the pass, deked around a defender, and fired a shot top shelf that the goalie had no chance of stopping.

The red light flashed. The horn blared. The Slashers bench erupted.

"YES!" I screamed, jumping up and pulling Coco with me. The rest of the WAGs were on their feet too, hugging and cheering.

When the celebration line broke apart, Cam skated to center ice and looked up – straight at our box. He couldn't possibly see me specifically from that distance in the dimly lit arena, but somehow, I felt his eyes find mine.

He raised his stick in a deliberate salute, and my heart practically burst through my chest.

"That," Trixie said with satisfaction, "was for you."

The game ended tied 1-1, sending it to overtime. Before the extra period could start, Coach Sully called the team to the bench for a quick strategy session.

When overtime began, Logan, Zayne, and Pietro took their usual positions for the opening face-off. But as they skated to center ice, Sully called Pietro back and sent Cam out instead.

"That's different," Shayna noted. "Bold move by Sully."

"Or maybe he just knows something we don't," Trixie said with a knowing smile.

Three-on-three overtime was always heart-stopping – wide open ice, end-to-end rushes, incredible scoring chances. Both teams had golden opportunities in the first minute: a breakaway for Boston that Fosse somehow stopped with his toe; a two-on-one for the Slashers that ended with Logan hitting the post.

Two minutes in, Boston got caught on a bad line change. Logan pounced on the loose puck and flew up the right wing with Cam on his left and Zayne trailing. The lone Boston defender backed up, trying to take away the pass to Cam while still challenging Logan.

Logan slowed just enough to draw the defender toward him, then slid the puck across to Cam. The Boston goalie pushed hard to his right, anticipating Cam's shot – but instead of shooting, Cam immediately sent the puck back across the crease to Zayne, who had continued his rush and was now wide open on the right side.

Zayne buried it in the empty net before the goalie could recover.

Game over. Slashers win.

The celebration was instant and euphoric. Zayne was swarmed by his teammates, disappearing under a pile of blue jerseys. When they finally let him up, the first thing he did was point to Cam, acknowledging the perfect pass that had made the goal possible.

Cam nodded back, then once again turned to look up at our box – this time raising both arms in triumph.

"I think that's his way of saying 'I see you,'" Coco said softly.

I nodded, not trusting my voice. The emotions of the moment were too raw, too overwhelming. Pride in watching Cam fight back from his early struggles. Joy at seeing the team – Cam, Zayne, and Logan especially – come together for a dramatic win. Fear about what would happen next. What I would say to him. What he would say to me.

Trixie touched my arm. "We should head back to the hotel right away. The boys will be a while with media and cooldown, and it will be better if you're not here when the press starts looking for you."

I hesitated, part of me wanting to stay, to wait for Cam, to finally face what I'd been running from. But Trixie was right – the middle of a hockey arena after my face had been plastered on the jumbotron was not the place for that conversation.

"Okay," I agreed. "Back to the hotel."

The extraction was as carefully orchestrated as our arrival had been. While most fans were still celebrating the win or filing out of the arena, we were escorted through service corridors to a loading dock where the SUVs waited. Trixie, ever the strategist, had arranged for decoy vehicles to wait at the VIP exit, drawing away the photographers.

On the ride back to the Four Seasons, I stared out at Boston's lights, my mind racing. After days of hiding, of shame and uncertainty, I'd made myself visible again – not just to Cam, but to the hockey world. There was no going back now.

"What are you thinking?" Coco asked quietly.

"That I have no idea what I'm going to say to him when I see him," I admitted.

"You'll figure it out," she said, squeezing my hand. "And for what it's worth, I think you being here already said a lot."

Once we were safely back in our room, I kicked off my shoes and collapsed on the bed, suddenly exhausted. The adrenaline that had carried me through the game was fading, leaving behind a bone-deep weariness.

"The team bus probably won't be back for at least an hour," Coco said, checking her phone.

"There's already media chatter about me being at the game, so they'll get extra questions, Cam in particular" I said. Quickly, I shot off a quick text to Coach Sully to ask him to remind the team again that the answer to any questions regarding Cam, me, or our relationship should be "no comment."

Not that the players should have any questions about what to say. I'd already texted and emailed them all multiple times with specific guidelines.

"Just so you know, once the guys get back, I'm staying in Logan's room tonight unless you need me. He's supposed to be bunking with Cam, so unless one of you calls me tonight to tell me to sleep in my *own* room, I'll assume all is well." Coco gathered a few things into her overnight bag.

I turned my head to look at her. "Are you sure? I don't want to kick you out of your own room."

She smiled. "Please. Besides, you and Cam need space to talk." She zipped up her bag. "I'll text you in the morning."

After she left, I raided the minibar, trying to calm my nerves and organize my thoughts. What did I want from this conversation with Cam? Closure? Reconciliation? A way forward, despite Montreal and the scandal and ten years of misunderstandings?

All of the above.

I sat on the edge of the bed, phone in hand, staring at the blank screen. Should I text him? Or just wait for him to come find me? What if he didn't want to see me at all?

No. I'd seen his face when he spotted me on the jumbotron. I'd watched him transform on the ice afterward. He wanted to see me as much as I needed to see him.

Taking a deep breath, I typed:

> ME: I don't need any more space. Room 1422.

I hit send before I could second-guess myself, then set the phone down and waited. For Cam. For answers. For whatever came next.

Chapter 23

The knock came exactly one hour and fourteen minutes after I'd returned to the hotel room. I knew because I'd been staring at the clock between checking my phone obsessively, pacing a groove in the carpet between the window and the door. I still wore Cam's jersey over my jeans, the sapphire ring on my finger like a security blanket.

My phone screen showed a stream of unread messages:

Team Group Chat:

LOGAN: Anyone heard from Murph?

PIETRO: He bolted from the bus like his ass was on fire

ZAYNE: ⌧

I'd changed positions approximately thirty times – sitting on the bed, standing by the window watching for the team bus, curled up in the armchair trying to calm my racing heart, back to pacing. The city lights of Boston blurred through my exhausted eyes. The hotel room felt too quiet, too empty, the hum of the heating system the only sound besides my own restless movements.

When the knock finally came, three soft raps, tentative in a way that was so unlike Cam's usual confident arrival, my heart slammed against my ribs. I froze mid-step, then practically ran to the door, stopping just short of yanking it open. My hand hovered over the handle.

Deep breath. Another.

The metal was cool under my trembling fingers as I turned the lock.

Cam stood in the hallway looking like he'd been through a war. He was wearing his post-game black suit and dark gray tie; his duffel bag was dropped carelessly at his feet.

  LISA DAILY

His hair still was damp from his post-game shower, curling slightly at his neck the way it did when he didn't bother to style it. A bruise was already blooming along his jaw from the fight, purple-black against his skin. Exhaustion carved lines around his eyes, and he swayed slightly on his feet like staying upright took effort.

But his eyes – those deep, ocean blue eyes that had haunted me for a decade – locked on mine with an intensity that stole my breath.

"Hi," I whispered.

"Hi," he said back, and something in his voice cracked like ice breaking.

That was all it took. I grabbed the lapels of his suit jacket with both hands and pulled him into the room, his bag dragging behind him. The door had barely clicked shut before his arms came around me, crushing me against his chest with a strength that felt cathartic. His face buried in my hair, and I could feel him breathing me in – or maybe that was me. Maybe it was both of us.

"Lana," he whispered against my temple. "I haven't slept for days and all I want to do is climb into bed and hold you."

His breath was warm on my cheek, and the scent of him – soap and hard-fought victory and that uniquely Cam scent underneath – made my knees weak. I could feel his heart hammering against mine, evidence that I wasn't the only one falling apart.

I pulled back just enough to see his face, my hands framed his jaw carefully, avoiding the worst of the bruise. "You're hurt."

"Doesn't matter." His hands tightened on my waist, fingers pressing into me like he was afraid I'd disappear. "You were there. You came to Boston. Saw you on the screen and thought I was hallucinating or something."

"Of course I came. I couldn't stay away." I said, and then his mouth crashed into mine.

This kiss was nothing like our controlled moments during the fake engagement. This was desperation and relief and two days of agony poured into the clash of lips and tongues and shared breath. His hands tangled in my hair, I felt a shiver run down my spine as I pressed closer to him, needing to erase every inch of distance between us. His lips met mine with an intensity that made my heart race, kissing me like a drowning man desperate for air. The world around us faded into a blur as the heat of his body against mine became my sole focus, every touch igniting a spark that made me crave more.

When we finally broke apart, both gasping, he rested his forehead against mine. His hands shook where they held me.

"When I saw you on that screen," he said roughly, "wearing my jersey, the ring still on your finger... Christ, Lana. The whole arena disappeared. There was just you."

"Come sit," I said, taking his hand and leading him to the bed. "You look like you're about to collapse."

He sank onto the mattress like his strings had been cut, pulling me down beside him. Our knees touched, and he immediately laced our fingers together, gripping tight.

"The last two days," he started, then stopped, shaking his head. "I haven't slept more than an hour at a time. Could barely choke down food. Logan said I was a zombie at practice. Coach threatened to bench me if I didn't get my head right."

"Me too," I admitted. "I wrote about fifteen different texts to you and deleted them all. Coco finally told me to stop being an idiot and just come to Boston."

"Remind me to send Coco flowers. Or a car. Maybe a small island."

Despite everything, I laughed. "She'd probably prefer tickets to Paris, honestly."

"Done," he smiled.

"What happened out there tonight?" I asked.

His face darkened suddenly. "When that Boston asshole said – " He cut himself off, jaw clenching hard enough that I worried about his teeth.

"What did he say?" I asked gently.

Cam's eyes went cold as arctic ice. "He made a crude comment about you being available now that your fake engagement was over. Said maybe he'd look you up when they played in Florida. Used some... *colorful* language about what he'd do."

"Cam – "

"And then he called you a puck bunny," he growled. "Said he'd like to...never mind. I'm not repeating it. I saw red. Nobody talks about you like that. Nobody."

My heart clenched at the protective fury in his voice. "So you tried to punch him through the ice?"

"Would've succeeded if the refs hadn't intervened." A ghost of his usual grin flickered across his face. "Zayne got some solid hits in too."

"I saw."

"Then, when I saw you up on the jumbotron, I couldn't believe you came... and then I realized... you weren't just wearing any jersey. You were wearing mine. Number twenty-two. My name." His voice dropped to a whisper. "My ring still on your finger after everything.

I lifted our joined hands, the sapphire catching the hotel room lights. "I couldn't take it off. Even when I was furious with you, even when I thought we were done. I couldn't take it off for more than a minute. It felt... wrong. Like taking it off would break the spell, and make everything really over."

Something shifted in his expression, raw vulnerability replacing the intensity. "After I saw you, it was like someone flipped a switch. One of the *ESPN* reporters said I played the last ten minutes like a man on fire. Everything clicked into place – every pass, every shot. I've been skating through fog since Thursday afternoon, and then there you were, and I could see clearly again."

"We do need to talk about Montreal," I said quietly, even though the words tasted like ash.

He sighed, the exhaustion showing more clearly now. His shoulders slumped. "I know."

"I can't tell you what to do," I said carefully. "If I say stay and you do, what happens in three years when you see what that money could have bought? If I say go and you listen, I'll always wonder if I pushed you away. It has to be your choice, Cam."

"But how can I choose when I don't know where we stand?" He turned to face me fully, shifting closer. "Would you... would you even consider coming to Montreal with me?"

My heart clenched painfully. "I thought about it. But Montreal's PR Director has been with the club for fifteen years and he's never going anywhere. And honestly? After this scandal, taking a lesser position and hoping to work my way up would be career suicide. I need to stay put and solve this, or I'm not going to come out of it alive.

"The NHL is your dream. I get it," he said.

"Since I was a kid," I confirmed. "I've always known the NHL was where I belonged. And St. Pete... my parents are getting older. Zayne is there. My whole life is there."

"Mine too," he said quietly. "The Montreal offer... it's going to be life-changing money. Ryan says it'll end up eight figures plus bonuses. But Zayne..." His voice caught. "Christ, Lana. He's the steadiest thing I've ever had in my life. Fourteen years of friendship. The closest thing to a real brother I've got. And more than that, even if you and I figure this out, things with him will change. That scares me."

I nodded.

"But for the record, if anybody can get Pandora back in the box, it's you." He squeezed my hand.

We sat in silence for a moment, the weight of all the complications pressing down on us. Outside, Boston traffic hummed, and somewhere down the hall, a door slammed.

"I need you to trust me," Cam said finally, capturing both my hands in his. His palms were warm, strong from years of stick handling. "I know I haven't earned it. I know I left you once before when I should have stayed. But I need you to trust that you're the most important thing in the world to me."

"Cam – "

"Remember what I said at your parents' house? About bad decisions?" His eyes locked on mine, refusing to let go. "Every choice I've made since that night in college has been about protecting what I thought I couldn't lose. But I was protecting the wrong things. I was so afraid of losing Zayne, of losing my place on the team, that I was willing to lose you instead. And that's the worst decision I've ever made."

My throat tightened. "What are you saying?"

"I'm saying I promise," he continued, his voice fierce with conviction, "I will not surprise you. I will not disappear on you ever again. I will not make any decision about Montreal without talking to you first. Without considering us first." He lifted our joined hands to his lips, pressing a kiss to my knuckles. "For me, Lana, you are second to no one. Not hockey, not money, not the team. No one."

His confession stole my breath. All my life, I'd felt like I came second – to hockey, to the family legacy, to everyone else's needs and dreams. But here was Cam, exhausted and bruised from literally fighting for my honor, promising to put me first.

"I'm not a lonely, scared kid anymore," Cam said firmly. "And you were never second. You were so far in first that I couldn't even see second place. That's why I ran. That's why I stayed away. Because I knew if I let myself love you, really love you, nothing else would ever matter as much again. And over the last few weeks, I've come to realize... I don't want to keep searching for a substitute family. I want to build *a real family*, with you."

My heart swelled. "Okay," I whispered, my voice thick with unshed tears as I kissed him gently on his forehead. "I trust you."

Relief washed over his face like sunrise. "Yeah?"

"Yeah." I touched the bruise on his jaw gently, and he leaned into my palm. "Now let me take care of you. You look like you got into a fight with the entire Boston Bruins lineup and lost."

"Technically, I won," he said with a crooked smile that made my heart flip.

I stood, pulling him up with me. He swayed slightly, and I steadied him with hands on his chest. "First things first – food. You just burned about two thousand calories out there, and you said you haven't been eating or sleeping."

"Lana, I'm fine – "

"Well, as the formidable Diana Decker loves to say, 'I'm hungry, so you can eat.' I grabbed the room service menu from the desk. "What sounds good?"

"Honestly? Everything. Logan forced me to choke down half a protein bar this morning, but that's all I've managed since..." He trailed off.

"Since the other morning," I finished softly. "Oh, Cam."

I ordered what seemed like half the menu – a strip steak with a side of roasted potatoes and a double bacon cheese burger and fries for him, pasta for me, truffle fries to share, and chocolate lava cake because nothing tastes better than a dessert someone hand-delivers to your bedside.

"And mozzarella sticks!" Cam yelled from the other side of the bedroom as I read off our order to the room service waiter.

"Thirty minutes," I said, hanging up. "Now, let's get you out of these clothes and see what other damage you're hiding."

He raised an eyebrow, a hint of his usual playfulness returning despite his exhaustion. "Trying to seduce me, Decker? Because I should warn you, I'm running on about two hours of sleep and pure adrenaline. Probably not my best performance, but for you, I'm pretty sure I could rally. I mean really, did you *see* me out there tonight?"

He winked playfully.

Aw. *There* was the charmer I knew so well.

"Trying to make sure you don't have any broken ribs, Murphy," I countered, but I was grinning right back at him. "Besides, your best performance is just existing. The rest is bonus."

His expression softened in a way that made my chest tight. "How do you do that?"

"Do what?"

"Say exactly what I need to hear."

As I stepped closer to Cam, I could feel the heat radiating from his body, a mixture of hours of exertion and the intense chemistry that always sparked between us. I reached out, my fingers lightly brushing against his shoulders as I helped him take off his jacket, the cool fabric sliding away under my touch. His eyes locked onto mine, holding me captive with their intense gaze. I could see the faint traces of pain etched on his face, but there was something else too – a hunger, a desire that mirrored my own.

With careful, deliberate movements, I began to unbutton his shirt, my knuckles grazing against the firm planes of his chest. Each button revealed more of his tanned skin, and I couldn't help but notice the way his breath hitched slightly as my fingers brushed against him. The air between us was charged, filled with an electricity that made every touch, every glance, feel amplified. It was hard to ignore the magnetic attraction that drew us together. As I pushed the shirt off his shoulders, my fingers lingered on his bare skin, tracing the lines of his muscles, feeling the warmth of his body. The room seemed to fade away, leaving just the two of us, caught in a moment filled with unspoken promises and a connection that was impossible to deny.

The overhead light revealed a map of bruises across his ribs – purple and blue blooming like violent flowers against his skin. A few were clearly from the fight, but others looked older.

"Cam, these look awful."

"Ran into the boards," he admitted sheepishly. "Wasn't watching where I was going."

"Because you were distracted."

"Because I was missing you," he corrected. "There's a difference. Doc cleared me already, promise. Nothing's broken, just colorful."

I traced a particularly nasty bruise gently, feeling the warmth of his skin, the rise and fall of his breathing. He shivered under my touch.

"I hate that you got hurt defending me," I said, tenderly kissing each bruise.

He caught my hand, pressing it flat against his chest where his heart beat steady and strong. "I'd do it again in a heartbeat. Every time. A hundred times. A thousand. Until every jackass in the league knows that you're off limits."

The possessive intensity in his voice sent heat through me that had nothing to do with anger.

"You're mine," he said roughly. "And I'm yours. And this isn't fake anymore."

"I'm yours," I murmured as I rose up on my toes, my heart pounding in my chest. "You're mine." I leaned in, pressing my lips softly to his, initiating a kiss that was slow yet charged with an electric desperation. Cam's hands found their way to my hips, his fingers sliding under the jersey to trace the bare skin underneath, sending a shiver of anticipation down my spine. I gasped softly into his mouth, the warmth of his breath mingling with mine. He took this as an invitation, deepening the kiss with a fervor that left me weak in the knees. His lips were firm yet tender, moving against mine with an intoxicating rhythm. I melted against him, careful not to press too hard against his bruises, yet driven by an irresistible need to be closer. The air around us seemed to crackle with the intensity of our mutual attraction, every touch and every breath heightening the powerful emotions and sexual chemistry that pulsed between us.

"You're killing me wearing this," he muttered against my lips. "My name on your back, my number... Do you have any idea what that does to me?"

I let my hand wander, tracing a slow, deliberate path down his torso. I could feel the heat of his body through his shirt, the subtle shift of his muscles as he responded to my touch. My fingers found the waistband of his pants, and I could sense his breath hitch as I lightly ran my hand over his suit pants – over the length of his cock – feeling it strain against the fabric and harden further beneath my touch. "Hmmm...well, I think I have *some* idea what that does to you," I teased, a playful smile dancing on my lips. The room seemed to grow warmer, the air thick with the obvious relief of being together, and the undeniable magnetism that had always been between us. Cam's eyes darkened with desire, and he leaned in closer, his breath hot on my skin. I let out a soft squeak as he nipped at my lower lip in retaliation, a mix of pleasure and pain that sent a shiver of anticipation down to my toes. Every touch, every glance, was fuel igniting the fire that burned between us.

His hands started to trace the curve of my waist, sending waves of warmth radiating through me. I could feel his breath, soft and rhythmic, against my neck, igniting a shiver that coursed down my spine. His fingers gently skimmed the edge of my jersey, teasing the delicate skin beneath, making my heart race with anticipation. I could almost taste the sweetness of his lips, just inches away from mine. My body yearned for his touch, especially after all the uncertainty of the last few days, and I suddenly felt like I couldn't get enough of him--like I'd *never* get enough of him. I had practically forgotten about food entirely, lost in the overwhelming intensity of our connection, when a sudden knock at the door sharply interrupted our moment, pulling us back to reality.

"Terrible timing," Cam groaned, dropping his forehead to my shoulder.

"Food first," I said firmly, though my voice was breathier than I'd intended. "Then... everything else."

"Everything else," he repeated with a movie star grin that made my stomach flip. "I like the sound of that."

We scrambled to the bathroom for robes, laughing as we nearly tripped over each other. I caught sight of us in the mirror – both flushed, hair messed up, looking thoroughly debauched despite being mostly clothed – and had to bite back a giggle.

The room service attendant maintained admirable professionalism despite our obvious state, setting up the food with efficiency before disappearing with a generous tip from Cam.

"God, this smells amazing," Cam said, already reaching for a mozzarella stick. He bit into it and moaned in a way that was borderline indecent and reminded me – vividly – of the last time I'd heard him make that sound.

"When's the last time you ate a real meal?" I asked, twirling pasta on my fork and trying really, really hard not to think about the sounds he was making. And how much I was looking forward to hearing them again in the extremely near future.

He thought about it while demolishing half his burger in three bites. "Breakfast on Thursday? Maybe? Everything's kind of a blur. I know Coco made dinner at some point, but..."

"Cam." I reached across the table to touch his hand. "You can't not eat. You need fuel, especially when you're playing."

"I know. I just...couldn't." He turned his hand palm up to lace our fingers together. "Everything felt wrong. Like the whole world was tilted off its axis. Logan threatened to force-feed me at one point."

"Good," I said. "Someone needs to take care of you when I'm not there."

"I'd rather you just always be there," he said simply, and my heart skipped.

We ate in comfortable silence for a few minutes, but we couldn't seem to stop touching – his foot hooked around my ankle under the table, fingers brushing as we shared truffle fries, his hand finding mine between bites. It was like we both needed constant reassurance that this was real, that the other person wasn't going to vanish.

"The team knows," Cam said eventually, dragging a fry through ketchup. "About us being real. They figured it out when I showed up to practice looking like death about the time ."

"What did they say?"

"Pietro started a betting pool on how long before we got married. Hendricks tried to give me relationship advice, which was alarming. Miller just said 'about damn time.'"

I laughed. "The publicist and the power forward. We're like a bad romance novel."

"No...the *best* romance novel," he corrected. "Though I'm still waiting for my shirtless cover shoot."

"I'll see what I can arrange," I said dryly. "Though after tonight's game, we might want to wait for the bruises to fade."

"Zayne cornered me in the locker room after the game," Cam said, sobering. "Wanted to know what the hell was wrong with me."

I tensed. "What did you tell him?"

"The truth. That I've been an idiot and nearly lost the best thing in my life because I was too scared to fight for it." He pushed the remains of his burger away. "He said I looked like shit and that I better fix things with you or he'd make the Boston player look like he got off easy."

"Zayne strikes again," I said with a small smile. "Though I appreciate him having my back. Both of you."

"He loves you," Cam said simply. "And despite his grumpy exterior, he wants you happy. Think he figured out how I felt about you at the beach house. He told me last night that he was tired of watching us dance around each other."

"Really?"

"Right after he threatened to end my career if I hurt you." Cam's smile was rueful. "But then he said something else. Said he'd never seen me as happy as I was during our little fake engagement. He said you guys had a long talk over pizza on Thursday night, and that maybe it was time he stopped trying to protect us both from something we clearly wanted."

My eyes burned with sudden tears. "He told my parents the same thing. So no need to freak out when we show up to Frank and Diana's for Thanksgiving, Zayne let the cat out of the bag last Sunday when we were still there."

"Your brother sees more than he lets on." Cam stood, moving to the window that overlooked the Boston skyline. The city lights painted his profile in gold and shadow. "Ten years, Lana. Ten years of watching you date other guys and pretending I didn't care. Ten years of letting you paint me as this player who couldn't commit, when the truth was I didn't want to commit because no one else was you."

I stood too, moving to wrap my arms around him from behind, pressing my cheek against his bare back. I could feel the tension in his muscles, the careful way he held himself. "We both made mistakes. We both let fear keep us apart. But we're here now. That's what matters."

He turned in my arms, cupping my face in his hands with devastating tenderness. "I love you," he said, the words hanging between us like a confession. "I've loved you since you told me at that house party my slap shot needed work.. I've loved you through distance and misunderstandings and a fake engagement that felt better than real. I love you in a way that terrifies me because I don't know how to exist anymore without it."

"Cam," I whispered, tears spilling over.

"You don't have to say it back," he said quickly. "I just needed you to know. Needed you to understand that whatever happens with Montreal, with the team, with anything – you're it for me. You're my person. My only person."

"I love you too," I said, the words coming easier than I'd expected, like they'd been waiting all this time to break free. "I've been fighting it for so long, telling myself it was just attraction or nostalgia or proximity. But I love you. Completely. Desperately. Against all my better judgment and professional ethics."

He laughed, the sound rough with emotion. "Against your better judgment?"

"Well, you are still a pain in my ass. Do you know how many carefully worded statements I've had to write about your penalty minutes?"

"But I'm *your* pain in the ass," he said, pulling me closer, hands spanning my waist.

"Yeah," I agreed, standing on my toes to kiss him softly. "You're mine."

The kiss deepened naturally, as if our mouths were made to fit together, our breaths synchronizing into one rhythm. I could feel Cam's heart pounding against my chest, echoing my own rapid pulse. His hands, strong and confident, slid down my back, tracing the curve of my spine and sending wave after wave of anticipation through me. His body, his breath, his scent were completely intoxicating.

We stumbled toward the bed, our bodies pressed tightly against each other, robes falling away. Cam's eyes never left mine, the intensity of his gaze making my breath hitch. He reached for the hem of my Slashers jersey, slowly pulling it up and over my head, his knuckles grazing my skin and leaving trails of fire in their wake. He tossed the jersey aside, his eyes widening in delight as he took in my teal bra – team colors, a little surprise just for him.

"Perfect," he murmured against my skin as he dipped his head and left a trail of kisses from my now-exposed collarbone down, down, between my breasts.

His fingers traced the edge of the lace, a feather-light touch that made my nipples harden in anticipation. He leaned in, his breath hot on my skin, and licked one taut peak through the fabric, drawing out a gasp from deep within me. He took his time, lavishing attention on each breast, his tongue and teeth teasing me until I was arching into him, desperate for more. Until I could feel the hot dampness between my legs, my body aching for his touch.

With a swift motion, he unhooked my bra, freeing my breasts to his hungry gaze. He cupped them, his thumbs circling my nipples, making me moan with pleasure. I reached for his pants, my fingers fumbling with the button in my haste. He helped me, shrugging out of them quickly, revealing the spectacular hard-on that had been pressing against me. I wrapped my hand around him, feeling the velvety softness of his skin, the rigid heat of his desire. He groaned, his hips thrusting forward, his body responding to my touch.

We tumbled onto the mattress, urgent and tender. But the desperation from earlier had transformed into something softer, more precious. We lay facing each other, our hands roaming over each other's bodies, exploring every curve

"Nice color choice," he murmured, fingers tracing the lace hearts of my teal panties, his fingers teasing me mercilessly, getting *thiiiiiis close* to where I wanted them.

"Go Slashers," I replied, my voice barely above a whisper, as Cam's fingers traced hearts on my skin, sending shivers down my spine. His touch was electrifying, awakening every nerve ending, making me hyperaware of his presence, his warmth, his scent – intoxicating and dizzying. I could feel his breath hot on my neck, his heart pounding against his chest, echoing my own racing heartbeat.

His hands wandered lower, exploring every curve and contour of my body as if it were a terrain he'd memorized but still marveled at. I could feel the rough callouses on his fingers, a testament to his strength, contrasting with the gentleness of his touch. My breath hitched as he trailed kisses down my collarbone, his lips soft and warm. I could feel the dampness between my legs growing, my body ready and eager for him.

"I want you inside me," I whispered, my voice thick with desire. Fire ignited in his eyes, a raw hunger that matched my own. He leaned down, his lips brushing against mine in a passionate, all-consuming kiss. His mouth moved to my hips, playfully pulling at my panties with his teeth. Ever so slowly, he began to pull them down, his mouth grazing my skin from my hip to my toes as he did so. The sensation was exquisite, a mix of pleasure and torment that left me gasping.

With a sense of urgency, Cam's eyes never left mine as he hurriedly removed his own briefs. His desire for me was evident and unashamed, and it sent another wave of heat coursing through me. He lowered himself onto me, his hard, muscular body fitting perfectly against my soft curves.

Cam's gaze locked onto mine, the intensity in his eyes reflecting the deep longing we both felt. Our breaths mingled, each inhale and exhale a shared, intimate rhythm. He gently brushed his lips against mine in a tender, lingering kiss that promised more.

I arched my back, my body yearning to be closer, to feel every inch of him. As Cam entered me, it was with a slow, deliberate movement that made me gasp. His cock filled me completely as our bodies joined seamlessly, as if we were made exactly for each other. This was more than physical; it was an emotional surrender, a raw and primal expression of the love we'd been denying ourselves and each other for too long. His tender touch spoke volumes, whispering promises of forever. The bond between us was palpable, a frequent and vibrant current that ran through every touch, every glance, every breath. I could feel his heart beating against my chest, his breath hot on my face. He made love to me slowly, gently, his eyes locked onto mine.

We moved together in a rhythm that was ours alone, a dance that was both passionate and tender. Each touch, each kiss was a testament to our love, our longing for each other. I could feel my body tightening, my release building with each thrust.

Cam's gaze held mine as we moved together, our bodies synchronized in a rhythm that felt as natural as breathing. Each touch, each kiss, was a testament to the love we'd confessed to each other. The room was filled with the soft sounds of our shared breaths, the rustle of sheets, and the distant hum of the city outside.

I could feel the tension building within me, a coil of heat and desire that tightened with each thrust. Cam's hands roamed over my body, tracing familiar paths that lit up every nerve ending. His lips found mine again, this time in a kiss that was slow and deep, filled with a passion that was both fierce and tender.

"I love you, " he murmured against my lips, his voice rough with emotion. "I love you so much."

The words sent a shiver down my spine, pushing me closer to the edge. I wrapped my arms around him, pulling him closer, needing to feel every inch of his skin against mine. "I love you too, Cam. Always."

Our bodies moved faster, the rhythm growing more urgent. The coil of tension within me tightened almost painfully, and then, with a final thrust, it snapped. Pleasure washed over me in waves, each one more intense than the last. I cried out, my fingers digging into Cam's muscular triceps as I rode out the storm.

Cam followed soon after, his body tensing as he found his own release. He buried his face in the crook of my neck, his breath hot against my skin. We lay there for a moment, our hearts pounding in sync, our breaths slowly returning to normal.

As the haze of pleasure began to fade, I snuggled into the warmth of Cam's body pressed against mine, the gentle rise and fall of his chest, the comforting weight of his arm draped over me. This was where I belonged – here, with him. No matter what happened with Montreal, no matter what challenges we faced, I knew that as long as we were together, we could overcome anything.

Eventually, Cam lifted his head, his eyes soft with affection and exhaustion.

But exhaustion was winning. I could see it in the way his eyes kept trying to close, the way his breathing was evening out.

"I'm so tired," he admitted, pulling me against his chest. "But I don't want to close my eyes in case this is a dream. In case I wake up and you're gone again."

"It's not a dream," I assured him, pressing closer until there was no space between us, skin to skin. "I'm here. We're here. And I'm not going anywhere."

"Promise?" His voice was slurred with approaching sleep.

"Promise." I pressed a kiss to his chest, right over his heart, feeling it beat strong and steady under my lips. "Sleep, baby. I'll be here when you wake up."

"Did you just call me *baby*, Cupcake Queen? Now look who's violating the 'ol no pet names rule..." he said groggily.

"Shhhhh."

Love you," he mumbled, already drifting off, one arm locked around me like even unconscious he needed to keep me close.

"Love you too," I whispered back, letting my own eyes close.

The sapphire ring on my finger caught the city lights one last time as I settled my hand over his heart.

For the first time in days, we both slept peacefully, tangled up together in the hotel bed, exactly where we belonged. The Montreal decision still loomed. The scandal fallout remained. The complications with the team hadn't disappeared.

But for now, at this moment, we had each other. We had truth instead of pretense, love instead of fear.

And that was everything we needed for now.

Chapter 24

My alarm went off at five-thirty Monday morning, though I'd barely slept. I stared at the ceiling of my apartment, mentally rehearsing the press conference I'd scheduled for nine o'clock. The professional part of my brain had crafted a carefully worded statement taking responsibility for the fake engagement without implicating the team or damaging Cam's image further. The personal part of my brain was still a jumble of emotions I couldn't begin to untangle.

I showered, blow-dried my hair into submission, and put on my armor: charcoal pencil skirt, white silk blouse, and my blazer in Slashers teal. I slipped on my favorite slay-all-day Christian Louboutin stilettos, the ones with the silver metal embellishment on their pointed toes. Perfect for kicking butt. As I fastened silver Tiffany hoops to my ears, my phone rang. My caller ID displayed "Joey Keegan – ESPN."

Joey was one of the most respected hockey journalists in the country. He'd been covering the Slashers for a decade, and unlike some reporters, he'd always been fair. Even during our worst seasons, he'd never gone for cheap shots or manufactured drama. I hesitated only a second before answering.

"Joey, good morning. I appreciate the call, but I'm afraid I can't comment until after the press conference."

"I know," he said, his voice serious. "And I wouldn't normally do this, but I thought you should know something before you walk into that room."

My stomach tightened. "What's that?"

"I know who leaked the story about your engagement being fake. It was Blake Churchin."

My hand froze on my earring. Blake Churchin was a recent hire, a coaching assistant who'd joined the team just before the season started. He mainly worked with the defensemen and had always been perfectly pleasant to me. It didn't make any sense.

"How do you know that?" I asked, fighting to keep my voice steady.

"He approached me last week, tried to give me the scoop. Sent me photos of the NDA documents. I declined the story – didn't feel right. Then, obviously Anson at *HockeyInsider* ran with it and it blew up."

I sank onto the edge of my bed. "Why would Blake do that?"

"That's the interesting part," Joey said. "After the story broke I circled back with him. He told me he'd done it to help the team. He'd thought it would torpedo Cam's Montreal deal and keep him with the Slashers. My bosses were pissed that I'd passed on the scoop, but even after it broke I could never confirm a second source."

I closed my eyes, processing this betrayal. Someone inside our organization, someone I worked with daily, had deliberately sabotaged Cam and me to manipulate his career decisions.

"I saw the game in Boston, Lana," Joey continued, his voice softening. "I was right behind the glass when Morozov said that shit about you to Cam, and I saw his reaction up close. I saw Cam's face when he spotted you on the Jumbotron. I've been covering this league for fifteen years, and I've never seen anything like the way he played after that moment."

I swallowed hard, remembering the intensity in Cam's eyes after he'd seen me, the way his entire game had transformed.

"You don't have to confirm anything," Joey added. "This is just a courtesy call, professional respect. But I thought you should know who was really behind this before you fall on your sword in a couple hours."

"Thank you, Joey," I managed. "I appreciate you telling me."

"For what it's worth," he said before hanging up, "I've never known you to lie to the press in all the years I've covered the team, and I sincerely hope you keep your job. Whatever you and Cam were doing, I don't think it was fake. Not really."

I sat there for several minutes after the call ended, turning Joey's words over in my mind. Blake Churchin. The leak had come from within our organization – from someone who thought he was acting in the team's best interest. The betrayal stung, but in a strange way, it was also validating. This wasn't just about me making a mistake. Someone else had deliberately tried to sabotage us.

The media room at Slashers Arena was packed when I arrived. The scent of coffee and electronics filled the air, mingling with the faint backdrop of ice and sweat that permeated every NHL arena. Cameras from every major sports network and gossip site lined the back wall. Beat reporters filled the seats, tablets and notebooks ready. Social media team members hovered along the periphery, phones poised to capture every moment. I spotted Marcus and Coach Sully in deep conversation near the side entrance.

I approached them, the paper of my prepared statement crackling slightly in my grip.

"Blake Churchin leaked the NDA," I said without preamble.

Coach Sully's eyebrows shot up. "How do you know?"

"Joey Keegan called me this morning. Said Blake approached him with the story and photos of the documents. Joey declined, but as we all know, Blake found someone else willing to run with it."

Marcus cursed under his breath. "That explains a lot."

Coach Rocco shook his head in disbelief. "Blake's been pushing hard against the Montreal deal in staff meetings. Thinks we can't afford to lose Cam."

"I'll deal with Blake," Coach Sully said, his voice ominously calm. "You focus on getting through the next thirty minutes, Lana."

I nodded, suddenly noticing movement at the back of the room. My parents and Nana Decker had arrived, slipping into seats near the wall. My mother looked fierce and determined, my father stoic as always. Nana looked ready for battle, her silver hair perfectly coiffed, her lucky Slashers brooch pinned to her cardigan. And beside them – Zayne. The last person in the universe I expected to be here today. He'd been incredibly supportive since the scandal broke, but showing up to a press conference was another level entirely.

As I made my way to the podium, I spotted more familiar faces. Logan and Coco were there, holding hands in the second row. Several other players had shown up too: Pietro, Miller, even Nick Fosse, our goaltender. The sight of so many team members, my extended hockey family, made something tighten in my chest.

I took my place behind the microphone, carefully arranging my statement and supporting documents on the podium. The camera flashes intensified and the room fell silent.

"Good morning," I began, my voice steadier than I expected. "Thank you all for coming. I've called this press conference to address the recent reports regarding my relationship with Cam Murphy."

I paused, taking a deep breath.

"As the team's Director of Communications, I hold myself to the highest standards of integrity and transparency. Recent reports have suggested that an engagement to Cam Murphy was fabricated for publicity purposes. I'm here today to correct factual errors in the reporting and take responsibility for my part in this situation."

I glanced down at my prepared text, acutely aware of the sapphire ring on my finger catching the light from the overhead fluorescents. I'd worn it today – for Cam, for myself, for us.

"The truth is that Cam and I have known each other for ten years, since our college days at Boston University. Our relationship has always been complicated – both professionally and personally. When the opportunity arose for Cam to secure the Redline endorsement deal, I agreed to help present an image that would satisfy the company's morality clause requirements. Neither Cam nor I made a single statement to the media, Redline, or anyone in the Slashers organization claiming that we were engaged."

I continued, "We've been informed that the source of the leak of certain confidential documents – which are standard practice in situations involving image management – was a member of our coaching staff hoping to impact Cam Murphy's standing with other teams in an effort to keep him with the Slashers."

The side door of the media room swung open with such force that it bounced against the wall. Every head in the room turned.

Cam stood in the doorway, breathing hard like he'd sprinted here from the locker room. He was wearing jeans and a well-worn, blue t-shirt the same color as his eyes, emblazoned with *Taylor Swift Fearless Tour* – hardly his usual press conference attire. His hair was adorably mussed, and the bruise along his jaw from the Boston fight was still visible. Our eyes met across the room, and something electric passed between us.

"I'm sorry I'm late," he said with his trademark grin, not to the room but directly to me.

Murmurs and chuckles rippled through the audience as Cam made his way to the front. Camera shutters clicked in rapid succession. I stood frozen at the podium, my carefully prepared statement forgotten.

"What are you doing?" I whispered as he approached.

"Something I should have done a long time ago," he replied, his eyes never leaving mine.

He stepped up beside me, and after a moment's hesitation, I moved aside to give him access to the microphone. The room fell into a hushed silence.

"I wasn't supposed to be here today," Cam began, his voice clear and strong. "Lana told me to stay away. Let her handle it. That's what she does – she handles things. Fixes problems. Takes care of every member of this team."

He paused, scanning the room. "But I'm done letting her take the fall for my mistakes. I'm done pretending. So here's the truth: This relationship didn't start like some romantic comedy, but if I'm being honest here, it was the best way I could think of to get her to go out with me again. Lana and I met a decade ago in college. And I've been in love with her pretty much since day one."

A collective gasp went through the room. I felt my cheeks flush as dozens of eyes turned to gauge my reaction. Cam continued, his voice gaining confidence.

"I made a lot of mistakes. I let her craft an image of me that wasn't real because it was easier than admitting how I really felt. I let her believe things about me that weren't true. I walked away from her once because I was too scared to fight for what I wanted. Her."

He turned slightly to face me, no longer speaking to the press but directly to me.

"But I'm not scared anymore. I don't care about some sneaker deal. Or the trade offer of a lifetime. I don't care what anyone in this room writes or tweets or thinks. The only thing I care about is you, Lana."

His voice softened, and I could see the vulnerability in his eyes.

"I love you. I've been in love with you since the day we met. That's not PR. That's me."

The room was so quiet you could hear a pin drop. Every reporter, every camera was trained on us, capturing this moment in high definition. But all I could see was Cam.

Cam, who'd fought for me on the ice in Boston. Cam, who'd held me through the night at the Four Seasons. Cam, who was standing before the entire hockey world, laying his heart bare.

"Lana?" he said, a question in his voice.

I stepped back to the microphone. My hands were trembling, but my voice was clear.

"Cam and I did date in college. Briefly. Intensely. It didn't work out for reasons that seemed insurmountable at the time."

I took a deep breath, feeling the weight of my next words.

"Over the years, I helped create an image of Cam that wasn't the full picture, and when it started to hurt him, I felt responsible. The truth is, Cam Murphy isn't the wild playboy myself and the media have portrayed him to be. He's loyal, thoughtful, obsessed with weird socks, and..."

I paused, my eyes locked with his.

"And... and I love him. I smiled, feeling lighter than I had in days. "If I'm being honest... I never completely got over Cam. And as hockey fans all across America already know... Cam Murphy is pretty hard to resist."

The room erupted. Camera flashes exploded like strobe lights. Reporters shot to their feet, shouting questions. But in that chaos, it felt like Cam and I were in our own bubble, the noise fading to a distant hum.

His smile – that devastating, heart-stopping smile – spread slowly across his face. He reached for my hand, his fingers intertwining with mine. When I smiled back at him, he brought my hand to his lips and kissed it softly, right where the sapphire ring caught the light.

"Cam, Cam," a reporter from *Sports Insider* yelled. "What about the ring? How does that fit in?"

Cam grinned, exuding his trademark charm. "The ring? Just between us? I'm still working up the courage to ask."

The room roared again, questions coming from every direction.

Coach Sully looked at me, nodded, and stepped up to the microphone, his authoritative presence immediately calming the crowd.

"I have a statement to make as well," he said, his voice cutting through the clamor. "This morning, we confirmed that Blake Churchin, an assistant coach who has been with the organization for three months, was responsible for leaking confidential team documents to the press. Blake has admitted that he did this in a misguided attempt to sabotage Cam Murphy's reputation with other teams, hoping it would kill potential trade deals and keep Cam with the Slashers."

Shocked murmurs swept through the room.

"Blake's employment with the Slashers has been terminated, effective immediately." Coach Sully's eyes found mine, and his stern expression softened slightly. "Lana Decker is as valuable a member of this team as any player or coach. Her integrity, professionalism, and dedication to this organization have never been in question."

He paused, his voice taking on the intensity he usually reserved for locker room speeches. "In hockey, when someone takes a cheap shot at one of our own, we respond as a team. We protect our own. I think the Boston Bruins can confirm that's true."

A ripple of laughter went through the room at the reference to Saturday's brawl.

To my surprise, my father stood up next. Frank Decker in his signature navy blazer and Slashers tie, the very picture of hockey royalty. The room immediately quieted – when Frank Decker spoke, people listened.

"My daughter Lana Decker has been part of the hockey world her entire life," he said, his deep voice carrying easily without a microphone. "She understands the game, the players, and the business better than most. I've watched her carve out her own place in this sport through her hard work and dedication."

He turned slightly to face Cam and me.

"Cameron spoke to my wife and myself last week after spending the weekend at our beach house with our extended family and asked for our blessing, which we wholeheartedly gave. He told us that while their relationship may have started unconventionally, his feelings for Lana were genuine and always had been. He wanted us to know his intentions were…serious."

I gasped, turning to Cam with wide eyes. He'd asked my parents for their blessing? Last week? Before the scandal even broke?

He shrugged, a sheepish smile playing at his lips. My heart was so full I thought it might burst. Cam respectfully nodded to my father, who acknowledged it with a nod of his own.

My mother dabbed at her eyes with a tissue, and even Zayne looked suspiciously misty.

Speaking of my brother, Zayne stood up next and made his way to the front of the room, shocking everyone, including me. The assembled media shifted forward in their seats – Zayne rarely spoke publicly outside of mandatory press appearances.

Who were these people impersonating my family?

"The first day I met Cam Murphy at BU," Zayne began, his voice gruff, "I told him I'd bury him in the equipment shed if he even *looked* at my sister. This has been my standard first-day-of-hockey-practice speech since I was in the third grade."

A laugh rippled through the audience.

"But I've never seen my sister or my teammate happier than when they're together," he continued. "Cam's been like a brother to me for years, and I'd be honored to call him my brother-in-law."

He turned to Cam, his expression deadly serious. "But if you hurt her, I'll still bury you in the equipment shed."

Cam nodded solemnly. "Understood."

The two men exchanged a look and Zayne surprised everyone by pulling Cam into a quick, fierce hug.

The press conference shifted into a more structured Q&A after that. I stepped back up to the microphone, my PR instincts taking over despite the emotional whirlwind of the last few minutes.

"We'll take a few questions now," I said, my professional composure returning. "Then we'll issue a follow-up statement later today."

Hands shot up around the room. I pointed to a reporter from *Hockey Today*.

"Is this going to affect Cam's decision regarding the Montreal offer?"

Cam stepped up beside me. "My agent and the teams are still in discussions, but I'll say this: St. Petersburg has always felt like home. Now more than ever."

I nodded to a journalist from *NHL Tonight*. "Lana, will you continue as PR Director now that you're in a relationship with a player?"

"Great question," I said. "The Slashers organization has protocols in place for situations like this. I'll be working with Marcus and the executive team to ensure there's no conflict of interest while maintaining the highest professional standards. The team comes first – that will never change."

"Is that the actual engagement ring?" shouted a reporter from the back.

I looked down at the sapphire on my finger, then at Cam. He raised an eyebrow, leaving it up to me how to answer.

"As Cam stated earlier, I believe he's, quote, 'still working up the courage to ask'. Let's not ruin his big surprise. Next question."

The room laughed, and Nana Decker blew me a kiss from the back. I fielded three more questions with professional ease, keeping the focus on the facts of the situation while acknowledging the emotional aspects that had captivated the hockey world.

When the press conference concluded, reporters rushed forward with follow-up questions, but I directed them to contact my office for follow-up. As security began clearing the room, I felt a hand on my shoulder. My mother pulled me into a tight hug.

"I've never been prouder," she whispered. "You handled that like the queen you are."

"Thanks, Mom," I said, returning her embrace.

My father was next, his hug brief but firm. "I told you that you belong here," he said gruffly, emotion evident in his voice despite his attempt to hide it.

Nana Decker pulled me into a hug and kissed me on the cheek, whispering, "The stars have all aligned for you two, darling. "

I laughed, turning to find Cam engaged in what appeared to be a serious conversation with Zayne and Logan. As if sensing my gaze, he looked up, his smile immediate and warm. He excused himself and made his way to me.

"You were amazing," he said, taking my hand. "Professional Lana is soooooo hot, by the way."

I rolled my eyes, but couldn't stop my smile. "That was quite the entrance you made."

"You know I love to make a splash." He squeezed my hand as we headed towards the door.

The heavy glass door of the media room swung shut behind us with a definitive click, muffling the continuing roar of questions and camera clicks. Cam's hand found mine, warm and solid, as we escaped down the service corridor toward my office.

Chapter 25

We walked hand in hand from the press conference to my office, both of us shell-shocked but in the best possible way. The hallway seemed to stretch endlessly, and I was acutely aware of every person we passed – their eyes widening, whispers following in our wake. Cam's hand was warm and steady in mine, his thumb occasionally brushing over my knuckles in a silent reassurance.

Once inside my office, I closed the door and leaned against it, finally letting out the breath I felt like I'd been holding since Cam crashed the press conference. The adrenaline was wearing off, leaving me slightly shaky but strangely calm.

"So," I said, meeting his gaze across the room. "That just happened."

Cam's smile was soft, a little uncertain. "Yeah. I kind of went off-script there."

"You think?" I laughed, the sound bordering on giddy. "Cam, you just declared your love for me on national television."

"Technically international," he corrected, taking a step toward me. "TSN in Canada definitely picked that up."

I groaned, but couldn't stop smiling. "The PR director in me is having a tiny meltdown right now. The rest of me..." I trailed off, not quite able to articulate the swirl of emotions – joy, relief, disbelief – coursing through me.

"The rest of you?" he prompted, taking another step closer.

"The rest of me has never been happier," I admitted softly.

His eyes darkened at my words. In three quick strides, he was standing in front of me, cradling my face in his hands. "Me neither," he whispered before his lips found mine.

The kiss was gentle at first, almost reverent, but quickly deepened as the reality of our situation – no more hiding, no more pretending – sank in. His hands slid into my hair, angling my head to deepen the kiss, and my arms encircled his neck, pulling him closer.

We broke apart at the sound of my phone buzzing – a constant, insistent vibration that signaled the media storm was already brewing. I glanced at the screen and laughed.

"What?" Cam asked, his arms still around my waist.

"Thirty-seven missed calls, sixty-four texts, and..." I checked my email notification. "One hundred and twenty-three new emails. All in the last twenty minutes." I set the phone face-down on my desk. "I think we might have caused a stir."

"Oh no! NOT A STIR," Cam laughed, looking utterly unrepentant.

Katie, my assistant, burst into my office without knocking, waving her tablet like a victory flag. "Have you seen Bluesky? Or Instagram? Or literally ANY social media?" Her eyes were wide, almost manic. "No more PR disaster – this is a PR MIRACLE!"

She thrust the tablet into my hands, and I scrolled through a seemingly endless stream of posts:

@PuckPrincess24: *I KNEW IT. I KNEW CAM AND LANA WERE REAL. I'M CRYING. #HockeyEverAfter*

@GoalieMom44: *Can we talk about how respectfully Cam loves her? Men, take notes.*

@HotForHatTricks: *When he said 'That's not PR. That's me' I ASCENDED. #HockeyEverAfter*

Someone had already created a fan cam zooming in on Cam's face during my line: "Cam Murphy is pretty hard to resist" – set to Taylor Swift's *Love Story*. It had over 150,000 likes in 15 minutes.

"The Slashers' social accounts have gained twenty thousand followers in the last hour," Katie continued, practically bouncing. "And Marcus wants me to tell you the merchandising team is already working on Valentine's Day special edition jerseys – his and hers."

"Tell them absolutely not," I said automatically, PR director instincts kicking in. "That's tacky and exploitative and – "

"I kind of like it," Cam interrupted, smirking as he peered over my shoulder at the tablet. "Just imagine: Murphy 22 and Murphy's 22."

I rolled my eyes, but couldn't stop my smile. "You're impossible."

"Impossibly in love with you," he countered, pressing a kiss to my temple.

Katie squealed. "Sorry! I'll go. Just... the press is requesting follow-up interviews, and *People* magazine wants an exclusive, and there's a hashtag trending – #HockeyEverAfter. I mean, how cute is that?"

"Katie," I interrupted firmly. "I need to catch my breath. Yes on exclusives for *People* and Joey Keegan at *ESPN* for now, so you can go ahead and get those scheduled. I also need to tweak my formal follow-up statement for this afternoon to include Cam crashing the presser... but I need a few minutes first."

"So romantic," she swooned. "Of course. Totally. Got it." She nodded, backing toward the door. With a final excited grin, she was gone.

Cam's arms encircled my waist from behind, his chin resting on my shoulder. "How are you really feeling?" he asked softly.

I leaned back against him, letting myself savor the solid warmth of him. "Overwhelmed. Happy. Terrified." I twisted in his arms to face him. "This is going to change everything, Cam. For both of us."

"Good," he said simply. "I'm ready for change."

A knock at the door interrupted us. Before I could answer, it swung open and Logan strode in, followed closely by Coco, both beaming.

"You two," Logan said, shaking his head with a grin. "Always have to steal the spotlight."

Coco pulled me into a tight hug. "I told you it was real," she whispered in my ear. "I'm so happy for you."

"Thanks," I murmured, squeezing her back. When we parted, she was practically glowing with happiness.

"My phone's blowing up with messages from my skating students," Coco told us. "They're all obsessed with you guys. Specifically, they want to know if Cam's as dreamy in person." She winked at Cam. "I told them he's okay."

"Just okay?" Cam clutched his chest in mock offense. "I'm wounded."

"Your ego will recover," Logan assured him, clapping him on the shoulder. "Nice press conference hijacking, by the way. Very dramatic."

"I learned from the best," Cam replied, nodding toward me.

My phone buzzed again with an incoming call from a number I didn't recognize. When it immediately rang again after sending it to voicemail, I sighed and answered.

"Lana Decker."

"Ms. Decker, this is Jess Riley from Sports Illustrated. I'd love to schedule – "

"Hi Jess. It's a little crazy around here today as you can probably imagine, but if you give Katie a call, she can put something on the books." She thanked me and I hung up, only for my phone to immediately ring again.

I immediately texted Katie: *Yes on SI and* shot Cam a look of exasperation. "I may need to turn this off for a while."

"Do it," he encouraged. "The world can wait."

My office door swung open again, this time revealing Pietro, Miller, and Nick, all grinning like idiots. "You guys broke the internet," Pietro informed us, scrolling through his phone. "And also my mom called to ask if I could get your autographs. Both of you. She's making a scrapbook. And she wants a wedding invitation. Please don't make me bring her as my plus-one."

"Tell her we'd be honored," Cam laughed.

"Also, Coach Sully wants you to know that any reporter who tries to get into the locker room today will be escorted out personally. By him." Pietro grinned. "I think he's kinda enjoying playing bodyguard."

Miller nodded. "He's all grumpy-proud, like when we won the Cup but he didn't want to admit he was emotional."

Nick, our typically stoic goaltender, simply gave us a thumbs-up. "Took you long enough," he said before wandering back out.

After they left, I turned to Cam with a laugh. "I can't decide if we're going to get any work done today."

"Probably not," he admitted, reaching for my hand. The sapphire on my finger caught the light, reminding me of all the questions still hanging between us.

As if reading my mind, Cam said, "About Montreal... "

The door opened yet again, this time revealing my brother. Zayne stood there looking simultaneously uncomfortable and pleased, which for him was practically exuberant.

"Z," Cam said, straightening slightly. Despite everything that had happened, there was still that moment of uncertainty – the decade-long fear of disappointing his best friend.

Zayne crossed the room in three long strides and, to my utter shock, pulled Cam into a rough embrace. "Took you long enough," he said gruffly, echoing Nick's sentiment. When they parted, Zayne looked at me. "You okay, Lan?"

I nodded, my throat suddenly tight with emotion. "Yeah. I'm good."

"Good." He cleared his throat, clearly reaching his emotional expression limit.

Katie poked her head inside my office. "Um, your nine-o-clock is still here. I'm so sorry I forgot to cancel her meeting on Friday with everything going on."

"Totally understandable. Sorry. Who am I meeting with again?"

She stepped inside, closing the door behind her and whispered, "The romance author? She's doing research?"

"Right, right, right..." I said, shaking my head to focus. "Send her in."

I looked at Zayne and Cam, "Stay a minute please guys, help me smooth this over."

Cam and Zayne nodded in unison,

I stood to greet her as Katie led the woman into my office. She wore a hibiscus pink sundress, wedge espadrilles, and her chestnut hair pulled up in a messy top knot.

She startled when she saw both Zayne and Cam standing in my office.

"I apologize for all the nuttiness this morning. We had a bit of a situation," I laughed.

"Shelby," she said, extending her hand. I shook it as she gushed, "Oh my GOD. Like, no worries at all. I watched the whole thing while I was waiting. I swear, it was the most romantic thing I've ever seen in my life. Really...incredible."

Her eyes were wide, like she'd just finished riding a roller coaster.

"Shelby, it's fantastic to meet you. I apologize that I'm not a bit more prepared for this meeting. This is Cam, and this is Zayne, two of our star players."

"I'm a fan," she gushed, shaking both their hands enthusiastically. Cam grinned, thanking her, and Zayne politely nodded."

Thanks so much," Zayne said, "It's always so great to meet the fans. Do you live in the area? Or are you visiting?"

"I'm local," she grinned. "Born and raised." Zayne smiled.

"Uh, would you like a photo?" Zayne asked. "With me... and Cam? Lana can take it."

Huh? What was this? Zayne was always polite and accommodating to fans because that's how we were raised, but in his entire life, I had never seen him like this. It was like watching a body double or something.

"I'd love it," she smiled. "That would be cool."

Zayne scooped my phone off my desk and handed it to me. Cam just grinned at me over Shelby's head. I posed them in front of the giant Slashers logo on my wall, and snapped a few pictures, Shelby in the middle, with Cam and Zayne on either side."Would you mind taking one with my phone too?" she asked, digging into her purse. "And is it okay if I post it to Instagram?"Just as I was about to answer, Zayne jumped in. "Just give Lana your number and she can send it to you." *What had gotten into him?* "Sure," I agreed. "These turned out great, I'll just text them to you. The guys, uh, have practice starting in a few minutes."

"Wow, thank you," she said. "Look, I know things are crazy around here this morning. Would it be easier on you if I came back next week?"

"That would be great," Zayne nodded. Cam was doing everything he could to keep a straight face.

"Do you mind?" I said. "I hate to have you come back, but things are a bit chaotic this morning since the presser. How about we get you scheduled for next week. I'll arrange for you to watch a practice, or we can bring you to a game if you'd like. I'll set up some interviews for you with a couple players."

"That would be amazing," she said. "I'll get out of your hair this morning."

"Thanks," I said, walking her to the door. "Katie – would you please get Shelby set up for a meeting next week? I'm going to attend a practice with her and we'll arrange a couple of player interviews." I tossed my phone to Katie. "Will you also please text her the pics we just took while I finish up here?"

"Sure thing, boss," Katie replied. Shelby thanked me, Cam, and Zayne again and gave a little wave as she disappeared through the door of my office.

Zayne nodded at Cam, "We've got practice. I'll see you down there."

My email pinged from Katie, and I instinctively glanced at my computer screen. The subject line read: "MEDIA ROUNDUP – MURPHY/DECKER."

Moment of truth. I clicked.

The email contained links to dozens of articles that had appeared in the last hour:

"Fake Fiancée, Real Feelings? Inside the Love Story Melting Hockey's Heart" – *People*

"Heartbreaker Off the Market: Cam Murphy and Lana Decker's Second Chance Romance Stuns NHL" – *ESPN*

"PR Genius! Lana Decker's Masterclass in Crisis Spin" – *Forbes*

"Hockey's Hottest Power Couple: Ten Years in the Making" – *Hockey Week*

"Murphy's Montreal Momentum: Will Love Keep Him in St. Pete?" – *The Athletic*

Cam leaned over my shoulder, reading along with me. "Hey, look at that. Forbes thinks you're a genius."

"Forbes thinks this was some elaborate PR strategy," I corrected. "They have no idea the last few days have been completely reactive crisis management."

"Maybe that's your superpower," Cam suggested. "Making catastrophes look like carefully executed plans."

I snorted. "That's definitely my superpower. It's pretty much my entire job description."

"Well, that and distracting me from hockey," he countered with a wink. He whispered conspiratorially, rubbing the hem of my blouse between his fingers, "Is it wrong that I want to tear all your buttons off with my teeth?"

Before I could answer, my desk phone rang. Ryan Keller appeared on the caller ID. I answered, putting it on speaker. "Ryan."

"Lana! Is Cam with you? He's not picking up his phone."

"I'm here, Ryan," Cam confirmed, pulling a chair beside me.

"Holy shit I can't believe you two started this morning in full damage control mode and then managed to make all of America fall in love with you in the space of 45 minutes. I just got off the phone with Redline." Ryan's voice practically vibrated with excitement. "The deal is ON. They're over the moon about this whole situation. They're calling it 'authentic brand storytelling' and 'leveraging genuine emotional connection' and a bunch of other marketing buzzwords that make the money go up."

"They're not upset about the...arrangement?" I asked, professional caution still at the forefront of my mind.

"Are you kidding? They're claiming they knew you two were the real deal all along! Said the chemistry between you two was off the charts. This is their dream scenario – the bad boy reformed by love, the college crush that never died, the second chance romance. They eat this stuff up!"

Cam's smile was radiant. "So the contract...?"

"Is everything we asked for, plus a bonus if Lana agrees to appear in some of the campaigns as your 'inspiration'. They want to tell your love story through sneakers."

"What does that even mean?" Cam laughed.

"It means six million dollars and your handsome mug plastered on billboards all over the country, hell if I know. I'll email you the deal memo, but bottom line: this is the biggest endorsement of your career, Murphy."

Relief washed over me. The very deal that had started our fake engagement charade was now secured – and better than we'd initially hoped.

"And..." Cam prompted, something in his expression shifting.

Ryan's tone changed slightly. "And I'll be talking to Marcus this afternoon about the St. Pete offer. Montreal is pushing hard, especially now; we still need to see if the Slashers can even make the numbers work."

My stomach dropped at the mention of Montreal. With everything that had just happened, the offer was still on the table. Still beckoning with its millions and prestige.

"We're taking everything under consideration," Ryan continued. "I'll keep you both updated."

After ending the call, Cam turned to me, clearly seeing the concern in my eyes. "Hey," he said softly. "It's going to be okay."

I nodded, pushing down the anxiety that threatened to overwhelm the joy of the morning. "I know. I trust you. We'll figure it out."

The words came out more easily than I expected, and I realized I meant them. After everything we'd been through, I did trust him. I had to.

"I need to get to practice," Cam said reluctantly, glancing at his watch. "Dinner tonight? My place?"

"Perfect," I agreed. "Pretty sure I'll be working late anyway."

He stood, hesitating for a moment before leaning down to kiss me. It was a brief kiss, but filled with promise. "I'll text you the address – though you've been there once before," he added with a wink.

"I think I can find my way," I assured him, my face flushing slightly as I vividly recalled the night we'd spent together.

"Also, just me or was Zayne being really weird earlier.""Oh no, not just you," I laughed. "*Total* weirdo."

With one last smile, he was gone, and I turned to face the mountain of work ahead. The world now knew about us, and there was no going back. Whatever came next, we'd face it together.

The rest of the day passed in a blur of congratulatory messages, media and sponsorship inquiries, and trying to maintain some semblance of normalcy in the midst of becoming hockey's hottest couple overnight.

Logan texted me:

> LOGAN: Coco says she loves Cam but if he hurts you she'll help Zayne hide his body.

Pietro sent a group message to the team:

> PIETRO: Can we focus on hockey now that Mom and Dad have figured out they're in love?

Coach Sully called me personally, his gruff voice softening when he said, "You did good, kid. You were in an impossible situation, and you came through. Both of you."

My parents called, insisting I bring Cam for Sunday dinner. "We always knew," my mother said cryptically. "A mother knows these things."

"I never thought I'd see my own daughter with a left wing," my father grumbled, though I could hear the grin in his voice. "But I suppose he'll do."

By evening, I was emotionally and physically exhausted. We decided to skip dinner out and order takeout to Cam's place instead. The idea of facing the public – even in a restaurant – was too much after the day we'd had.

We had to slip out through the service entrance of the arena to avoid the cluster of reporters and fans who had somehow gotten wind of our location. Cam kept his arm around me protectively as we hurried to his Range Rover, his massive body angled to shield me from view.

"This is insane," I muttered as we finally made it into his car. "I'm usually the one managing this kind of circus, not the main attraction."

"Welcome to the other side," he said with a wry smile, navigating carefully through the parking lot. "Now you know what it's like when you send us out to 'just answer a few questions.'"

"Touché." I leaned back against the headrest, finally letting the exhaustion of the day wash over me.

Cam reached over to take my hand. "For what it's worth, I think you do a great job protecting us. I've just never appreciated it until I saw you on the receiving end of the frenzy."

The drive to Cam's was quiet; both of us were worn out from the past few days. As the Tampa Bay skyline appeared in the windshield, glittering against the deepening twilight, a sense of peace settled over me. Whatever happened next – with the media, with Montreal, with us – I'd never felt more hopeful about the future than I did in that moment.

Cam's modern waterfront home was unusually tidy, I noticed as we walked in. The spacious open floor plan with its floor-to-ceiling windows overlooking the bay was a study in masculine elegance – comfortable yet sophisticated, with muted blues and grays reflecting the water views. When we'd spent the night together before, I'd been too distracted by, well, *Cam* to fully appreciate his space. Now I took it in properly.

Unlike the playboy image we'd cultivated, Cam's home reflected the real him.

The walls featured photos of him with various teammates over the years from peewee hockey on up, with his BU hockey team, and several with Zayne and Logan. I was surprised to find that I appeared in the background of several of his framed photos. Interestingly, while the players in the foreground were sometimes slightly blurred, I was often perfectly in focus – as if the photographer had been aiming at me all along. I smiled to myself as I explored the rest of his living room. There were books everywhere – spy novels, biographies, a few cookbooks. A massive floor to ceiling wall of old-school vinyl records. A large, comfortable sectional faced both the breathtaking bay view.

As I settled on the couch, my eye caught something unusual on the kitchen island – a glass cake dome on a pedestal containing six delicate purple-frosted cupcakes, and a tupperware container nearby with a dozen or so unfrosted cupcakes.

"What's all this?"

Cam rubbed the back of his neck. "Ah, that. Well..." He walked to the island, picking up a piece of paper covered with what appeared to be a recipe, along with a bunch of scribbles and measurements. "I wanted to surprise you. I've been trying to recreate those lavender vanilla cupcakes you love so much from Sweet Caroline's."

"Really?" My heart melted. "So that explains all the baking supplies I saw the morning after I spent the night."

"Yeah. I've been practicing since that day at the bakery during our little selfie tour." He hesitated. "I still can't get the frosting quite right, though."

I crossed to the kitchen and wrapped my arms around his waist from behind, pressing my cheek against his shoulder blades. "You are full of surprises, Hitman."

He turned in my arms. "I like to keep you on your toes."

"I think the key is the lavender infusion time – who knew?" he said. "Sweet Caroline's frosting has this texture that's somewhere between buttercream and whipped cream."

I marveled at this side of him I'd never known about. Cam Murphy – NHL star, league heartthrob, badass enforcer – meticulously piping lavender frosting onto homemade cupcakes because he knew I loved them.

"Want to taste?" he asked, pulling a covered bowl out of the refrigerator. He grabbed a small spatula from a drawer, opened the container, and presented me with a small dollop of pale purple frosting.

"Wait, wait..." he said, "this is the best part!" He looked so proud of himself as pulled a tiny, sparkly white crown made from sugar and carefully placed it on top of the cupcake. "For my cupcake queen!""Aw." I leaned forward and let him feed me the sweet confection.

The delicate floral notes mixed with vanilla and butter bloomed across my tongue. "Oh my God," I said, genuinely surprised. "That's really good. Like, really close to the original."

His face lit up with pride. "Yeah?"

"Absolutely." I reached for the spatula again, but he playfully held it just out of reach.

"Payment required," he teased.

"Oh really?" I raised an eyebrow, slipping into the easy flirtation that had always simmered beneath our professional relationship. "What kind of payment?"

His eyes darkened slightly. "I think you know."

I stepped closer, sliding my hands up his chest. "Would this work?" I asked innocently, pressing a soft kiss to his jaw.

"Getting warmer," he murmured.

Later, we sat on his couch eating takeout lasagne which paired remarkably well with lavender cupcakes and prosecco. With my feet in his lap, I found myself admiring the sapphire ring again. The ocean blue stone caught the light from the floor lamp nearby, sending prismatic reflections bouncing across the ceiling.

"I hate to admit it," I said, swirling my hand to make the light dance, "but I'm actually going to be sorry to give this back. I've gotten kind of attached to my fake ring."

Cam's hands stilled on my ankle. "Who says it's fake?"

I froze. "Wait. What?"

He finally looked up at me, his expression completely serious. "It was never fake, Lana. I picked it. Paid for it. The second I saw it, I knew it was yours."

I stared at him, stunned. All this time, I'd assumed it was a prop – something borrowed or rented for the charade. "But, why would you buy a real engagement ring for a fake engagement?"

He set down his fork and took my hands in his. "Because I hoped, somewhere deep down, that it wouldn't always be fake. That maybe this whole ridiculous plan would give me the chance I'd been too scared to take for ten years." His fingers brushed over the sapphire. "The guy from Tiffany said mermaid sapphires represent hope for a long and happy relationship. I sort of thought that was fitting, since that has always been my hope for us too."

I blinked rapidly against sudden tears, the full meaning of his gesture hitting me. "You romantic idiot," I managed, making him laugh.

"Your romantic idiot," he corrected, leaning in to kiss me softly.

He smiled that devastating smile. "So... about that ring..."

My heart skipped. "What about it?"

"I know we started this whole thing backward, but what do you think about making it real? Not right away," he added quickly. "We can take our time. Do it right."

I looked at him, this man I loved. Who made my heart soar and my knees weak, and fit in with my family so well it was like he'd always been there. "I think... I'd like that." I kissed him tenderly, my heart so full it felt like it might burst. "Of course, you'll have to clear it with Nana Decker, she's still angling for a June wedding. After all, Venus *will* be in Cancer. Or something."

"It's Mars. We could make that work," he grinned, leaning over to kiss me softly. "I've been pining after you for ten years, so I'm just trying not to seem too...eager."

I laughed.

"But I am."

"And I'm still not sure how I'm going to maintain professional distance at work when all I want to do is drag you into my office and – "

"Please continue that thought in explicit detail," he interrupted with a wolfish grin.

I laughed. "You're incorrigible."

"Part of my charm," he agreed, pulling me closer.

We sat in comfortable silence for a while, watching the lights of boats moving across the bay. Tomorrow would bring more questions, more media attention, more decisions about how to navigate our new public relationship alongside our professional responsibilities. But tonight was just for us – no cameras, no reporters, no expectations.

Just Cam and me, finally real. A love story ten years in the making. And it was only just beginning.

The cupcakes, the mermaid sapphire, the bay view, how easy it was to be with Cam – all of it felt like pieces falling into place.

He held me in his arms, and kissed me playfully until it deepened. His lips moved against mine with an unhurried gentleness that made my heart flutter in my chest. The taste of cupcakes still lingered between us, sweet like the moment we were sharing. I felt incredibly happy – complete and belonging in a way I'd never experienced before.

When Cam took my hand, his fingers intertwining with mine as naturally as if they'd always belonged there, I followed him upstairs without hesitation. The wooden stairs creaked softly beneath our feet, but I barely noticed, too captivated by the warmth of his hand and the quiet affection in his eyes when he glanced back at me.

His bedroom was bathed in moonlight, reflected off the water and streaming through the large windows, casting everything in a magical silvery glow. The bay's distant waters shimmered beyond the glass, a perfect backdrop to what felt like the beginning of forever.

Cam drew me close, his hands sliding reverently up my sides. "You're the most beautiful person I've ever known," he whispered, his voice thick with emotion. "I can't believe you're finally here. With me."

I reached up to trace the curve of his cheek, feeling the slight roughness of evening stubble beneath my fingertips. "I've always been yours," I admitted quietly. It felt good to say it out loud.

We kissed again, slowly sinking onto his bed, our bodies finding each other with the certainty of puzzle pieces clicking into place. His weight above me felt like an anchor, grounding me to this perfect moment. We took our time undressing each other, each newly revealed patch of skin explored with gentle touches and softer kisses.

When I straddled him, looking down into those impossibly blue eyes, I saw everything I'd ever wanted reflected back at me – desire, yes, but also tenderness, admiration, and a love so clear it brought tears to my eyes. Cam reached up to brush away a tear with his thumb, his touch feather-light against my cheek.

"I love you," he said, the words floating between us.

"I love you too," I whispered back, leaning down to kiss him as we began to move together.

Our bodies rocked in a gentle rhythm, finding a tempo as natural as breathing. This wasn't just sex – it was communion, the physical manifestation of the connection we'd been fighting for years. My hands splayed across his chest, feeling his heart thundering beneath my palm. His hands gripped my hips, guiding me, supporting me, worshipping me.

When we both reached our peak, it wasn't with the explosive urgency of our earlier encounters, but with a deep, soul-shaking intensity that left us both breathless and clinging to one another, unwilling to let even an inch of space come between us.

We lay together in his bed afterward, spent and happy – my head on his chest listening to the steady beat of his heart, his finger absentmindedly twirling a lock of my hair.

Nothing outside his bedroom door existed in that moment – there was only us, wrapped in each other's warmth, finally home.

"Lana, I need to tell you something," he said quietly, his chest rumbling beneath my ear. "We're talking to Montreal in the morning..."

My heart stuttered. "And?"

"And I'm telling them I'm staying in St. Pete."

I sat up in bed and stared at him. "Cam, that deal is – "

"Life-changing, yeah." He shrugged. "But you know what else is life-changing? Feeling like I have a real family for the first time in my life. The Slashers made a strong offer for me to renew my contract. It's not Montreal money, but it's more than fair."

"But – "

"No buts," he said firmly. "This is where I want to be. With you. With my team. With your entire extended family at the beach house. Thirteen years of friendship with Zayne and half as many with Logan. A Cup-winning team. The smartest PR director in the league. And bonus, sunny Florida versus frigid Quebec means a lot more opportunities to see you in that little white bikini.

I kissed his forehead tenderly and snuggled deeper under his arm, looking up at him – at this beautiful man who'd crashed a press conference to declare his love for me, who'd chosen me over money and opportunity, who'd finally allowed himself to be seen for who he really was. The real Cam Murphy. My Cam.

The hockey heartthrob who broke my heart and somehow put it all back together again.

Chapter 26

I awoke to a blast of sunlight streaming through Cam's bedroom windows. No blinds, right on the water. Yeesh. I stretched, instinctively reaching for Cam's warmth, but found his side of the bed empty. The aroma of coffee and something sweet – cinnamon? – drifted up from the kitchen.

Two days. It had been exactly one week since our lives had been turned upside down, inside out, and somehow landed exactly where they were supposed to be. The fake engagement scandal, the press conference, Cam's public declaration – it all felt like a lifetime ago and just yesterday at the same time.

I smiled, running my fingers over the sapphire ring that hadn't left my finger. It sparkled in the morning light, sending blue reflections dancing across the ceiling. Real. It had been real all along.

Wrapping myself in Cam's discarded T-shirt from yesterday – a BU hockey shirt that had become my unofficial pajamas – I padded downstairs to find him.

The sight that greeted me made my heart do a little somersault. Cam stood at the kitchen island, concentration etched on his face as he meticulously arranged blueberries on top of a golden pancake. His game-day ritual was in full effect: left sock first (today featuring little sharks with sunglasses), specific playlist humming softly from the speakers, and precisely timed breakfast three hours before light practice.

"Morning," I said softly, not wanting to break his concentration.

He looked up, and his face transformed with that smile that still, after everything, made my knees weak. "Morning, beautiful." He gestured to his creation. "Blueberry pancakes. The berries are arranged in a '22.'"

I walked closer and saw that indeed, the blueberries formed a perfect jersey number atop the pancake.

"That's..." I tilted my head, "actually really impressive. Do you always make number pancakes on game day?"

"Uh...no?" He looked at me sheepishly, flipped the pancake onto a plate, and slid it toward me. "Because that would be... *embarrassing*. And today's a big day."

Today. The first home game since our press conference. The first time we'd appear publicly at our home arena as a real couple. The official announcement of Cam's decision to stay with the Slashers despite Montreal's monstrous offer. The game against Pittsburgh, our biggest conference rival. And just minutes from now, the official signing of the Redline deal.

The doorbell rang, ending our domestic breakfast moment. Cam's agent Ryan arrived with his usual hurricane energy, designer suit impeccable, tablet already open to the Redline contract, a Fedex box under his arm.

"Ready to make history, kids?" Ryan asked, not waiting for an answer before spreading papers across Cam's kitchen island, carefully avoiding the pancake station.

The next thirty minutes passed in a blur of signatures, legal language, and Ryan's excited commentary. The contract was exactly what they'd promised – six million dollars, creative control over Cam's image in the campaign (my suggestion), and a clause that specifically mentioned me as a potential participant in select promotional activities. (I'm still not sure about that one.)

"And here," Ryan said with a flourish, opening the box, "is your first official Redline package."

Inside were two identical pairs of sleek, black sneakers with teal accents – Slashers colors. The right heel of each shoe featured a tiny embroidered "22," while the left heel had a delicate embossed hockey stick.

"They're not launching the Cameron Murphy line for another six months," Ryan explained, "but they wanted you both to have the prototype."

Cam pulled out the larger pair, turning them over in his hands with something like wonder. "They really did it. Every detail we talked about."

"They're really good at listening," Ryan said, glancing between us with a knowing smile. "Especially when it comes to authentic stories. Pure Cameron Murphy, hockey enforcer and devoted romantic."

After Ryan left, promising to meet us at the arena, Cam pulled a bottle of champagne from the fridge. "It's too early to drink, especially on game day," he said, "but I think we need to mark the moment."

He poured just a splash into two flutes, then handed one to me. "To us," he said simply.

"To us," I echoed, clinking my glass against his. "And to the Slashers for the next three years."

Cam's eyes widened slightly. "You heard about the contract terms already?"

I nodded. "Marcus called this morning while you were in the shower. Three years, eight million per year. He wanted me to know before the press release went out at noon."

Cam set his glass down. "And?"

"And what?"

"What do you think? I know Montreal was planning to offer almost twelve per year."

I set my glass down too, then took both his hands in mine. "I think you made the decision that was right for you. For both of us." I squeezed his hands. "I know what it means to you to stay here, with this team. With Zayne and Logan. With me."

His expression softened. "I dunno," he teased gently. "Four million a year is a lot to leave on the table."

"Oh no," I started to freak out. "Are you regretting it already? I mean, it's also not like you'll be struggling to make rent," I pointed out. "Besides, there's no state income tax in Florida. And you don't have to learn French."

He laughed, pulling me into his arms. "I'd have learned French for you."

"Je t'aime," I said, one of the few French phrases I remembered from college.

"I love you too," he murmured against my hair. "More than hockey. More than money. More than anything."

The way he said it – so simple, so certain – made my throat tight with emotion. Cam Murphy, the man who'd been through so many broken homes he'd stopped believing in forever, was promising me exactly that. Forever.

The arena was buzzing with energy when we arrived – separately, because we didn't want to mess with the usual routine. Cam with the team for pre-game preparations, me to handle the media and last-minute PR details. But this time, we shared a steamy kiss next to the stairs before parting ways.

"For luck," he said with a wink.

"You don't need luck, Hitman." I straightened his tie. "But I'll take that kiss anyway."

Inside, Katie was waiting for me with a tablet full of interview requests and a sparkling water.

"You're a goddess," I said, taking the water gratefully.

"You look happy," she observed, falling into step beside me as we headed toward my office.

"I am," I said simply.

"Good. Because you've got seventeen interview requests, *Sports Illustrated* wants you and Cam for a cover story, and *People* is still pushing for that exclusive."

I nodded, shifting into work mode. "Let's prioritize hockey press for today. *ESPN*, *The Athletic*, *Hockey Night*. We'll consider the lifestyle angles next week after we've seen how tonight's game coverage goes."

Katie made notes, then glanced up with a sly smile. "Oh, and that package you ordered arrived. I put it in your office."

The package – the special surprise I had planned for tonight. "Perfect. Thank you."

My office felt like a haven of calm amid the pre-game chaos. I took a moment to center myself, going through my game-day checklist with practiced efficiency. Press box arrangements confirmed. VIP accommodations for special guests arranged. Social media monitoring rolling.

A knock at my door interrupted my rhythm. I looked up to see Coach Sully standing there, his imposing figure filling the doorframe.

"Got a minute, Decker?"

"Of course, Coach." I gestured to the chair across from my desk.

He sat, his expression unreadable. "Quite a week you've had."

I nodded, unsure where this was going. "It's been... eventful."

"That's one word for it." He leaned forward slightly. "I've been coaching a long time, Lana. Seen every kind of drama, distraction, and disaster you can imagine. What happened this past week could have torn this team apart."

I tensed, bracing for criticism. "I understand, and I – "

He held up a hand. "Let me finish. It could have torn this team apart, but instead, it's brought us closer. The way you handled the press conference, the way Murphy stepped up, the way the team rallied around you both – I haven't seen this kind of unity outside a Cup run."

Relief flooded through me. "Thank you, Coach."

"Don't thank me. You earned it." He stood, straightening his Slashers tie. "And for what it's worth, I've never seen Murphy play better than he has in practice this week. Whatever you two have, it's good for him. Good for the team."

After Coach left, I sat for a moment, absorbing his words. Then I reached for the package Katie had mentioned – a flat, square box delivered from a custom t-shirt shop in downtown St. Pete. Inside was exactly what I'd ordered: a simple black t-shirt with "PUCK DADDY" emblazoned across the chest in the Slashers' teal and white.

It was ridiculous. Completely unprofessional. The exact kind of thing the old Lana would never have considered wearing to a game.

I tucked it into my bag with a smile.

On my way to the arena floor, I ran into Logan, who gave me a warm smile.

"Hey, PR guru," he said, already in his warm-up gear. "Team's buzzing about Cam staying. Hometown discount and everything."

"He loves it here," I said simply.

"He loves you here," Logan corrected with a knowing look. "But we'll take it either way. The Slashers are a family, and you're both part of it."

By game time, the arena was electric. Every seat filled, the crowd a sea of teal and black, buzzing with anticipation. I took my usual spot behind the bench, clipboard in hand, mermaid sapphire ring catching the arena lights every time I moved.

The Penguins were a formidable opponent, currently leading our division by a slim margin. Their enforcer-turned-scorer, Mike "the Vike" Bracken, had been featured on the cover of last week's Sports Illustrated, much to our marketing department's chagrin.

I spotted Cam during warm-ups, his golden-brown hair visible beneath his helmet as he circled the ice with familiar grace. My eyes found him instantly – my number 22, moving with purpose, focused and intent.

When the teams lined up for the national anthem, Cam glanced over to where I stood. Even from this distance, I could see his smile. I touched the sapphire ring, our private signal. His smile widened before he turned his attention back to the ice.

The first period was fast and physical, Pittsburgh dominating early. Mike "The Vike" lived up to his reputation, scoring on a breakaway that left our defense looking flat-footed.

As he glided past the Slashers' bench, he struck his hockey stick against the boards, his thick auburn beard billowing with the motion.

"Tell your captain to keep his head up tonight," he called to Cam with a smirk.

Cam just gave him an easy smile – the kind that used to make me nervous because it usually preceded him throwing a punch. But tonight, he simply nodded and said something I couldn't hear.

"I swear to God," said Reaper to no one in particular. "I'd give up a year of playing professionally if I could have that glorious fucking beard."

The Slashers fought back, with Logan netting a power-play goal to tie it up, only for Pittsburgh to score again in the final minute of the period.

During the intermission, I checked in with Katie, who was monitoring social media from the press box.

"Mentions of Cam are through the roof," she reported. "Everyone's watching him tonight."

"And the Redline announcement?" We'd timed the press release about Cam's sneaker deal to drop during the first intermission.

"Already trending. Lots of positive buzz. Oh, and Marcus just forwarded an email from *Sports Business Journal* – they're calling you 'the PR mastermind who turned a potential scandal into the feel-good story of the season.'"

I couldn't help the proud smile that spread across my face. After everything we'd been through, my professional reputation wasn't just intact – it was enhanced. I headed up to the VIP box to sit with my mom and dad, Coco, and some of the other WAGs. The moment I stepped through the door, I was engulfed in a flurry of hugs and congratulations. Mom pulled me into a tight embrace, her familiar perfume wrapping around me like a warm blanket.

"I knew it would all work out," she whispered, her eyes shining with pride and maybe a few unshed tears. "You two are perfect for each other – I've known it since the moment he walked into our home."

Dad, never one for excessive displays of emotion, gave me a gruff but heartfelt hug. "The Slashers have a solid chance at winning the Cup again with Cam staying on," he said, his voice thick with approval. "And I'm proud of you, honey. The way you handled everything – pure Decker grit." He clapped a hand on my shoulder. "Cam's officially part of Team Decker now, whether he likes it or not."

"I think he likes it," I said softly, as my dad nodded knowingly.

Coco bounced over, her enthusiasm infectious as always. "So are you coming to the team celebration after? Logan says everyone's riding high after the trade news and your press conference love fest."

Before I could answer, the Redline executives approached, their faces beaming with corporate delight. "Lana, we can't thank you enough," the marketing VP gushed, shaking my hand vigorously. "This whole situation has generated more authentic engagement than our last three campaigns combined. We're absolutely thrilled about working with both you and Cam moving forward."

I smiled, feeling a weight lift from my shoulders. At my lowest point, I'd been ready to resign from the job I love. Now, I was surrounded by support, love, and the promise of something real with the man I'd been denying my feelings for all these years.

The second period started with Pittsburgh still leading 2-1. Cam seemed more focused, his skating more fluid, his passes sharper. Midway through the period, he set up Pietro for a beautiful goal that tied the game again. The crowd erupted, and as Pietro celebrated with the team, Cam pointed up to where I stood, making my heart skip.

Then, disaster struck. A controversial call sent Zayne to the penalty box for tripping, and during the ensuing power play, Pittsburgh scored again. 3-2, with momentum slipping away.

As the period wound down, the tension in the arena was palpable. The Slashers needed something – a spark, a game-changer. No better time for my surprise.

I texted Marty in the broadcast control room. During a TV timeout, the arena's giant screens showed fans in the stands, as they always did. Stadium cameras panned across sections, catching people dancing, cheering, holding signs. When the camera suddenly swung to me, I was ready.

With a deep breath and a silent prayer that I wasn't about to embarrass myself to an unrecoverable degree, I stood up right next to the glass and slowly opened my blazer to reveal the "PUCK DADDY" t-shirt underneath.

And there I was, back on the Jumbotron.

The crowd went wild. Gasps, then cheers, then full-on roaring laughter and applause. On the bench, players turned to see what the commotion was about. And there was Cam, head thrown back in laughter when he saw the shirt, eyes bright with surprise and delight.

Katie, who stopped by the box to get my signoff on media credentials for a late-arriving features reporter, stopped dead in her tracks, mouth open in shock before dissolving into giggles.

"Oh my god," she whispered. "Is this the same Lana Decker who once made me change my shoes because they were too 'casual professional' for a game?"

I shrugged, unable to stop smiling. "People change."

"For the better," she said, giving me a quick hug before hurrying off.

The moment lasted only seconds before the camera moved on, but the energy in the arena had shifted completely.

The crowd started chanting *PUCK DADDY! PUCK DADDY! PUCK DADDY!* and as play resumed, the Slashers skated with renewed purpose. By the end of the second period, Zayne had scored on a slap shot from the blue line, tying the game 3-3.

"Ladies and gentlemen," the announcer's voice boomed during the second intermission, "tonight's attendance is a season-high 19,257! And I think we all know they're here to see if our PR director has any more surprises up her sleeve!"

I blushed as several people nearby gave me thumbs-up or knowing smiles. Hockey was serious business, and I'd always maintained the utmost professionalism at games. But tonight was different. Tonight was about celebration, redemption, and yes – a little bit of fun.

The third period was a battle of wills. Neither team gave an inch, both goalies making spectacular saves. With two minutes left in regulation, Coach Sully called a timeout, gathering the team around him at the bench.

I couldn't hear what was said, but when the players returned to the ice, there was a different energy about them. Cam, especially, seemed to radiate intensity. His eyes focused in that way that made me think of a predator tracking its prey.

With just forty seconds left on the clock, Logan won a face-off in the Penguins' zone, sliding the puck back to Zayne, who fired a pass to Cam positioned near the right circle. What happened next unfolded like a movie scene.

Cam received the puck, deked around one defender, then another. The Penguins' goalie slid to the near post, anticipating the shot, but Cam hesitated – just a fraction of a second – before firing the puck into the top corner of the net.

Goal.

The arena exploded. 4-3 Slashers, with thirty-one seconds remaining.

"What a goal by Cameron Murphy!" the play-by-play announcer shouted over the roar of the crowd.

His color commentator chimed in, "Looks like someone's found their center off the ice, too. That engagement ring might be the best equipment upgrade of the season."

Cam's teammates mobbed him, a tangle of teal jerseys and sticks raised in triumph. When he emerged from the pile, he skated to the glass directly in front of where I stood, pounding the logo on his chest twice before blowing me a kiss.

I caught it, pressing my hand to my heart, not caring who saw or what they thought. This was our moment – real, unscripted, and perfect.

The final half-minute was a blur of defensive plays and cleared pucks, and when the horn sounded, sealing the Slashers' victory, the celebration was deafening.

In the post-game media scrum, reporters crowded around Cam, microphones thrust toward him as camera lights bathed him in artificial brightness.

"Cam, great game," one reporter said. "What's changed in your approach?"

Cam, still in his jersey, sweat dampening his hair, smiled. "I'm just playing like I'm home. When you're with the people who matter – your team, your family – everything becomes clearer. The ice feels right. The puck feels right. I'm just... right where I belong."

A reporter from *Hockey Night* asked, "Your decision to stay with the Slashers despite Montreal's significant offer has surprised many. Was that decision influenced by your relationship with Lana Decker?"

I watched his eyes on the TV screen in the VIP box. "Lana is the most important person in my life. So yes, she was a factor. But so were my teammates, the organization, and the city of St. Pete. This is home. And I just finally realized that home is worth a lot more to me than a bigger paycheck."

After the interviews, after the showers and changed clothes, the team gathered at Ocean Prime – a team tradition after important victories. In a private room with views of the bay, players, coaches, and staff celebrated not just tonight's win, but the journey of the past week.

Logan raised a glass, the captain's voice cutting through the chatter. "To the Slashers – and to Cam & Lana who FINALLY figured out what the rest of us have been seeing all along."

"The Slashers," everyone echoed.

As the night wore on, I found myself sitting beside Zayne, who had been uncharacteristically quiet.

"You okay?" I asked, bumping his shoulder gently with mine.

He nodded, watching Cam across the room, deep in conversation with Coach Rocco. "Yeah. Just thinking."

"About?"

"How things change." He turned to look at me directly. "For the better, I mean."

I smiled, warmed by the rare openness in my brother's expression. "They do. Sometimes when you least expect it."

Zayne sipped his beer. "You know, when I first saw you two at the NHL awards, I was ready to kill him. More than a decade of friendship, and I was ready to throw it all away."

"I remember," I said dryly.

"But watching you two together – it's different than what I thought. He's different with you." Zayne set his beer down with surprising gentleness. "He loves you. Not just saying it. I can see it."

"I love him too," I said softly.

"I know." Zayne's lips twitched in what might have been a smile. "And as weird as it is to say, you both deserve this. To be happy. Together."

Before I could respond to this shocking and unprecedented display of emotional openness from my brother, Cam appeared beside us, sliding an arm around my waist.

"Everything okay here?" he asked, looking between us with slight concern.

"Fine," Zayne said, resuming his usual gruff demeanor. "Just telling Lana that you better make me best man. And I guess I'm going to need a date for the wedding."

Cam's eyebrows shot up, and I felt my cheeks warm. "The wedding?"

Zayne stood, patting Cam's shoulder. "Don't play dumb, Murphy. We all know where this is heading." He gestured vaguely at my ring. "Just don't rush her, okay? And if you do anything stupid..."

"...you'll bury me in the equipment shed," Cam finished his sentence. "Got it."

"Lana, I just wanted to say... I know you need one of the guys to do an interview with that writer, Shelby. So...I just wanted to, uh, tell you...I'm good to help out. If you want."

"Thanks, Zayne," I replied. Stunned.

With that parting shot, Zayne wandered off to join Logan and Pietro, leaving Cam and me shocked and amused.

"Did my brother just give us his blessing?" I asked incredulously.

"I think he did." Cam pulled me closer. "And threatened my life in the same breath. Classic Zayne."

"And, am I crazy or did he just volunteer to do an interview with a romance author? Without me even *asking* him?"

"Yes, yes he did," Cam grinned, taking a sip of his drink.

Later, as we stood on the restaurant's terrace, the night air warm and salt-tinged from the bay, Cam wrapped his arms around me from behind, resting his chin on my shoulder.

"So," he said, his voice low and intimate in my ear. "Puck Daddy, huh?"

I laughed, leaning back against him. "Well, you know how much I love the pet names..."

"I loved it, Cupcake Queen" he said, pressing a kiss to my temple. "Almost as much as I love you."

I turned in his arms to face him, reaching up to trace the line of his jaw. "You were amazing tonight. On the ice. With the press. With my brother."

"I had good motivation." His hands settled at my waist, warm and steady. "I'm playing for more than just the win now. I'm playing for us. For our future."

The word *future* stretched out between us, full of promise and possibility. Marriage. A home. Weekends at the beach house with my extended family. Maybe someday, a family of our own. I held the sapphire ring on my finger, no longer a prop but a promise.

"Our future," I repeated softly. "I kinda like the sound of that."

Cam's smile – that devastating, heart-stopping smile that had been my undoing from the very beginning – spread slowly across his face.

"Me too," he said, before closing the distance between us with a kiss that felt like... well, like coming home.

Zayne & Shelby's Story

And how to get your hands on the smuttiest sex scene I've ever written...

Hello Awesome Reader,

Thanks so much for reading *Cold Feet,* book 2 in the St. Pete Slashers series I hope you loved it!

If you did, please **consider leaving a review** on one of the major bookselling sites. Reviews help readers find new books to love, and they help your favorite authors make a living, and, you know, eat.

If you adore contemporary romance books as much as I do, please join the swoon squad -- my free newsletter where you'll get sneak peeks of my upcoming books, book swag, and TONS of free giveaways of your favorite romance authors like Christina Lauren, Helena Hunting, Emily Henry -- and of course, me! **Plus, you'll get a free book! Sign up here:**

Open the camera app on your phone to scan this QR code to get your free book, Fifteen Minutes of Shame!

Deleted Scene: The Smuttiest Sex Scene I've Ever Written

So... you know that scene after the press conference where Cam and Lana go back to his place? Well, it started off a lot smuttier. Like, *a lot* smuttier. The scene ended up being cut for length (no pun intended) but if you'd like to read it (you *know* you want to), you can check it out here:

Open your phone's camera app to scan this QR code to read the deleted scene from COLD FEET

Up next in the St. Pete Slashers series, Zayne and Sheby's story: BREAKING THE ICE

Star St. Pete Slashers player Zayne Decker is not exactly a people person. Or a romance person. Until he meets *her,* an *all-about-exploring-the-feelings* romance author.

Happy (swoony) reading!

xoxo Lisa

What to Read Next
From Lisa Daily

www.ingramcontent.com/pod-product-compliance
Lightning Source LLC
Chambersburg PA
CBHW021214310726

48971CB00006B/1560